THE SPEED OF CLOUDS

THE SPEED OF CLOUDS

MIRIAM SEIDEL

NEW DOOR BOOKS
Philadelphia 2018

NEW DOOR BOOKS
An imprint of P. M. Gordon Associates, Inc.
2115 Wallace Street
Philadelphia, Pennsylvania 19130
U.S.A.

Library of Congress Control Number: 2017916108
ISBN 978-0-9995501-0-6

To Steve and Ethan

And to my mother, Barbara Scheiber,
for showing the way

THE SPEED OF CLOUDS

Ladies and Gentlemen, Humanoids, Cyborgs and Androids, Reptilians, Gonfarians, other respected members of the known Universe, and any otherwise embodied Dear Readers:

I'm happy to announce this, Issue Nine of "Voice of the Cyborg"! We got a little behind schedule, but you know how it is with getting a zine printed, stapled, stuffed and mailed. Maybe some future zine will be able to whoosh through the ether to your email inboxes! Think about it: we've got just a few months to go till the year 2000 kicks in. Some people are spreading doom about the Y2K bug, saying we're heading for massive computer crashes when the digital calendars click over at midnight this coming New Year's Eve. I choose to be optimistic. The way I see it, the future is getting closer, ready or not!

Back to our new issue, let me welcome a new writer to our pages, Tad Fishkin. Tad's story involves some kind of showdown between the Santak and the Mesh—two of SkyLog's more fascinating alien species. He's done his homework, so let's give a high five for this brand-new contributor to the Voice. Even though his story doesn't include our beloved Roi, IMHO the best cyborg of the 23rd century. But I promise this look at the Mesh, who are all cyborgs, of course, will be illuminating. Roi isn't the only one we can learn from—we're open to all corners of the SkyLog universe! Send us your androids, your romance bots, your battle-weary Meshers yearning to be free!

We've also got a new installment of Angie Madden's Roi–Dr. Braxton romance, set in the alternate timeline where Roi is secretly still able to feel emotions. Whoa, is it getting hot in here? I call timeout to cool down.

Lastly, where are all you contributors? Seriously—this issue's coming out a bit thinner than the last one. We've got to keep going, now more than ever, since the Disastrous Cancellation Event that cut down *SkyLog: Century 23* in its prime. It's up to us to imagine what happens next, and even what might have happened, like Angie's doing in her new story. Plus, "Voice of the Cyborg" should be a place where we can throw around the big questions that attracted us in the first place, before we got hung up on attractive cyborgs and other non-conventional creatures. Are you all too busy consoling yourselves with old SkyLog episodes in syndication? We've seen a couple of zines biting the dust in the last year or so. If things don't pick up here, I may have to inflict some longer editorials on you.

Don't forget, I'm accepting submissions by email now—except for artwork of course. Till I get a better modem, just snail-mail that to me.

One more note: This publication is no longer associated in any way with the Cyborg Appreciation Society. The Society will conduct their fannish business separately, and I am publishing and editing "Voice of the Cyborg" myself. So I expect an appropriate increase in respect around here.

Reporting some anomalous signals from the outer shell—radiation barriers may be affected . . .

"WHAT IS IT, MA?" I hit save and close but don't turn around. I know she's standing in the door of my room.

"I've been calling you for the last five minutes."

"Don't exaggerate."

"I called a couple times, you didn't answer." She picks her way around the bed. "Don't you want to eat before your meeting?"

She leans over my shoulder and squints at the screen, as if narrowing her eyes could force it to make more sense. How could such a little woman have given birth to me? Her head barely clears the monitor. Even with me in the wheelchair, Janine's face isn't that much higher than mine. If I could stand up next to her, I'd be way taller, I think. It's been a while.

"I'm not going to the meeting."

She turns to me. "Honey, you look so nice! What did you do to your hair?" Did she even hear me? I want to bat her hand off my head. Why did I get dressed up anyway? Regulation Transortium Fleet officer's uniform. I guess it's my way of saying I'm still the Commander here, even if Sheryl's in charge of the club.

"I told you I'm not going, Ma."

"But—it's Thursday, right? You always go to your meeting the first Thursday of the month."

I turn the chair so I can see her straight on. Other than the alarm on her face, she's looking kind of perky, with a flowery blouse over her turquoise leggings.

"What are *you* all dressed up for?"

She looks down at her outfit. "Your father is coming over later. He's gonna help me bring some boxes down to the basement." Message received, Captain.

"I'll be in here. You and Irv can have your fun, or whatever. You won't even know I'm home."

"Do you want him to do anything for you while he's here? Move those boxes?"

"Negative." She means the boxes of old issues of "Voice of the Cyborg" stacked next to the desk. But I like having them right there in case I get a request for a back copy. I glance around the room, at my bookshelf, overflowing with my prized sci-fi book collection, including the SkyLog novelizations from the first TV series. The *SkyLog II* poster right over my bed, since it features the *Century 23* cast's introduction to the big screen. My collection of autographed headshots of SL stars from both series, which I got personally at various Cons over the last ten years. I can tell you which of them were nice, who was cruising on autopilot, and who were high or beery while signing their photos. Okay, my desk is a bit overcrowded, but that's "Voice of the Cyborg" HQ.

"Mindy, honey—you haven't missed a meeting in, what—a couple of years! Except when you were in the hospital that last time . . ." That was for the kidney infection. No big deal, in the scheme of things.

"I'm not going, okay?" I turn back to the monitor.

"What happened? Did something happen?"

"I told you already! I'm not the Commander anymore," I say, trying to keep my voice level. "Sheryl's in charge tonight, and I don't want to spoil her party."

"But you're friends! Aren't you friends with Sheryl?"

"No, we are not friends." I mean that to sound frosty and cyborgish, but it barely comes out at all. Before, I would have said all the members of the CAS were my friends. Obviously Sheryl wasn't, I see that now. What kind of friend goes around behind your back, contacting everybody, campaigning to throw you out of office?

"But your meetings are—so much fun for you!" By which she means, they're the high point of my social life and her last hope for me to meet some nice boy, even though the club is over ninety percent female.

"I'll still be doing the magazine."

"Right, you said." Janine takes this in. "Then you can have supper with us—I'm making ravioli."

"I'm not hungry. And don't ask me again, I really don't want to eat anything."

She looks at me with her raised eyebrow thing. I know she wants to touch my cheek, but she's holding back.

"I'll bring you something later," she says. "And you'll come out and say hi to your father."

"Whatever." Lots of static. Signal's breaking down, we can't hold the com feed much longer.

The door shuts. I turn back to the screen, and start up the artificial-life program that Zuzana gave me, watching it as it generates growth patterns by itself. From just a few little random lines, pinwheel shapes start spiraling out. And the colors keep changing, on some hidden algorithm: now they're pink going to red at the tips. You never know how they'll end up. I've been thinking of asking Zu if she could make it work as a screensaver— but I'd probably go right back to my old, classic advancing-stars screensaver anyway. I always do. Zuzana's still my friend, I think. She emailed me a few times after the meeting, but I couldn't figure out what to say to her, too embarrassed over the whole thing. Remembering, I squeeze my eyes shut, and the forms curlicue along on the inside of my eyelids, glowing a sick yellow-green.

I wheel over and shut the bedroom door. Before I can turn around, I'm caught by the reflection in the mirror on the back of the door. It's somebody I don't know. That SkyLog uniform is stretching in all the wrong places like some cheap Halloween costume—the top over the big boobs and middle, the pants stretching too tight over those thighs. The face, weary and off-kilter. Is this what happens when my rank is taken away—I crumple down into my chair like some crucial part of my skeleton was removed? Or did I look like this before and didn't notice, only seeing the Fleet officer in the mirror? I feel old. Next birthday I'll be twenty-four, which rounds up to twenty-five. Then it's just a step till thirty. Nerdy girl in a wheelchair, living with Mom. Without the CAS, what have I got? The zine, I remind myself and that person grimacing back at me, for the hundredth time since the last meeting. My fanzine. The place where SkyLoggers can let loose and bravely imagine things that are about more than how we look.

Stupid fucking mirror. I jab the light switch off. That's better, cloaked in half-darkness, the curtains drawn. But now I'm back in the meeting, caught again in that horrible moment—the fluorescent lights buzzing in the silence as I look around the table in the library's conference room, at the raised hands among the eight members who showed up, except for Zu, voting Sheryl in as our new Commander. Sheryl avoiding my eyes as she declares herself the winner. It happened so fast. First she introduced the new bylaws, new because we never had any before, and written by her. Right after that, she called for a vote. And then she just kept talking in her droning-on monotone, moving past the vote like it was no big deal, right into something about planning for the next Con. I sat there, my skin turning cold. Couldn't say anything, like my voice was stuck in my throat, making it hard to breathe. Me, with the zingers always ready, couldn't say a thing.

I started the CAS, for fuck's sake—it never occurred to me to step down after a while. And Sheryl, mousy little Sheryl, who joined just last year, who said she left the Synergy because it was so disorganized. Not that we were super-organized, but we're smaller than the Synergy. She showed up for the meetings every month, and was always so helpful in her ultra-quiet way. I figured she was a fellow Roi lover, even though she didn't say much when we talked about his important episodes, things like that—but she did jump in to talk about planning for the next Con, membership dues, or to point out when we wandered off the agenda. She volunteered to do the minutes—nobody wants to do the minutes. Then she offered to clean up the various lists: the Voice subscriber list, the membership list, and to send out subscription and dues reminders. That's when I should have started worrying. With the membership records, she went around to everyone behind my back, setting the whole thing up. Up till the last meeting, the worst thing that had happened this year was *SkyLog: C23* getting canceled. Which was upsetting enough, even if the constant rumors about that meant it was no surprise.

In the near dark, the blue hush of the monitor calls me back. The growth program kept going without me, the pinwheels now paisley-shaped blotches bumping against each other. The screensaver will come on soon. There it is: the white pinpricks of stars moving toward me from the blackness of space, unending waves of them.

THE DOOR OF my cabin pings. I know who it is.

Enter, I say.

The door slides away as he walks in, then shuts behind him. Roi.

He stands there in the doorway, with his grave expression and putty-gray skin. His Wuvian antenna buds exposed on his hairless skull.

Come and sit, I say. He walks over, not too slow or too fast, no wasted movement. I know he unnerves many of the ship's crew. It's not only how he looks and moves but what he represents. For me, though, instead of being disturbed, I'm fascinated by how he sits on the uneasy boundary between humanoid and artificial life-form. An Enmeshed humanoid—the only one ever to escape the Mesh alive.

I put my hand on his, feeling his hardened, leathery skin.

I'm happy to see you again, I tell him.

He looks at me, says nothing. I tell myself again that the emotional responses he was born with have been crushed, twisted beyond recognition by his Enmeshment. He can't respond freely to anything. Can't prefer anything, or make any choice between options that are presented to him. Even after all this time on the ship, he needs to be told what to do.

To fill the silence, I talk. I tell him about the mission I just returned from, to the Ixaran moon colony. The sting of failure, the shame of being kicked off Ixara 3, victim of my apparent inability to read the intentions of the colony representatives. Dr. Braxton says it's good to talk about my feelings with Roi. She thinks that hearing humanoid emotions described in real time as they're experienced will help to rehabilitate his own damaged functioning. Watching his face, I don't know. I only know he's listening.

I stop talking, and look around the cabin. Stark and cool, with only one decorative touch—the branching figurine on the table, its tips lazily shifting colors. There's the never-ending hum of the ship, reminding me that I'm a tiny unit in a much larger mission. But even here, with Roi beside me, the pain of my recent mission failure wells up. Sighing, I signal the lights to lower. Nothing will happen unless I demand it.

I feel sad, I say. I need you to comfort me. He knows what this means. I lie back on the couch and pull him to me. He circles me with his arms, strokes my hair. We kiss. I want him to want this too, but he can't want anything, not after what he's been through. I pull off his tunic and trace the raised line that runs up and down his arms on both sides. I know it continues down to his feet, the same line that meets at the top of his bare head. It's the most visible reminder that he's a creature both of pumping blood and coursing electricity. We start to move together. It's a relief to both of us not to have the burden of talking anymore. I wait for the zing of electricity, the charge that escapes from him, a sign of his rising excitement. It's a charge that can stun or even kill someone at full force. We move faster. There it is. The buzz, frightening and exciting both at once, a taste of his own hybrid being moving through me.

THIS WORLD IS harsh and dry. The air sparks with static and the wind shrills in my ears, slapping my hair across my face. I squint up against the skyline: ragged brown mountains against the white sky, the giant sun lowering quickly toward the horizon. The mountains could be miles away. The plain travels out from here, zigzagging with cracks big enough for a podcraft to land in. The temperature will drop like a stone when night falls—I've got to make my contact soon. I want to explore, but my orders keep me at the entry coordinates until I'm approached. Where are they hiding?

It's always the same with a new mission, learning a new world. With the heavier gravity here, my boots feel magnetized, holding my feet to this slab of rock. My brain is overstuffed with briefing data, and no sense of how they'll play out in the reality of first contact. My nerves are pulsing. Outside, if anyone is looking, they see a Transortium Fleet Mission Officer Grade II, cool and professional. Tall and beautiful, if they share human aesthetic standards; long honey-colored hair whipped to one side in the wind. Alone. My superiors know by now that I work best alone. So I stand on the promontory, looking at everything and nothing—the mountains, the lowering sun, the slightest movement in the shadows, waiting.

"MINDY!"

"What?"

"I said, what's that one you've got?" It's my mother, squinting at me from the far end of the couch. I look down dumbly at what I'm holding—a technicolor movie still, half-stuffed into a clear plastic sleeve.

"Um, it's Annette Funicello and some guy." The wind still whistling in my ears. I push back a stray strand of hair, hold up the picture. My mother leans toward it.

"Oh, that's *Pajama Party*. So that's—Sweetie!" she calls. "Who was it with Annette Funicello in *Pajama Party*?"

"Tommy Kirk," comes my father's voice from the kitchen. "American International, 1964." He's emptying the dishwasher.

"Your father knows everything," Janine reminds me. "It's not signed, is it?"

I look again, shake my head no. No sign of any inscriptions. Maybe I should explore further?

"Honey, you know it only goes in the sleeve if it's signed. Just put it in the box." She throws me another appraising squint.

"I know, Ma." Jeez. We're getting ready for the Cherry Hill show. It's going to be her first time there, and she's worried. The ashtray's already full of mangled butts. I've probably missed a couple of stories about other dealers who might be there. The photos and lobby cards are in piles on the couch and the coffee table. I'm sorting autographed glossies from the unsigned ones, putting the autographs in plastic sleeves. Janine puts them into the appropriate looseleaf binder or box. Two binders for random Hollywood movies, A through M and N through Z, by actor. One for horror movies, one for TV shows.

Then there's the SkyLog binder—a nod to me, plus she knows it's good for business. And the one red binder for her beloved Mary, who can turn the world on with her smile. This one gets Janine's loving attention. The pictures are all in chronological order, starting with a rare shot from *Richard Diamond, Private Detective*, her first TV series, where Mary plays the sexy answering-service girl, but only her legs appear on camera. Then, stills from *The Dick Van Dyke Show*, and finally *The Mary Tyler Moore Show*. That's the Mary I guess my mom fell in love with, the cute, struggling career girl. Ma was cute, and she definitely had her struggles, but she never had a career. Till now maybe, if she can make the move from the flea markets into collectibles. Sometimes people call her the Mary lady—she always sets up a kind of shrine at the center of her table, with the *TV Guide* cover issues fanning out around the framed, personally autographed MTM head shot Janine wrote away for when Mary was on *The Dick Van Dyke Show*. That'll never be sold. The stuff in her Mary binder is a little pricey too.

Irv comes out of the kitchen holding his coffee, turns up the TV. It's *Jeopardy*. "Who was Bessie Coleman?" he asks the TV. A moment later, Alex Trebek indicates that he's right, she is indeed the first African American aviatrix. My father does know everything, or it seems that way. His first job was working on the UNIVAC computer, which makes him the ultimate computer geek. And he sometimes seems like a computer himself with his prodigious data-storage capacity. My dad's the one who explained to me about the Y2K bug and its possible disastrous consequences inside computers all over the world as their timing devices move into the new century. It's July now, five months to go. I'm glad he's monitoring the situation. He slides a cardboard box from his armchair onto the coffee table and sits down to help us with the sorting.

This room may give the impression that we're a bunch of batshit-crazy hoarders. But it's more that Janine is a loyal member of the Church of the Flea Market Circuit, whose members hold the belief that Anything Can Be Resold, Eventually. Even though she's graduating herself up to the memorabilia shows, the flow of stuff into our house has kept up the usual pace: vintage blenders and toasters, mostly nonworking, stuffed animals and dolls of all kinds—Beanie Babies, Holly Hobbies, don't even start on the Barbies—mostly not in mint condition. Mystery boxes piled behind the couch. A lava lamp she claims is original, and a Kiss poster leaning against the wall next to me. She knows I need a clear path to get from my room to the kitchen, but sometimes I'll get stuck on a Transformer or a runaway Smurf.

That's another thing that makes us different: Ma's in love with old things that remind her of when she was young and even before. Being surrounded by all these little blasts from the past seems to invigorate her. Whereas I've got my head in the future. I don't mind some sci-fi memorabilia or a signed still from SkyLog, but I'd prefer our environment more streamlined, like on the *Encounter*. In terms of the house, right now the past is winning.

Irv is somewhere in the middle between me and Ma on the past-future axis. He's into sci-fi like I am, and he's all for progress, but he's never met a computer he could throw away. My theory is, all the piles of stuff that Ma kept bringing home from the shows just got to be too much for him. And Ma's yelling, of course—that was part of why he left. Whatever it was, it all happened the last time I was in the hospital, for the kidney infection, which is why I don't remember the exact moment. When I got home that time, he'd moved out to the little apartment by the Blue Route where he lives now. The weird thing is how they still seem to think of themselves as a couple.

I glance over at the SkyLog binder on the table. Ever since *Century 23* got canceled, that binder has been making me weirdly uncomfortable. The ratings were slipping, they said. They had just hit the magic number for syndication. But that meant they had to wrap up the storylines fast, and now we'll never get the answers to the Mowg foray into Santak territory, or whether Roi gets a ship's rank on the *Encounter*—except in the fanfic universe, and that's not canon. But it's something else that's bothering me: now there's no SkyLog on the air to guide us into the new millennium. Here we are on the verge of a new century, and instead of giving us stories for the future, it looks like SkyLog may be done. Slipping into nostalgia, like all the other things Janine and I traffic in at our flea markets. That's not right.

I TAKE A DEEP BREATH. The sky that was dazzling white before has turned ash-gray. The last of the sunset, just a line of molten light brushing the cliffs. The dry crack-lines on the plain are softer now. The natives live inside those crevices, I know, but it's hard to imagine. I shiver, and wonder again why I take on these missions, never knowing how they'll turn out. But I know the answer: I was chosen for this. They trained me, enhancing my unusual abilities in reconnaissance, tracking, establishing trust with beings unfamiliar with the Transortium.

Eyes watch me from the shadows. I can barely make out the few dark shapes moving closer, slow and soundless. Maybe my briefing was wrong, and daylight encounters are taboo. I hope this is just a matter of politeness. They're closer now—five or six, all much smaller than me, I have to take care not to frighten them. No sudden moves. I rehearse the lines of greeting again in my head.

"WHO COULD THAT BE!" my mother says. The doorbell rings again. She takes another drag, kills the butt in the ashtray. "Irv, honey! Get the door, I can't get up here." Her lap is overflowing with slippery photos. Irv lopes over, his eyes still on the TV.

"What are the Geneva Accords?" he mutters, pulling the door open.

It's Zuzana. My tall, thin friend, her moon face framed with flyaway, reddish-brown hair. Wearing her summer uniform—denim cutoffs and a T-shirt, this one from the last Beastie Boys concert. She stands at an angle, her body as usual a beat behind or ahead of its mental instructions. Her eyes catch mine and then dart off to the side, like I'm one of her nun teachers from grade school and I've caught her at something. I don't know what I look like; I look down at the photo in my lap. Elizabeth Montgomery in *Bewitched*. Signed. I stare at her perfect features. She totally doesn't look like a witch.

"Suzy! Mindy, it's your friend Suzy. Irv, close the door, you're letting all the hot air in." Too late, the heavy summer air is already humidifying the room.

"Hi, Mr. Vogel, Mrs. V."

"Come on and sit down, honey." Janine paws at the stuff on the couch. "It's been such a long time. Here, sit down. Mindy, it's Susy."

"I see that, Ma."

Zu fumbles her way onto the couch. Photos slide into her thighs, her knees poke into the coffee table. Looking at her caught there, her thin, knobby body pinned, I almost feel sorry for her. I send a withering glare at my mother, who thinks she's so clever and devious.

"You want something to drink? Irv, get her a Sprite! Do you want a Sprite?"

"No, really, that's okay."

Silence.

"So, how's the piano coming along, Sue?" My father sets down her drink, spiked with the usual two ice cubes.

"Pretty good, I guess." I can barely hear her. She hasn't played piano for a couple of years, as far as I know, not since she hooked up her MIDI system. Zu only plays found sounds now, as she calls them. TV static, traffic noise, old SkyLog sound tracks, snatches of her favorite composers and groups—they all go into the blender, morphing in and out of each other. She'll call me up and play back what sounds to me like a few bars of noise into the phone.

"So what brings you here?" Janine presses on. Instant translation: How did my mother embarrass you into showing up here?

"Mindy—I just wanted to tell you, I'm sorry about what happened, with Sheryl and all . . ."

"What? I'm cool with it. I was getting bored running the meetings."

"I didn't vote for her," she says. We both know that already. Zu and Sheryl never hit it off. Sheryl came over here a couple of times to help with mailing out the Voice—that's what gave Ma the idea she was a friend of mine.

"Of course not, you girls are best friends," Janine says. "Maybe you'd like to go out somewhere?"

"I don't care who you voted for," I say. "I don't care who anybody voted for."

"Some people," Zu says in a small voice, "said to tell you they hope you'll come back."

"Irv and me can finish this up without you, honey." Janine pulls the sliding photos and binders toward her side of the couch. "Why don't you two go out and enjoy yourselves?"

Zuzana stares at me.

"So they want me back, just not as Commander."

"What about Spudz?" Janine is unstoppable. "You two like going to Spudz sometimes."

"Ma! We're talking!" As if anything could shut her up. "Who said they wanted me back?"

"Ah—Annemarie. And Cleo." But they're inseparable, so that only counts as one opinion.

"You could talk things over at Spudz."

"Ma!"

"And—" Zu hesitates, "um, Sheryl." Sheryl! My chest squeezes tight. So she wants to take away my position and also have me stick around and smile while she leads the meeting, my meeting? Fuck that. Then something else hits me.

"How do you know?" She talked to Sheryl after the last meeting?

"Are you sure you don't want to go somewhere tonight?" Ma, again.

"Jesus, Ma!" My head is pounding.

"Come on, J," my father says. "Let them talk." He starts scooping up photos and plastic folders, throwing them into the box on the coffee table. Ma follows him into her bedroom.

"I want you to come back," Zu says in a tiny voice.

I can't talk. The thought of Zu calling Sheryl after what happened sticks in my throat.

"Mindy, c'mon," Zu says. "You've been there so long."

I take a breath. "Look, I'm done with Sheryl, and I'm done with the CAS. I decided I'm just gonna put out the Voice myself from now on."

"But—" she says, then clamps her lips together.

"What!"

"Sheryl's taking over the zine too." My skin prickles, and a wave of heat travels up my back.

"She can't! I started it. I'm the Editor!"

"She said she wants it to be more, um, entertaining—with, like, puzzles, and contests, and more news . . ." I stop hearing her as the meaning of this settles in. Of course, Sheryl got the subscription list too.

"What about the next issue? It's ready to go to the printer!" I'm starting to panic. Sheryl can't stop me from getting the next issue out. But what's the point, if she's in charge of the zine?

"I'll help you." Zu's thinking about the practical part. I've never done it all myself, it's always been a group effort—other people helping with the pickup, the packing, the labeling. I guess I was thinking some people would help me out of loyalty. But there's another looming problem that's crossed my mind, and now it comes into blinking-neon focus.

"What about the Con?" Our eyes lock. She understands.

"How'm I going to sell the Voice there?"

"There's gotta be some way . . ."

"Shit. I don't believe this." I've got some subscribers, but the zine can't pay for itself without all the copies that are sold at the Con. And the booth rental is paid out of the club's membership dues. I guess I've been assuming Sheryl would let me sell the zine from their table, out of guilt. But that won't happen if she's putting out her own version of it.

"What am I going to do, rent a booth myself?" But the picture I see in my head is me with a pile of zines in my lap, wheeling around the crowded aisles, trying vainly to catch people's attention. Alone. Cast out of the ship, into the void. Worse, a void where everyone can see my sorry-ass, exiled self.

"It's another three months till the Con, Mindy. We'll figure it out."

"No! I can't." Can't deal, can't talk about this now. Look away, can't let myself cry in front of my friend. "Just go," I manage. Zu stands up, but doesn't move, looking at me.

"Sorry . . ." my mother says, slipping back in from the bedroom. "What, you're leaving so soon?"

"Yes, she's going, Ma! Is that a problem?" My voice loud and raw.

I have to get out of here. I jerk my wheels hard to the right, too fast. A front wheel catches on the base of the lava lamp. The lamp tips in toward the wheel, then falls in my path, its fat pinky-orange teardrops swimming around in slow motion. I'm blocked in. Zuzana, behind me, jiggles the handgrips up and down to free the wheel, but she's too strong, and we're pushing at cross-purposes. I'm listing to one side and forward, holding on to keep from sliding to the floor. Gene Simmons sticks his lizard-like tongue out at me from the old Kiss poster. I hear my mother yelling, then my father saying something as he grabs my shoulder.

"Get away!" I yell.

WHY AREN'T I ABOARD the ship? The high shrill of the wind and the twittering voices around me die away into quiet and darkness, and I feel the all-over tingling shudder that comes with entering sub-cell travel. I'm in the void, alone.

FROM: tadmesh@deepnet.com
TO: MindRoid@comet.net
SUBJECT: NEW STORY
DATE: 7/10/99 8:43 PM

Dear Mindy or should I call you MindRoid,

Here is another story, well really it is more of the story I
sent you before, Shadow of the Mesh. I hope its okay. I am
not sure when you're next issue is coming out but here it is
anyway.

- Tadmesh a.k.a. Tad Fishkin

OKAY, AT LEAST this one writer hasn't abandoned me. I open
the attachment, feeling eager and also relieved at getting an
unsolicited submission.

Shadow of the Mesh, Part 2
by Tad Fishkin

Pak looked around, and listened for any sounds outside of his
room. He pulled the comtron from the heal of his boot where
it was hidden and whispered into it.

"Interim Mission Report, Timespace axis 2238107.FN084062.
No one suspects me of being Under-Officer Pak of the

Transortium Fleet. They still think I am Squadron Leader Gonon of the Santak home world, assigned here after honorable duty in orbit around Waarnen V. They do not suspect that the real Gonon was killed in surprise skirmishing with Transortium personnel in which I took part with them. Since then I have tried to become Gonon, even though I was raised and trained as a loyal Transortium member, serving along with my uncle, First Officer Bokun.

"I am gathering intel on the administration of this colony according to my orders, even though I am opposed to Santak colonization on principal. But this new evidence of Mesh intrusion is pretty disturbing. Request response as soon as possible on how to precede. I will transmit this as soon as it is safe."

Oh boy. Now I remember how this guy writes. I can see him now, a zit-faced kid sitting at his keyboard, putting off studying for his physics finals. Blowing off English since middle school. Lucky he's got me for an editor, saving him from embarrassment by going where Spell Check has never explored.

Did he say he was majoring in aeronautical engineering? There are so many like him at the Cons, with their gawky necks sticking up out of their crewmen's jerseys, cruising the vendor tables alone or in pairs, their fingers roaming lovingly over the collectibles as they debate tach speeds and metaspace waves.

I start reading again. What the frell? This is all about the San-tak! Now he's gone into a full-page discussion of Santak history—the split that happened after they liberated themselves from the 100-year rule of the Mowg. But my readers should already know all about how the Santak split into two factions, the ones who imitated their Mowg Overlords and started building their own space empire, and the smaller group, the Dissenters. I can cut this back. All we really need to get here is how uncomfortable Pak is seeing the Santak Imperium in action, which makes sense since his clan is part of the Dissenters, who've joined the Transortium and are trying to redefine their traditional ways. "He felt like an alien among them"—that's tasty. The Santak are so not my favorite

SkyLog species, though. Coming from a Class IV society, barely out of the feudal level. Big chip on their shoulders from being conquered by the Mowg, always have to prove they're the best. To my way of thinking, the whole point of traveling into the future is to be part of more advanced ways of life. Okay, maybe they could work as enemies of the Transortium, but they just don't fit my idea of Fleet material.

Just then Pak heard footsteps coming towards his room. It was Rel a lower ranking Santak.

"I came to alert you, Leader. That we have received another signal which matches the earlier signal that we received."

Pak fingered his Santak chest plate, it was much thicker and heavier than a Transortium Fleet uniform.

"Why did you not bring me this information sooner!" he yelled. Rel flinched but then stood straight and spoke with honor. "I came as soon as I could be relived of my post."

"Next time make it faster! How do you interpret the data?"

"It bares the unmistakable signature of a Mesh transmission."

"What! The Mesh have never been that close to this star system, and besides ever since the Terran-Mesh conflict they have not returned to this quadrant!"

"There is no error. The data collection was performed with honor." Rel was a subordinate, but he had little fear.

"Well struck. Give me the readouts and then go," Pak growled. He laid down on his bunk, but he could not get the thoughts of the Mesh out of his head. He had seen vids of the Terran invasion. He could never forget the dead gray skin and colorless eyes and how they moved so fast like they were on automatic pilot, all together even stepping in sync, grabbing at the humans, then the flash as they stunned the victims then threw there limp bodies back behind them. The survivors ended up worse then dead, since they got turned into Meshers themselves with the neuro-electric insertions and hardened skin, and then became part of the Mesh to serve the next invasion. Pak never felt comfortable with Roi when he came on the Encounter. Even after they began to learn from him about how life with the Mesh had worked, his dread of the Mesh did not diminish. If the Mesh was really coming toward this planet, there was little time to loose.

Okay, it seems like he's building up to some cyborg action here. But what's the point? I can't do anything with this right now anyway. "Voice of the Cyborg" is stalled, sitting on the runway with its engines off. I could clean this story up and tack it onto the first part. Then what? Go back to Sheryl and beg her to include it in her new, improved fanzine, or should I say overblown club newsletter? This is exactly what I've been trying not to think about.

I remind myself of my new cyborgification project: I will no longer need humans, with their messy fleshiness and sloppy feelings. I'm rebooting my inner structure. All sore spots will be smoothed out, replaced with synth organs, neurids and the rest. Emotions neutralized. I sit in my mobility device, dealing with the flow of incoming information from the screen in front of me. This computer feels like a gift from the SkyLog future, with its invisible threads of connection and its instantaneous movement of data that somehow erases time and space like some metaspace transportation system. This Tad could live in Hong Kong, or Antarctica, it won't matter. All I need is words, and some images, no more of that face-to-face contact thing than necessary. I'm evolving, part of some human vanguard, learning to live in this new, Roi-like way.

FROM: amadden@uokla.edu
TO: MindRoid@comet.net
SUBJECT: crazy
DATE: 7/12/99 1:27 AM

Hey Mind, howz it going!! Im going crazy here in the stacks they have me indexing some old letters and stuff. Glad u liked that last story I sent u. I mean, Roi would not even be with us if it wasnt for Dr. Dina's stubbornness not to mention her mad medical skills. This is a feminist issue right? Don't let men write the history of the future! Yeah!!! We're standing up for the rights of all SkyLog fan-chicks. I would kill for a big Con right now, Normal I mean Norman is driving me over the edge. Thinking of going to the Chicago Con, are you? Insert Wuvian salute here, Angie

FROM: MindRoid@comet.net
TO: amadden@uokla.edu
SUBJECT: Re: crazy
DATE: 7/12/99 10:11 AM

Angie, you know I loved your story, it's gonna be the headliner in the next issue of the Voice. It should have been out by now, and it will be, right after I'm through dealing with some stupid delays. There may be some changes here as I have recently severed relations with the CAS. But I know I can count on you for your great contributions!! Otherwise everything is cool here. Don't think I'll be getting to Chicago, I'm cutting back on my personal appearances, ;-). Well, hang in there. Remember, if you happen to hear anything else, I'm still editor of the Voice. Cyborgs 4ever, Mindy

FROM: drzuz@ultranet.com
TO: MindRoid@comet.net
SUBJECT: read this
DATE: 7/12/99 11:22 AM

No, I'm not gonna read that. Can't face anything from Zu right now. Goddamn human feelings scorching my veins, corroding my synth organs. Must stop this now. I turn off my desk light. In a minute, the monitor will fill with stars.

THEY SKATE BY against the blackness to either side as the leading edge of the ship slides forward. I look back from the screen. Roi sits beside me in the darkened cabin, his eyes gazing out the window.

What are you thinking? I ask him.

I was watching to see if I could recognize any major stars.

Sometimes I like to just watch the stars moving past the ship, I say. Like shooting stars. It helps me feel calmer when I'm worried about something.

He doesn't pick up my cue about being worried. I remember the windy planet again—being surrounded by the small hooded figures, the size of a six- or seven-year-old Terran child, and their dry touch as they pulled and nudged me underground. Staring at me, giving no response to my questions.

I need your help, I say. I'm not sure if I should continue this latest mission or not.

We could go over the Salient Factors, he offers. That's something he is good at.

I summarize for him: This was meant to be an exploratory mission, to test the cultural levels of the Night People, as they call themselves. The Mowg, who recently claimed the planet for resource extraction, are setting up a mining operation not far from the settlement I visited. The moment of First Contact is looming, and the Mowg are famously indifferent to the rights and needs of indigenous beings. But now our ship has received orders to leave for the Eridani System. I could ask the Captain to let me stay behind and be picked up later, but I have to put in my request by 2400 hours.

He questions me about what we know of the Night People, then begins laying out his own SSF—Summary of Salient Factors. They seem to be a Class II society, he says. Tools and weapons level A or B, organizational level C. Political and religious leadership still combined in one person. Abstract reasoning still undivided from cosmic-spiritual understanding. No written numbers or alphabet. Have they ever made a treaty?

I'm not sure, I answer—that's something I'd have to find out.

The Transortium treaty with the Mowg is still in force?

Yes, I tell him. But they've continued to expand their operations, and they haven't responded to our request for a statement of intent.

He asks more questions. This is Roi's Wuvian mind shining through, let loose by my request. Showing that famous Wuvian gift for deep analysis, looking for the pattern hidden in the messy jumble of facts. A special species trait that would have been prized and preserved by the Mesh, not crushed along with the ability to act on his own responses.

As we talk, the main point becomes clear—the Night People are no match for the Mowg, either in diplomacy or in war. And the Mowg will be happy to displace them, or worse, if they can get away with it.

I wish . . . I stop.

He looks at me.

I wish I had your ability to take things in and examine them like you do, so easy, with no emotions interfering.

But we have emotions, Kat. He's slipped into using We, the way the Mesh think of themselves.

I was thinking of myself, of course—what a relief it would be to be free of emotion sometimes. His own situation is painful to contemplate: He's told me how the neural connections between his emotions and his main nervous systems were microsurgically severed. This means that he and other Meshers can feel anger, terror or fear, according to their original genetic makeup, but have lost the ability to follow through on them by any internal pathway. When I try to imagine this, it feels like being stuck in a terrible nightmare. To be under the complete control of the Parents— the collective of artificial intelligences that lies at the heart of every Mesh ship. It's the Parents who oversee the Enmeshment of new members. For reasons we don't yet understand, Enmeshed beings can't reproduce biologically, so they can only add to the Mesh through Takings. The Parents regulate the recharging pro- cess of the individual Meshers in their banks of regeneration beds. They communicate plans for future Takings and oversee off-ship deployments. They call this stream of communication the Lul- laby, Roi told me. They issue the orders to cull any beings who fail to Mesh. Roi and the others had to act on all these orders, no mat- ter how scared or angry they might feel.

Before Roi, we knew hardly anything about the lives of Mesh- ers, only what we learned from the survivors of their invasions. The Meshers captured alive always died within hours, as if they couldn't survive separation from the Mesh. But Dr. Braxton stubbornly worked on Roi to keep him alive, replacing his shattered leg and leaving his altered neural and metabolic functions intact. It was months before he talked at all. Almost a year passed before he told us anything about life in the Mesh. The doctor fashioned a regeneration bed for him in MedBay with jerry-rigged inputs for his neuroelectric system, which he seems to like. Instead of the stream of energy and data from the Parents, he receives a feed from the ship's computer. Now he works with Dr. Braxton most days.

What have I gotten myself into? Being part of Roi's intimate circle can be as challenging as any away mission, and could be just as important. Maybe I should stay on board for a while. But the Night People need me too.

I circle my arms around him, and hold this strange being close, crooning softly in his ear—my own attempt at a Lullaby.

W E'RE DRIVING INTO the sun. Dead ahead, it's broken through the haze hanging over the horizon. It was dark when Janine dragged me out of bed, but now at last it's daytime. Sunlight sparkles on the shingled roofs of the pizza shacks and chain restaurants, the gas stations and seedy mini-malls, the overblown Jersey diners with their chrome and neon facades—like that could cheer me up.

"Is this the Black Horse Pike?" Janine frets. "I hope I didn't miss the turnoff."

"It's okay, Ma. We've been on it for the last ten minutes."

"Check the map, will you please, honey?"

Not being a morning person, I'm in no condition to check anything. Staring at the sun, which keeps cranking up the brightness as it rises, is about all I can handle right now. Why can't the van have some onboard computer telling us what turn to take, and our estimated arrival time, like on the *Encounter*? The Collectorama! flyer, with its tiny map and written directions to the show, is in my backpack. But Janine went over the directions so many times at dinner last night, I kind of memorized them.

"I'm telling you. You stay on this road till we get to the mall. Then we turn and follow the signs."

She gives a hard sigh and scrunches up closer to the wheel. I know she needs a smoke, but I've declared a secondary-smoke ban in the van.

My body is cramped and stiff; I've been waiting in this small antechamber for hours, and I'm starting to regret my decision to return alone to the planet. Finally a door opens, and a small hooded figure approaches me and twitters softly. I'm meant to follow him, or her. It feels good to get up and move again, even if the cavern's ceilings aren't high enough for a tall Terran female. Following my guide down the winding passage, I have to duck to keep from catching my hair on the rough rock. Light comes from hidden pockets in the wall surface, whether from flame or phosphorescence I can't tell.

We enter a big chamber, the first real room I've been in. This space is lit by daylight from openings in the ceiling. Beyond the slashes of white and the dusty haze, I make out an old figure crouching against the far wall, looking at me. My guide gestures me toward a mat placed in the light. I sit, on display in the center. I'm surrounded by others, I realize—dozens of them, pushed up against the walls of the chamber, rustling in the darkness. I must look like a giant to them, with huge pale face and limbs and a mass of gold hair on top, so wildly different from their little fuzz of hair all over. I draw myself up and give the brief speech of greeting I've memorized. The seated one doesn't answer, but the swishing sound of other voices surrounds me, along with the piercing whistle of the wind blowing over us on the surface.

The van screeches, knocking me toward Janine as it makes a hard right turn. We're pulling into the Holiday Inn parking lot.

"Jeez, Ma!"

"I asked you if this was it, a couple times!" she yells back. She's right. I'm the navigator. Luckily, the only fallout is the lady in that late-model Honda glaring at us. We lurch into the last free handicapped spot; now the lady's really mad. Look at the plates, Ma'am, we're legit. Janine gets out, pulls my chair out of the back of the van and brings it around. When my mother's quiet, I know she's hit the top of her anxiety scale. She holds my chair steady while I do my vehicle-to-solo-mobility-device maneuver. Rigid arms, swing the body down—I'm good at this. Feet hang loose till touchdown, but my legs have been staying obligingly bent lately, which makes it kind of easier. It's the muscle tightening Dr. O'Malley talked to me about. I know, I should have been exercising. She's been trying to get me to do surgery to correct it. Says that way I'd be able to have getting around on crutches as an option. She means well.

Janine lights up her last Slim for a while, and puffs through our regular routine: unloading a box into my lap, handing me some shopping bags to hold, then looping some more bags over my handles, and finally balancing some posters off the back. We set off at a snail's pace for the doors. We'll do this two or three times to get all our stuff inside. This is one time when you could say being in a wheelchair is an advantage. We never have to go looking for a hand truck, and people hold the doors for us without being asked.

I've tried to explain to Dr. O'Malley, it's my choice. Maybe it wasn't a deliberate choice at the time. There was so much going on—Ma finally talked Irv into moving back to Philly right after high school, then that last big operation on my neck, and the long, uneven recovery. With all that going on, I somehow never got back to the crutches. Now it makes more sense to be on wheels. I've got better things to do. I'm sorry, I tell Dr. O. in my head. Life's just too short. I've already done way more than my quota of hospital time.

The room is like the few other indoor shows we've been to, nothing fancy. I always check the floor first; this one's a thin old carpet with random soft-drink stains kinking up the flower pattern.

"Look, it's the Tee Shirt Heaven people. Hiya!" Janine calls to a couple unpacking at their table. She's been on the alert for familiar faces. "Remember, honey?" she stage-whispers. "They've got a store in North Jersey, but they do shows."

The lady looks up and waves our way. Everybody always remembers us. What do they say to each other—Look, there's that Mary Tyler Moore Lady and her crabby paraplegic sidekick? I've got plenty of crabby to spread around today.

"How ya doing, Marcy?" Janine bubbles. "This is my first time here."

"You'll do fine," the lady says. She and her partner are wearing their own T-shirts, with matching blowups of a *Mars Attacks* trading card, the one where the bug-eyed Martian grabs at a screaming woman in a tight red dress. Marcy, under her very blond hair, looks old enough to have been that young thing. We head down the row toward our table, just past the video guy with his animé, blooper tapes and *Mystery Science Theater 3000*–worthy horror movies. Ma flaps her lucky tablecloth out over the table: the faded yellow one with lacy edges that belonged to her mother. Its claim to fame is that Frankie Avalon had lunch on it once, in my grandmother's tiny rowhouse in South Philly. His mother and my grandmother were friends, or at least that's what Janine says. I start unpacking our stuff, leaving room for the MTM shrine in the middle, which Ma always does herself. Binders up at the front, then our miscellaneous stuff like the lunch boxes to the sides; posters go up behind, leaning on the back table.

You could call my mother a generalist, aside from her Mary memorabilia. Piece for piece, she can't compete against someone who just sells posters, like that guy against the far wall. I've been pushing her to specialize; I think she could make a go of it with lunch boxes and other school memorabilia. But she can't help it, she loves everything. This is so important to her. I see her over in the corner, talking earnestly to the guy who organizes Collectorama! and some other shows. C'mon, Ma! I've got the table pretty much laid out, but I can't do the posters by myself. And I need something to eat, I wasn't hungry when we left this morning.

THEY'RE APPROACHING ME slowly, from all sides, coming out into the light. I try not to look around, just keep my eyes on their leader, who's still sitting motionless against the wall. I feel a light touch on my shoulder, and another on my back. Then a hand darts out, and slender fingers rip my comtron from my neck. Hey! I cry out and grab toward it without thinking. But they've already retreated back into the shadows. They probably think they've captured a pretty piece of jewelry, but if they stumble on its function, then I've violated Principle One on First Contact. And in any case,

I have to get it back or I'll be stranded here. I slip my hand over the pocket where my weapon is hidden.

"WELL, DO YOU want it or not?" My mother is waving a gigantic bran muffin a few inches from my face. My usual breakfast— she must have brought it from home. I free it from its wrapping and munch, looking around. A couple of early-bird visitors wander past.

"Sweetie," my mother says. "When you go for your bathroom break, I want you to stop and talk to that poster guy. Maybe he's interested in buying one of ours. I think his name is Burt, or Bart, I remember him. He looks nice, doesn't he?" She still hasn't given up trying to fix me up with somebody nice.

"Whatever." I glance over at the guy—he's not even my type. Too skinny, and his hair looks dyed blond.

Pretty soon people are stopping at our table, Janine is chatting them up about their favorite canceled TV shows, I'm riffling through piles and notebooks to find stuff for them, and we've made our first few sales.

My digital watch beeps at eleven, reminding me it's time for my first bathroom break. I ease out into the aisle, which has filled up with a good crowd by now. Some lunch boxes catch my eye— The A-Team, Barbie, Smurfs. Another Barbie. Wow, and a Bionic Woman! For some reason, you don't see too much Bionic Woman stuff. Lindsay Wagner was my faithful lunch companion when I was a kid. Once I discovered *The Bionic Woman* in reruns, I badgered my mom till she found the lunch box somewhere. I'd pull out my sandwich and chips, stand the box up with the picture facing me, and me and Jaime Sommers would go off on our adventures. Actually, me *as* Jaime, tall, gorgeous and partly metal and plastic, would go off and save the world. I was clumping around in my crutches and braces then, and knowing they could make replacement parts for her made me optimistic for my own parts. Hah. Still, I want this box—I'll come back later when I have some cash.

I find the ladies' room and ease into the big stall. Get myself on the toilet, then pull out the plastic bag with my catheters and wipes and do my thing. I've been pretty good with the bathroom breaks, but I usually wear a pad just in case. The accidents I used to have when I was a kid—those were the worst. There's no snappy comeback to other kids when you wet your pants. When I was in with the kidney infection a few years ago, Dr. O'Malley told me about some new surgery that's supposed to give you more control. I had to remind her of my No More Elective Surgery policy. She's okay, but sometimes she forgets.

Wheeling back through the lobby, those childhood dreams of bionic freedom keep coming back to me. I know now that replacement parts aren't in the cards, but the whiff of that old fantasy got me a little high. No, it's either wheels or crutches on the horizon. I could go back to the crutches if I wanted, like I did up into high school. That memory comes back: Me struggling up the aisle at my high school graduation, scared every second that the damn gown would catch on the crutch tips. My parents sitting there, Ma just about fluorescent with pride. Yeah, I made it, Ma, your little spina bifida baby who couldn't move her legs when she was born. They said I'd never be able to walk, that there might be brain damage, that I'd always be small for my age. At least that prediction was wrong. I forced myself up that aisle, under the rounded gym ceiling. The only high school in America, they said, with a geodesic gym building. Where I spent many a gym period on the sidelines of some game, staring up at the interlocking steel-beam triangles, imagining it as some UFO interior, or a planetary colony's artificial-weather unit. But I was looking down at graduation, had to keep watching the crutch tips and the edge of the powder-blue gown.

Damn it, this remembering is not what I wanted. I turn away from the aisle with the lunch boxes and head toward the poster table. I will be cool and professional, bringing a complete report back to my superior.

The poster guy's table is at the end of the aisle. He's got a *Star Wars: Phantom Menace* poster up front and center. Flanking it on either side, older offerings for the connoisseurs. Blood of the Vampire—No One is Safe. And a vintage *Man in the Iron Mask* poster—not the pathetic remake with Leonardo DiCaprio. Behind

This Hideous Mask . . . He Yearned For Love. The prices aren't bad. Burt or Bart is writing up a receipt. Long pale face, spiky hair, stubble beard.

"With you in a minute," he says without looking at me. I see the item being purchased as he rolls it up for his customer: the poster from *SkyLog III: Revenge of the Mowg.*

"That one was a dog," I say. It just slipped out. I have very definite opinions about the SkyLog movies. Plus, since it didn't do as well as the others, there hasn't been another SkyLog movie since. And now, with the *Century 23* series canceled, it's just another reminder of the precarious situation we Loggers find ourselves in at this point. So I may have a grudge against this particular movie.

The customer turns to me. Beer gut straining his black T-shirt over the worn big-guy jeans. At my eye level, I've had a ringside view of many beer guts, as well as the rear views; his are standard issue for this crowd.

"Don't tell me," he says through his overgrown mustache, fixing me with an aggrieved glare. "You're a Dr. Dina Braxton fan." Good shot, big guy. Thank God you're wrong—she's not my type at all. What the Captain saw in her, I can't figure out.

"Can't get one past you," I say. "Okay, let me see; you must be one of those overgrown Bokun groupies." His nervous chuckle tells me I've scored a direct hit. Bokun is the only Santak officer on the *Encounter.* It was an easy guess, since *SkyLog III* features a visit to the Santak home world. And I've noticed how Santak wannabes tend to be plus-size. You can't miss them at the Cons, with their orange makeup, shaggy hair and chest plates, towering over all the Transortium Fleet crewmen and officers. It's never been my thing. If you want pseudo–Dark Ages escapism, stick with Hercules and Xena, I say. This one hasn't combed his hair in a while either. He's still standing there, sizing me up.

"Right," he says. "I bet you've got a big Mary Sue thing going on!"

"I do not!" My face flushes hot.

"Yeah!" he nods. "You're all about the girl hero saving the Fleet!"

I feel like I've been slapped. Being called out for a Mary Sue is like the worst putdown in the world of fan fiction. Mary Sue isn't even a character on the show—she's just an insult fanfic writers throw around at each other. In my circle, nobody ever accuses anybody else of writing a Mary Sue, which basically means inserting yourself as the brilliant, sexy heroine of your own story. That would wipe out at least half of what's gone into "Voice of the Cyborg," since we've always had more women authors than men. What is a fanfic writer who happens to be female supposed to do—put in a main character who's stupid and cowardly and not good-looking? And this guy is double wrong, I don't even write fanfic. I used to put one of my stories in every issue, even had a couple published in other zines, but not anymore. What goes on inside my head is my business.

The guy raises his fist in a casual Santak salute and saunters away. I feel like my shirt's been ripped off, and I'm furious at myself for not thinking of anything to hurl back at him.

"So what can I do you for?" Bart/Burt asks. I will myself to stop blushing, which doesn't work.

"Nothing," I mumble. "Just thought you might be interested in a rare Kiss poster. We're at Table 12."

"Don't do rock posters, sorry."

I wheel on back, blocked every few feet by the growing crowd of browsers, wishing I could just run them over. My attempt at cyborg cool has been shattered by one asshole, someone who clearly knows nothing about anything that matters in the Transortium. In my head, I subject him to some choice insults. Rounding the bend to our row, I see Janine sitting, looking up at some guy, a big smile on her face.

"Mindy, there you are!" she calls, waving me in. "Nick, this is my daughter, Mindy. Mindy, this is Mr. Nick Costa, the King of Comics!" Right, I passed his booth before. A double-wide—he's got a lot of inventory, but the few mint issues were way overpriced.

As he turns toward me, I clock the smooth recovery from his initial surprise: very good time, Mr. Nick Costa. We'll give it an 8.

"What a lovely girl," he purrs. He's small, with thinning black hair falling to the shoulders of his white shirt.

"I was just telling your mom what a nice collection she's got."

"Oh, no, Nick. I'm just a little fish compared to you." She's wriggling like a fish too.

"No, really. You've got the makings of a good setup here. I've always been a big fan of Mary Tyler Moore." He taps the framed picture. She never lets anyone touch it, but she doesn't flinch.

"Stop by later," he adds, slapping a business card down as he leaves. *KING OF COMIX—Stick with Nick, It won't Costa Lot, Over 5,000 Back Issues.* His store's in Secaucus. Janine leans toward me. "He says my stuff is distinctive."

"Right."

"And he says he might be able to get me into the Atlantic City show." She looks straight at me, her pupils wide, like the guy's hypnotized her.

"Really? And how would he do that?" I can't take any bullshit right now.

"He said he knows some people there." Luckily, a customer asks her about one of the *TV Guides.* Maybe she'll forget about Atlantic City. It's the biggest antiques and collectibles show around, no way are we ready for it. The booth rental alone would kill us.

"So, did you see the poster guy?" she asks after she's made the sale. "Is he nice?"

"Not my type." Both of the poster guys were assholes.

"Did you talk to him? What's his name, anyway?"

"Bart," I lie.

Another customer comes up, and after that it's a steady stream of people looking or buying, and I get into the show zone, where I'm not thinking about anything except where something is, what's the price, and how much I'll bargain down, with a little people-watching thrown in. We're a good team—Janine the chatty one, me more down to business. When the crowd finally thins, I'm punchy and stiff. It's about four-thirty, past time for my bathroom break—we were too busy when my watch went off.

"How're we doing?" I ask.

"Really good, I think. Here, you count." She hands me a wad of bills. Not bad, I can tell by the feel of it: maybe a hundred dollars. That means we paid for the table rental, and then some. We do okay, between my SSI payments, the flea markets, and Irv helping out when he can, but we've had a few tough spots here and there.

"So, Ma, now you're a real collectibles dealer."

"Knock on wood. There's still tomorrow."

"I'm going for a pit stop. Do you want something to eat?"

"Okay, maybe some fries. And a Sprite. I'll start putting some things away."

I wheel out and down the aisle, heading for the booth selling that Bionic Woman lunch box. But it's gone. Damn it, I should have asked them to hold it for me. Stupid, stupid. The vendor turns away to another customer, and I rouse myself to roll away. What is wrong with me? I shouldn't be this upset over a damn lunch box. Now my cafeteria memories come back with a sharper edge. Lunch hour was truly the worst. In middle school I usually had a book to bury myself in, and then in high school I had a couple of friends I sat with. But there were always the kids at the other tables—the boys whooping it up, the girls leaning in to share secrets.

After my pit stop, I head back in with our fries and drinks, and I pick up the A-Team lunch box for a good price, but it doesn't pull me out of my funk. Now my brain has circled back around to Sheryl. The truth is, I did think she was my friend. She came over, though we didn't hang out like I do with Zu. She never invited me to her place, but I never thought much about that. She lives with a roommate, somebody she met in college, I think. She always had to leave the CAS meetings at the same time to catch the bus home. It's just that she seemed so *interested* in me. Isn't that part of being a friend?

I find myself stuck in a small knot of people, staring at a clear plastic tote bag with hot-pink stripes swirling around it, stuffed with various tchotchkes.

"Aren't you Janine's girl?" I look up. The old lady attached to the tote bag does look familiar. A cap of white curls surrounds her pudgy face, which is accessorized with round red-framed glasses.

"Is it Millie?" she tries.

"Mindy." Now I remember: she's a veteran of my mom's flea market circuit, a real diehard, so regular that she and Janine had struck up a friendship. But I haven't seen her in years.

"Remember me? It's Roxie, your mom's friend." She looks older, but her voice is the same. Kind of like a gas-powered lawnmower.

"Hi, Rox. Long time no see."

"I was not too well for a while. But things are looking up. What'd you get?" She grabs the lunch box from my lap, turns it appraisingly.

"It's not like I'm a big Mr. T fan," I say in my defense.

"Look what I found," she says, reaching into her bag with the swirly lines—it's kind of neo-psychedelic, or maybe vintage. She pulls out a couple of little Japanese robot toys, one in the original box. Very nice. And, last but not least, a *Lost in Space* robot. Not from the pathetic remake—an old one from the original TV series.

"Wow, that's really rare!" He's like the classic ugly robot icon; I have a guilty-pleasure soft spot for him. Bots and androids are another one of my things.

"I went wild today. I'm in the middle of my robotic period," Roxie says. "How's your mom?"

"She's right over there, go see for yourself. Second table on the right."

"She's got a table here?"

"Yeah, we're getting into collectibles. She'll freak when she sees you. In a good way." I point her in the right direction, and weave my way back through legs and purses, doing one last scan for interesting material. When I get back, Roxie's standing with Janine at the table.

"Min!" Janine beams, gesturing toward Roxie. "Isn't this great?" Like she found her long-lost sister. "Did you know that Roxie's an artist?"

"I just got back to it," says Roxie. "I was a painter before, a long time ago. Now I make things out of other things," she explains, raising her tote bag like a champagne glass.

"You make art out of shopping bags?" Janine tries.

"No, found objects." She jiggles the bag. "I call them my lost-and-found objects, actually. They're lost till I find them." She must have a huge amount of tchotchkes in reserve by now, I think, remembering her old buying habits.

"So." Roxie turns to me. "Your mother tells me you're a writer?"

"No." I toss Janine a glare, which bounces off her. "Well, I do write my editorials, but that's all."

"But, honey, you write stories, too!"

"No I don't!" Why can't she remember that? It's a sore spot, and it keeps getting poked today. "I put out a zine, so I work with a lot of writers." My voice comes out thin and even, that's good.

Roxie is giving me a blank look.

"You know, a fan magazine. It's SkyLog-related, for the community of cyborg appreciators." At least I'm still putting out my zine—Sheryl can't stop me. But I still haven't figured out what to do about selling it at the Con.

"Oh, SkyLog!" she says. "Flying into the future, finding other worlds!" At least she's heard the tagline.

"We're giving Roxie a ride home!" Janine says.

"We are?" Where the hell are we going to fit her?

"She lives right near here!"

"You really don't have to," Roxie says. "I can call Morris."

"Stop it, of course we'll take you," Janine says. "You don't mind sitting on a box?"

A half hour later, the van is packed, we're all crowded in, and we set off for the home of Roxie and Morris Grunwald. Roxie leans between us, and she and Ma start in on a serious catching-up chat. It seems that Roxie had trouble with her left leg and her heart, and these or some other stuff have kept her in and out of the hospital the last few years.

IT'S NIGHT. I'm sitting beside the Old One now, wearing some woven thing around my neck. This might be a gift, meant in exchange for my stolen device. I feel the Old One's eyes sliding up and down my body as I watch the proceedings—some kind of greeting or entertainment for their strange visitor. The others have slipped off their hooded robes, leaving them naked except for belts, bracelets, and the hair-fuzz all over their bodies. They're starting to dance, their limbs and torsos snaking gracefully as they weave complex patterns. It's mesmerizing, with the shooshing voices and padding feet lulling me after the long hours of waiting. Hey—that's my comtron, hanging on a string around a dancer's neck! So it's just an exotic piece of jewelry to them. Would it be so terrible if I let them keep it, if I stayed on here, an honored guest, desired by their chief? To live in this simpler world, where I appear to be wanted, maybe even revered? No—I have to get past this moment that always comes in my exploratory missions. I have to be careful. And I must get the comtron back.

"MINDY! ROXIE's asking you a question!"

"I'm just wondering," Roxie's hand grips my shoulder. "Since I have the pacemaker plugged into my heart, does that make me some kind of android?"

"No." I have to be patient, she is an old lady. "An android is made up totally of synthetic parts. You'd be more like a cyborg. That's, you know, when you start out with a humanoid organism and add machine parts or digital elements. Sort of like Lindsay Wagner in *The Bionic Woman*." I feel the pang of loss again. It's just a damn lunch box, I tell myself.

"Is this where we turn?" Janine speaks up.

"Yes! Turn, turn!" Apparently they missed it the first time. We're in a neatly clipped development of older, one-story houses. Roxie navigates us past the cul-de-sacs and horseshoes, and finally to her house. It's pretty much like all the houses we've passed, except that it's painted the color of the inside of a ripe cantaloupe. In the late-afternoon light, it gives off an eerie sun-drenched glow. As we pull up the driveway, I see that the side of the house is painted a different color—a light grayish blue. Wow. Maybe it's from being inside the hotel all day, but I feel a little dizzy, like I've slipped into a dream.

"That's some house you've got," I say. Roxie is pleased.

"I think of it as my homage to Edward Hopper," she says, pointing at the side wall. "In his paintings, when the sun hits the house, it looks orange in the front, blue on the shaded side. See?"

"That's pretty radical."

"I'm very radical," she answers as she slides open the van door, then lets herself carefully down onto the asphalt.

"What do the neighbors think of it?" Janine asks, dubiously eyeing the other houses on the block, which are basically all white.

"Screw the neighbors. They're a bunch of bourgeois airheads, with the color sense of lemmings." My mother's eyes go wide—she always says this is a "very nice" area.

"I may have to live in Cherry Hill," Roxie goes on, "but I don't have to fit in here. Why don't you ladies come in for some coffee?"

My mother never turns down an invitation—hey, she doesn't get that many. Even though we're both cross-eyed tired, sweaty and spacey from our day at the hotel, we enter the cantaloupe-colored house.

The first thing I see is, there's no rug. That's definitely a plus. Then I see the paintings on the walls, all sizes, popping with color—kind of abstract but you can recognize figures, houses, trees here and there.

"Those are my old paintings. Morris!" she calls. "He must be lying down, I'll go get him, you ladies make yourselves at home." She shuffles down the short hallway. Wheeling through the sparsely furnished living room, I try to makes sense out of the dining room, or what would be the dining room. It's only got a single nylon lawn chair. But I can't go inside—the place is totally colonized with toys, pieces of Plexiglas and curling ribbons of different-colored telephone wire. They're on the floor, hanging from the ceiling, even traveling tightrope-style from one wall to another. A Barbie hangs over the doorway, naked and trailing silver and gold pipe-cleaner strands. The ceiling is black, with swirls of glitter like nebulae. How the hell did she get glitter on the ceiling? And climbing the back wall, a small fleet of robots, all different shapes and sizes. Down on the floor, a herd of plastic dinosaurs roams across a sheet of green-painted plywood.

"What do you think? Something else, eh?" I turn to see a rumpled old guy, stooped, not much hair. Blinding white sneakers on his feet.

"That's my husband, Morris," calls Roxie from the kitchen, clanking cups and plates. He shakes hands with us, all courtly. "Are you two artists?" he asks.

"Oh my gosh, no!" Janine giggles. "We didn't even know Roxie was an artist till today."

"I never know what she'll come up with next," he says, waving a hand at the dining area. "Of course, we always ate in the kitchen anyway." I look around us at the piles of toys and odd things in the corners—more dinosaurs, plastic soldiers, martini glasses, old gilt picture frames—and then back at the insane giant diorama in the dining room. It's like our house, I think, but different: like the toys and junk had decided to climb out of the boxes and make a statement.

Roxie appears at her husband's side, reaches up to straighten his crooked collar. "Yeah, you've put up with me all this time, babe," she says to him.

"Roxie, if you don't mind my asking, what is this?" Janine asks, peering into the other room.

"It's my newest experiment. I was making little sculptures out of these things—they're all in the back room. Then, I don't know, I wanted to put them together into something bigger."

I wheel right up to the edge, trying to see how this could be art.

"I call it 'Green World, Black World.' See?" She points first to the dinosaurs on their grass-green field, then up to the black ceiling. "This is where we came from, and that's where we're going." I crane my neck again at the ceiling, with its cosmic whirls of glitter. "But then," she adds, "the black also refers to the dark side of our new technologies, like nuclear war."

"What about the robots?" I ask, studying the bunch of them climbing the far wall on bits of wire.

"I'm not sure about the robots. That's why they're on the wall, in between. What do you say, Mindy?"

I feel a little exposed. "I'm with you," I say. "Put them in between for now, see how they behave."

"Did she tell you about her show?" Morris asks.

"It's no big deal, it's at the Senior Center. The last time I had a real show was twenty years ago."

"Isn't that something," Janine says. "Are you going to put your paintings in too?" She's wandered back into the living room.

"No, this will just be my current work." Roxie reaches up to fiddle with a curly red wire.

"But—the paintings all say 'Greenworld,'" Ma says.

"That's just how I sign my work. Greenworld sounds better than Grunwald." She leans in toward me and adds in a low voice, "I used to hang around with these musicians when I had my studio in Philly. It just came to me one night, when we were smoking weed." She straightens up. "Morrie saved me from all that." Then she disappears back into the kitchen.

"I'm afraid I'm not much help to Roxie anymore," Morris says. "It's the back. Can't help her hang things, can't get down to my workshop to cut the big pieces for her. Bum back, bad eyes. Getting old is crap." I hear you, Morris. You don't have to tell me about body parts that don't work. Maybe by the time I'm your age, sometime in the next century, I'll be able to follow through on my dream of replacing various parts with improved synth materials. Maybe it's just too soon to attempt.

We're called into the kitchen, to sit around the table for coffee and apple cake, which is pretty tasty. In the glare of the fluorescent light, Roxie and her husband look smaller, just a couple of senior citizens having a snack. But I feel strangely stirred up.

"You know, I have a friend who would like to see your work," I say. "She's kind of trying to do something similar, but with sounds." This reminds me how Zu and I haven't talked or emailed since the night she came over.

"Tell her to call me. I've been thinking it would be nice to have some sound as part of the show," Roxie says. "And all the musicians I know are dead," she adds, licking crumbs from her fingers. Thinking of Zu and what happened between us, my appetite's gone.

As we're leaving, Roxie calls, "Wait!" and shuffles over to her psychedelic plastic bag, next to the couch.

"This is for you, Mindy," she says, and presses the *Lost in Space* robot into my hand.

"But you just got this!" I protest. I know I'm going to keep it.

"I've got more than I need," she says. "Just promise me you'll tell me when you figure out where the robots go."

As we drive home, I turn the little robot over in my hands, looking at the clunky, faceless head, the fat tubular arms, the primitive tank-tread mobility hack. An obsolete dream from an earlier time. An artificial lifeform always watching out for danger, trying to protect its human companions.

THE CEREMONY is over. I'm resting in a room off the Old One's chambers, trying to make sense of things. I've reached that point where I'm exhausted and overwhelmed by the encounter with a new culture, the newness and the ballooning uncertainties. I feel a pang of loneliness that makes me curl in on myself. I miss my cyborg, the one who watches me with such quiet concentration from across the divide of our histories.

Shadow of the Mesh, Part 3

5

Pak strode into the briefing room and saluted Commander Varm. The Commander had very impressive nose bones, with four separate spikes, and his chest plate carried the carved insignia of many battles.

"Gonon," Varm said without looking up from the readout. Good, he doesn't suspect me, he still thinks I am Gonon, Pak thought. He silently thanked his ancestors for giving him sharp enough nose bones to pass among the Santak, even though he was part human.

"Why did you show me this intercepted transmission," Varm asked.

"Because I think it is from the Mesh, Leader," Pak answered. The Mesh's official warning, "You Will Be Mesh," rang in his head. This is the announcement they gave right before any invasion.

"But this is a mere fragment of a signal" said Varm. But didn't Varm remember the Mesh invasion of Kepler-62-IV! The Mesh was almost unstoppable.

"We must go into full mobilization now," Pak said. "If we wait to receive an official signal from the Mesh it will be too late."

Varm grabbed Pak by the chest plate and pulled him close. "I make the military decisions here, Slime-worm!!"

"I am your servant," Pak said which was hard because he was choking. Varm finely let go and went back to the table, Pak gasped for breath and rubbed his throat. Then Varm told Pak about the report that was just received of a group of rebels. The rebels in the Honzhin territory were fighting against the Santak rulers. How ironic Pak thought. Just the same as the Santak had fought against the rule of their Mowg conquerors.

"The rebels claim that they already made contact with the Mesh" Varm said. "If their claim is true, they must have some secret form of sensing technology." Maybe they modified there metaspace sensors, Pak thought.

"We will arrange for you to be captured by the rebels," Varm told him. "You will find out their secret technology and return to us. It could be extremely useful if the Mesh really are approaching." He still does not believe, thought Pak. If only he knew what Pak had learned from Roi: that the Mesh evaluated every society on its warlike characteristics, and adjusted the Taking plan accordingly. These aggressive Santak would be treated worse than others.

Several hours later, Pak was standing on a trail through the forest with his hands up, looking down the barrels of four energy guns. The figures behind the weapons wore rags in different shades of red which made them blend in with the orange and red leaves of the trees all around them.

"I'm unarmed!" Pak yelled.

The leader shouted, "What are you doing in the contested area!" The voice revealed it was a female. With the thick band of rags around her head and covering her body he hadn't noticed. Now he could see she was tall, and really beautiful, if you didn't mind the magenta skin of the Honzhin natives. Even under the layers of rags he could make out her pleasing shape and muscular limbs.

"I got separated from my party." That was what he was told to say. The leader looked him up and down with her orange eyes. "I don't believe you," she said. "Take him."

They tied his hands and pushed him along with an energy gun poking into his back. As he stumbled forward Pak thought, "Soon I'll know about there sensing technology. Either that or I will be dead." As his uncle Bokun had tried to teach him, there are many ways to become a Santak warrior.

FROM: MindRoid@comet.net
TO: tadmesh@deepnet.com
SUBJECT: Your Story
DATE: 7/22/99 6:39 PM

Dear tadmesh,

Thanx for your new story, looks pretty good. Okay, I have to admit that this zine doesn't come out often enough to print your stuff separately at your current rate of production. Is it okay if we bundle a few of these together? And I hope we're gonna get to see some of the Mesh soon. My readers are into artificially enhanced lifeforms, remember? Also, the Voice may be changing its name for the forthcoming issue. I'll let you know.

Your loyal editor, Mindy

FROM: amadden@uokla.edu
TO: MindRoid@comet.net
SUBJECT: new girl hero
DATE: 7/23/99 1:42 PM

Mind,

You will not believe what happened. They had me working in this dusty old storeroom in the library basement, and I found these old letters and papers and stuff in a box way in the back and I sat and read them right thru lunch. All from this woman Catherine Weldon, seems she lived with Sitting Bull on the reservation about a hundred years ago. It was hard to read the old handwriting, but I got in the zone. I am peeing my pants here. This single white lady from NY moves out to live with the Indians. THIS IS MY KIND OF WOMAN! And then she got mixed up with this Ghost Dance thing that was happening, then she was kicked off the reservation, she had all kinds of problems. Then she got forgotten, just like Dr. Dina never gets the credit she deserves for saving Roi. That's HIStory for you! And then my supervisor Lillian says this is a really important find, because the guy that published her letters back in the thirties, Mr. Vestal, he kind of mislaid the originals. And all they had in his archive upstairs was some typed copies, so of course this box of original stuff is a real find. Maybe there's even some new ones he never typed (more likely his wife typed them, lol). So Lillian took the box and locked it in her office, probably gonna hold a press conference or announce it at her next Librarian conference or something. I already copied some of them for myself. But Mindy, holding those letters in my hands felt like TIME TRAVEL.

abundant life, angie

FROM: MindRoid@comet.net
TO: amadden@uokla.edu
SUBJECT: Re: new girl hero
DATE: 7/23/99 3:37 PM

Angie—

Props on you, that is way cool! You're like Indiana Jones there. Obvi you should get the credit for this, not your boss. Okay, I don't know that much about Wild Western history or the Indians, but this Catherine sounds pretty awesome. Maybe you could work her into a "real" time travel story?? xoxo Mindy

I always thought working in a library would be the perfect job, being surrounded by books all the time. Finding some lost letters would make it even more awesome. I did try taking that Intro to Library Science course at County Community. Big mistake, I should have known anything with the word "science" in it was not for me, if it's not science fiction, that is. That was after we moved back to Philadelphia, after the last big surgery I had, after my headaches had died down. The campus was accessible enough, but not knowing anybody was hard. And then I had another kidney infection, took the Incomplete and said to hell with it.

FROM: botsy@skymail.com
TO: MindRoid@comet.net
SUBJECT: Inspiration Strikes Again!!!
DATE: 7/24/99 10:05 AM

Hey Mindy! Ready or not here it comes, another poem for your pages!! Well, it's kind of really a filk duet inspired by Barbie Girl, but I think it works as a poem too.

Hi Bottina!
Hi Roi!
Do you want to go for a ride?
Sure Roi.

I'm a cyborg girl, in a cyborg world
Life is plastic, it's fantastic
You can kiss my face, then we'll regenerate
Don't care if we're machines or people now

Come on Roi, let's make some noise!

You're my doll, rock 'n' roll, we don't need emotion,
Kiss me here, touch me there, put it all in motion.
You can touch,
You can play,
Just don't go away.

I'm a cyborg girl, in a cyborg world
Life is plastic, it's fantastic

We can gravitate, we'll gyrate till real late
Don't care if we're machines or people now

Come on Roi, let's make some noise! (Oh oh yeah) . . .

I tried to keep it PG-13 for you. But if you want the R version
let me know. ;) Now I gotta start thinking about the costumes
for me and Trevor if we're gonna sing this at the Con!

Love ya, Patty aka Bottina

The costume contest! It's only the high point of the whole Con,
with people dressing up as Meshers, Wuvians, Gonfarians and
other various SkyLog species including Terrans. Some contestants sing filk numbers too, like Patty and Trevor. The CAS never
went all out, just a dignified lineup in our Transortium uniforms,
even if we sometimes had more than one Roi. I don't miss the idea
of getting up on stage in front of everybody, but right now I can't
imagine even sitting in the audience and having to watch my former club up there, whatever they're planning.

Patty's not in the CAS—she lives too far away. I think I can
count on her as a contributor, even after she finds out about
Sheryl's takeover. But I wish she hadn't mentioned the damn Con.
I keep thinking I've got things under control, and then I get reminded of some other thing.

TO: MindRoid@comet.net
FROM: jammin@ultranet.com
SUBJECT: Bash
DATE: 7/24/99 10:22 PM

Mindy,

Okay, it's me. Just wanted to make sure you'd read this.
Here's the deal. Remember according to your calculations,
how a week from tomorrow is the negative 250th anniversary
of Roi's Mesh Liberation Day? How about I pick you up and
we have a little party at Spudz to celebrate. Just you and

me. This has ZERO to do with the CAS, which I have resigned from. Knock twice for yes.

xo Zu

FROM: MindRoid@comet.net
TO: jammin@ultranet.com
SUBJECT: Re: Bash
DATE: 7/24/99 11:14 PM

Knock knock

6

"So, are you working tonight?" I ask, looking out the car window at a playground, almost hidden under trees that look exhausted in the heat.

"No way," Zu says. We're in her boxy old Toyota, metallic blue. It was a dumb question anyway. Zu works the midnight-to-eight shift, doing overflow keyboarding at one of the big law firms in town. A whiz on any keyboard.

Silence. I usually carry the conversation, but tonight I feel shy. Like we broke up, and now we're trying to reconcile. Or I am, anyway.

"So I met this old lady," I say. That sounds stupid. "She's actually very interesting, she's an artist."

"What kind of art?" Zu asks. This stops me.

"I don't know what it's called. She used to do paintings, but now she like puts a lot of things together, old toys and things, it takes up the whole room."

"Sounds pretty out there."

"Exactly, it's very bizarre. Anyway, she's looking for a musician to work with, and I mentioned your name."

"To do what?"

"I don't know, okay? Maybe some kind of background music, or sounds—you're good at sounds."

"I guess I could talk to her, find out what she wants."

"She's really a trip," I say. "Her name's Roxie." Seems like Zu's accepted my little peace offering.

More silence. We're on the Pike now. Spudz is up ahead a couple of miles, a dozen or so traffic lights. When we first moved here, there were still a few chunks of open farmland. Now it's just about all paved over. But it keeps changing: that little building was a gas station, then I think a florist, and now it's a Java the Hut. Some things just close and stay closed, like the Cinderella School of Beauty, with its stucco walls cracked like a network of varicose veins, and weeds coming up like rude bits of body hair. Other buildings disappear, and some fancier, glassier building pops up. It's disorienting. Reminds me somehow of when Marty McFly travels to the past in the first *Back to the Future*, and sees his family's development—but it's just a bulldozed field with a sign at the road promising the Home of Tomorrow. Except this is in reverse. Going into the future can be just as bizarre as traveling into the past. Science fiction's one thing, but in my experience actual time travel can feel pretty bumpy.

I LEAN MY HEAD back. My long hair fascinates them, and two of them stand on either side of me, swaying and humming, twisting it into coils and knots. Their long digits tickle my scalp. Without my comtron, I've had to follow them very closely to figure out what they're doing, and I've started picking up a little of their language. They call themselves the Night People because they hunt at night, when the wind dies down, and there are other groups who don't. They won't let me go along, though—I'm the honored guest of the Old One, living with his family. I feel the days ticking by. I have to speak to the Old One soon.

WE PULL IN the Spudz parking lot. Zu helps me up the curb cut and through the double doors. Sounds and smells greet me like an old friend: clattering plates, roar of voices, aromatic frying fat. The hostess takes us to a table by the wall—a pretty good approximation of sitting in a booth—and gives us two oversized menus.

"Hey, ladies!" It's Ronni, one of the waitresses. "Where've you all been keeping yourselves?" she asks, setting down glasses of water and straws. Zu blinks and looks at the menu, her mouth cinching in a frown. Why didn't I think up an answer to that in advance?

"Oh, you know . . . been pretty busy," I say. Well, Zu probably has. "Zu's deep into her new, um, electronic compositions." Zu tosses me a look.

"Cool," Ronni says. "What can I get you ladies?" I order a Rolling Rock, and Zu gets a St. Pauli Girl. Then we put in our usual orders—for me, a baked Spudz with bacon bits and broccoli, and obligatory side salad, and for Zu her usual purist fare, plain burger and a plain baked Spudz. A few years back, Zu and I hit on the idea of honoring Roi's Mesh Liberation Day, since birthdays aren't celebrated by either Wuvians or Meshers. Instead, we counted back from the date he was brought on board the *Encounter*, kind of being born into his new post-Mesh life. Raising a glass with Zu for the occasion is way better than sitting in my room.

"To the best cyborg in the known Universe!" There are a few other recognized cyborgs serving in the Fleet—not Meshers, of course, but some Gonfarians with enhanced functioning thanks to prosthetics and implanted software. But we're loyal to our Roi. Then we move on to evaluating the latest non-SkyLog performance by Van Dawkins, the guy who plays Roi. Once she's done with her burger, Zu pulls her Walkman out of her backpack to play me part of her latest musical work in progress, which mixes in part of Mac the Navigator's ukulele solo from Season Five of the first series—okay, that's good. Then she turns over the tape and presses Record.

"Is this an interview?" I ask. She laughs, holding up the Walkman, her elbow on the table.

"No! I'm sampling the background noise." Of course she is. Who knows what it will sound like once she's done with it? I sit back, regarding my mostly finished Spudz and half-finished glass of beer, glinting gold in the low light. Me and beer is mostly theoretical. Goes right through me—I better check the facilities soon. But I'm feeling mellow, or at least close to mellow. The table between us is littered with Zu creations: paper straw covers, flattened into circles and linked in a tiny chain, plastic straws remade as equilateral triangles. Her fingers keep going even when they're not working a keyboard or a console.

I take a breath. "So I was wondering. Do you think you could help me distribute the zine when we're at the Con?"

"Sure, but—"

"But what?" I knew it—she's going to say she went back to the CAS.

"Well, if Sheryl brings out her own Voice—"

"I really don't care about that, as long as you're not part of it."

"Hey! I told you I wasn't going back!"

"Okay, fine. So my zine will be for sale at the Con, just under a different name. To avoid confusion."

She takes this in. "What's the new name?"

"I was thinking, A.L.L., 'Alternate Lifeforms Log.'"

She nods, repeating it. "It's good." She's the first person I've tried it out on, and she's Zu, so I'm glad she likes it.

"I mean," I say, "that way there's no problem with including all kinds of aliens, maybe even some non-SkyLog species . . ."

"So, are you gonna rent a table then?"

"I have to see if they'll give me a special rate, or maybe a freebie. For all the support I've given to the Con over the years."

"Okay." She leans forward. "But Mindy, what about the next issue? You won't have the club to help. And you know Sheryl's gonna be in touch with the subscribers, and the contributors, if she hasn't already. Who knows what she'll tell them?"

"Screw Sheryl." My face is hot. "I already got a couple more pieces in—another one from that Tad guy, and one of Patty's filk things. And Angie Madden, from Oklahoma, she's working on something." That's half-true—who knows where she's going with that Indian thing she's into now.

"What about you?" I say. "You used to give me good stuff."

"I told you, Mindy, I don't have time to write anymore!" I know that—Zu's all into mixing sounds now—but I'm desperate.

"I don't care what you write. Any kind of slash is fine: Captain Tanaka and Roi, Roi and Bokun, it's all cool." Now she's getting red. That was her specialty, slash fiction—Tanaka/Roi, Roi/Bokun, Dr. Braxton/Ensign Nema. Stories that spliced same-sex characters together into romantic couples that would never get written into prime time. Stupid network censorship. But fanfic writers like Zu rushed right into the vacuum. It doesn't do much for me, but a lot of people like it. You could say slash fic extends the principle of Abundant Life in Many Forms even further, into the characters' private lives. And Zu's stories were good.

"What about you then?" Zu says. "You used to write good stuff too. Why'd you stop?" I feel a needle-stab in my gut.

"I told you, I got bored with it."

"That's bullcrap, Mindy."

"I just felt funny about publishing my own stuff in my zine." Another thing I've told the few people who asked about this.

"Double bullcrap. Nobody cares if the editor puts their own story in, as long as it's good."

"Can we just drop it?"

Ronni swoops in, eyes on the table, and starts stacking our plates. I never told Zu, never told anyone what happened. How I started getting letters to the editor, typed, with no return address. Explaining to me in punishing detail how my stories were so Mary Sue it was painful to read them. How my Mission Officer, Kat Wanderer, was so disgustingly brilliant, beautiful, heroic, seductive, that they should rename Mary Sue after her. Urging me to kill her off, for the sake of fandom. How, as the editor, I should hold myself to the highest standards. The letters were all signed A True SkyLog Fan. I never printed them in the zine. But after getting letters from True Fan over several issues of the Voice, I did kill off my brilliant, beautiful heroine. Not really, but Kat Wanderer's adventures never got written down again.

"You ladies want dessert? We've got the Boston cream pie."

Zu glances at her watch. "Um, not for me." I shake my head no. Ronni slaps the bill on the table.

"I thought you were all clear tonight."

"I wasn't sure when we'd get done," she says. "But there's a meeting tonight. If you want to go."

My face feels suddenly numb. "Not the CAS."

"No!" A spot of red flushes on each of her round cheeks. "Jesus, Mindy! What's with you?"

"Then what?"

"There's this other group, I went to a couple of their meetings."

"What, the Synergy? The Isaac Asimov?" This is embarrassing—I feel like she's cheating on me. But she's not, I have to keep remembering, I'm group-less.

"It's the Lrak." She bobs her head down.

"That Santak club?" I stare at her. She nods, peeking up at me.

"I just," I stumble. "Wow. I never thought you . . ." I know the Lrak—they do Con security duty sometimes—but I never mixed with them, given my general feelings about the Santak.

"Anyway, I thought maybe you'd come along," she says. Now I feel dizzy, though it may be partly the beer.

"I'm just trying to figure out, have you *joined* this group?"

"They're really all right, Mindy," she says in a rush. "I wouldn't have gone, but this guy Bradley, he's in the mailroom where I work but he's really a musician—"

"Oh, I see." She's been wanting to tell me all this.

"There we were at the office, both into SkyLog but different parts of it, you know. I just figured—"

"You figured I'd want to go too."

"Uh, yes?" Her long fingers are spread out on the table.

"Do I have a choice?" My jaw's tight. I can't drive myself home. Couldn't commandeer the car, can't drive period. This could be a case of kidnapping.

"I could take you home and then go. But that'd make me late."

"Take me home."

"Shit, Mindy . . ." she shakes her head. "Do you have to be such a hard-ass about everything?"

"I'm only a hard-ass when you try and twist my arm!"

She looks away, then back. "You know, you've been really bitchy lately." That stings—I thought she liked my zingers, or at least had a high tolerance for them.

"Well, this hasn't been such a great time for me," I say. "You try getting kicked out of your own club."

"That was like two months ago. You're not the only one with problems, Mindy."

She's right. I've been stewing, and maybe taking it out on

other people. I stare down at the table and let out a hard breath. The shiny tabletop, cleared of our dinner, is like a tableau of my life right now. A flat landscape of crater-like beer rings, with ruins of paper chains and plastic-straw triangles. A lonely, abandoned planet. The thin atmosphere of my zine-world isn't enough to sustain me—not to mention that its future is shaky. And I need Zu. It's more than just her being helpful, like agreeing to help me at the Con, which I know I can't handle myself. She's my best human friend. I can't give her another reason to give up on me.

"I guess I can survive one Santak meeting."

"Okay, cool." She tries to hold back her smile.

"And I'll try and tone down the bitchiness." That could be hard, though. "Just," I say, "I need you to let me know when I'm getting out of hand."

"I can totally do that."

THEY PULL ME to my feet, coaxing me along, twittering softly. It is time, they're saying. I hear sounds coming from the big chamber where I first met the chief—singing voices, clapping, chattering.

He's in the chamber, standing this time, waiting for me. Dressed in a decorated cloak and wearing a headpiece of twisted fibers. They did my hair for this, I realize. Several others come out of the shadows, trailing a long robe or cape, holding it up in front as high as they can. They've made it for me. With a fine weave, combining the colors of this world, sand, gray, orange, in a flowing pattern. My guides pull me to the center of the room, into a circle of burning fat lamps. I say the words of thanks, hardly hearing myself over the other voices. Others step forward to the stamping rhythm and move around me in a slow circle. They're dressed, or rather undressed like before, in belts and bracelets. My guides are pulling at my sleeves. Others come up behind me, reaching, pulling at my uniform, on my back, my legs. The voices rise to a higher pitch. What—they want to undress me! My uniform will only unfasten at my command, but they don't know that. What if they could just rip it away? I feel suddenly aware of my breasts, my skin under the tunic. More pulling and stroking. I look at the dancers circling me, their short hairs glinting in the lamplight. And the chief—what am I to him?

The Old One raises an arm and speaks. He wants me to be his mate. No! I'm so stupid not to have seen this coming! I can't think straight. As a Transortium Fleet officer, it might be best for me to go along with this, quietly observing as I seem to take part. But I can't. I fight the feeling of rising panic—I'm in over my head again. Sweat pops out on my neck, my chest, my hands.

One of the dancers grabs for the seamlock of my uniform. Without thinking, I smack the little dancer away, sending her flying into the rock wall. The room goes quiet and still. I feel their eyes on me.

I LOOK AROUND. We're off the expressway now, winding our way through smaller streets. I'm feeling sweaty, Zu's air conditioner has about had it. Heavy green of overhanging trees. At the end of a street with angular modern houses peeking through the foliage, we pull into an institutional driveway marked by a tastefully small wooden sign.

"We're going to a Unitarian church?"

"Yup. And it's handicapped-accessible," she says, turning into a parking spot. There's a low ramp leading up to the modest concrete building.

"I'm going to meet a bunch of Santak Unitarians?" I'm nervous, can't shut up.

"They just use the building, Mindy," Zu says wearily. "Unitarians are super-tolerant. They'll let anyone use their building, even the Santak." I let this go without a snappy comeback—must dial down the bitch-o-meter. I wheel myself up the ramp and into the lobby, then follow her down a short hall, through the final door into a smallish meeting room. No table in the middle, just folding chairs and a vinyl couch. Ten or twelve people already here. We've come in on the tail of one guy's story, and the room explodes in loud guffaws. Nobody wearing a Fleet uniform, except for one kid in the corner. But one guy's wearing a Santak chest plate over his T-shirt, and another one has a curved blade sticking out of his boot—metal or plastic? I don't want to know. They look like a bunch of beer-bellied bikers. I did notice a couple of bikes in the parking lot. That's the Santak—Biker Trash of the Transortium. I'm ready to back out, rehearsing what I'll say to Zu as she chases me down the hallway. But it's too late, we've been seen.

"Hey, Zuzana," somebody says, and "Zu, you made it." Eyes on me too. At least I'm not sticking out because of my size; instead it's Zu standing out here with her beanstalk silhouette. Size comes in handy on security detail at the Cons: you don't want to cross one of these guys looming over you in full uniform, with their long locks and spiky noses.

"Who's your friend?" somebody asks.

"Wait. I know," says a guy planted on the couch. "It's the President of the Dr. Dina Braxton Fan Club." He's scowling right at me. Oh, shit. It's the guy I insulted at Collectorama!—the guy who bought the *SkyLog III* poster. Dressed the same, black T-shirt and jeans, same unruly black hair, still uncombed, and droopy black mustache.

"No, she's the—" Zu stops as I send an elbow into her bony thigh. "Ah, this is my friend Mindy. Mindy, Len."

"Yeah, we've met," I mutter. He's still glowering at me. I feel a little sick, remembering the insults we traded at the show. This is the second time tonight I've been forced to think about my Mary Sue issues, making it a pretty bad night so far.

"And that's Vlad," Zu goes on, nodding toward a truly giant guy with a bushy beard sitting next to Len. Vlad has on a tan shirt with "Vlad" embroidered on the pocket.

"Yeah, I know you," says a woman standing next to us. "Didn't you do the front table at the last Valley Forge Con?"

"That's me," I say. Mindy the Unforgettable. I glance at Zu, who looks away. Zu blends into a crowd. You could meet her three, four times without remembering her. She can show up here and start fresh, no problem, no past history. I don't have that luxury. I'm Mindy the Memorable, the Extremely Visible. Now I'm super-aware of what I'm wearing, a T-shirt and sweatpants. Thank God I didn't put on my Fleet tunic tonight.

"So, you're coming over to the dark side, huh?" says the woman who recognized me, giving me an appraising look. "I heard a lot about you already. You guys are really good friends." She throws a glance toward Zu.

"We go way back," I say. Zu has a funny look on her face.

"Welcome to the Lrak," the woman says. "I'm Trish. Well, around here, I'm Nalip." Trish is short and solid, with a heart-shaped face, Goth-black hair and black nail polish. "Don't worry about Len," she adds. "He bites everybody's head off."

"I've noticed."

Trish perches on the arm of the couch and leans over toward me. "You know," she says, scrutinizing my face, "I think you'd look real good with some nose spikes. Bradley, don't you think she's got the face for it?" she calls across the room. A tall dreadlocked black guy, sitting loose and angular in one of the folding chairs, looks at me impassively and gives a nod. So that's Bradley. Bradley the mailroom guy, musician and card-carrying Santak. The guy I can blame, indirectly at least, for my being here.

"He's our Jedi master in the makeup department," Trish tells me.

"I'll pass on the spikes for now." Impersonating a Santak would violate my cyborg loyalties. Neurid-enhanced brain function still gets my vote over their primitive, barely controlled emotional workings. I look around the room, trying to get my bearings. That kid over in the corner, the one wearing the full Fleet uniform, is staring at me. Looks about twelve. Maybe he got dragged here against his will by his Santak parents, and he recognizes another kidnap victim.

The guy with the scimitar tucked in his boot stands up, and the conversation quiets down. He's a little older than everybody else, with long brownish-gray hair pulled in a ponytail, and a short same-color beard. He could really be a retired biker. He pulls out the blade, brandishes it high. Dear God, I think it's real.

"I am Kagash, Captain of the Class One Raptor Lrak!" he says in a twangy voice. "Anyone wishing to challenge me for this blade, let them do so now." He holds the blade straight out and stares around at each person, even locking eyes with me for a long second, but this seems like part of the ceremony—no one makes a move.

"Okay then." He lowers the blade. "We'd like to welcome a visitor who's on board tonight . . ." He turns toward me again, and continues after a whispered prompt, "Mindy. She's a friend of Zuzana, so she's okay. I want you all to give her the full welcome of a Santak ally." Some hoots and claps follow this. Zu's sitting next to me, looking down at her hands, which are wedged between her knees. Boy, you think you know someone. The Captain goes on to cover some club business, an upcoming party, a makeup workshop to be run by Bradley. This guy Kagash knows how to run things, even if he's a little grim. Change the details, and it's just what I did at the CAS. There's an art to running a meeting, and I was pretty good at it. But that's gone now. The loss hits me again, and I fight it back down.

"And Trish is gonna bring some of her Nadibian casserole that was such a big hit last time, right, Trish?" he teases. A little humor doesn't hurt.

"So we have a preliminary Polg ceremony tonight," says the Captain. He points toward the door, and somebody kills the overhead fluorescent light. Three or four cigarette lighters click on in the sudden dark, like at some U2 concert. I wonder what the minister would think about this part of the evening's agenda. Do Unitarians have ministers?

The Captain nods to Zu. She gets up and stands next to him in the middle of the room, her shoulders curving forward like she's trying not to be so tall. Their faces are lit yellow by the little flames, with funny horror-movie shadows. He holds out the blade to Zu.

"Are you ready to claim your new name?" he asks. She takes the blade and holds it out. "With this I take my name," she answers, her voice small but steady. It hits me—they've adapted that thing from the episode where Pak claims his Santak name, except they're holding lighters instead of torches. I can't believe what I'm seeing—Zu's in deeper than I thought. This feels like some kind of cult. I would grab her and roll out of here if I could.

"Speak your new name to your Santak brothers and sisters," the Captain says, "so they can hear it."

"Kadep!" she shouts, the loudest I've ever heard out of her. The name gets echoed around the room, with a few yells and ululations. She steals a look at me, and I understand: she had to know this was going down tonight. She wanted me to see this, my best friend transmogrifying into a Santak.

"And how do you seal this claim?" he asks. Zu takes the blade, lifts it to her head and saws off a strand of her reddish-brown hair, grimacing. So it's a working implement. She holds out the strand.

"With this," she says. Someone holds out a lighter, and she touches it to the flame. The smell from the burning hair rises on a thin smoke-whirl and spreads over the room. I look around at all the faces, intent, their features flickering like Zu's. Mine must be too. The Captain says a short phrase in Santak, then, in his singsong twang, "The honor of this name is as delicate as smoke. Use it well." There's that honor thing of theirs. I guess it's part of their code—how they hold back their warlike urges. Like when the Santak had renounced war and replaced it with the Butak'La competitions, at least until they were conquered by the Mowg. And now some of them, at least, have revived the tradition.

The Captain takes the blade from Zu and nods again; the lights go up, and I blink in the sudden glare.

"Of course we'll do the whole ceremony at our next full-dress meeting," he says. Will they use real flaming torches for that one?

He's done, and everybody gravitates to the corner where there's a table with cookies and a plastic jug holding some neon-blue drink. I wheel over that way, past Zu, who's getting a big bear hug from Trish. When Zu comes over to me, she's still smiling, charged up. Till she sees my face.

"You could have given me some warning," I say.

"Right, like you would've come with me then!" She catches me with her eyes. "Find Other Worlds, Mindy." That's just it—right now all I want is something familiar. Somebody grabs Zu away by the elbow. Somebody else hands me a cup of blue Kool-Aid and a cookie.

"Are you the Mindy that publishes 'Voice of the Cyborg'?" It's the kid in the T-Fleet tunic—*Century 23*, under-officer rank—and matching pants.

"Yeah, that's me," I admit, staring at the cookie.

"I'm Tad. Tad Fishkin. One of your contributors." He has an oddly precise way of speaking, so his "contributor" rhymes with "spore."

I look at him, trying to compute this. I thought he was a college kid at least. Maybe high school. Is it a hormone problem? No, he looks like a perfectly normal twelve-year old, all elbows and wrists, thin ribcage under the green tunic, straight brown hair slicked back.

"You're Tadmesh?"

"I don't go by that here," he says. "Here I'm Pak, Clansman of Bokun. Kind of a Transortium liaison." Just like in his story: Pak, half-Santak, half-Terran, undercover with the Santak. He's put himself in an admirable but difficult position.

"Weren't you majoring in aeronautical engineering?" I'm still struggling with the difference between the Tad in front of me and the one in my head. Maybe he's one of those genius kids that enrolled in college ten years early?

"Well, I plan to," he answers. "I do like to read about it a lot." This is all pretty unnerving. But it's nice to be reminded of my zine here—the one thing I've still got a grip on.

"So, are your parents here?" I look around, trying to match him with anyone in this room.

"My dad dropped me off. He's over at the Denny's, grading summer school papers. He should be back in like," he checks his watch, "twenty to twenty-five minutes."

"So what do you think of this club?"

"It's excellent."

The Captain appears at Tad's side, holding a paper cup. "Roger," he says. Oh—he's introducing himself by his real name.

"This dude's all right," he says, punching Tad in the shoulder. "We just got to beef him up a little, so he can pick up a full-size blade. Right, man?" Tad smiles for the first time, a little embarrassed. I feel a pang of protectiveness toward him—he's my contribu*tor*, after all.

"I heard you're straight-up Transortium," Roger says to me. "Our door's always open to Sorters."

"Really? I thought a Santak Imperium ship like the Lrak would never let Transortium crew on board."

"What about me?" Tad pipes up. "I'm here, and I'm from a Dissenter Clan, I mean Pak is. Roger says he might have me do the bookkeeping, and then I'd get a real ship's rank, maybe even officer."

"Whoa, slow down there," Roger says. "He's right though," he says to me. "We take Imperial Santak, Dissenters, and anybody else who's willing to do the Polg ceremony."

"Good to know." Hah. I'm more likely to join the Mesh and get sucked into the group mind. That might be a relief right now. Still, it's nice to know they've opened their doors to a Transortium-leaning kid like Tad.

The rest of the meeting goes by with the usual mix of Con gossip, rehashing of recent reruns, and some trivia questions. I keep my mouth shut even when I know the answers, which is hard. Part of me is still seething at Zu. It's all weirdly familiar yet strange—kind of an outcast, Bizarro version of the CAS. Sort of like the Santak's uneasy position in the Transortium, I guess.

As the meeting breaks up, I see Tad go up to a guy standing at the door—must be his dad. Glasses, trim hair and beard, a ringer for HAL's psychiatrist in the sequel to *2001: A Space Odyssey*. Tad is pointing me out to him. I start turning my chair to wheel over and say hi, but my wheel is blocked. That guy Len has rooted himself in front of me. Mr. Nice Guy.

"So. I bet you think this is all pretty stupid." Arms folded, eyebrows practically meeting in the middle. He might have overheard me complaining to Zu.

"Look, I really don't need this. If it starts your engines, fine."

"You're one of those TSNs, looking down on the Santak."

"I am not a TSN!" TSN is short for Transortium Snob. I hate that term, and now he's made me say it. What is it with this guy? He's a genius at hitting people's sore spots. "Besides, I can't very well look down on you," I shoot back, looking pointedly up at him. That was unfair, but it works the way it usually does: he takes an off-balance step backwards, rolls his eyes and looks away. I scan desperately for Zu; she's right behind my shoulder.

"Are you guys coming with us to the Acropolis?" Trish asks Zu. "We're gonna get some pizza."

"Can't," I say.

"Yeah, it's been a long night," Zu says, looking my way. "We came right from a party." I know that was for me, but I don't care. I've got to get out of here, now.

W E'RE SITTING IN a low bowl of land: me and
the Old One, and about ten of his followers perched on the little ridge all around us. He
knows I miss the daylight, and he's taken me here to see the sunset. The others squat on the ridge around us to watch for daytime dangers. The shallow gully protects us from the wind, too.
We hear the wind but can talk over it.

Since my violent lapse, showing how easily I could throw one
of them, they've been more careful around me. Right after it happened, wanting to show them I meant no harm, I undressed myself and let them examine me, even touch me. They could see for
themselves our similarities and differences. This led to some misunderstanding, since taking off my clothes should have been the
next step in my acceptance as the chief's mate. But, with a few
words and firm gestures, I convinced them that wasn't going to
happen.

He nods to one of the followers, who scrambles down to us
and hands me something—my comtron! I turn it on. Its translation function is intact. I'm swamped with relief.

We can understand each other now, I say, and watch his face
open up with wonder, and some fear.

This is a powerful magic, he says.

Yes. Now we can talk about the important things.

Good, he says. Why didn't you agree to be my mate?

Damn! He hasn't given up on that! I have to be careful what I say. The planet's sun touches the mountain ridge.

I already have a mate, I say, thinking of my Wuvian-cyborg companion. He's a lover, and I think I can call him a friend, but a mate? A life partner? Wishing won't make it so.

Leave that one, he says. I will treat you well.

I'm sure that you would. Let me think about this, I say to buy time. The sun is gone, leaving a crown of pale pink over the ridge.

You would be my Most Respected Mate.

I search the nuances in this term. It sounds more like Advisor or Councilor. That is what I want, isn't it?

So you would listen to what I say then?

He agrees. But we don't have time for games.

Please listen to me now. I adjust the comtron to view mode and do a quick search. There's no off-planet signal—the ship isn't due back for at least a week—but I find the briefing images and holo feeds I came with, and hold the comtron toward him. It glows in the quick-falling darkness.

This is happening across the mountains, I say. The Mowg are working there, digging out metals. They've come from very far away. There are many of them. I watch him scowl as he tries to understand what he's seeing. Finally he looks up from the holo-screen.

We know about this already.

How?

The mountain scouts.

And you know they want your land too?

Yes. They want all the sacred lands. Now it's his turn to look closely at me with his deep-set eyes, to make sure I understand. The thing you call metal is sacred to us. It runs under our home, like a river under the chasm. That's why we live here.

This is worse than I thought. Our scans showed the ore under their land, but not their attachment to it.

If you want your people to live, you have to move. The Mowg will destroy you.

He is silent, and I hear the rushing wind.

We have a plan, he says.

What is it? I imagine them throwing their spears against the Mowg's giant treaded extraction drones.

It will make everything right again. But it is not for an outlander to know.

I understand. If I agree to be his highest Mate, I can be part of the plan. It shouldn't matter. Strategically, it's the right thing to do. But I keep seeing Roi in my head. I wish I could talk to him now, but I can't—I'm cut off from him and anyone on the ship or in the Fleet. Trapped in this stone-age world. Except for my database and translator, I'm stuck here in a tiny orbit, reaching out only as far as I can walk, touch or speak. I shiver under the darkening sky.

I OPEN MY EYES—the monitor's gone black. Look around my little room, my world—dresser, desk, bookshelf, bed. My stuff, piled on surfaces and attached to walls—posters, autographed pictures, the books and zines I'm reading now. It's all right here, safe, familiar. My fan-girl cave. But now it feels cut off, suffocating for lack of oxygen. I remind myself of all the ways I'm connected to the bigger world from here: the phone, of course, and my clock radio, and the computer, even if the modem is whiny and slow. I spent a couple of hours online, checking in on different SkyLog message boards, signed in as SpaceKat today instead of MindRoid. Online, I'm the queen of the zingers. I'm fearless, ready to trade barbs with the most wrongheadedly opinionated of SkyLoggers. So why is it so different in real life? I think sourly of that guy Len again— a perfect example of how I go into brain freeze when somebody throws something nasty at me. Whatever I end up saying is never what I want to have said, once I figure it out later. It wasn't just him, the whole meeting left me feeling that way, off-balance but unable to put a name on what's wrong.

It's not that bad, I remind myself. I got to meet one of my contributors, which was pretty cool, even if he put one over on me as to how old he is. And Zu said she'll help me at the Con. I look over at the box of old, unsold Voice issues next to the desk. And then it hits me, what I'm trying to do. It's not the same, it won't even be "Voice of the Cyborg" anymore—it'll have a new name, and it will be a zine without a group behind it. Just me. And my room here, my little planet, is just too small. I'm stuck in some far-out, lonely orbit, like Kat, on my own crazy mission, trying to pull things off too far from the galactic signal. Don't panic. Don't panic.

FROM: MindRoid@comet.net
TO: drzuz@ultranet.com
SUBJECT: virtual zine
DATE: 8/4/99 8:42 PM

Zu,

It just hit me, I need a website. Not sure what to call it, but I need someplace to be online, like a central command for MindRoid on the Web. A place where I can tell people what's going on with the Voice, I mean the A.L.L., or whatever we call it. Where anybody can find me. Maybe if I use the royal We, they won't even figure out that it's only me behind the curtain, LOL.

So, how do you do that? Yours is pretty nice. I want to try and get it up and running before the Con if I can. Needless to say, my budget on this would be very micro.

- Mindy

T HE SIGN GREETS US in the lobby, hand-
lettered on poster board, held up on a spindly
metal easel:

SENIOR CENTER ART EXHIBIT
OPENING TODAY, 2 TO 4
"MS. ROXIE GRUNWALD: GREEN WORLD—BLACK WORLD"
SOCIAL ROOM

with an arrow pointing to the left.

"Excuse me," Janine calls to the girl behind the desk, who's
wearing a cardigan sweater—the air conditioning's on full blast.
"Do you know where the art show is?"

"Down this way, Ma!" I wheel on ahead, needing to put distance between us. She'll catch up after she's done chatting up the
girl. The door to the Social Room is propped open, so I can go in
myself.

The Social Room has never looked like this before, I'm pretty
sure, and probably never will again. The ceiling is covered by several lengths of black cloth, billowing down from where they've
been tucked into the acoustic tile framing. Swirls of gold-glitter
Milky Ways travel across the black surfaces. A couple of fluorescent ceiling lamps have escaped the cover-up, or we'd be plunged
in real darkness. Little spaceships hang on strings here and there.

I spot the flying Barbie from Roxie's dining room up there too, dressed only in a few twisting pipe-cleaners, coiling behind into her comet trail. Funny how Roxie always makes me look up first.

On the earthly level, a motley crowd mills around me. It's a metal traffic jam, with several old ladies gripping tight to their aluminum walkers, their faces showing varying stages of bafflement. And a couple of old guys in wheelchairs, their expressions completely unreadable, parked in the middle of the room—must be from the Assisted Living facility next door. I so don't want anybody to associate me with them. I'd like to scoot around the room, check out the artwork in this new setting, but I'm stuck a few feet in from the door by the growing crowd.

A couple of grandmas next to me lean in toward a small sculpture on a white pedestal. One of them adjusts her glasses and whispers to her buddy, who puts a hand up to her open mouth. I lean around to see: they're looking at one of Roxie's tchotchke-sculptures, a purple fur teddy bear standing up, wearing a jaunty tutu and holding out a real martini glass like for a toast. A toy dinosaur swims in the glass, in what looks like jelled vodka. Then I see the small rocket ship poised for liftoff between the bear's legs. Through the crowd, I can see other sculptures dotted around the room, and a big orange Plexiglas lightning bolt traveling up from the floor, its tip petering out near the ceiling.

"There you are, kid." It's Roxie. She appears before me like a tricked-out alien ambassador in the sea of pantsuits: little white leather boots, white stretch pants and a silver lamé, shoulder-padded top, cinched at her rounded middle by a wide black belt studded with an asteroid-sized silver buckle. She's carrying a little silver purse, and a wreath of sparkly pipe cleaners glints through her white curls.

"Hey, Rox. You really outdid yourself."

"It was a complete nightmare," she says, glancing around the room. "They wouldn't even let me put nails in the walls, God forbid I should paint them a different color. It should really be all black in here. Do you know anything about black lights?" she asks, giving me an accusing stare.

"Sorry."

"Oh well," she says. "I might do that in my next piece. Shoot high, then do what you can, I say. At least they sprang for the refreshments, and they're not taking any commission on sales." Sales? Does that mean there are people who would actually buy any of this?

"So, where's your sidekick?" she asks me.

"I think I lost her back that way." Just then I hear Janine yell "Roxie!" She runs up and blankets Roxie in a big hug, then pulls back, still holding her by the hands.

"Look at you! This is so incredible!" she gushes. "I've never been to a real art show before." Now that I think of it, I haven't either, but I'm not announcing it to the world. "Is everything for sale, or what?" she continues, wandering ahead.

Roxie turns back to me. "So, your friends were a big help," she says. "Thanks for hooking us up."

"Sure, no problem." Zu told me that she'd been in touch with Roxie and that she'd be here today, that's all. Where is Zu anyway? I spot her, huddled over some equipment in the corner. "I'm gonna go see how she's doing, okay?"

"Just behave yourself," Roxie answers, looking around the room. I begin the journey across the room, a foot or two at a time. I pass another tchotchke-sculpture, this one involving a rounded chrome toaster and half a dozen detached Barbie legs. Two middle-aged women are frowning at it, one wearing nurse's whites, the other in a denim jumper.

"How in God's name did she get to show here?" That's the nurse.

"She's a member." The other one nods in Roxie's direction.

"Excuse me, ladies, coming through." Them I don't mind pushing aside. In a clear space in front of me, a bigger piece sits on a low, wide base. Rising from its mirrored surface is a forest of Plexiglas tubing of different colors—green, blue, orange. The tubes emanate their own light, like fiber-optic strands. Some of them are blossoming little rubber balls, with swirling paint patterns like tiny planets. One of the rubber balls sprouts a thin metal rod, on its tip a little plastic astronaut in his white spacesuit—a spacewalker with no ship. Through the crowd noise, I can just hear a low, slow-moving chord buzzing around the piece. A good sound track for this space diorama, sort of like the music of the spheres. That must be Zu's work.

A few feet away, Zu stands next to a guy who's kneeling on the floor, his pants hanging dangerously low, bending over a clump of wires. Then, with a start, the little astronaut begins turning on his wire, making a small orbit around his planet. He looks piti-fully small, yet giant in contrast to the little ball-planet, kind of like the baby floating in space at the end of *2001*. I feel a shiver and a prickling up my neck, like at the end of a good SkyLog episode. What is it about Roxie's work that gets me? That's it, I guess: like the way a good episode brings up big questions and lets them float around you, her work somehow throws things together that add up to questions, even if they're not in words. There's no words at the end of *2001* either, I think.

"That did it," the guy says, coming out of his crouch. Oh jeez— it's Len, the obnoxious Santak guy. Damn it, why did Zu have to bring him along? If she was going to ask anybody for help, I thought it would be Bradley. Bradley said he would help me design my website; Zu says he's better at that stuff than she is.

Zu and Len gravitate over to the piece I've been looking at. The three of us gaze on the astronaut as, with tiny shudders on the bouncing rod, he does his celestial micro-orbit. Len gives Zu a high-five. Looks like he put on a clean black T-shirt for the occasion.

"Hey, Mind. What do you think?" says Zu, indicating the room with a turn of her head.

"I think Roxie's ready for a seat on the Galactic Council."

"Do they take artists?" Len asks.

"They should."

"Len really helped out a lot," Zu says. "I didn't think we'd get that thing working."

"The wiring was a little messed up." He crosses his arms. "She's got some great ideas, she just needs a little help with execution."

"I'm gonna go fire up the keyboard," Zu says to me. "She asked me to play something live for the opening." So that was a record-ing I just heard. She backs away toward the corner, where I see her equipment set out. I've only ever seen Zu play in her apartment. She's good enough to be in a band—okay, some weird electronics band—but she claims she's too shy to get up on a stage.

"Seriously, Roxie's really cool," Len says, absently stroking his mustache. He looks across the room to where Roxie's talking to a couple of grandmas. Morris is with them, looking natty in a beige sport coat, his little bit of white hair slicked back. "Zu said she's a friend of yours."

"Oh yeah, Roxie and me go way back."

"She was telling us all these stories, like how she used to know Bucky Fuller." Roxie and Buckminster Fuller? This is news to me.

"Sure, she told me all about that," I lie, feeling a thin stab of jealousy. I've known her for years—well, sort of. This guy met her, what, last week? She's already spilling her secrets to him.

"Bucky is like my ultimate hero," Len is going on, "and here this little old lady, I mean this very cool old lady, she knew him pretty well. I guess she told you all about how he got one of her paintings."

"Yep, heard that." The second lie is supposed to be easier. What else don't I know about her? Even when he's not insulting me, this guy somehow succeeds in throwing me off.

"I mean, imagine Roxie giving Bucky her interpretation of the tensegrity principle. What I wouldn't give to hear that conversation."

"Is that like geodesics?" I try. "My high school had one of those, a geodesic dome. Over the gym. They said it was the only school in the country to have one. At the time, anyway." Now I'm looking up at the dome of my high school gym, with its huge web of triangular beams.

"I think I heard about that one. Down in Virginia?"

"Maryland. Farnsworth High." Yeah, I spent many hours in that gym, watching some stupid game, the whoops and calls of the running girls making harsh echoes off the dome, their thin legs flashing out from their gym shorts. By senior year, they gave up and let me go to study hall instead.

"—one of the biggest geodesics built up to then," he's saying.

"Right before the American building at the Montreal Expo in '67." He turns to look at me.

"Farnsworth, as in Philo T.?"

"Yup." What high school gets named after an inventor? I'll take Weirdly Named Landmarks in Ionia, Maryland, for $200, Alex. Ionia, the gem of the suburbs, the futuristic planned community where everything was supposed to be in balance—people, nature, businesses with tasteful signs, of course no billboards. Irv was so excited about it when he found us a place to live there, after he got the job managing the mainframe computers at the government lab outside Washington, DC. He hadn't been happy since his old company, the one that made the UNIVAC computer, merged into Unisys. And I was hopeful about making a new start in a new place, even though it meant leaving everything I knew. I was young and dumb.

Len's staring at me, hands on his hips. "Big fancy high school, putting up a geodesic dome. Rich neighborhood, huh? What, did everybody walk around inventing stuff?"

"We weren't rich!" He's getting it so wrong, I can't even tell where to start. I felt so disoriented when we moved there, with all the pretty curving paths lined with trees—super pedestrian-friendly, but not that friendly to somebody on crutches. Ma hated it too. At least Ionia had a decent shopping mall with an okay bookstore. And the high school had a sprawling, one-story layout. I see myself clumping through the halls on my crutches, invisible to just about everybody else, part of the background noise to their chattering.

Just then, thankfully, a different noise washes over us—a louder version of the long, low chord from before. It curves out big, then fades as Zu adjusts some knobs. Other sounds come in under and over the big chord. Some sounding like voices, conversations coming over a great distance through clouds of static, like astronauts transmitting from deep space back to Earth. Along with electronic blips and ticks, and snatches of tunes careening in and out: the Beverly Hillbillies theme song, something from an Irish Spring commercial, and some big orchestral thing. The only thing it doesn't have is a beat. Zu's stuff never has a beat. This is not anything new for her, but it has a nice all-over feeling, and I like hearing it in a bigger space than her bedroom, the different patches of things all building together into this one big wave. Something about Roxie's work inspired her, I think.

Then, turning to look for Roxie, I see the music crashing over people in a sonic tidal wave—their mouths open, hands pressed to ears, mouthing words to their nearest neighbors, but they could be yelling. Old ladies steering their walkers toward the door in a slow-motion stampede. The men in wheelchairs look around in wonder, finding themselves in a strange room on planet Earth. The staff person, the one in the denim dress, rockets across the room toward Zu, and I see them earnestly conversing, with lots of gesturing. Then silence.

"—you really must—" the denim lady says into the sudden silence; hearing herself, she turns back toward us. "I'm very sorry, people. It was just a misunderstanding." Zu looks down, frowning as she adjusts some knobs. "Why don't you all have some cookies," the lady finishes lamely.

The remaining guests cascade toward the refreshment table. I wheel over to Zu and her silent pile of equipment.

"I thought it was really good."

"Yeah, thanks," she says, plucking a cable from the back of her keyboard.

"Look, you almost got those guys to get up and boogie," I say, waving toward the interplanetary visitors in their wheelchairs, who've already subsided back into their stasis fields. Zu makes a soft snort.

"Don't take it personally, kid." It's Roxie, who's come up to us with Morris. "Good art is rarely understood by the masses."

"It's okay," Zu says. "She just said it was too loud. The thing is, this piece needs to be loud for it to work."

"Don't you ever compromise," says Roxie. She looks around the room again and clomps away in her white boots.

"You girls did a great job," Morris says, gallantly including me in the screwup. He leans toward us and lowers his voice.

"Roxie's just a little distracted. She's still hoping Philip might get here." He checks his watch, a solid one with a twisty gold band.

"At this point, it doesn't seem likely." Seeing our blank faces, he goes on: "Philip, our son. He teaches. In Baltimore. Art History."

"Well, that is a pretty long haul," I say, feeling uncomfortable for Morris. Baltimore is the closest real city to Ionia, so I know exactly how long it takes from there.

"He said he might be busy, with the end of the summer session." The thought of Roxie as a mother, let alone a grandmother, was never part of my picture of her. Plus, I don't remember her ever mentioning any kids. Morris clears his throat. "You know, Roxie keeps saying this is no big deal, but it is. This is her first solo show in almost twenty years."

"At least she got a big crowd," I say.

"The Center was very nice. But we hardly know a soul here. Roxie would commit hara-kiri before she'd take a class at this place. And her artist friends from Philly are all gone, or they can't get themselves out to New Jersey."

"It's their loss," says Roxie. She's back, trailing Len, her arm entwined in his. "Right, Leonard?"

"Damn straight," says Len. He's actually smiling. Big white teeth.

"I used to know a Leonard. Lenny Krazwicki. Remember, Morris? Did woodcuts, played bocce? Do you think you're any relation?" she asks Len, pressing her arm into his side. If I didn't know they were only serving fruit punch, I'd guess she was a little tipsy.

"Leonard's my right-hand man now." She squeezes his arm. "Morrie can't cut it anymore. I mean the Plexiglas!" We laugh nervously.

"Roxie!" It's my mother, approaching us with her always-great timing, waving a cup of something. "Who's this nice young man you've been keeping from me?"

"This is my new collaborator, Leonard Grimes."

"Griffith," Len corrects.

"From now on we're going to be inseparable," Roxie continues. "Like Sonny and Cher." Len blushes deep red, right up to his forehead.

"Easy, Roxie," Morris says. "Don't scare the kid away."

"No, really. You're very good," she says to Len. "You just gotta have confidence in yourself. Everybody's an artist, somebody said that. Now Sue, she's already got the confidence." Zu shrugs and twists, making herself a few inches shorter.

"The three of us are gonna go places."

"Like ABBA!" Janine says.

"There's four of them, last time I checked," I mutter. Roxie leans in toward Zu, pulling Len along with her, and bends down to include me.

"Just remember," Roxie stage-whispers, "never, ever let the Philistines get to you." Now I do smell alcohol. Has she got a flask stuffed in that teeny silver purse? She straightens up and looks around the room. The guests are all gone, and the denim lady is straightening things up at the refreshment table. She waves to us and walks over, wiping her hands on a paper towel.

"I think it went pretty well," she says, in a tone that means she wants it to be done, now.

"I guess so," Roxie says. "Considering I couldn't put anything on the walls, and you—" Morris puts a hand on her shoulder and cuts in. "We certainly appreciate all your help, Dottie."

Dottie nods. "Will you be needing any help with this?" she asks, nodding toward Zu's equipment.

"I got it," says Len, recovering his default Genghis Khan scowl.

As they start gathering things up, I wheel over. "Why don't you hand me the keyboard," I say. "We do it that way all the time at the shows."

"I said I can handle it," Len says. Fine, fuck you. I wheel around to see the guest of honor and her consort at the door, Morris surrounding Roxie with one arm. A plastic rocket ship wobbles over their heads in a breeze from the door. Morris plants a kiss on her forehead.

"Congratulations, sweetheart. It was a great opening."

FROM: amadden@uokla.edu
TO: MindRoid@comet.net
SUBJECT: C Weldon
DATE: 8/14/99 5:28 PM

Hey Mind,

Remember those old letters I found? I read through all the
ones I copied and they are so fricking wild. First this lady
Catherine Weldon comes out to Dakota Territory all by herself.
She ends up living with Sitting Bull and his family. Nobody
can figure her out, white people or Indians—she's caught in
the middle. Then the Agent kicks her off the reservation just
to get rid of this uppity white woman. Meanwhile the Ghost
Dancers are going hotter and heavier. This Ghost Dance
thing is really insane, I've been talking to Hank about it, you
remember him Hank the history grad student. I've been
trying to educate him in SkyLog lore, but he claims to be only
interested in Star Trek, you know, that series in the 1960s
that lasted just two seasons? Well, it's someplace to start,
anyway. Last week me and Hank and a couple more of my
dubious pals took some sixpacks and sneaked up on the roof
of the library to watch the meteor shower. They said it would
be good this year and they were right. Those shooting stars
making their little white pencil tracks looked like they were

falling right down to Earth to hit us in the face. I lost count after a hundred. It was better than any screensaver.

But about those letters by Catherine Weldon—Hank told me it was this Indian guy, Wovoka, out west who had a vision and thought up the Ghost Dance. He predicted all the white people were gonna get plowed under by this ginormous tidal wave of earth, but the Indians would be lifted up and dangled in midair then floated back down, and then they would all get to start over fresh like before the white people came. Now I don't know about where you live Mindy, but out here in the Bible Belt people getting lifted up in the air sounds an awful lot like the Rapture. A lot of folks here are really looking forward to it, mainly the Good Book-reading white folks that expect to be dangling their toes up there while the wicked ppl like me get our comeuppance down on the ground.

Anyway the Ghost Dancing was supposed to give people a preview of the good times to come, like if they wore special clothes and danced around in a circle they would fall down in a trance and see their dead relatives coming back to visit them, same as they would after the white people all got washed away. That's why they called it the Ghost Dance. And it was really catching on big time on the Rez. See, so many Indians had died, and then they were forced onto the reservations and things were looking really bad. No wonder they got into this crazy thing that sounds like the rapture. Hank gave me a book about it. He's into all kinds of Indian stuff, he's part Cherokee, around here everybody says they are. He says I probly am too, I don't know.

Then when the Ghost Dance got to the Dakotas Catherine freaked, like she knew it wouldn't end well. And she was right, Sitting Bull got killed by the Agency men and then the Massacre at Wounded Knee happened right after. Damn. Our Catherine is in there but in the histories she's just like a *tiny* footnote can you believe it, so typical. She gives her heart & soul & life for the Indians and all she gets is a crappy little footnote. As you can see, I've been really getting into this, I was gonna start a new story about Roi in the Mesh but all this stuff got me off the rails.

What's going on Mindy, I got something from Sheryl at CAS that they are "still" publishing Voice of the Cyborg but it is going in a different direction. Are you still the editor or what? Let me know.

abundant life, angie

FROM: MindRoid@comet.net
TO: amadden@uokla.edu
SUBJECT: Re: C Weldon
DATE: 8/14/99 8:55 PM

Angie,

Forget anything Sheryl says. I'm still publishing the real Voice, only with a new name. Zu Hagendorf is helping me on it, you remember, she used to write some great slash for us. And I'm working on getting a website of my own, a place for various musings and news about the zine. If you get back to that prequel story about Roi when he was in the Mesh, I want to see it!! This Tad guy is supposedly doing a series about the Mesh, but so far not a single Mesher has appeared. What the hell is everybody so afraid of? They only want to Take every living being they can and turn them into Meshers, lol! Anyway, just keep sending me your stuff, I don't care what it's about.

Catherine sounds totally cool. Almost cool enough to be a character in some SkyLog episode. I could see her up against the Santak somehow. Speaking of which, Zu dragged me to a Santak meeting last week. And now she's all over me to join this Santak Raptor squadron. Not my thing.

Abundant life,

Mindy

FROM: tadmesh@deepnet.com
TO: MindRoid@comet.net
SUBJECT: NEW INSTALLMENT
DATE: 8/17/99 8:48:12 PM

Dear Mindy:

I never expected to meet you at the Lrak meeting. It would
be fun to talk sometime, since I see you are into a lot of
different SkyLog stuff like I am. I havent seen you in the Mesh
or Santak chat groups, dont you like to hang out online, or do
you use another name? Anyway here is another Chapter of my
Shadow of the Mesh series. I think this is going to be my first
novel. I hope you like it. After camp ends I will have more time
to write.

May You Strike With Honor,

Tad

Shadow of the Mesh, Part 4

Night had fallen on the rebel camp. A pile of red-hot stones
offered a tiny bit of light under the dark trees.

"I tell you, I am Transortium. You have to believe me," said
Pak to the leader who he had learned her name was Anki. His
voice was hoarse from talking and also thirst. He decided it
was best to tell the truth, since these rebels deeply hated
their Santak overlords. Only how to prove it. He left his
comtron behind, fearing that it might be discovered. So he
spent a long time describing details of the Encounter to this
raggedy female. She stared at him with her orange eyes, they
looked like the eyes of a Terran cat. And her magenta skin
had thin yellow stripes. She stared again at his nose bones.
"If you are really Transortium, you should have no problem
killing a few Santak," she said.

Pak swallowed. Of course his primary allegiance is to the
Transortium. But he is also Santak, and being here has given

him new respect for them. Then he remembered Varm, and he felt Varm's powerful hand squeezing his throat again.

"I will do it" he answered. Anki told him that a Santak vehicle would be passing near here early in the morning. If he would throw an explosive devise into the vehicle she would believe him.

"In return I ask one thing" said Pak. "That you will show me the technology that allowed you to learn of the Mesh approaching this planet."

"You know of this?" Anki's orange eyes narrowed.

"If you want your people to survive you must tell me. The Transortium maybe will able to help."

"When you prove yourself, we will reveal the technology." She gave a little smile.

They took off into the forest and walked for many hours. Finally they came out at the crossroads where they waited in drizzling rain till they heard the distant sound of a motor. Anki handed the explosive device to Pak. His hands were shaking. Now he could see the vehicle approaching. Pretending to be an automaton like a mindless Mesher, he threw the device. Direct hit! A fiery mass of sparks and pieces of metal flew into the air. Pak was relieved it was still dark so he did not have to see the bodies. In his mind he sang a brief Santak death chant for them. Then he saw Anki staring at him. Her orange eyes looked like two flames in the reflection of the burning wreck. She grabbed him by his hair and kissed him. "I believe you now" she said fast. No one else noticed.

FROM: MindRoid@comet.net
TO: tadmesh@deepnet.com
SUBJECT: Re: NEW INSTALLMENT
DATE: 8/17/99 9:26:12 PM

Tad,

It *was* nice to meet you, put a face on tadmesh. Just, what's a nice kid like you doing hanging around with the Santak? Whose side r u on, anyway?

And, nice piece of writing. Good to see we are getting a little closer to the Mesh. It may be a while before I have enough material on hand for another issue. You're going too fast for me! ;-) Things have been way busy here, I am working on making a website for me and the zine real soon. To answer your question, I used to spend serious time in various SL chat rooms, but I got tired of dealing with all the pigs, present company excluded. Now I keep to a few where everybody isn't always making jackasses of themselves. Watch for MindRoid or SpaceKat.

SkyLog 4ever,

Mindy

I TRY TO MAKE SENSE of what I'm looking at, but it keeps all smooshing together: lots of < and > symbols, slashes and equal signs, along with mysterious abbreviations, taunting me like the longest math formula I could never solve. I feel an algebra headache coming on.

"Can't you go back to the regular view?"

"This is the regular view," Bradley says, typing away on his laptop, squeezing in more weird symbols on one line. "The other one is just the wysiwyg."

"That's what I want then, the wysiwyg thingy."

"Chill, Mindy," Zu says. "Let him do what he has to do." We're sitting around the kitchen table, there wasn't room for all three of us at my bedroom desk. I let out a sigh. I've been getting little glimpses of the web design, then losing them again in this coding maze. Bradley finally convinced me to have a lighter background instead of black for the text blocks; he says it's easier to read. I wanted the writing to appear like out of the blackness of space. Since he's not charging me for any of this, I gave in.

"We can still have the stars in the background, right? Around the top and the edges, I mean."

"Oh yeah. Billions and billions of stars," he says, sounding distracted as he types. We're all leaning in toward the screen. I'm aware of Bradley's arm near mine, like a buzzing, low-level force field. His skin a warm mahogany-brown, his long fingers moving on the keyboard. I can hear him breathing, a sort of half-humming commentary on what he's doing. I remind myself that he's Zu's friend. The two of them are even shaped the same, both of them with gawky thin arms and legs, all angles hunching forward. She's watching the screen intently, like it actually makes sense to her.

"Okay, here we go." He pushes a few buttons, and the code disappears. There it is: my web page. Along the top, in glowing gold letters against the stars: ALTERNATE LIFEFORMS LOG. A menu bar, then the lighter block below with my introduction: "Welcome to A.L.L.—a place to discuss all forms of life in the SkyLog universe and beyond." I stare at it, taking it in. This is it, my spot in the cybersphere. A glowing node, a place of my own in the encompassing no-place of the Web. I won't be just a visitor anymore; I'll be a location other beings can visit. It doesn't have my name on the URL—that would be weird. But still. It feels like a hangout where I could hang out.

"Wow," I say finally.

"Whew!" Bradley says, pushing my shoulder. "You had me going there, girl."

"I mean— Wow," I repeat.

"I think she likes it," Zu says.

"Okay, just save a couple of Wows for when we're done." He toggles back to the coding and starts typing again.

"How's everybody doing?" It's Janine. She comes up to stand behind Bradley, fastening one earring. Maybe it's because I've been staring at the screen, but she seems to be in high focus, somehow brighter than usual. She's wearing her oversized red button-down shirt, pulled in with a gold belt, over tight black pants—her version of Mary's outfit from an old *Television Magazine* cover. Since the show was in black and white, photos are the only way to know the colors she wore. Ma's going out with Nick again tonight. She and Mary don't have anywhere near the same build, but this is a good look for her.

"Hey, Mrs. V.," Zu says. "You look really swank there." Bradley starts unfolding himself out of the kitchen chair.

"Don't get up!" Janine protests. "What a well-mannered young man! Where did you meet Suzy again?"

"We both work at Spenser Darmstadter, Ma'am." Bradley towers over her.

"Please, call me Janine!" I'm feeling an itch of embarrassment and irritation. Why does she have to be so friendly to everybody?

"Where are you going, Ma?"

"Do you think it's okay?" She smooths down the front of the shirt. "We're going somewhere very nice, in Philly."

"You look fine." I just want her to leave.

"Are you getting hungry? I've got some chicken in the fridge."

"No! We're just gonna order some pizza." My thank-you to Bradley, since he wouldn't let me pay him.

"Do you want to see Mindy's website?" Zu asks. Bradley slides back into the chair, pushes some buttons and reveals my home page. My mother leans over his shoulder.

"That's beautiful." Ma pronounces it the old Philly way, *byou-dee-ful*, which makes me self-conscious. "But how will people see it?"

Bradley takes a thoughtful breath, realizing what he's dealing with. "Well, right now, it's just on my computer. But then, when it's done, I'll upload it to the Web," he says, stopping as he sees Janine's expression. "I'll send it through wires up to the Internet. And then anyone can see it. Anybody who's got an Internet connection."

"Does this have anything to do with the cyberspace?" she asks through pursed lips. I roll my eyes clear over to the refrigerator.

"You got it!" Bradley sounds relieved.

"Because I keep asking them—Mindy, and Irv, my husband, but they never explain it to me. I mean, where is it exactly?"

"Well, it is hard to explain."

"Hey, I've tried!" I say. It just bounces off her, anything technological, from the toaster on up. But then I'm not one to talk when it comes to knowing how the wires and signals actually work.

"I guess you could say it's a place for digital information," he tries. "But not a physical place."

"So it's in our imagination?"

"Good question. Um, not exactly."

"Give up now," I warn, "before your brain explodes." But now my mother's got me going. I stare at the screen again. Where is a website, where will mine be? I feel dizzy. How can I go into cyber-space if it isn't there?

"I'll let you finish up," Janine says, allowing Bradley off the hook. "Gotta go put my face on." She disappears, and Zu and I exchange a look. Thank God somebody understands.

"I could order the pizza now," I say.

"No, let's get through a little more," Brad says. I like the way he includes me, even though I'm not doing anything.

"I still think you could do more with your menu, Mind," Zu says. "Show her my website again, Bradley." We've got the kitchen phone line plugged into his laptop. He dials up with the usual bleeping and screeching and navigates to the home page for Zuzana's Audio Zoo.

"See what we did?" she says, taking over the keyboard. "I've got an image map for the list instead of buttons." I've seen this before. It looks like a short chunk of piano keyboard set on its side, each key marking a different choice on the list, from the top of the scale—"Old TV Themes"—down through "Famous Quotes," "Sounds from Space" and "Theremins." Theremins? The lowest note on the sideways scale is for "Zuzana's Latest Piece."

"What the hell's a theremin?"

"It's this amazing electronic instrument. It's like the first one ever invented. You know, the Beach Boys, 'Good Vibrations'?" She taps the keyboard. "Here." On the last click, a strange sound ema-nates from the computer, a kind of tinny animal wail. "You move your hands around in the air to play it," she says, waving one hand like a conductor. "But you really have to hear it in person to get the effect. I'm gonna get one. Bob Moog is selling them now, you know, the guy that invented the Moog synthesizer?"

Bradley's smile just got wider. "That's all you need! You are a crazy woman!" She smiles crookedly.

"So what do you think?" she says to me. "Not piano keys. Maybe little spaceships?"

"I don't know. I don't have much of a menu." Right now it's just Home, About, News, and Links. "Let's just keep it simple."

"You got it." Bradley clicks on the Links button, and I see the list of links I gave him to the major SkyLog sites and forums.

"I'm not seeing any Santak links here," Bradley says. "What, are you prejudiced against us?"

"No! They're, they're just like any other—"

"Members of the Transortium, right. So?"

"I'm not prejudiced against anybody!" I'm blushing.

"Some of your best friends are Santak, right?" Zu says. She's just teasing, but it hurts. It's true that the Santak are distinguished by their dark-orange skin as well as their impressive nose spikes. But my not liking them isn't that kind of prejudice—is it? Now I feel awful.

"Okay, fine, put in a link to the Lrak."

Zu already showed me the Lrak's website, which Bradley designed for them. He adds it, clicks on the link. There it is: A deep-purple banner, with the title inside the outline of a hovering Santak Raptor. Very cool.

"Yeah, Zu ratted on you already," Bradley says. "She told me how you hate on the Santak."

"I just think they're kind of medieval. They don't fit in the 23rd century."

"Yeah, so they were a medieval-level society when they were invaded by the Mowg. And then, being forced to serve their Mowg overlords for so long, that didn't help."

"Hey, I'm familiar with Santak history."

"Those old-time principles—honor, loyalty, ready to fight if necessary to protect what we love?" He ticks off their virtues on his long fingers. "That makes us good allies."

"They're just another alternate lifeform, Mindy," Zu says.

"So, you gonna give us another chance?" He looks at me. I know he's asking, will I go to another meeting?

"All right, I'll go!" I let out a hard sigh, so he'll get what this is costing me. But I do owe him.

"They're just Loggers, like everybody else," Zu goes on. "A bunch of geeks."

"Really? Didn't look that way to me," I say, thinking of Vlad. And Trish.

"Okay, not everybody. But Bradley. And Tad, for sure. And

Len, he works for the cable company. You saw how good he is with wiring."

"I said I'll go!"

The doorbell rings. Janine screams from the bedroom, "Somebody get that!" Zu goes to the door.

"Well, hello!" It's Nick. "Nick Costa. And you are?" Zu mutters an answer and excuses herself, but Nick follows her back to the kitchen.

"Mindy, you never told me you had such a pretty—" He stops as Bradley gets up and introduces himself, and they shake hands.

"So what's going on here?" He looks puzzled—maybe our crew is too motley for him.

"They're helping me design a website."

"Really! I'm thinking of getting one of them." He leans over Zu, looking at the screen. "Could you help me?" He puts a hand on her shoulder. I see her body stiffen.

"No, but Bradley can," she says. "He's starting his own business."

"We're kind of busy here, Nick." Nobody hears me, it's like I'm on mute.

"See," Nick says, still talking to Zu, "I'm thinking of branching out, starting a store in Philly, and maybe down the Shore in Jersey. So then I should definitely be on the, what do you call it?"

"The Web," Zu says, her voice tight.

"That's right. The World Wide Web." Did he just squeeze her shoulder?

"Look—" she shifts and turns toward him.

"Oh, you're here!" It's my mother again. Her face is set on Maximum Damage—major mascara, tightly outlined lips. Nick straightens up and turns to Janine with a big smile.

"Don't you look nice!" he says, taking her elbow and moving toward the door.

"Where are you going, Ma?"

"Morton's," Nick answers for her. "Best steak place in town."

"I've never been there!" she breathes.

"And we'll drive around, check out some locations for the

new store." This gives me a chill. I don't want to hear him making more excuses to see Janine.

"Be good!" Janine throws back at us. The door shuts behind them.

"Sorry about that," I say. "He's a true slimeball, as you can see."

Zu shrugs, not looking at me. "But if he really wants a website . . ."

"No way I'm working for him." Bradley shakes his head.

"And I don't think that's what he wanted," I add, then feel bad when I see Zu's face.

"Hey! Report to Command Deck! We're still not done here," Bradley says, back to typing already. "Mindy."

"Yes, sir."

"Zu says you've got skills with your editorials."

I shrug. "Maybe."

"So, you could put your editorials up too. Give people a taste of the next issue."

"It's just text, Mindy," Zu says. We agreed already, it's too complicated to put the whole Voice, I mean the A.L.L., on the website, not to mention expensive—the more content you store, the more it costs, and pictures especially are space hogs.

"See," Bradley says, "we put it on the menu, and call it, what? The Editorializer?"

"Hm."

"MindRoid Speaks!" Zu says.

"You don't have to call it an editorial. I could set it up as a blog."

"Yeah. What is that exactly?"

"It stands for weblog. A lot of people are doing it. You can write anything you want about anything, anytime."

"And anybody can see it, anywhere!" Zu says.

"Whoa, whoa. Why would I want to do that?"

"Because you're a good writer?"

"I can't even think about that now." Doesn't Zu know how much this scares me, the idea of writing anything other than an intro to the zine?

"So, no blog." Bradley raises an eyebrow.

"Come on, Mindy."

"No blog. Just editorials." I'm feeling wrung out. Zu leans toward the screen, asking Bradley questions. She may be shy with Nick, but she's a Chatty Cathy with Bradley. I leave the table and get some sodas out of the fridge while Bradley types on. I have to go to the bathroom before I drink mine.

"Okay, see?" He points to the screen. In between the arrows and squiggles, I see "MINDY, PUT EDITORIAL HERE."

"Just type it right in there, or cut and paste."

"Got it."

Bradley clicks over to the wysiwyg view. How did he know I needed to see it again? There it is, my website, quietly existing there, almost ready to pulse out into the imaginary yet somehow real no-place sphere.

Greetings Humans, Cyborgs, Shapeshifters, Vogons, and Sentients of all kinds!

You have made contact with A.L.L., the Alternate Lifeforms Log. Here we express our commitment to the highest goals of the Transortium, hoping that all lifeforms will be able to mingle and learn about each other without fear and suspicion. Whether your nose is spiky or smooth, whether you have antennas instead of ears, or horns instead of hair, we hope you will feel welcome here. If you're under four feet tall, have gray skin and a huge head with big bug eyes, that's okay too. Same with means of locomotion: we invite bipeds, quadrupeds, centipedes, those who move on wheels and all-terrain treads. Please note, A.L.L. asserts the right of hybrid synth-organic beings as well as non-carbon-based sentient beings to call themselves lifeforms and to explore with us the meaning of life.

Who are we? We are MindRoid and her loyal contributors. (We are not connected in any way to "Voice of the Cyborg" or the Cyborg Appreciation Society.) We are the website for A.L.L., which we hope will become one of your fave zines for speculation and conversation inspired by but not limited to the SkyLog universe. Come here to find out when the next issue will be available, read editorials, and maybe excerpts from our best stories. This is the future, people. Cyberspace is a very big place. We're ready to fly into the future and find other worlds.

The first issue of A.L.L. is going to the printer shortly. To subscribe, email MindRoid **here**, and I'll tell you where to send the check. And look for us at the next SkyLog Con in Philly. Future issues will include a new installment of Tad Fishkin's "Shadow of the Mesh," which looks like it's turning into a novella. Also, an interesting story from new contributor Hank Hendricks about experimental cyborgs in the 22nd century. Hank is a friend of our longtime contributor Angie Madden, so we know he's okay. Hopefully, there will be more from Angie and all our regulars including Patty Noska, and the usual great art.

Comments on the zine and the website are welcome, as well as submissions! Any compliments on the website should go to web wizard Bradley Carter, who is available to work on a website near you, at **koolpages4you.com**.

Check out our **amazing links**.

Return to **A.L.L. home page**.

Go back to top and **read this again** (makes you an honorary member of the MindRoid Fan Club).

W ALKING DOWN THE ship's corridor. The soft squeak of my shoes gripping the floor, the hiss of a cabin door, the sheen of the curving wall, the smooth all-over light—all this is so familiar, like putting on your old, comfortable clothes. My stride is easier, more confident than it's been. I nod crisply to a passing crewperson. And yet I still hear the wind, still feel the sandy grit on my skin. It's like I'm in both places at once—back on the planet and here on the ship. I remind myself this is normal after an off-ship mission.

I passed Dr. Braxton's reentry medscan with no red flags, changed into a clean uniform and went straight to my debriefing with the Captain. He listened to my report from behind his desk, half turned away in his seat, looking out at the stars. I may not have shared all the details of my stay with the Night People. The problem, the Captain reminded me when I was done, is that the Mowg are our allies. We have no agreement with the Night People. If I can't persuade them to move away from their underground home and the mineral trove it holds, there may be no more we can do. In spite of my relief to be back on board, I found myself arguing for one last visit, one last try. Now I have to submit a detailed report and recommendation, ASAP.

The doors to Deck 6 All-Crew hiss open. As I enter, the ambient roar of conversation goes silent. But it's not me anyone's looking at. Someone gasps, and I push through the crowd toward the sound. I spot Roi standing there, the still center of a tense stand-off. His face drips with the drink that's been thrown at him, and the rest of it runs dark down his tunic. A crew member still holds the glass in her hand, shocked at what she's done. I scan the faces around them—one crewman murmuring to another one, who's smirking. It's Crewman Adwaaan. The little shit! He's figured out that whispering a command softly in Roi's ear makes it much more likely he'll obey; it mimics the all-consuming Lullaby he lived with on the Mesh ship.

What is Roi feeling now, still unable to connect any of his emotions—humiliation, disappointment, rage—to a deliberate action? This isn't the first time Adwaaan has pulled this prank, getting Roi to repeat some obscene insult to someone else, then stepping back to watch the blowup. But it's the first time I've caught him at it. I launch myself toward Adwaaan, shouting, showing the rage that Roi can't. I land one good punch before I'm stopped, hands grasping at my arms, other voices rising around mine.

LIGHT FLOODS IN as the shouting subsides. I'm looking up into the face of a Santak warrior. I take in the impressive spikes protruding from his nose and up to his hairline, the dreadlocks cascading away on either side. A benign mahogany-brown face under the harsh angles, dark almond eyes looking at me with concern. It's Bradley. His long fingers are hovering on either side of my face.

"Where were you?" he asks softly.

"On the ship." I never talk about that—he caught me off guard. There's a buzz of low voices around us.

"Welcome back," he says with half a smile. Then he purses his lips and lifts something with both hands from my face. Right, I'm getting fitted for my Santak facial extensions. Now I feel my face all clammy with Vaseline.

"Almost lost that one, huh, Doc?" It's Trish, calling from somewhere off to my left.

"Oh no, the patient and nose bones are doing fine." Bradley holds up my newly formed prosthesis for all to see. I look at the bright white of the plaster, tracing the seam of bone spikes—not too big, just the right size for my face. He did a good job. Oohs and aahs come from around the room.

"Done with Honor!" That's Roger. I'm lying flat on my back on the couch, so when I turn my head toward him everything looks sideways: Captain Roger's legs, some other pairs of legs, and a bunch of bodies lying on the floor beside me, laid out in a row on a big sheet. Zu is lying there, closest to me, then Tad's shorter body next to her, and someone else, a guy I just met today, don't remember his name. I had other things on my mind. Zu might have mentioned something about making Santak face extensions at the next meeting, but I didn't think much of it. Definitely didn't figure it would involve me having to get out of my chair, two guys lifting me over here to the couch, Zuzana taking me under the knees—she knows I'm self-conscious about the way my legs don't quite straighten out. Then—oh jeez—realizing that I really can't lie down straight anymore. Zu improvised a couple of couch pillows under my knees to disguise the fact that they wouldn't go down. I guess I've been sort of working around it at home, letting myself believe it wasn't a big deal. But it is.

Then I had to lie still for like a half hour while the plaster set, flashing back to the many times I've been stuck in a hospital bed. Especially my last big surgery, the one right after I graduated from high school. That one, I had to lie on my stomach for the operation while they cut my neck open and took out some bone to give my brain more room. It happens sometimes with spina bifida. It worked—got rid of the bad headaches I had all through that summer, and the weird feelings in my arms that made it harder to use the crutches. But they don't tell you about the pain you'll feel after surgery. Or how you might still have headaches for a whole year, making it hard to think about anything like going to college or learning to drive, which I thought I'd be doing. Fucking disaster. And somehow I never got back on the crutches after that either, it was just easier to wheel around. That's when I made my No More Surgeries resolution. And I've kept it except for the kidney infection a few years ago, when my fever was so high I couldn't make an effective protest. Dr. O'Malley says once you get past age thirty with spina bifida, the health problems tend to stabilize. We'll see.

Bradley swabs my face with a damp cloth.

"You okay?"

"Fine. I'll be sure and ask for a Santak doctor next time I need one." He nods, and turns to Zu and the others. Zu, sitting up: "What do I look like?" Her grin is ridiculously wide.

"An albino Santak," I say. The white nose ridge extending across her already pale face is pretty striking. Trish holds a makeup mirror in front of Zu's face, and she bursts into giggles.

"Hey," Trish scolds her. "Rule number one, Santak officers don't giggle." Trish looks pretty cool herself, with her black hair curling around her orange-painted face extension, purple lipstick, and a First Officer Bokun T-shirt showing off her fabulous big-girl figure. Zu collects herself while Bradley, down on one knee beside her, gently detaches her new face extension.

"Actually, I think you look like Rem," Tad says. "When she came on the *Encounter* in 'The Wolves Among Us.'" He's lying on his side, head propped on one fist and looking at Zu. On his smaller face, the spiky protrusions look even more improbable. "If you had all the makeup on—"

"And a nice low-cut leather jumpsuit, right, Tad?" Trish cackles. Zu would need a serious pushup bra to get anything going in that area. Unlike me, or Trish. But the tease bounces off him. "I was thinking of some fake teeth—can you do that?" Tad asks Bradley.

"That all depends on what she wants," says Bradley. "Now hold still, dude." And he pulls away Tad's plaster prosthesis, spanning it with one hand. By itself, the white plaster looks like part of a little dinosaur model.

"I got a killer idea," Trish says. "Zu goes to the Con as Rem, and Tad goes as Torm, her bratty little nephew." That's another thing I haven't been wanting to think about, what I'll wear to the Con. I guess I figured I'd just go in my Transortium officer's uniform. It feels nice and official, like when I'm helping at the front table, stamping the hands of civilians, or guarding the V.I.P. seats. The way I see it, Cons are really Transortium territory, and Santak and the occasional gray-suited Mesh are the interlopers. Even though, I have to admit, the Santak have some pretty impressive getups.

And now, here I am with the makings of a Santak nose ridge. Is this my group now? Could I really show up at the big Fall Con with the Santak contingent? I try to imagine myself in full Santak regalia, selling my zine. And then Sheryl will be there, commanding the CAS table. It's hard to imagine her actually commanding anything, but I've been rehearsing the part where we come face to face. I can't always be trying to avoid her. Maybe dressing up like one of the Lrak crew would give me some kind of armor against her. But imagining that churns my gut. Grabbing the back of the couch, I hoist myself up to a half-sitting position and then wrestle my legs back down so my feet are on the floor.

"Oh, sure you could," Trish is saying.

"Don't push the kid." It's Len, standing by the door in his usual black T-shirt and jeans. "He's got his own sense of honor, that's all."

"You should talk," Trish shoots back. "You're not even wearing your nose bones."

"Hey. I don't get dressed up for fun. My gear is serious stuff." Sounds like he's used this excuse before.

"It would just make me very uncomfortable to play anyone who's betrayed the Tribe of Bardim," says Tad. Bardim, of course, is the Santak tribe that Pak and his uncle Bokun belong to. Even for the Santak who joined the Transortium, the old clan ties are strong. Maybe especially for them. Tad's sitting up now, scratching at the bright-pink skin of his human nose.

"And besides," Tad says, "I was thinking of going to the Con as a Mesher." The buzz of voices around us stops.

"You sure you want to say that in this room, man?" That's Roger, who's touching up his own mask with dabs from a small paintbrush.

"Actually," Tad says, straightening his Transortium tunic, "I was considering going as an Enmeshed Santak." He doesn't know he's just thrown a grenade. Roger moves toward him, as if to protect him from the explosion. "Well, you know, kid," he soothes, "that's fighting words in here."

"No, listen to him," I say. As his editor, I've got to defend the precocious little bastard. "It's a good question. Is it possible for a

Santak to be successfully Enmeshed?" It's a question that Tad will have to deal with soon in his story. I personally think the answer is yes. Neurids and electronic implants will win out over flesh, any flesh, spiky or smooth, orange, pink, brown or magenta, every time. But the chorus of No Way's and boos from outraged Santak warriors tells me I'm in the minority here.

"A Santak warrior would die before he's turned into a Mesher," Len says.

"But what if he didn't have a choice?" Tad counters.

"Yeah, remember," I say. "You Will Be Mesh. That's how they roll."

"Enmesh. Or die. That's the choice. A Santak would always choose to die," Len says, his eyes locking onto mine. He looks like he's ready to settle this outside. How does he cross my wires so bad? When that happens I can't think straight, can't talk. I remind myself it's Tad who's on the line here.

"Okay," I say. "But what if like one Santak accidentally got captured before he was able to fall on his blade." This brings a pained look to Len's face. "Would a full Enmeshing of a Santak be possible? I mean, maybe some races go Mesh better than others." I'm getting warmed up.

"You tell it, Mindy." It's Bradley; he doesn't look up from the mask and the nail file he's sanding it with.

"Yeah, we're too nasty, man." It's Vlad the giant over in the corner. "We'd short out the damn Mesh implants."

"Too gamey," somebody else says. "They need softer meat."

"But assuming he could be Enmeshed—" Tad starts, but Vlad interrupts: "He'd be the baddest son of a bitch in the whole damn Mesh!" That gets some appreciative whoops.

"He'd end up like all the other Mesh," Tad finishes. "The first thing they do is suppress the emotion centers. No matter what the species. Then, whatever individual characteristics are interesting get vacuumed up into the core for further study and possible future applications. So, basically, the individual always submits to the Mesh." He's up on his knees, giving this little lecture. Eyes bright. Fearless.

"Where'd he get to be such an expert?" Trish says, nudging me in the arm.

"He's majoring in Mesh," I mutter.

"In the meantime," says Bradley, approaching Tad with a newly trimmed prosthesis, "we're gonna submit you to this damn group."

Tad fingers his new, alien skin and frowns solemnly into the hand mirror that Bradley holds up. Now it's Zu's turn. Looking at her new face, she can't suppress another wide smile—it spreads so big it jumps over and colonizes Bradley's face. She catches my gaze and rolls her eyes. Yeah, I feel you. I can't believe it either. Then the new guy gets his—Kevin, that's his name. "That's really freaky," he says slowly to the mirror. Finally Bradley comes over to me.

"Now who's the fairest one of all?" he asks, holding up the mirror as I balance the new facial feature on top of my old ones. The plaster cool and clammy against my skin. Kevin's right, this is really freaky. This is not me, it's somebody else. The lower face is familiar: the squarish jaw that Janine always said I got from her aunt Vera who went into the convent. The thin straight mouth. But the spikes traveling up my nose and beyond make everything else new and strange, even the gray eyes staring back at me.

NOW WE'RE SITTING in the living room of Captain Roger's house. It's a reduced off-ship contingent. At least Zu gave me a choice about coming along this time. Tad, despite protesting to his dad, wasn't able to join us, and some people went home. The Captain sits in what must be his favorite chair, an old mousy-gray wreck. Zu's over on the sofa with Bradley, their four knees sticking up at the same stork-like angle; Trish perches on one arm of the sofa, leaning against the wall behind Zu. Len backwards-straddles a kitchen chair, and Vlad stands in the corner, looming over everybody. I'm in my mobile seating device. Yellow glow from a standing lamp lights the beery flush on people's faces. I don't know how many more this room could hold anyway.

It's an old house, with bowing wood floors in here and cracked linoleum in the kitchen. I heard Roger works in construction, but apparently he doesn't practice his skills on his own house. The small yard out front is mostly gravel, with two motorcycles leaning against the wall—Len's along with Roger's. The gravel was rough going, and the wooden steps were not great, but Bradley managed to get me up onto the porch, and I took over from there. Zu's strong enough to get me down a few steps, but going up is hard for her.

We chipped in for two large Acropolis pizzas and settled in to watch the tape Roger made of the last *Century 23* episode. This reminded everybody of all the storylines left hanging, not to mention the insult of the cancellation itself, and our general frustration channeled into a rowdy argument over what the next series should be about, what time period, etc. Of course, the majority agreed that it should take place on a Santak Raptor, so I had to stand up for the Transortium. Inside, I'm feeling a bit down, wondering if there will ever be another SkyLog series. Somebody suggested the fans should all write letters to the producers. Roger put in a tape of the latest *Babylon 5* episode, maybe hoping it would calm us down. I'm starting to fade. I haven't been out this late in a long time.

Something catches my attention down below. I do a discreet one-arm pushup, separating my butt from the seat, and slide my other hand underneath. Oh, Christ. I did, I wet myself. My watch beeped during the meeting, and I let it go, and then I didn't remember till we were sitting in Zu's car in the church parking lot. Cars were pulling out, Len was revving up his motorcycle, and I didn't want to hold things up to go back inside. When we got here and I eyeballed the narrow hallway to the bathroom at the far end, I realized my mistake.

Usually, the pee just sits in there till I remember to go. But I forgot how beer goes through me. Damn, damn. It's been so long since I had an accident, I got overconfident and didn't wear a pad. Wishful thinking, Mindy. If I can smell it, anyone else can too, or will in a minute. I've got to get myself in that bathroom somehow, get cleaned up, get the hell out of here. I think I may have a pad in the bottom of my backpack.

I pull back, wheel around and head down the tight hallway. Luckily there's no junk on the floor to block me. But opening the bathroom door reveals the next, bigger problem: there's no way to get the wheelchair into this tiny room. Shit. This is like an old, bad memory from long ago. I guess Janine and I have mostly been frequenting hotels, malls, hospitals, gas stations, places that have to comply with the Access for the Handicapped stuff. Okay, don't panic.

"Hey, Zu!" I call, trying to sound casual. "Can I see you for a minute?" Why did this have to happen now? Did anyone else notice? I hear her rustling up from the sofa. I don't think this has come up for me since we've been friends.

"What's up?" she says from behind me.

"I can't get in the goddamn john," I half-whisper. "I think I can slide myself onto the toilet, but the chair won't fit in there."

"Do you want me to stand here so nobody can see?" She's half-whispering too.

Ha. That would be like a carrot hiding a loaf of bread. "Just wait till I get on, then pull the chair out of the way and shut the door." With her help, we angle the chair in as close to the toilet as possible.

"You guys need any help?" It's Roger, standing at the end of the hallway.

"We're fine," Zu says. I manage to lift up, balancing between one armrest and the toilet tank lid, and scrunch myself into place, still with my pants on. Now she can see what's happened, if she didn't already guess—the seat of the chair is dark with pee.

"Okay, hand me the backpack."

As the door closes, I see Roger leaning casually against the wall at the end of the hallway, his eyes on the TV. Thanks, Captain. He'll make sure no one gets near us.

I take a deep breath and slump back against the toilet tank. In front of me, a little white porcelain sink, exposed pipes underneath. Beside me, a metal shower stall with a heavy curtain. A smoky mirror above the sink, too high up to reflect my face, all I can see is a fringe of hair and the top of my forehead.

Okay, let's get to it. I have to take off the shoes and everything before I can take off the soaked underpants. I ball them up and throw them in the pack.

"You okay, Mind?" Zu's voice comes through the door.

"Oh yeah, everything's great." Usually I do my toilet maneuvers on autopilot. Now, everything feels hyperreal, flooded in the garish light of the fluorescent bulb. My hand holding the wipe, my pale belly and thighs. Everything's going in slow motion. I feel the whomp, whomp of blood rushing in my head as I pull on my pants, with a pad wedged into the crotch.

"Okay, mission accomplished." I push the door partway open and Zu moves the chair into place. She's turned over the seat pad. I settle back in, with the backpack draped over my lap.

"Let's get out of here," I say.

"But—" she glances into the room, "—*Babylon 5* isn't over. Can we wait till the end?"

"Yeah, fine." But I'm itchy to leave. My haze of good feeling has dispersed into the ether. I roll through the living room past the small group. Zu edges back onto the couch, but I keep going into the kitchen, where a screen door lets out onto the front porch. As I grab the doorknob, a hand appears above me, swinging the door out wide.

"Lemme get that." It's Len. He must have been in the kitchen, getting another beer.

"I don't need your help!" I say, sharper than I meant to. I push out onto the porch and hear the screen door whack hard against the frame behind me. I roll right up to the steps, as far as I can go. It's dark now. The vehicles are looming shapes on the gravel. Past that, a murky row of high, overgrown shrubs. Just beyond the bushes, cars roar by, unseen except for a little headlight glare twinkling through the brambles. This is one of those old houses built right up to the road, long ago when the only traffic was horses. Now it's like living on a highway median. Between the car sounds, the metallic buzz of voices from the TV, earnestly discussing the fate of the known universe.

The door shuts again, softer this time.

"So." It's Len. "I guess it's pretty tough, dealing with the wheelchair all the time." If you only knew, Santak Guy.

"I get around."

"Right." He takes a chug from the beer bottle.

"I used to use crutches," I say. "I could always go back to them if I wanted to." The words leave my mouth with a sour, electric tang, telling me this is a lie. I've got myself bent in the shape of the goddamn wheelchair. After my big operation, I didn't keep up with the exercises my physical therapists gave me—told myself they weren't that important—and at a certain point Ma stopped nagging. So I never did get back on the crutches. Dr. O'Malley didn't mind, she said that was my choice. Over the last few years, my muscles have slowly customized themselves to match my artificial mobility device. I didn't want to notice it, but I'm starting to become one with the chair. I'm turning myself into some kind of cyborg, more Mesher than Santak. I feel a chill.

"Why don't you use crutches then?" Len asks. "It seems like stairs and bathrooms and stuff would be easier." So he did notice.

"There's nothing wrong with being in a chair!" I launch into my wheelchair speech. "It's faster, for one. I can leave you in the dust on the straightaway. And it's a lot easier to carry things." I glance down at the backpack in my lap. "In my case, it's more comfortable, since I don't have to wear braces if I'm wheeling. That way I have more energy left for the important stuff."

"Oh, I get it." He's facing me now, leaning his back against the porch post. "You're, like, one of those disability activists."

"What's wrong with that?" This guy's always getting under my skin.

"Hey, nothing." He raises his hands in mock surrender. Shouldn't I be proud of that label? I never thought of it one way or another, never went to a protest or wrote my Congressman or anything.

"Look," I say. "It's a choice. Some people choose crutches, some people choose wheels. I choose wheels."

He's staring at me, brows knitted into one line, frowning. When the hell is that show going to be over? I hear Commander Sinclair and Ambassador Mollari raising their voices.

"It's just hard to picture you on crutches, with your knees locked up like that." Crap. Of course, he saw me struggling to get horizontal for my facial extension.

"It's called contractures," I say, my voice thin. "It's just something that happens sometimes when you've been in a chair for a long time. There's a surgical procedure that can take care of it."

"Then why don't you do it?"

"I just said." Slowing down to emphasize every word. "I choose to be in the chair." He doesn't have to know about my no-more-hospitals promise to myself. Not unless it's life-threatening, and even then they might have to knock me out and drag me there unconscious. This contracture thing is elective, they cut your tendons and reattach them, then you're in casts for weeks. I wasn't listening too hard when Dr. O'Malley went through the whole thing. I knew I wouldn't be doing it.

"I guess I don't get it," Len says, still frowning. "You're talking about mobility, right? So Bucky's Dymaxion principle should apply. A wheelchair reduces friction and gains speed, so it's more efficient that way. But what it gains there, it loses in flexibility and access. To maximize your mobility, it seems like you'd prefer crutches. If it was me, I'd do the operation and get up on the crutches."

"You're right, you don't get it," I snap. "I didn't ask to be this way. It happened to me, okay? It was my freaking bad luck. And till somebody comes up with some Bucky Fuller jetpack, I'm gonna be in this chair."

He scowls down at the steps. A truck's screaming brakes and high beams take over the little yard, then disappear.

"See, that's where I disagree with you," he says. "Bad luck is just a way of saying something is part of a bigger thing that we haven't figured out yet."

"What, you think I was the victim of some bizarre top-secret government experiment or something?" That was actually a fantasy I entertained for a while when I was a kid.

"No." He shakes his head. "You're not a victim of anything. It's more big-picture than that."

"Are you saying I somehow screwed up my body myself, like before I was born?"

"No! I don't know. Bucky calls it class-one evolutionary trending. Everything fits together, everything moves us forward. So yeah, maybe we don't know what caused it, and maybe we don't know how much we can change it. Which means it's up to you."

I feel like he's punched me. "You do know that's total bullshit," I manage to get out, breathing hard, my voice rising. "You just said the worst thing. I did not make this happen to me. And nobody gets to lay that kind of guilt-tripping, you-can-do-it-all shit on me!" We stare at each other in the sudden silence.

"Okay, I see," he says. "It's okay for you to dump on everybody else. But if somebody wants to offer another—"

"Fuck you!" I can't let him finish. "Just fuck you!"

I hear fast footsteps through the kitchen, then the door creaking open. Len turns toward Zu. His face looks like it's caught between two or three expressions, none of them right.

"You ready to go?" she says to me, low and fast. I nod, can't talk now. As we bump down the steps and across the crunching gravel, past the hulking motorcycles, I clutch my backpack with the wet underwear and the Santak face extension, willing myself not to cry.

12

ROI LIES NEXT to me on the floor pad. We're in a Total Sim of the *Across the Slirrhian Sea* series, rocking gently inside a two-person Slirrhian skiff. I desperately needed something that felt like a vacation, and since I couldn't get any shore leave after my long absence, I traded with someone for their Sim time. And I thought this concentrated dose of pleasure would be good for Roi too. His leathery skin looks softer in the pearly Slirrhian light, and a light breeze brushes across us. The other characters in the story aren't due to arrive till nightfall.

I turn on my back, let out a long breath and stretch, feeling every muscle. Above us, layers of gauzy panels adjust the skiff's movement—now we're just bobbing in place in a quiet spot. We're both wearing the traditional short robes of Slirrh, made of a feather-soft fabric that floats away from you when you move, just like it did in the holo. I turn back toward Roi and open my arms wide. He pulls me closer, skin to skin.

I've wanted this so long, I whisper. To be held by you. No Fleet, no reports or regulations, no drills. Just the two of us. He runs his hand through my hair, then slips it under my robe and down my body. I shudder, and a sigh escapes me as I let go into the feelings he's giving me. So grateful that he doesn't need to be told what I want. We kiss. The boat rocks along with our movements, and the sails pinwheel out above us, like we're inside a flower. We move together, our intensity held in the enveloping softness. I give in to widening waves of pleasure.

Afterward, we lie close, our faces almost touching.

Are you happy?

I can't believe I just asked him that. But I really do want to know. How could he not feel something of what I'm feeling? Now that the words are out there, I watch him.

This—this—he struggles to speak—this place, being here with you—it gives me some— He winces. —Some sense of—

I put my hand to his mouth, sorry now. We don't have to talk about it, I say.

But he wants to say something. He looks away.

It has an echo of the Lullaby, he says.

Oh. That awful moment in Deck 6 All-Crew comes back to me. Roi's Achilles heel, and his greatest experience of bliss. The Doctor believes that the Parent-Mesher connection is cemented by an element of supreme pleasure—and that the trauma of losing this connection lay behind Roi's early catatonic state. It might be part of the reason for the failure of other captured Meshers to survive.

I hope that's a good thing, I say, trying to make things lighter.

It's a good thing. And a bad thing.

Why?

Because it reminds us of the Mesh, he says, reverting to the plural.

So, is it more good thing, or bad? I push. But I know the answer—it's both.

He looks at me, his face a well of sadness. He's remembering. As deep as this sadness goes, that's how great the ecstasy of oneness with the Mesh must have been for him. That was the compensation for the loss of his will, for his submission to carrying out the horrendous actions involved in the Mesh Takings.

You still miss them, I say.

He nods.

This was selfish of me, wanting to share this experience with him. But part of me still hopes to find a way to help restore his crippled emotional circuits. Is that selfish too? I close my eyes against the soft light of Slirrh, and hear the water slapping the sides of the skiff, and the chick, chick of the slowly turning masts.

MY EYES OPEN to a blinding white haze. I shield them with my arm. Lying here baking in the sun so long, I feel woozy, like I'm ballooning out, seeping over my edges. There's the chick chick chick of the rotating sprinkler. The lawn chair beside me is empty, except for the cardboard box and the stuff lying next to it: a Mac the Navigator mug, some costume jewelry, a raygun-shaped water pistol.

A gushing sound, then "Shit!" My mother's wrestling with the sprinkler in the middle of our backyard, her halter top and shorts spattered in the spray. Finally she sets it down on a patch of dry brown grass and backs away, waving her hands and lifting her feet in a little "Boy, am I wet" dance.

"Oh my God," she says, all breathless. Standing next to me now, still shaking her hands, her elbows high. Little droplets flick onto me, refreshingly cool.

"That always happens," she says.

"Because you never turn off the sprinkler first."

"It's not turning all the way around, so I had to move it." The sprinkler's been doing this half-cocked semicircle thing for a while.

"Why don't you get Dad to fix it?"

She fingers through her wet hair, ignoring me. "I'm gonna go in and dry off. You want something to drink?" She turns and looks at me. "You should go in soon, honey, you'll get a burn out here."

"I'm fine."

"I'll get you some lotion." She opens the screen door and goes inside.

I look around our little yard, backed by the neighbors' chain-link fence with the green-and-white aluminum weave that blocks the view of their annoying dog and everything else. The dog's old and fat now, I hardly ever hear him barking, and the family's two kids are sulky teenagers. Now all I can see is the top of the un-used swing set. Ma put in flowers—geraniums lining the fence, and rose bushes at either corner—but they look limp and dejected.

Janine's interest in her garden comes and goes in a kind of wave-like curve, and we're in one of her troughs.

Ma's right about the lotion, though. I'm fair and sunburn like crazy, whereas she turns a nice all-over nut brown. Not that I'm outside enough most days for it to matter. But today I needed the sun, had to just bake in the melting heat. It's as close as I'll get to lounging on the beach anytime soon. And it's been so long, I didn't think of putting on any sunscreen. By tomorrow my exposed parts, face, arms, legs, will be hot pink. It's been a long time since I actually burned myself, I mean really burned. It was a day like today, even hotter maybe, back in high school when I was getting around on crutches. I had on shorts, sat down on a wrought-iron chair in our neighbor's yard. Of course I couldn't feel my skin singeing on the hot iron, in stripes on either side of the braces.

There's a threatening tinge of pink on my legs already. I've been trying not to look at them. Even on this form-fitting lounge chair, my knees are sticking up, and my feet curl down awkwardly to one side. Which reminds me again of the other night. Zu said over and over that no one else noticed I had wet myself, other than Roger and Len. But everybody must have heard when I lost it with Len and yelled at him. You would think I'd be immune to embarrassment by now. The problem is, I was starting to like most of the people in the Lrak, and now the thought of seeing them again makes my teeth grind. And on top of that, I'm still carrying on the argument with Len in my head. Where does he get off bringing up some random Bucky principle and applying it to my personal situation? Even if it does make sense in a certain way. He's got no idea, none of them do, how hard it is for me to choose to go back for more surgery.

I hear the muffled *vroom* of Irv's Mitsubishi pulling into our driveway. Was he coming today? The car door slams. A few seconds later, there he is, nailed in the sun like some pale butterfly. Looking smaller in the glare, with his quizzical expression, his short-sleeved office shirt and pants—the man has no weekend clothes. Even his graying hair looks more faded. When did his hair start to go gray? After we came back to Philly he had a hard time finding a job—fewer mainframes around to manage, I guess. He worked for himself for a while, and then finally got a job with a little computer-networking company downtown. Way below his pay grade.

"Hey, Ace." He steps up onto the patio. "How's it going?"

"Not bad. How 'bout you?" He nods in answer, surveying the yard.

"Where's your mother?"

"She got a little wet, trying to fix the sprinkler." He glances at it and goes right over to turn off the spigot. The sprinkler slows to a stop as Irv wades over and squats down, his loafers turning shiny in the wet grass. Pulling out his keychain with the all-in-one tool, he sets to work on the thing.

"Hey, Pop?" He grunts.

"I've been thinking," I make myself go on.

"About what?" he asks without looking up.

"You remember about the contractures, right?"

"The thing with your legs. Sure."

"I'm thinking of talking to Dr. O'Malley. About doing the surgery."

He looks up. "You sure?"

"Just talking to her. Go over my options."

He gives a little nod. "Sounds like a good idea." I needed to hear that.

Irv gives the sprinkler a finger-whirl and goes to turn on the water again. Success—it turns, a slow full circle, then settles into an easy rotation. He sits down beside me.

"Did you mention this to your mother?" Looking over the fence.

"Not yet." It's not something we talk about, but Irv and I both know she doesn't welcome the idea of me having surgery any more than I do.

"So did you get the Captain's book yet?" he asks. Henley Ito, who plays Captain Tanaka on *Century 23*, just came out with his memoir. We jump on that topic, speculating on how much he'll reveal about how and why the show got canceled.

Janine pops the back door open with one hip and backs out with a tray balanced on the other, holding three cans of Sprite, the sun lotion and her box of Slims. She's changed into a big T-shirt— one of mine, I see—that covers her shorts, so it's just her toast-colored legs coming out the bottom.

"I heard you two talking out here!" she says with a glance at Irv.

"You told me to come over today, remember?"

"Sure, because we had to work late at that show yesterday, right, Mindy?" I look blank, won't tell a lie for her. Irv usually comes on Saturdays, but last night Janine went out on another date with Nick, the King of Comix. Seafood Shanty, her favorite.

"Actually," she says, "we met somebody who might help us get set up at the Atlantic City show." Proud of her little subterfuge. She and Nick were supposedly getting together to discuss the possibility of us doing Atlantic City. All week she's been going on about how he might want to share a booth with us there. I'm thinking it's something else he wants to share with her.

"I tried explaining it to her," I tell him. "The booth rental is totally out of our league."

"Well, if you decide to do it, let me know," Irv says. "It's a pretty big haul to the Shore."

Maybe they've already started the other kind of "sharing." Nick's not the first guy to come around since Irv stopped living with us. Janine and I are both grown women, and it's her business who she sleeps with. But something about this guy really cranks me. And he's got her wound up too: since they started dating, she's been organizing and rearranging things around here. Now instead of piles of boxes, there are things on every surface, displaying the Janine Vogel Collection of mid- to late-twentieth-century artifacts. As soon as Irv goes in the house, he'll see the difference—except in my room, I wouldn't let her touch anything in there.

"Did Mindy tell you?" Janine sips from the can. "She went out again, with her new friends!"

"Ma!"

"New friends?" Irv cocks an eyebrow.

"Just some people from that Santak club, I met them through Zu."

My mother hands the tube of sun lotion to Irv.

"Are you gonna join this club?" Irv asks, rubbing lotion on his nose.

"I mean, they're Santak, Pop." I hate how uncomfortable I'm feeling.

"But isn't that still SkyLog?" my mother protests. "They're all members of the same, the Transparency . . ."

"Yes, Ma! The Transortium." My father looks at me, and our eyes catch for a quick, awkward moment. Better to bring it up while he's here. My stomach flip-flops.

"Anyway," I start.

"I'm sure they'd be happy to have you as a member," she says.

"Ma! Will you listen for one second?"

"What?"

I let out a breath. "Me and Dad, we were just talking about me maybe having that surgery."

"What surgery?"

"For the contractures."

"I thought you didn't want any more surgery!"

"Of course I don't!"

"What are you saying then?"

"She just wants to talk to Dr. O'Malley about it," Irv offers, handing the lotion back to my mother. "Scope things out."

"I think they're getting tighter," I say. All eyes turn to my knees, sticking up from the raised contours of the lounge chair.

"Oh. All right," Janine says. "I'm just surprised, that's all."

"So I'll call to make an appointment." I watch her face. "Just to talk." Her mouth is scrunched up. She squishes a big blob of lotion into one hand and stands there, looking lost.

"Sure," she says. She reaches with the lotion toward my face.

"Jeez, Ma!" I push her hand away, knocking the tube to the cement.

"You're gonna get burned!"

"I can do it myself!" She left a smear of lotion on my cheek. I rub it in, mixing it into my sweat-slick skin.

"Fine," she says. She picks up the tube. "You don't need me." She leans over again, picking up the SkyLog mug, the raygun, the plastic jewelry, putting them all on the tray. "I see you got everything decided without me." She stands there, her eyes bright, glittering daggers at me, then Irv. She picks up the tray and heads for the door.

"J, that's not the way it was." My dad beats her to the door and pulls it out wide for her. The door creaks shut, leaving me out here alone. But I can hear them yelling from inside the house, every word. Just like old times. She's blaming everything on him, he's taking the heat for me. Then the voices muffle, they've gone into the bedroom. I shouldn't have done it this way, using Irv as a buffer. It's just hard dealing with her sometimes. I shift up to sitting, put my feet down on the cement, and lean over to hoist myself back into my chair. On the way back in, I lean over to turn off the spigot, and the sprinkler chicks to a stop.

13

'M LYING ON my back, looking up at the night sky. A wash of stars sprinkles across the deep indigo. The huge lilac moon looms to one side, frosting the mountain ridge with lavender. Hearing the pounding of the mining pumps under the sound of the wind, it comes to me: I'm on the other side of the mountains from the Night People. Our diplomatic mission to the Mowg may have succeeded, but dealing with them has left me exhausted. And I don't trust their assurances that they will leave the valuable seam of ore in the Valley untouched. What am I doing here, away from the settlement? I must have slipped off from the others, half-sleepwalking. The vibrating stars and the ever-present wind are telling me what I have to do: cross the mountains, find the People and warn them. If I tell them what I've seen here, they'll understand. I try to get up, but it's like I'm pinned down. I can't move! What's happening?

Now I'm back on the ship. Did they travel me up without my knowing? I'm lying flat on my back, on an examination couch in Med Bay. The doctor stands, her face contracted with concern, her scanner clicking as she draws a curve in the air just above my stomach.

So, do I pass? I ask. I really want to ask what the hell I'm doing here. The doctor ignores my comment, just keeps moving the device over me. Being scrutinized like this makes me uncomfortable. I can't move at all—the couch hugs me tight. Finally she stops and looks up at me.

This isn't a routine post-mission check, is it?

There seems to be an old injury in the lumbar spine, she says, glancing at her device. I don't know why we never picked this up before.

It was just a childhood accident, I say. This isn't right! I mean, I know about this, but she's not supposed to. What's going on?

I didn't think it would affect anything . . .

The scan doesn't lie, Kat. I'm just amazed we never picked it up before. And you somehow got past the officer's training exam—

I'm fine, really! It's no big deal!

—so nobody ever ran the next level of tests that could have revealed the aftereffects.

No!

She turns away, leaving me lying here alone and trapped.

I'M IN A DIFFERENT PLACE. A bare room, in half-darkness. Still lying flat. Bars on either side of me—some kind of jail? Am I in a Total Sim program? But I'm breathing convincingly stale institutional air, with notes of wintergreen disinfectant and pee. A few blinking lights, a beeping sound. From somewhere I can't see, a gurgling wheeze and a machine humming. I have a headache and feel all dried out—my skin, my mouth, my eyelids. Okay, so this is me, Mindy, in a twentieth-century hospital room. What time is it? By the half-light, it could be early morning or dusk. I can't make out the clock face.

I look down: casts cover my legs from the thighs down to the feet. It's coming back to me now in all of its sordid clarity. I did it, I had the surgery. This is the former Mercy General, now a branch of HealthNet MidAtlantic. We Care About Your Wellness. It's a double room, with somebody's ragged wheezing and the swish of a respirator coming from behind a curtained divider. I can't stop looking at my legs, how they lie there on the bed, flat and docile as a sleeping cat, a long, low, blanketed double ridge. No stubborn bends at the knees, hips or feet. It's been a long time since they've looked like that. So the operation was a success. Moving my fingers around where the casts end, I discover my legs are still numb and unfeeling down there, like they've always been. What did I expect? This is twentieth-century medicine here.

Someone's looking at me. Hunched in a chair beside the bed—it's Irv. How long has he been there? I hope he didn't spend the night in that little chair.

"Hey, Ace." His tone is soft. "How you doing?"

"Hey, Pop." My throat feels gravelly, my words barely audible. "I've been better." I heave out a sigh. He gets up and holds a Styrofoam cup to my mouth, and I sip the last bit of ice water.

"You comfortable enough there?"

"Oh yeah." It's not a question of pain. It's just that I'm having massive buyer's remorse. I can't believe I put myself back here in a hospital room, where all the other times I've ever been stuck here are whacking together in my brain, a giant train wreck of memories.

"Dr. Hsu said everything went real good," he says.

"Who?"

"The surgeon, Dr. Hsu? He said he'd come in this morning." How am I supposed to keep all the doctors straight? They're all bouncing around in the train wreck, including that doctor from Med Bay.

A fit of strangled coughing comes from behind the divider. Irv crosses to the other side. "You all right?" he asks. "Sure you don't need anything?" No response, but the coughing subsides and he returns to his chair. "Hip surgery," he whispers. He pulls something out of the old NPR tote bag leaning against the chair. "I brought you this." It's a book—that new Henley Ito memoir.

"That's so cool. Thanks." It's the hardback, he didn't even wait for the paperback.

"He is your favorite Captain, right?"

"Yeah." Irv will always be loyal to the first Crew, which I only ever saw in reruns. I lean the book against my hip, not in any shape to read now. Irv brought me to my first Con when I was still in middle school. He somehow got me up to the front row, where we had a close-up view of the first Captain. The shock of seeing him in the flesh, sharing our space-time continuum, wearing a Hawaiian shirt instead of his Fleet tunic. Then Daddy being his usual patient self while we waited so long in the autograph line afterward. Lying here, I feel about as old as I was then; there's a lump in my throat.

"Hey, Pop?" My voice still small and hoarse. "If anybody ever tries to get me in a hospital again, will you promise to lock me in my room or handcuff me to my chair or something?"

"But you decided to do this, babe." He looks stricken.

"It was a big mistake. Can we just leave now?"

"Oh, babe," he says. "It doesn't get any easier, does it?" I shake my head no, squeeze my eyes shut to hold in the tears. He's been in hospital rooms like this with me so many times before. But it's not always just the two of us.

"Where's Ma?" I ask.

"She was here last night."

"Why does she do that?" In the half-dark, my thoughts seem to flop right out of my mouth.

"Do what?"

"You know. What she does. Flake out when I'm in the hospital." He sighs. We've never talked about this.

"First off, I made her go home."

"You know what I mean." I'm seeing Janine, standing outside a hospital room, yelling at the doctor, her face discolored, neck taut, eyes bulging; the doctor towering over her, talking low and rapid. When was that? It could be several memories mixed together.

"You probably don't remember all the times when you were little," he says. "She was always here. Wouldn't even sleep."

"Okay, but then the time after high school—" That was the big one, when they said that basically my brain was leaking into my spine. I was so sick and scared then, not knowing what was going to happen. And in the hospital I couldn't see much, because they had me lying on my belly or on one side, in a post-surgery haze of pain and confusion. Ma pacing the room, yelling, I remember that. Then long days without her. Irv brought me home.

"Where the hell did she go?"

He shakes his head. "It just got to be too much for her." He sounds very tired. He's never going to tell me what happened. I see now how hard it was for him, juggling my recovery with what-ever my mother was doing. I never thought of that before, how much energy I sucked out of him.

"It's my fault."

"What? No!"

"Yeah it is. Me getting sick all the time, all this." I wave a hand out from my body to encompass the room and the hospital around us.

"No!" Surprise and hurt mash together on his face. "Don't ever say that, Mindy! We're in this together. You, me, your mother."

"But," again I can't stop myself, "how come you left after the last time?"

He grimaces like I've hit him. "It just seemed like . . ." It's the start of his generic bullshit explanation of why he left the house after I was in for the kidney infection, but he trails off. Actually, he moved out while I was in the hospital; when I came home, Irv and his stuff were gone.

"Your mother and I," he tries again. "She was under a lot of pressure."

"So was I!"

"Mindy—she, things were starting to get violent."

"Oh." I know Irv would never hit anyone. "She hit you?" His grimace gets worse.

"Tried to. She's little, but she's strong." This somehow doesn't surprise me, and that makes me sad. I turn my head away.

"Mindy. We all make mistakes. But you know I'm not going away. I'll always be here."

"I still wish you hadn't moved out."

"I think you two do pretty well without me."

"Oh yeah, two crazies going to flea markets."

He picks up the book from the bed, puts it on the end table. Stands over me, looking out the window.

"Okay, yeah. Your mother's a little crazy," he says finally. "But when she freaks out, it's because she loves you so much. She just can't stand it, seeing you . . ."

I know this. I know how hard this is for her. How hard it was for her, right from the start, always afraid she might lose me, her baby. But my own feelings are swamping me. I want us to just be a family, like before. If Irv were still living with us, then Janine wouldn't have started seeing the slimeball Nick.

The harsh coughing starts up again on the other side of the curtain. Irv heads out to the hallway to flag down a nurse, who quiets the old lady with a drink of water, then asks her in a loud voice, "How's your pain level on a scale of one to ten?" The woman doesn't understand. The nurse repeats, slower: Pain level. One to ten. I'm not sure how I'd answer that. I'd have to know what kind of pain.

"AM I INTERRUPTING ANYTHING?" This is another doctor, I know her. There's a good feeling here, a weak flashlight beam in the fog.

"That depends."

"On what?"

"Which ship we're on, I guess."

"Okay," she says, laughing a little. I recognize how the skin crinkles around her smile—it's Dr. Teresa O'Malley, my twentieth-century doctor. She's not old, but her hair is the color of aluminum, falling straight like a helmet around her thin face. Her knobby wrists protrude from the white sleeves of her medical uniform.

"I hear you're doing really well, Mindy." She puts her hand on one of my legs appraisingly. Looking at her is nice—the little crinkles around her eyes, how she looks sideways when she talks.

"So when do you spring me?"

"Not so fast," she says, laughing again. "Can you pull yourself up on your side? I want to get a better look here." She's challenging me, testing my strength. I grab the bars and heave up on my side. Now I'm facing the divider, its fabric curving like old drapery.

"The physical therapist should be coming in to see you tomorrow," she says. "I want you to get started right away this time."

"Can't you just use neurospray?"

"What?" she says absently. "Mindy, we went through this. Whether you decide to go back to the crutches or not, this is part of taking good care of yourself."

I shrug. "I'm not really seeing the point." The legs are the same—still zero feeling. Dark Ages medicine.

She moves around to my side of the bed and leans in on me. Her eyes a little red-rimmed, but they always look that way.

"Mindy. You said you wanted to give it a shot this time. We talked about this. You said you thought it through and you wanted to have the option of, what was it, greater mobility and access. Remember?"

"Yeah. Damn Dymaxion theory."

"I don't know about that," she says. "This was your decision. But it won't work if you don't commit to the physical therapy. Even if you decide to go back to mainly using the chair, which is fine with me, you have to do the PT. And keep it up. Otherwise you'll just be back where you were, looking at more contractures down the road."

"I just can't think about it right now, okay?"

"Okay. You talk to the physical therapist." She straightens up. "Nice card! Who's it from?" She hands it to me.

It must be from Roxie. It's like one of her artworks but in miniature: the card surface is covered with safety pins, bits of paper doily, a cutout dinosaur, and little springs dangling off the paper. Like it's being held together and bursting apart at the same time.

"It's from an artist I know."

Dear Mindy,

Sorry I couldn't come in to wish you Get Well Soon. Nothing personal, more like something personal I have against hospitals. I told you about how they had to open up my chest and put in this machine the last time I was there. No Fun. But you probably know what I'm talking about. Your mother says after this operation you might go back to walking with crutches, not like you don't do great already. I read some of the "zines" you gave me, and you've got a way with words. Take care of yourself, things will look up soon I'm sure.

Your pal, Roxie

ONE MOMENT HE wasn't there, and then he's there. Standing in front of me at the foot of the bed. The air crackling blue around him, blurring the edges of his body. This sparking cloud is coming from him, out of the electrical seam that runs up and down the outer edge of his limbs. His head glows neon-bright, throwing off a tingling corona. Is this a Mesh thing I haven't seen before? I don't understand how he got here. Did the sparking cloud somehow open up a link between our time periods? He looks around, taking in the details of this centuries-old medical facility: the overhead TV, the pockmarked acoustic ceiling tiles, the cutesy-bright flower painting on the wall, the tubes tethering my body to the boxy monitors. He moves to the side of my bed, lowers the metallic railing and sits on the mattress beside me. So close, I can feel the waves of energy jittering off him. He's come all this way. I know it's impossible, but I don't care.

I'm so happy to see you, I say. He doesn't answer, just looks at me. I follow his gaze as it moves from my face, down my body, over the rumpled hospital gown, to my legs lying flat under the thin blanket.

I'm sorry I didn't tell you about this, I say. It seems like I didn't want to understand it myself—the extent of the problem, I mean. This is the best they can do.

He reaches his hand out to touch my thigh. I feel it—the energy coming through him, into my skin, spitting through nerves small and sharp like tiny bee-bites. This can't be happening. It's the same crackling power designed to stun the captives of the Mesh. Is he here to Enmesh me? But this is gentler—the energy's a conduit for something else. The outlines of his hand slither and tingle as it moves, and I feel the bee-bites swirling down my leg. I shouldn't feel them there. I give up trying to understand.

A LOUD RUMBLING in the hallway overtakes the drone of the TV. Seconds later, a hospital utility cart wheels into my room, with a smallish black device sitting on top. The person pushing it is familiar. Reddish hair, flat moon face: it's my friend Zuzana. My good, good friend Zu.

"How'd you get in here?" I say. All this reality switching is wiping me out.

"What, I told you I was coming by tonight," she answers, looking at me. "Your mom said you were well enough for visitors." Oh right—it's dark outside. Irv had to go to work, said he'd be back later.

"What's with the, the medical equipment?"

"You mean this?" She puts her hand on the black thing, which sports some knobs and shiny metal outgrowths. "It's—" she glances toward the door as two more visitors enter: one tall and thin, with a mane of dreadlocks poking out around his brown face; the other one shorter and more solid, black hair flopping over his thick black eyebrows. Bradley and Len. They hover awkwardly by the door, each holding a bulging shopping bag. Then one more comes in behind them, the black-haired Santak female—Trish. The room feels suddenly tiny, crowded to bursting. Trish pushes the wheeled divider back against the other bed.

"Hey, hey! Watch out there!" I say.

"Nobody here but us Santak." Trish pulls the divider out so I can see—the other bed's empty. What happened to the old lady? People are materializing and dematerializing around me.

"I told you this was a stupid idea," Len growls.

"Be cool." That's Bradley. "Zu's the Off-Ship Officer here."

"Santak don't do errands of mercy," Len states, folding his arms.

"No, man," Bradley says quietly, "it's a Jan-Le ceremony, re-member." It hits me that Zu probably used some subterfuge to get Len here, the same way she dragged me to that first Lrak meeting.

"Which loosely translates as Get Well Concert," says Zu, switching off the TV with a quick sideways tap. "Let's do this."

She kneels down near me, fiddling with something close to the floor. "Hand me the power strip." Boy, she is the mission commander. Even so, I see in her face, hovering close to mine, a dizzy lightness.

"So, are you gonna hook me up to that thing?" I'm half back in the sparking cloud. Maybe it's some kind of signal booster, sent by my 23rd-century friend to enhance his hands-on treatment. Zu looks at me again, smiling but evaluating me too.

"Mindy, it's my theremin." When I look blank she goes on, "You know, the new instrument I've been telling you about? I played it for you over the phone a couple of times." The thing is just a low black box—looks like an antenna poking up on one end, and another one weirdly looping out from one side.

"So this is going to involve sound," I say.

"Yeah, there's gonna be some sound," she answers, laughing. "But we'll keep it down as low as we can." Bradley's setting up a keyboard on my food tray table. Len pulls an amplifier about the size of a toaster out of the bag, and Trish is holding some kind of small drum.

"It's a tabla," she says with a shrug, seeing me staring at it. Len's down on the floor, threading wires around.

"Okay, that's it," Len says, coming up for air right at the night table. He spots my one and only get-well card.

"It's from Roxie," I explain.

"Of course." A big white-toothed smile spreads under his mustache. When he smiles he sort of reminds me of Teddy Roosevelt but without the granny glasses. He gently boings one of the springs, which makes the card vibrate. "Excellent. How's she doing?" he adds, still watching the card.

"No idea. I've been kind of tied up."

"Right. How are *you* doing?" he asks, looking at me, his cheeks flushing a little.

"Okay, I guess." I look at his face, the eyes lurking under those black eyebrows. "Actually, this is kind of your fault," I say, the words still flopping out of me. His blush holds.

"Yeah, well. I know I said some dumb things—"

"You did," I say, cutting him off. "But your Bucky Fuller bullshit did get me thinking."

"Can't argue with Bucky," he says with a nervous laugh. Well, yeah, you can. You just can't necessarily win. Bucky's streamlined simplicity cuts through other kinds of bullshit like a Swiss knife. Unfortunately, it all led me to here.

Len's eyes drift down to my legs: "Looks like it worked, anyway."

"Are we ready?" asks Zu. Bradley signals yes. "Hey, Trish," he calls, "get the door?"

With the door shut, the corridor sounds gone and the TV off, it feels like we're inside a sealed box.

"Okay, this is something I wrote for synthesizer and theremin," Zu says. "It's for you," she adds, ducking her head. She nods over to Bradley. He lays down some bass chords on the keyboard, then slowly pulls in a higher, floating cluster of sound like an unhinged accordion. Some light, dancing beats from Trish's drum. Then I hear a strange high note spiraling down like a slide whistle. Zu's hand is moving near the antenna thing sticking up from the black box, but never touching it—like she's conducting, coaxing some invisible musician to shape the sounds to her hand gestures. Her head is cocked, her face expressionless but superintent. She and the box are in sync: as her hand moves away from the antenna, the sounds go lower; then they go higher again with her approaching hand.

The sound hooks into me, cutting me open to the raw nerves. The thing sometimes sounds like a human voice, then wails higher like some plaintive wild creature. But not quite like either of them. Every curving note is completely, eerily not from the human or the animal world, or from any carbon-based lifeform. It's the voice of the living machine, the cry of all those conscious entities constructed but not given mouths to speak. The sound probes inside me like my cyborg visitor's electric touch. That blue haze tingles in the air again. I close my eyes, scared. My filters are shredded, the sound is mainlining into me, plucking, sawing, keening. It's so intense, I'm feeling it as pain now—but the pain is tangled up with the connection, his touch on me, his desire to touch me.

The sound stops. I open my eyes to the hospital room. No blue in the air, thank God. Zu is still in her listening trance, both hands hovering at the antennas. She comes to, turns a knob, nods to the others. I see faces at the door.

"That was incredible," Len says softly. Standing by the door, he hasn't noticed our audience. Now they come in—a nurse and a tech.

"What *is* that thing?" asks one of them with a look of wonder. They all talk at once. Zu: "It's a theremin." Bradley: "A musical instrument." Len: "It's a special device—be careful!" I say nothing, can't talk. I still feel skinless, almost vibrating, like a bell after it's been struck. The nurse, in spite of Len's warning, approaches the theremin, looking hypnotized. The other one speaks up: "Whatever it is, you've got to keep it down. There are patients resting on this floor."

"Sure, no problem." Bradley's soothing voice.

"We're just trying to cheer up our friend here," says Len. "It's no louder than the damn TV."

"Just keep it down," she repeats. "I don't know how many rules you're breaking, but I can find out." She moves toward the door. But her buddy has edged closer to the mysterious machine.

"Girl, that is something," she says.

"Want to try it?" Zu offers. The nurse moves her hand gingerly toward the antenna and Zu turns the theremin back on, then fiddles with a dial, bringing down the volume. The sound wiggles upward as the nurse's hand does the same, and her giggles ping around the wobbling wail. I try not to panic as I feel it ricocheting around inside me.

"It's just like in the horror movies!" the nurse cries.

"Yeah, it was used in a lot of those old soundtracks," Zu says patiently.

"You coming, Keesha?" It's the tech, leaning through the door.

"Oh! Right!" Keesha breaks herself away. "I do not believe that thing," she says as they move out into the hallway.

"Okay," says Zu, pulling out some sheet music and handing it to Bradley. "Since they didn't kick us out, here's one more. It's a little more laid back." This time I'm determined to keep my eyes open, hoping that might protect me from the sonic invasion. Bradley begins again, pulling some expansive chords up from the low side of the keyboard like they're trying to stretch over huge spaces. When the otherworldly voice enters again, lazing down toward the cascading chords and the light popping rhythm of the drum, I know there's no defending myself against it. I surrender, pierced all over again. But this time, with my eyes open, something else happens. The electricity that started with Roi's probing cyborg touch is in the air now. Zu's standing there with her eyes unfocused, looking somewhere past my head, Trish is a little behind her, Bradley's staring down at his keyboard, Len still guarding the door. Nobody's looking at each other, but the electricity is forming lines connecting them. Thin and luminous, the same as what just traveled through my neural network. The music is traveling along these lines, maybe somehow creating them. And then I'm stunned by a shock that licks through me like a rogue line of lightning—Oh my God! I'm seeing the love traveling between humans. What's causing this, what am I seeing? It must be Bradley and Zuzana. Of course I know what it means, being in love. But I've never seen it, felt it before with this blinding directness. It's happening right now, in front of me. Do they know? Is the yawning, pulsating music telling them? I feel like crying, it's all too much. I close my eyes and turn my head to the side.

"You okay?" It's Len, his voice low, just over a whisper. He must be kneeling right next to me. I don't want to open my eyes.

"No," I say, shaking my head, then, "I don't know." The theremin gives a long sigh over a last, achingly slow chord, and the music ends. I am so alone. My entire body sore, swollen with confused, vibrating pain.

14

FROM: amadden@uokla.edu
TO: MindRoid@comet.net
SUBJECT: sorry
DATE: 9/15/99 1:22 PM

Mindy,

I'm sorry I haven't sent u anything yet. Cant get myself to
start writing. I'm stuck in the goddamn computer pod every
day and crawl home at nite. Then alls I can do is fall on
the couch, suck on a beer and watch reruns. Plus that guy
Hank is putting the moves on me to get serious, he doesn't
understand I'm a traveling girl, I got to have my fun and then
move on to the next planet. Just feeling generally down,
thanks for listening. I think maybe Catherine Weldon is rubbing
off on me. She got such a hard hand to play with. Did I tell
you the part about her getting kicked off the Sioux Rez for
meddling with the Ghost Dancers? She was one feisty lady.
But then after she left on the steamboat, her son Christie
got lockjaw and died, just a 13 yr old kid. So then she's
completely alone, writing super-sad letters back to Sitting Bull
that he never answered, missing her son, and "far from all my
Dakota friends" as she said. Did I tell you about how Sitting
Bull wanted her to be his wife? I guess he wanted to make
her an honest woman since she was living in his cabin with

him and his other wives and children. But she got all offended and turned him down. Here she goes out west finding other worlds and getting chewed up, it's all too alien for her. And then there's nothing—no more letters from her, and nobody knows what happened to her after that. But we do know what happened to Sitting Bull and the Indians. Since he wouldn't come out against the Ghost Dancers the Indian Agent had him shot, right outside his cabin. And then the worst thing, because the Indians wouldn't stop dancing the army came in and shot them all at Wounded Knee Creek. This was in the middle of winter so the bodies twisted and froze in the snow, old men, women, babies and kids. All they were trying to do was see their dead relatives again, and instead they got to be dead too.

It's all like a massive downer. And Catherine writing to Sitting Bull, not even knowing that he's about to be arrested & shot. I'm guessing one of his wives kept the letters, then one of the kids gave them or maybe sold them to Mr. Vestal many years after all this went down.

abundant life, angie

FROM: MindRoid@comet.net
TO: amadden@uokla.edu
SUBJECT: Re: sorry
DATE: 9/15/99 3:49 PM

Angie,

Don't worry about sending anything in, it'll be a while before I get the next issue together. Your Catherine is really something. I still feel like she could be a SkyLog character somehow, going off and getting into trouble in various parts of the galaxy. Meanwhile, I'm back home from another surgery. Lots of lying around, except when I undergo torture by physical therapy three times a week. Only two more weeks and five days before I get the stupid casts off my legs. It's the first time I did an operation on purpose, but that didn't make it any easier. For now, there's lots of time for me to lie around and think about things. Nothing as bad as Catherine went through, it's just that I seem to have lost my superpower of ignoring bad memories. They keep coming back, rerunning like some second-rate series. Well, I've had various old friends stopping by. And this guy Len came over after work a couple of times.

- Mindy

These memory loops are driving me crazy, I wish I could re-forget them, take an amnesia pill or something. It's like the pins and needles when your arm has been asleep and starts waking up again. Except that usually goes away after a few minutes, and these needles seem to be sticking pretty deep. I'm subjected to random scenes from that third-rate show *Mindy Goes to High School*. Me going up to the front doors, hoping they'll be open so I won't have to struggle with them. Down the long main hallway, past the trophy cases, past the kids yelling each other's names. Or me in the cafeteria. No longer protected by my Bionic Woman lunch box, sitting at the table at the back, where there's less traffic. I ate alone or with my friend Mary Ellen, she had picked me out to be friends, and a couple of other girls. Mary Ellen was very nice, the only problem being we had zero interests in common. All around us, the girl tables and boy tables, and a few combined. The girls so breezy and quick moving, leaning and arching in their little out-fits. Screeching to each other, dipping their chins and laughing up at the big boys when they stopped by, the boys hulking there with backpacks hanging off their shoulders. The popular girls, so pretty. Kimberly presided at the popular girls' table, her gold-highlighted hair swinging as she turned to examine newcomers.

Or Me at My Locker. Balancing myself on the crutches while I pull books out. The girls crowding around to one side of me, inches away—I'm invisible to them. I grab onto the locker door in case I get pushed. *You don't really like him do you? Did you see what she was wearing? So who's coming on Friday night? Who's driving?* Staring into my locker, waiting for them to leave, so I won't get pushed.

I always get back to the science room. This is where the Science Fiction Club met, in Mr. Schechter's physics class. That one year, Ma picked me up Wednesday afternoons so I could stay late for the meetings, under the silent gazes of Max Planck and Niels Bohr. Mostly boys, of course. An assortment of geeks and weirdos: one guy with a mohawk, and the other two girls wore a lot of leather. I wasn't there long enough to move up in the ranks, but it was okay. First time I was part of a group where I was actually into what was going on. The thing is, something else happened in that science room. I hate this part. I came in early to class, propped the door open with one crutch. There's Kimberly, queen of the cafeteria, standing in front of Mr. Schechter's desk, talking to him. Her back to me, she doesn't see me. She's my lab partner too, and I've been doing most of the work, which is funny considering it's not my forte. *You've got to change me*, she's saying to him. *I just can't stand working with her.* But Mr. Schechter has seen me, his gaze locks with mine. Sticks deep into me. I want to take his embarrassment away but can't move or talk. She turns, her eyes sliding over me, as they have a dozen times before; shakes her shiny hair as if to say, *I mean it.* On Monday I had a new lab partner.

Which brings me right back to Sheryl. I pretty much knew where I stood with Kimberly—never imagined we were friends, though it was interesting being inside the blast radius of Miss Popular. But I thought Sheryl was on my side. Yes, I let myself overlook her strangeness. She worked her way in quietly, deliberately. Always helpful. Coming over to my place to help collate and staple, stuffing zines into big envelopes for the mailing. Janine even invited her to stay for dinner one time. I felt sorry for her, Ma peppering her with questions—what does her roommate do, what's it like working as a bookkeeper, did she ever watch *The Dick Van Dyke Show?*—when clearly Sheryl hated talking about herself. Maybe there were warning signs that Sheryl was not my friend, but I missed them. I know what a real friend is, from Zu. Somebody who calls me on my crap and tells me straight out how she's feeling. Except now, since I've realized something's going on with Zu and Bradley, I feel like I'm losing her too. I haven't said anything, don't want her to feel like I resent her being happy. But it's hanging between us. And right now that hurts as much as the stuff with Sheryl.

Was that what I was thinking with this operation? After all these years, that it might make me able to keep up with other people? Yes, standing up does put you at eye level with most everybody else, more like a standard-issue human. But I still can't do it without metal and plastic: the crutches, the braces—artificial bones and joints, you might say. My not-so-high-tech exoskeleton, far from a Bucky jetpack.

I look around my room. It feels like it's gotten more overstuffed while the rest of the house is getting leaner and cleaner, with Janine packing more and more into boxes. Lately, I'm even having trouble finding some things, like my 20th Anniversary SkyLog compendium that came out when *Century 23* was starting, with commentary from the producers of both shows. And a couple of *Amazing Stories* issues. They've got to be here somewhere.

FROM: amadden@uokla.edu
TO: MindRoid@comet.net
SUBJECT: parallel reality
DATE: 9/16/99 12:19 AM

Hey girl,

So who is this Len guy. Don't hold out on me now Mindy, is he one of those Santak you were telling me about. They have gotten a bad rap, if you ask me they are a lot more reliable than most humans.

Me and Hank had a big fight last night. He wants me to move in with him and give up my dubious lifestyle. I told him I'm too old to settle down. He knows I'd like to get out of Normal, but he wants to stay here till he gets his dissertation approved, which is just bullshit, since that's like a receding event horizon. I truly don't know how much longer I can take it here.

What I'm saying is I can't think straight right now, let alone start on another story. Honest, Mindy, I wonder. Is there any point? I mean writing stories about characters in a TV show. Am I crazy spending my time writing fanfic? No offense to you and your zine which is great.

SL4EVER,

Angie

FROM: MindRoid@comet.net
TO: amadden@uokla.edu
SUBJECT: Re: parallel reality
DATE: 9/16/99 11:32 AM

Ange -

No!! Writing fanfic is not crazy!! Well, maybe it is, but good-crazy, just like being a fan in the first place is. Sorry I can't give you any advice in the guy department, but I can tell you, don't stop writing! Your stories are great, people want to read what you do! Maybe I'm just being selfish here, I want to keep publishing your stuff. But I mean it too.

- Mindy

My own question is a little different: Is it crazy to write fanfic if you never even write it down? I wonder if that's been making me a little crazy. I liked being able to slip in and out of my different worlds, between this one and that other one, several light years and centuries away. I might miss some conversation, people might think I was spacing out. But in the hospital it started to go haywire—all that sliding around, with bits and pieces colliding from my different worlds. I couldn't keep anything straight, and it was starting to get scary.

So I've started writing it down again, Roi and Kat. Hoping that will help me get things sorted out. Fuck the True SkyLog Fan, whoever that was, accusing my writing of being too Mary Sueish. And fuck me worrying about Kat Wanderer being a Mary Sue.

That's not exactly true—I'm still worrying about that. Which is why I haven't told anybody about this, not Angie, not Zu, nobody. I started writing in an old school notebook. Then, when Irv brought me his old laptop computer so I could work on things in bed, I went digital. Whatever I write goes in a folder called Random Notes.

They've made a feast for me. I've picked my way through what I can eat, and now I sit back against a moss-pillow. They're teasing me, telling stories I can't follow about the Giant Far-walking Woman. The torches throw fingering shadows on the rock walls. When I got back here, they swarmed around me, patting me softly, making sure I was real and whole. They led me down into the crevice, holding onto me so I wouldn't slip on the tiny steps. Walking the familiar corridors, I felt the tug again. The pull to let go and just be here, on this world. I can never really be a part of it, I know—but they're so happy to have me back. I'm seen and appreciated here in a way I can't remember anywhere else. This makes my mission feel even more urgent—I have to find a way to persuade them to leave this place where they've lived so long. If I stay with them, I could try to guide them to a similar, safer environment. I have to stay focused: I need to make them see that their defense, if you can call it that, against the Mowg will lead to disaster. I've got to speak with the Old One. But he didn't sit beside me at the feast. He gave a short welcome speech but hasn't looked at me or talked to me since.

Finally our eyes meet. Now I know: he's closed himself off from me. After I left, he made his own calculations on the dangers faced by his people. I'm no longer helpful to him. If the scouts saw me coming from the direction of the Mowg compound, he must think I've betrayed him. A line of ice trickles down my spine. In the middle of the celebration, I'm completely alone.

15

PULL ON THE green elastic straps. Bring my hands down slow to my shoulders, taking a deep breath in. It's so damn hard, and they keep raising the tension on me. Have to get the upper body strength up, they say. Now that I've got the casts off, the PTs are really on my case. I let go, move my arms back out gently as the cords contract. But lately I've been releasing them faster, with a sharp breath out—it feels like my arms are punching something. Or somebody. Now it's Cafeteria Kimberly, my so-called partner in science lab. Her face turning toward me, her slack-mouthed look of disdain, shattered with the second blow. She collapses down and backwards, her limbs loose like a doll. It replays on a loop with my breath: in and out, windup, punch. Just keep repeating that moment of surprise, the falling back. Then I might do Sheryl. She stands there, her mouth open like she's about to explain something to me. Her pale face opens with surprise, the eyebrows shooting up. My breath thrums out, fist connects with chin. Her hair flies out, her glasses sail off. Catch my breath and pull down again.

"Hey." It's Jennifer, my physical therapist, putting a hand on my shoulder. "I think you went way past twenty there." She's got the most incredible long curly blond hair. Looks like she's just out of high school, but she must be older than that.

"Do I get extra credit?" I'm still panting.

"Sure do," she says, "As long as you give me that much between the parallel bars too."

"That would be cruel and unusual." I stare glumly at the walker she's pushing into place in front of me. I hate that old-lady contraption. It really does feel like I show up here three times a week to get persecuted. I give a big sigh.

"Can't I just use the crutches?"

"Yeah, well, show me your stuff with the parallel bars first. Then maybe we'll try them again."

Okay. I lock the knee braces so my legs are straight, grab the front of the walker, heave myself up. I'm standing—still feels weird to be at this height. Throw the walker ahead, swing my legs forward. That's where the arm strength comes in. I must really be getting stronger, that part's easier. Do that a few more times, till I get to the parallel bars, then grab onto them. They stretch ahead of me, far too long. Jennifer whisks the walker away, my lovely assistant readying for the magic trick. Except there's no magic here, this is all grunt work.

"Okay, give it to me," she orders. "One down and one back." I start down the bars. Here's the funny thing: I do seem to have a teeny bit more movement in my hips and upper legs than I remember. It gives me more control in swinging my legs. Jennifer said I should consider trying to train myself for walking mode with the crutches, one foot in front of the other. I told her just getting myself on my feet was enough change for now. Still, swinging my way down the bars, I wonder. Could I have moved like this all along, and I just didn't get strong enough to do it? Did I get so used to not moving that I forgot how it felt? Or is it something new? I remember the visit from my cyborg friend, his electric touch. Maybe I'm benefiting from some medical knowledge dating centuries in the future. Another thing I won't mention to Jennifer, or anyone else.

Made it to the end. I stand there, winded and sweating through my T-shirt.

"Great," Jennifer says. "Now try coming back, moving just one arm at a time."

"I hate you," I breathe. I lean on one bar and turn myself

around. At this moment I do hate Jennifer, with her confident body, muscular legs and thick, flowing yellow hair. And I hate Sheryl and Kimberly. Was Sheryl more deliberate in what she did to me? No, they both knew what they were doing. I let the anger ripple through me, it helps me swing myself along, heart beating hard, juice flowing in my burning muscles. Then there's Nick. That asshole. Takes my mother to the Atlantic City show without me—okay, there's no way I could have gone with the casts on. But she comes back even more under his spell. Talking about merging their inventory. What the hell can she be thinking? Don't want to think about that.

Jennifer gives me a thumbs-up from the sidelines. I don't really hate her. She showed me how to massage my legs so they won't tighten up again, wants me to do it at home. Sometimes she throws in a quick back rub, exquisitely painful. But I do hate physical therapy.

I've made it back to the other end. Zu's here, standing just inside the door. Holding my reward, a decaf double latte, and a cappuccino for her. Leaning against the cinderblock wall, looking tall and relaxed, none of her usual awkwardness. Compared to her I feel like a sweaty, breath-sucking lump of flesh.

"Hey, Mind." Zu sets the latte on a magazine table and comes over. "Looking good!" No, I'm not.

"Yeah, wow," Jennifer says. "You're really hot today, Mindy."

"Huh." I gulp in air.

"So, you want to try the crutches?" Jennifer holds them up: brushed black metal with the forearm cuffs. A lot better-looking than the wooden ones I used in high school, which are stuffed in the back of my closet. This kind reduces the stress on your arms and shoulders, they say.

"How about you take them back across to your chair," she suggests. I nod. The wheels look pretty far away. She places the crutches in front of me, holds them as I slip my arms through the cuffs. I feel her attention on me, and Zu's, like a floodlight. Me staying upright and walking, even on the crutches, is so new. The feeling is like a small, fragile thing I have to shield from anyone else, keep secret and safe until I've started to understand it. But they're crowding me—I feel their bodies, one near each of my elbows. They need to be there in case I stumble, but they feel way too close. They're pressing on the force field radiating out from my hot, anxious self. When Jennifer touches my elbow, I blow.

"Get off me!" I push out in both directions. "I need some room here!" But Jennifer grabs my arm, steadying me.

"Damn it, Mindy!" It's Zu. She must have jumped back, and the cappuccino in her hand went flying. Now it's on the floor, an empty cup in a puddle widening on the linoleum. She stalks off, muttering about paper towels.

"Okay." Jennifer's voice low and deliberate. "Let's just get over to the chair." I push forward. She's still there, but hovering at a point just beyond the force field. Better. Place the crutches. Swing forward, land my feet. It's all slightly off from the old crutches. Bring one forward, then the other. Swing the feet again. Taking no chances. There's that scary moment with each step where it feels like I'm standing. Upright, by myself. Place the crutches, swing forward again. There's my familiar chair. Grabbing its arms, I let her help me now, snapping off the crutches; then I unlock the braces and sit down heavily.

"That's great," says Jennifer, cool and careful.

"Yeah, it's a breeze." My whole body pulsing with the effort I've just put out, and the concentration. It's hard to imagine doing this all the time.

"Maybe I'm too old for this," I say, looking away from Jennifer. Zu's standing over by the parallel bars, holding a wad of brown-stained paper towels, looking deeply exasperated.

"No way, Mindy." Jennifer kneels in front of me so I can't avoid her. "It's true, more people your age, with spina bifida I mean, are moving from crutches to a chair, probably. But you're strong. I know you can do this. Look how good you're doing already." She must have gotten an A in Pep-Talking Your Patients. She lets me go after I promise to come back in two days, promise to do the exercises at home. I wheel out, crutches stowed in back of the chair, past a couple of guys ambling along on the treadmills, through the waiting area. Zu walks beside me, still carrying my latte. She won't push me now, which is just fine.

"Okay," she says once we hit the lobby. "You've definitely hit Code Red in bitchiness."

Right, I asked her to let me know. I give the wheels a few turns down the straightaway, stop at the exit doors.

"Sorry. I thought I'd get some slack for going through PT hell."

"It's like you want everybody else to suffer along with you," she says, moving through the automatic doors with me. The cooler outside air hits my face like water after the stale inside air. I stop to breathe it in, then roll on more slowly. It's that brisk, quick-turning weather of fall that could turn right back into August-type heat. Across the way, on a traffic island in the parking lot, the trees are swaying. The leaves on their top branches rustle in the wind, some turning over to show their pale undersides. Bright blue sky. I just want to take in this air. It's like my body needs more of it, with all this exercise. I follow Zu to her car.

"I owe you a cappuccino at least," I say, staring at the door handle.

"Yeah, you do," she says, opening my door. I hear in her voice that she's not flaming mad anymore, even if I'm not close to being forgiven. I take one last deep breath, some parking-lot exhaust mixing with the fresh stuff, before getting into the car. Zu hands me my latte, then takes care of the wheelchair. We pull out of the parking lot in silence. She doesn't speak till we've eased onto the road: "You want me to take you on Friday, then?"

"That's okay. I can get my mom to do it." I think I can. My mother's been even more unpredictable than usual. Sometimes she's fawning all over me, making me special foods like her grandma's potato gnocchi even though it's usually a no-no on my diet, and other times she's off in her own world, going on about her new life with Nick, which she seems to assume will include Irv still coming around to help. She never asks what I want—even if I'm not sure myself. I need some space to figure it out.

"Are you sure? Cuz I'm free then."

"It's okay, really." I've got to give Zu a break from my bitchy side. Can't afford for her to be mad at me. I pull the lid from the latte, take a careful sip.

"Cool, I can sleep late," she says. I look at her. Why didn't I notice before? She's been coming over at odd hours, blowing off our semi-regular Sunday video nights with lame excuses about music practice. Between work and her new social life, I guess she must be pretty wiped out.

"So, did Trish call you?" she asks.

"Trish?"

"About the costume contest."

"Oh! Yeah, she did. Did you put her up to it?" Zu knows I've never been big on displaying myself on a stage.

"No way," she says, a little too firmly. "She's the one that organizes it for the Lrak." She turns onto a connecting road.

Just about every club enters a skit or a tableau in the Con's big costume contest. It's gotten pretty elaborate in recent years, more like a talent show really. Of course, anyone can compete as an individual, but that's a much bigger undertaking, putting a greater burden on the fabulousness of the costume. When I was Commander of the CAS I went along with it only if I could wear my usual Commander's outfit. Never really enjoyed it. But the Santak get so dressed up for the Con anyway, with the makeup and the nose spikes, and sometimes wigs.

"So?" Zu asks.

"I told her I'd do it." She turns to look at me—she was all revved up to try and talk me into it. "I've already got the nose bones," I say. "And Trish promised to help me with the costume."

"That's great, Mind!"

"Yeah, I guess this is it," I say. "This is my club now. Might as well go all in."

Zu nods. She knows what a big deal this is for me, committing to another club. When they came to see me in the hospital, that counted. They're stand-up. I still have major qualms about other parts of the Santak culture, but I've told myself I can work on that from within.

"What about you?" I ask Zu. "You're gonna be in the show too, right?" Her head shrinks back against the headrest.

"I'm doing the music for it," she says. We're stopped at the light that lets us onto the main road back to my house.

"That's the saddest excuse ever. If I'm getting up there, you're going with me."

"No, Mind," she protests, pulling out onto the Pike. "There isn't any part for me."

"I'm sure that can be arranged." She lets out a hard sigh.

"In fact," I go on, energized by her discomfort, "I'll check with Trish on it, ASAP."

"You don't have to, I'll talk to her," she says, speeding up to make the next light.

"All right! You know it'll be awesome." Now I'm seeing both of us, in our extravagant Santak outfits, up on the stage. There I am, standing up. Standing next to tall, sexy Zuzana, supported by my sleek black crutches. That's the point of all this agony, isn't it? To be able to stand up with everybody else. But am I ready to go public like that? Let everybody see what I'm just taking little baby steps toward, still working on figuring out myself? Zu will have Bradley there with her—I'll be flying solo.

"Maybe you and Bradley can have matching accessories," I say.

"What?"

"At the contest. You know, because you're . . ." We still haven't talked about them being a couple.

"Me and Bradley?"

"Going together," I mumble.

"What?" she says again.

"Is it a secret?"

"Mindy, we're not—where'd you get that idea?"

"You're always playing music with him . . ." That sounds stupid, but I'm seeing them playing in my hospital room again, Zu on her theremin, Bradley on his keyboard, feeling the whip-crack of connection between them. The zinging clarity of it.

"He's my music buddy!" She gives a harsh laugh. "He's going out with one of the paralegals at work!" She pauses. "Okay. It's Trish. I'm seeing Trish."

My insides do a slow somersault, then get stuck.

"Trish?"

"Yes. She's a girl, I know." Her voice is weary. "I should have told you."

Should have told me!

"I just . . ." I give up trying to talk, still replaying Zu's theremin concert in my head. I know what I saw, what I felt. Could I be wrong? Maybe the bolt of emotion I felt was real, but I got the poles of connection mixed up? I'm reeling, still trying to unspool the relationship I've been assuming since then.

"I'm sorry, Mind." We've stopped at a red light. There's Spudz, on the other side of the street. "I was going to tell you."

"I just can't believe . . ." Trying to take in this new information—of course I know women can be gay—but Zu! My best friend—what does this mean? My skin prickles. "When? When were you going to tell me?"

"As soon as I was sure. But it happened pretty fast. And you were in the hospital, and then you were recovering from surgery . . ." So it was right around then. What I felt was real—I just jumped to the wrong conclusion. But that doesn't matter now. I feel betrayed, can't think straight. I can't even begin to unravel what this means for Zu and me, for our friendship. I shake my head, trying to clear it.

"I mean, when were you going to tell me you're gay?"

"It's not that easy, Mindy."

"Right, I get it. It's easier not to tell me."

Zu flings her head back, looks away, then back to the road. "Okay. I was with a girl in high school. Then a boy when I was at Holy Family. That was so weird that I got disgusted with the whole thing, sex, relationships, whatever, and decided to be a monk. Just work on my music and do SkyLog for fun. So I never really decided I was one way or the other."

"Did you tell anybody else?" I ask, afraid to hear the answer.

"No. Not my parents, nobody."

I sit quiet for a bit. We're stuck at the left turn as cars whiz by, then finally we turn into the quieter street that leads to my neighborhood. I can totally see Zu not telling her parents anything. She's already like a mutant in her family, the only one that's into music, the only one to go to college, even if she didn't finish. Idiots. When will the creatures of the twentieth century learn to just get along, like they do in the Transortium, where beings of all places of origin, skin types, protrusions and presumably sexual orientations have learned to coexist peacefully? Then something else hits me.

"So, is that why you were writing slash?" I ask her.

"Jeez, Mindy—I don't know, maybe!" It's making sense to me now, sort of—her skill with writing about intimate trysts between Roi and the Captain, or between the Captain and Mac, the navigator. I just thought Zu had a great imagination.

"But then why . . ."

"—didn't I do girl-on-girl slash?" She gives a loud sigh. "I don't know. Maybe because the girl characters on SkyLog just aren't as interesting. Maybe it was just more fun."

"Huh." I can't think of anything to say. Too much to deal with. I feel untethered, turned upside down—everything looks strange. Zu's changing, moving away from me. I'm caught in some bizarre relativity experiment: me moving forward with her in the car but actually stationary, stuck in one place, while Zu travels out, away from our familiar lives, a galaxy rushing out with the expanding universe, wheeling away as it dopplers out from the center. My life is changing too, I remind myself—but that slams me cruelly back to the me lumbering along on metal crutches, thudding across the physical therapy room in a bad parody of forward movement. Tears press into my eyes. We're on my street. Home is the last place I want to be.

16

FROM: tadmesh@deepnet.com
TO: MindRoid@comet.net
SUBJECT: NEW INSTALLMENT, SHADOW OF
              THE MESH
DATE: 9/28/99 5:05 PM

"Its time for you to keep your promise," Pak said to Anki after they got back to the camp. She said nothing but took him by the arm and walked him to the edge of the clearing. But there was nothing there, just a few boxes of supplies, and the smallest of the rebels, a puny male still curled up asleep.

"Is this where the secret technology is hidden?"

"Yes," she said and smiled, then she leaned down and shook the young male by the shoulder.

"But where is the receiver?" Pak asked.

"Here," she said. "Ozi is a Hearer."

"Yes but how does he hear them?" Anki looked at him like he was stupid.

"Ozi has the Hearing from his fathers and mothers, from eight times eight generations back." So it was a very old technology.

"Now be quiet so the Hearing can begin." Ozi sat up looking half asleep, his eyes were pale yellow. They sat for several minutes in silence. Pak felt the others creeping up beside him. Finally Ozi spoke in a strange high voice.

"The Mesh is one." This made Pak shiver. "The Mesh speaks with many voices, but has just one mind." How did he know this?

"Where is the Mesh coming from?" Pak asked.

"The Mesh comes from far away, so far, it cannot be measured." Great, no coordinates.

"But where is the Mesh now? How many are there," he asked.

"The Mesh approaches with the speed of the sun's rays. I hear many voices. The Mesh is one."

"Can you at least say how many vessels it is traveling on?"

"Only one vessel." That was good, if this guy was right. A fleet of ships would mean they might as well give up now. He pictured the Mesh ship, far bigger than the Encounter. With its fat body and strange spider-like arms and dark non-reflective surface so that it seemed to disappear in the surrounding space.

"What else can you hear?" Pak asked.

"You Will Be Mesh, it says. We will be One."

"No!" Pak shouted. He was making them sound friendly or something, which the Mesh definitely was not. He pictured the dead eyes of the Meshers, the hairless bodies and flashing lines of electricity running down there arms, and the super strength that could crush you like a bug. He shuddered to imagine how it would feel to be Enmeshed. Would he automatically see everything from the Mesh point of view? Would any of him survive?

"We will be One, just like with Ooshan." What was he talking about now? Anki whispered, "Ooshan is the Sky Dragon. We have been waiting for Ooshan to return for many many years." Just then Ozi leaned forward quickly and put his hands on Pak's head, covering his ears. Pak felt like a tiny shock going through his skull. Then Ozi slumped forward.

"The Hearing is finished," said Anki.

Suddenly everything went dark, and Pak found himself walking inside a huge chamber glowing with a soft gray light. There were other beings around him, there skin all light gray, lying propped up in long rows, not moving, there eyes staring straight ahead. Each one was connected by the tube that exited from the top of the skull to a kind of port just above the head. Up above, pipes sparked and flashed with lines of energy, the only bright light in the room. Pak heard a whooshing sound all around him, mixed with breathing. There was also a soft buzzing that sounded like voices, but he couldn't make out any words, it all mushed into one big sound that seemed to envelope him and everyone else. He wanted to shut it out but he couldn't.

Then he was in the camp again sitting with Anki and Ozi. They both stared at him.

"What just happened?"

"You have the Hearing," Ozi said. "I knew when I saw you."

"But—where was I?"

"You were with Ooshan."

"No." Why was Ozi talking about that fairy tale dragon? Pak realized that he already knew where he was, in this flash he had seen and experienced the Mesh ship that was even now approaching this planet.

"Ooshan and Mesh is the same," Ozi said. "Ooshan comes here in the form of Mesh." Ozi looked into Pak's eyes again, trying to make sure he understood. "Ooshan sweeps away all of the bad things, the bad people. We waited many centuries for the sky dragon."

"No! You're all wrong!" Pak shouted. "I don't know about your dragon, but I know the Mesh. They sweep away everything, not just the bad people. You will be dead or you'll be Mesh yourself."

"Yes," answered Ozi. His yellow eyes glowed. "We will be one with the Mesh."

Anki stood up. "You must come with us now. All the Hearers are needed to welcome the dragon."

Pak felt sick and afraid. Yet even though his heart banged in fear, he had to know more. And he could only learn more by following this raggedy group of rebels and their Hearer. If they are right, Pak thought, this would be a good time for me to sing my Santak death chant.

I pull back from the screen, squeeze my eyes shut and press a hand to my forehead. It's getting harder for me to sit at the computer for hours on end. Maybe I need glasses? But no, it's a kind of restlessness. I should go and get something to eat. What the hell is a twelve-year-old doing thinking about stuff like this? Or thirteen, whatever he is now. I've been nudging him to get to the Mesh in his story, and now I'm not sure I want him to. His writing seems to be getting better, though.

The screensaver comes on, the new one I downloaded from SETI. A field of tiny blocks, a multicolored digital landscape, blips up and down, while my hard drive analyzes one millionth of the night sky for anomalous radio signals. One chance in a billion, my computer will have the big Contact moment, catch the first signs of intelligent life, find the first of the other worlds waiting out there to be found.

Zu told me about the SETI software and sent me the link. She's always a step or two ahead of me. But how am I supposed to follow her now? It was bad enough to feel left out when I thought she had a boyfriend. Getting my mind around her being gay—I'm working on it. Of course she's the same person, even with this new thing about her. It's just that I've been thinking back, remembering us sitting next to each other on the couch watching videos, huddled together in front of my computer, etc. Am I gay too? Is that what drew us together, and I just didn't get it? I've admired Zu's slim body curving into the glow of the monitor, I've even pictured her in a gauzy Ren-faire dress that would match her wispy reddish-brown hair, knowing she'd never ever dress up like that. Then I'm thinking, was she into me that way? And if she was, would it matter? Maybe I should just feel pleased. And pleased for her finding somebody, of course. But it still feels like I'm losing her. I can't deal with this, and we haven't talked about any of this since she told me.

Looking around, my room seems very small—too much stuff in here, hemming me in. There's hardly room to maneuver with the crutches, so I've been leaving them by the door. With my braces on I can pull myself along, swinging from one piece of furniture to another, the dresser to the desk or whatever. Right now I'm parked in the wheelchair at my desk. My room is just too damn crowded, too small. I need to get out of here. I whirl the wheelchair around—my mother is standing in the doorway.

"Shit, Ma!" She's peering over me at the wall behind the desk. She tiptoes in like a hunter tracking hidden prey. The wall holds my rogue's gallery of SkyLog actors, smiling or grimacing depending on the character. The photos all crowded together, edges curling up on their autographed signatures. I should have taken better care of them. But I wanted them out here where I could see them.

"Just checking—" she says. "Do you have all the head shots from the first series?"

"All the ones that matter." From all the cast members who ever came to a SkyLog convention I attended, anyway. "Why?" She's inched over to the desk, forcing me to retreat behind the foot of the bed.

"Well, they'd be more valuable as a group, wouldn't they?" She pats her neck thoughtfully, examining a very young headshot of Colin Scully as the first Captain.

"Of course they would, if I was going to sell them."

"You should really frame them." I know that too. She drums her fingers lightly on the few inches of free desk surface, then turns to my bookshelf, clogged with books, magazines, loose papers. One shelf holds SkyLog novelizations and reference books, on another there's a choice selection of my sci-fi favorites—Philip K. Dick, Ursula Le Guin, Larry Niven—and on the bottom, old issues of *Asimov's* and *Amazing Stories* and a bunch of fanzines.

"Are any of those books autographed?" she says.

"What the hell, Ma!"

"I'm trying to do an inventory of our good stuff. For Nick." She pulls a book out of the shelf and thumbs to the front. I feel cold creep up the skin on my arms.

"Our stuff? This is *my* stuff." My words come out slow and somehow muffled.

"What do you mean, Mindy? You've got some real collectibles in here."

"I know. This is my stuff, Ma," I say, still on low speed. Every-thing's flipped. I was just feeling suffocated by all the stuff in here, and now I'm protecting it. My mother's drumming her chest, fingers tapping her purple I Heart New York sweatshirt, looking over the posters. Something occurs to me.

"Did you take my 20th Anniversary SkyLog compendium?" I still haven't been able to find it.

"No! What are you talking about, Mindy?"

Now I wish I hadn't mentioned the compendium—she'll assume it's valuable. Maybe she'll go looking for it behind the furniture when I'm not here.

"Well, it's not for sale," I say. "None of it, the books or anything else. My stuff is not for sale." She looks straight at me, finally.

"Mindy, it's very important for us to put our best foot forward now," she says. "I want Nick to see I'm a real dealer. Surely you can spare a few things." The chill digs into my arms, scrapes my cheeks. She's never asked me to sell anything of mine, defined by being in my room.

"I'm not talking to you about this."

"What I mean is," she tries again. "We need to work together. This is like a brand-new start for us."

"Us! You're only thinking about yourself!"

"How can you say that, Mindy!" Her face reddens. "I'm always here for you!"

"Oh. Really?" My chest constricts, I push the words out. "Then why do you always crap out when I'm in the hospital?" Now I've done it—brought up the thing we never mention. Her face crumples.

"What are you talking about?"

"You know. Every time I go in for something. When I wake up, you're gone. Irv always makes excuses for you. Where did you go this time, to stay with Nick?"

"You don't even remember all the times!" She's yelling now. "All the operations when you were little—closing up your back, cleaning up the scar tissue. I was there next to you, as soon as they let me in, your father couldn't get me to go home." She lets out a breath and sits down heavily on the bed. "I prayed," she goes on. "I prayed so hard for you. I prayed to God to make you get better." This is a shock—I've never heard my mother talk about God. She glances around and pats her pockets, searching for a cigarette.

"I guess I used up all my prayers. And then it didn't get easier, it got harder."

"How about for me?" Now I'm yelling. "You have no idea what I'm going through!"

"I've taken care of you the best I can." Quiet now, her eyes pleading. Maybe that's the problem—I've been letting my mother take care of me. It's hard to imagine things being any different.

"Okay, Ma. Can you just leave now?" There's so much I have to figure out. She stands up, drawing herself straight.

"I'm going up there tomorrow," she says, dropping the words like coins between us. "To Secaucus, with Nick. We're looking for an apartment."

"C'mon, Ma. Get serious!"

"It'll be your new home too."

No. This is too much. "I can't believe this. Just get out of my room. Please!" I reflexively push at the wheels, but there's nowhere for me to go. I twist around, looking away from her.

"That's why I thought you could put some of your stuff into the inventory. It would be a nice gesture."

"I said no! And you can't just leave the house."

"Why not? We'll sell it. Or your father can buy back my half and move in if he wants." Her scheme is crazy—we both know Irv couldn't afford that—but at the moment I can't come up with anything in its place. The idea of me tagging along to her love nest in New Jersey makes me dizzy.

"Did you tell Irv about this, this plan of yours?"

"I was going to," she says. "As soon as we find the apartment."

"Why not just move in with him?"

"His apartment's too small." For him to move in with us would be massively worse, so I don't bring that up.

"Sweetie—" she reaches toward me.

"Don't! Just don't. This is insane."

"This is what you do when you love someone!" Her words hit me like a slap.

"Do what you want." I'm furious, my voice comes out too loud. Still can't move the wheelchair. I grab at the base of the bed with one hand, the edge of my desk with the other, and pull myself up to a precarious standing position. This is so weird—I'm looking down at her.

"Please," I say, separating each word, "get out of my room, now."

She backs into the doorway.

"I know you'll get to like him," she tries.

"I can't talk to you!" I yell, holding onto the desk now with both hands. "You think this is all actually gonna happen, you think I'm gonna just leave here, just leave my life, and go up there with you! You're crazy!" She starts backward, and her mouth goes small.

"And look at you!" she spits. "Living in your dream world." She stalks away. I stand there shaking, trying not to lose my balance.

L EN'S DRIVING with the window all the way
down. The wind has whipped up his hair,
stiffening it into little black sails going off at odd
angles. His face is a silhouette against the trees zipping past us,
their leaves a blur of green, yellow and orange.

My window's up, but the air hits me from his side. Len drives a
lot faster than my mother or Zu. Now, zooming along with heavy
metal blasting from the radio, I feel like I've been sprung out. This
is my first sort-of social occasion since the surgery, other than the
Lrak meeting last week. We're on our way to Roxie's house in New
Jersey. Len's helping her with the new piece she's started, and she's
been trying to get me to come out and see it. I won't be much help,
but that's okay.

His van's different from ours. The engine's loud, the hood
looks like it's vibrating. And there's a lot of stuff in the back. Technological detritus—phones, circuit boards, a clunky beige computer monitor dark with grime, loops of orange cable. And tools: a
circular saw, a plastic bucket filled with nails, bolts and such, and
a serious-looking black toolbox. Maybe he needs all the ballast to
keep from lifting off.

"I told you, I cleaned it up," he says, his voice loud over the van
noise and Korn's screaming guitars.

"Yeah, thanks."

"You couldn't have sat there if I didn't."

"So, I'm guessing your work van doesn't look like this."

He barks out a laugh. "That'd get me fired."

"I guess there's other cable companies."

"For now. Cable's on the way out."

"You're kidding, right?"

"Oh yeah. Fiber optics is the next big thing." This leads to another one of his Bucky rants. Bucky foresaw the magic of fiber optics, of course. There's even a molecule named after him—Fullerene, or the Buckyball or Buckytube depending on its shape—that Len claims would make great fiber optic switches. But I'm still thinking about the possibility of him losing his job.

"So when cable goes away, you'd what? Fix people's fiber optic switches?"

"I don't know, we'll see what happens."

"But fixing cables—or whatever you do," I stumble, "you couldn't do that for somebody else?"

"Fixing something anyway. I was always good at fixing things, any kind of wiring. I built a whole radio when I was like twelve. But it's only a matter of time before the robots start fixing everything too." He laughs silently. Apparently thinking about being made obsolete makes him laugh.

"What would you do then? Seriously."

"I don't know. Maybe fix stuff for people at a flea market. Toasters. Blenders. Computers."

"You could get a table next to ours." He finds that funny too. He's so cool about this, but to me it's not funny at all. I'm thinking about Irv and how his whole department disappeared when computers got smaller and more powerful. Maybe it's just what's going on at home that's making me feel so shaky. Janine and I are hardly talking. She's made a few more trips to see Nick, says they're still looking for an apartment. I really doubt that she could pull off such a big move by herself. And even if she did, it's hard to picture her getting through a week without Irv helping out—repairing appliances, sorting things out, sending checks. I went along with her to a show last Saturday, trying to be helpful at least. Even that felt off. Without my chair, I couldn't help her move things back and forth from the van, and I had to be extra careful moving through the aisles on the crutches. Bottom line, I'm having a hard time keeping my balance.

"You're not gonna believe what she's doing," Len says. He must have moved on to talking about Roxie.

"Try me." Past his head, a stand of trees with a thin cover of leaves winks by. He's wearing his old brown leather jacket.

"She's got these things that look like X-rays, but they're not," he says. "They're just photocopied onto Mylar—words, constellations, that kind of thing."

"Mylar." I'm trying to remember what that is.

"You know, the clear plastic sheets. I got a bunch of them for her." He taps his open palms on the steering wheel. "I never was really into art before," he adds. "Never knew it could be this interesting." He's practically bouncing in his seat. I haven't seen him like this before—talkative, almost kidlike. Being with him right now feels like a warm beam on my skin after all the stress with my mother. I already told her I won't live under a roof with Nick. Could I live on my own? Run my own household, get places? A number of scenarios have been swirling in my head: Moving into Irv's cramped apartment. Irv moving into the house with me. Getting a little apartment of my own, maybe near Zu. That one gives me butterflies—having my own place is a fantasy I've entertained for some time in the future. Something I let myself think about when Ma's driving me insane. But I'm not sure I'm ready for the reality. I know I have to talk to Irv about all this. But when he called yesterday, the words wouldn't come out of my mouth. The Janine and Nick part, I just couldn't say it.

"Roxie says everyone's an artist," Len announces.

"Yeah, I heard that." I look at him, still bouncy and light, like he's connected by an invisible thread to the ceiling of the van, his hair pointing in various directions. I imagine how it would look if he combed his hair back. Or grew it longer.

"So what do you think?" he asks. "About what Roxie said," he adds when I don't answer. I think it's just one of her things, part of the Roxie package, but I don't want to say that.

"Maybe . . . Maybe everybody's an artist, but, um, we're not all created equal. Some people are more artist than others. I don't understand half of what she says anyway."

He laughs. "Me neither! She keeps trying to explain to me about subliming, how it's so important to the new piece. It's something that can happen to ice in space—it can evaporate without ever turning to water. Like it skips a step."

"Cool."

"Yeah. But how it relates to her piece, I don't get it. I'm trying though."

We go quiet for a while, letting the chugging and wailing of the music blast over us. This is Anthrax, I think. Zu told me she's been trying to turn Len on to noise rock, like Sonic Youth. I can see really far across the fields here, with a line of woods behind them. The sky's a crystal-sharp blue, like the inside of a geode, just a few puffy clouds high up.

"This is a lot like where I grew up," Len says. "Down in Delaware. Me and my dad used to spend time in the woods. Hunting." Somehow that makes sense, Len carrying a rifle in the woods. We pass a little white house sitting way back from the road, a pickup parked in the yard. This countryish part feels familiar to me, too. When I was a little kid, Irv drove me along roads like this, for hours it seemed, going nowhere in particular. We'd fall into long, comfortable silences, kind of like this, with me looking out my window. We counted cows, or I'd jabber away, making up stories featuring my dolls and the SkyLog action figures Daddy bought me. He would listen, sometimes ask a question. Now that I think of it, he was probably taking me out to give Ma some time off. I must have been tough to handle then.

I look over at Len again. In the right clothes, with his hair and mustache a little longer, Len really could pass for Genghis Khan, or one of his lieutenants. His eyes even have a little slant to them.

"What?" He glances over at me with a crooked smile.

"I was just trying to imagine you in full Santak uniform." It's pretty close to the picture in my head.

"Yeah, well." He's looking straight ahead. "I only take out the gear for serious stuff. Everybody in the club knows that."

"So the costume contest is pretty serious, then?"

"Where'd you hear I was doing the contest?" He glances in his side mirror, slides around another car.

"Trish said."

"Okay, the contest is a Lrak tradition. It's upholding the honor of the ship. So yeah, that's serious." He takes the exit, and we swing into a long, wide turn. At the straightaway we hit a strip of gas stations, mini-marts and liquor stores. He speaks up again: "What about you? I never saw you in Santak gear."

"I just defected from the Transortium, remember?"

"That's no excuse."

"Well, I am doing the costume contest, it so happens. Trish said she'll help me get ready."

"About time you got a uniform."

"The thing is," I start, looking out at another treeless field.

"What."

"It's just . . ." This is hard to talk about; it came to me after I had already told Trish and Zu that I'd do it. "I keep thinking about the Santak and their attitudes toward anyone who isn't, you know, in top fighting condition. Look at how they dumped on Pak just because he was small."

"That wasn't it," he counters. "They disrespected him because he was klutzy, and a lousy fighter."

"It just seems to me, a Santak with a disability is, like, a contradiction in terms." I said it. If I'm going to get up in front of people in the likeness of a Santak, I have to deal with this. The braces can be hidden under my clothes, but the crutches are right out there. And it seems clear to me that Santak are not big on physical handicaps. I guess this wasn't an issue when I was wearing my Fleet uniform. The Transortium's committed to diversity of all kinds. It's like their brand.

"Untrue! That's bullshit, Santak do not discriminate!" His face is getting red. "It's how you perform your duty that matters. Duty and Honor. What about Larm?" That's the captain of a Santak Raptor on the show. "He's got a major limp, and he's captain of his own Raptor."

"But if someone couldn't get around on their own, couldn't walk—"

"Bullcrap, Mindy. Besides, you get around just fine. I'm telling you, it's how you hold up in the pinch, on a Butak'La team or in any standoff that matters. Everything else is irrelevant. And anyway," he adds, "I bet you could kick ass in the Butak'La." Does he mean in real life? If so, that's ridiculous. There's a regional Butak'La competition for Santak clubs every June. People show off their blade work, throw heavy objects and do some hand-to-hand combat. But I don't say anything, partly because I've got a lump in my throat. He's ambushed me—behind the usual Len-like belligerence, he's sticking up for me.

I turn my head away. Out the window, a stand of woods rises between two farms, then disappears. That feeling comes to me again, like when I was in the car with Zu: the sense of going two different speeds at the same time. But this time I feel like the two of us, Len and me, are in sync. We're moving forward yet sitting still together. High white clouds are hanging out, miles above us probably. They look like they're standing still, or somehow keeping up with us at the exact same speed. But really they're going at their own pace. How fast are they moving, what's their perception of speed, of the tiny cars below? I'm wobbling on the edge of understanding something.

We've gone over the bridge into New Jersey, the shopping centers and diners crowding in on the fields. Then gas stations and convenience stores filling in. We reach Roxie's neighborhood, with its rows of one-story houses on neat lawns, and a single tree parked in front of each house. As Len noses along the curving roads, I start mentally rehearsing getting out of the van. I haven't done it with the crutches that many times, and never from this vehicle. Here we are. Roxie's melon-colored house, looking psychedelic against the royal blue sky. I open the door, scooch myself around, slide the crutches out from beside the seat. Lock the legs straight, plant the tips on the asphalt. Slide down. Yes. Len stands a few paces ahead, half-watching me. We head up the path.

Roxie pulls the door open. She's rocking skinny jeans and an orange cable-knit sweater. I'm looking down on her for the first time. She's hardly taller than Janine.

"I've been waiting for you," she says, grabbing Len by the wrist and pulling him in. I stay by the door while she drags him over to the far end of the room. She's never seen me on the crutches, isn't that worth a little comment? I'm also eyeing things, trying to figure out the best way to negotiate my way in—the front room has turned into an obstacle course since I was here. I start to pick out what must be Roxie's work in progress, the one she's been telling me about. Her older paintings are stacked to one side, a clash of bright colors. The room is crisscrossed over our heads with clear nylon string, like tiny clotheslines. Hanging from them by clothespins, what look at first like X-rays, but they're not. Instead of bones, it's like stars winking and shining, white on the dark sheets: pinwheel galaxies, nebulas, star clusters. This must be the Mylar stuff Len was trying to explain to me. Tacked on the wall are some of the original space photos she must have copied—black and white glossies and magazine cutouts—with more in piles nearby.

Roxie's high-volume laugh pulls me around. "Everything's geodesic to you!" she says, batting Len on the shoulder. He's balancing a big sheet of translucent Plexiglas, the color of skim milk, against his chest.

"No, really," he says. "This curve here makes a classic geodesic line," he says. "You know, like he said in his book on Spaceship Earth." Behind the foggy sheet I can just follow the outline of Len's body, a darker mass in the milkiness, the coastline of some hidden continent.

"He's a real Bucky-head, you know," she says to me.

"Yeah, I got that."

"Wait!" She trots toward me with her little shuffling steps. "You can't look at it till I turn on the lights!" Like she just realized I was here. Then, to Len: "Bring that over here." He hoists the sheet over, and with Roxie directing, holds it upright in front of several bare-bulb clamp lights on the floor. She directs me to move a little to the right, then clicks on the lights one by one. The sheet glows softly, like haze with sun behind it. And the X-rays come alive, the stars bright, almost pulsing. Roxie steps back beside me, pinching at her chin.

"I don't know." She frowns. "They were clearer the other way."

"You have to play with the distance," Len says.

"This room isn't big enough," she says. I spot more stuff up near the ceiling, from Roxie's Senior Center show: the comet-trailed Barbie, a toy spaceship, a plastic astronaut, and two dinosaurs, spray-painted gold, hanging in a line from another nylon filament. Looking around, it feels like if I could see everything here in the right way, it would say something to me, some important sentence about things. Each thing—each toy, each space photo, each string—would be a word in the sentence.

"So what do you think?" Roxie looks at me like she really wants to know.

"Len said it's about sublime something?" I'm groping.

"Right, subliming! I saw it in one of Morris's science magazines, and I couldn't stop thinking about it," she says. "But it's really hard to show that, where it's about something disappearing. Melting directly into nothing. I figured," she says, peering at the nearest X-ray, "since it happens in space, I'd put the stars in . . . Where's that article?" Her eyes dart around the room. "I want to show Mindy. Morris! I can't find anything in here!"

She wanders around, picking her way over toys and snaking extension cords, and chooses a pile of papers to attack. "There's too much stuff here. Morris!" It's no surprise Roxie managed to lose something in here. But how do I lose stuff in my little room? The SkyLog compendium is a pretty big book, hard to miss. I don't even know when it disappeared. And I'd remember if I lent it to somebody, wouldn't I? When did Sheryl come over? I see her standing there, staring at my bookshelf, not saying anything. Then at the next meeting, I think, she made some semi-sarcastic comment about my vast library. Did she take it? What kind of person does that, takes somebody's books without asking? This is crazy, I'm being paranoid. But she did steal the club from me.

Morris is holding a magazine out to me. His hair even more flyaway than usual—looks like Roxie woke him up from a nap. He's opened the magazine to show the article about subliming in space. I stare at the picture—an artist's imagining of the rocky surface of a comet, with vapor jets swooshing out where, I guess, the subliming thing is happening.

"So that's where the comet trail comes from?"

"Right," Morris says. "Why don't you sit down, it'll be easier to read."

"Well, I still think it relates to Bucky," Len says, "his idea of ephemeralization. Everything, technology and all, tending toward being less physical. That's what I see, anyway," he trails off, a little sheepish. Meanwhile, I've maneuvered myself onto the sofa. Staring at that picture, trying to understand. It makes me feel a little shivery, this space mystery dancing around on top of the disturbing thoughts about my missing book and Sheryl.

"I'm gonna take this back with me," Len says. He hefts the sheet of Plexiglas. "No offense, Morris, but my bandsaw's better than yours." He hauls it outside to the van. Morris joins me on the sofa.

"Who needs a living room, anyway?" he says, sweeping his head around the room. "I'm just a little concerned about when Philip comes up next weekend with his girlfriend."

"He's not coming," Roxie says flatly, taking off for the kitchen.

"Why do you say that?" Morris raises his voice toward the kitchen. "He told us he's coming. With Judith."

"He says he's coming, then he doesn't." Her voice rises over clattering dishes. "It always happens."

"That's ridiculous," Morris shouts. Then, to me, "She just gets nervous."

Roxie hustles back in with two mugs of coffee. I hold mine up to my face, needing to feel the heat. But there isn't any—it's barely warm. She stands there, a hand on her cheek, gazing at her unfinished work. From here, I can see into the dining room where "Green World, Black World" still hangs, with the dinosaurs and robots in their places.

"So, Roxie," I say, wanting to get us away from the subject of Philip. "I don't see any robots in your new piece. Are you turning your back on artificial lifeforms?"

She considers this and laughs. "I don't need robots. I'm the robot now. Or, what do you say, android?"

"I think you mean cyborg. An artificially enhanced human."

"That's it, cyborg. With this heart machine they put in. I can feel it pumping, boom, boom, boom, same speed all day, all night, like that steam hammer that killed John Henry. It's going too fast."

"Roxie," Morris protests. "You just saw Dr. Friedman. He said the pacemaker's working fine."

"What do doctors know?" She pulls down at the edge of her sweater and fiddles with the nearest hanging X-ray. "I'm telling you. This thing's making me go faster. It's very uncomfortable. I wake up at two, three in the morning and it's still going, boom, boom, boom." Maybe she's right, the thing is pushing her like a big windup toy: she hasn't stopped moving since we got here.

Morris sets his mouth and sighs. "I can't talk to her," he says.

"But look at you, Mindy," Roxie says, turning back to examine me like I'm a new element in her piece. "You're walking around now! And not only walking but moving into cyberspace!"

"Yeah, the website's up." That's a good thing. I have a place of my own in the Internet, even if not IRL. I've been adding things, putting in links. Pasted in a few of my favorite stories from old issues. I've even gotten a few emails from the website, one of them from New Zealand. Who knew there were SkyLog fans in New Zealand?

"Look at how great she's doing!" Roxie announces to the room. "I think you should celebrate."

"No way, Roxie. The timing isn't good." It sucks big-time, to be honest.

"You can't wait for the timing. Just go ahead and do it, as they say."

She turns to Len, who's come back from the van. "I told Mindy she should have a party, celebrate all the good things she's doing."

"Sure, sounds good," he says, smiling his toothy smile. But he doesn't look at me, or he'd see the alarm on my face. I feel a strong urge to spill everything to Roxie, tell her all about Janine and Nick and her crazy moving plan, and how hard it is feeling so unsettled while I'm just learning to get around this new way, and how nervous I am about coming out as a Santak at the Con. I want to have her sit next to me and take my hand like a grandma, want to lean on her shoulder. But it's hard with Morris here, as nice and gentlemanly as he is, not to mention Len. And Roxie isn't sitting down anytime soon. Now she's twiddling the end of a nylon string to tighten it. Len lifts another sheet of Plexiglas.

"You want some coffee?" Morris asks him.

"In a minute." Len heads out the door again.

"So how about it then?" Roxie pushes.

"I can't have a party now. There's stuff going on at home. It's complicated."

"Have it here," she says. "I'll help you. We had some great parties in the old days, didn't we, babe?" But Morris has gone into the kitchen. She turns to examine me again.

"Such a nice-looking girl. You know, you don't give yourself credit," she says. "You should at least get some new clothes for your new you." I've got my usual sweatshirt on—my navy and white Penn State, Irv's alma mater—and it is getting pretty old. Since I went back to the braces, I've been wearing these snap-away track pants.

"Maybe I should get something for the Con. The SkyLog convention, it's next weekend."

"There you go. We'll go to the mall, you'll get some new things for your convention."

"Okay, sure." The idea of going shopping with Roxie is actually cheering. Maybe we could talk then.

"Morrie will take us. I'm very good at putting outfits together."

"I know," I say, remembering the silver lamé top and little white leather boots she wore to the Senior Center opening. Maybe I *could* manage a little celebration of my own. My birthday's coming up next month, I haven't even thought about that. But I won't tell anybody about this half-formed idea, especially Roxie, she'd be out buying party decorations. I glance back up at the little Barbie, proudly naked, flying forward into the void like Supergirl, her pipe-cleaner comet trail subliming behind her.

THE MAGIC-DOOR ENTRANCE of the mall slides open to let me through. Ahead are scattered shoppers—geezers, moms with little kids in strollers. The teenagers will descend later. I move around the low fountain, with some aluminum thingy spraying water out in spirals like our backyard sprinkler, then concentrate on scanning the shiny floor ahead of me as I get into my forward rhythm. I wanted to get here myself, but the bus schedules didn't match up. So I laid it out to Janine that she could drop me off here and go on to the old racetrack, where they have a flea market in the parking lot every Wednesday. Of course she wanted to come along and see Roxie, but I told her this time was just the two of us. Clothes shopping is a sore spot between me and Ma. She's been careful with me, really trying hard, and she didn't make a fuss about this, but we did agree that she'd meet us back here in the food court for lunch. Of course this kind of thing would be easier if I could drive—I've been thinking about that more. It would have to be an adapted vehicle. Irv talked to me about that after high school. He would have taught me to drive, he would have built the damn hand controls himself if I'd wanted it. But it all seemed too hard then, when I was so down after the big surgery, and I just let it slide.

I've reached the central atrium. Roxie's sitting there on a bench, looking small next to a ficus tree in a humongous planter.

She spreads around the middle when she's sitting down, like one of those little birds that fluffs out when it's cold. She's wearing a canary-yellow windbreaker, carrying an old-lady snap purse and her psychedelic tote bag.

"Hey, Rox."

"There you are!" She lifts herself up and gathers her things. "Let's get going. Lerner's is having a sale, I checked the paper." We head for the elevator. She seems to be rushing, but her steps are so small, it's easy for me to keep up with her. I can even stop and rest a little as she catches up.

"So," she says at the elevator. "You're going to a convention."

"A SkyLog convention."

"And what do people wear at these conventions?" The elevator dings, and we enter it with a thin-mustached guy and his small son.

"Other than SkyLog costumes? Nothing special. I mean, except when you're in costume, it's pretty casual." The little boy peers out, hands pressed to the glass elevator wall as we rise higher in the atrium, while his father watches us intently. The Con is a pretty poor excuse for a shopping trip, really. Trish already helped me get my Santak costume ready.

"You'll need a nice top," Roxie says. Out of the elevator, Roxie's immediately sidetracked by one of the novelty stands. She's got to browse through the loopy hot-pink drinking straws, the erasing magic markers and dishtowels with risqué slogans. She buys five of the drinking straws, which go into her see-through vinyl bag. Maybe they'll end up as part of a sculpture. We rejoin the thin stream of shoppers.

"So, you're going with Len?" she asks.

"What?" I practically trip.

"To the convention."

"Not exactly," I say. "We'll both be there, that's all."

"You're not going together then."

"That's what I said."

"I mean going together. Dating." Damn it, doesn't she know I still have to concentrate when I'm walking with the crutches? I steady myself.

"Me and Len?" I laugh, sounding like a tinkling cocktail-party laugh from an old movie. We've passed under the archway into the department store. Roxie angles over to a rack of sweaters and examines one, lifting the sleeve and rubbing it expertly between fingers and thumb. She checks the collar for the label.

"Made in Sri Lanka. What do they know about cashmere?" We forge on into the store's interior.

"He likes you," she says, her eyes scanning right and left.

"What are you talking about?" My indignation sounds even fakier than the laugh.

"I can tell these things."

"I don't think so, Roxie."

"No, I've got a talent for it."

"I mean, no, I don't think he, he's interested in me." She veers off to the left, forcing me onto a carpeted area.

"They'll have your size over here. What are you, anyway?" She stops and turns to appraise me.

"Fourteen. Or sixteen." Most of what I've been wearing comes in small, medium or large, or in other words, large. Lately I've avoided shopping completely, except for T-shirts and such that I buy myself at the Cons. Other things, Janine just brings home for me. I've seen how some websites are selling clothes online, which seems pretty cool.

Roxie pulls a long purple dress from the rack, holds it up.

"Try this on," she says. I panic—nobody said anything about dresses.

"I can't."

"How else are you going to see how it looks?"

"I can't try on a dress. No way, not with the crutches and all." And the braces. I hadn't thought that far into this. Not to mention that I haven't worn a dress in years, too girly for me. Not liking girly stuff is one of the things I was worrying over, but I concluded it's got nothing to do with whether I'm gay or not.

"Okay, we'll find a mirror." She pushes off to the right, zigzagging toward a mirrored column. I don't think I could have gotten this deep into the racks in the wheelchair. At the mirror, Roxie holds the dress in front of me. I actually like it.

"Not a good color on you," she says, frowning. "Stay here, I'll be right back." She disappears with the dress. I glance at myself in the mirror. I'm not a fan of full-length views of myself, but I look. Denim jacket, navy turtleneck, fanny pack, black track pants. Hair held up in back with a clip. Not bad. This is about as dressed up as I get, other than when I wear my Transortium uniform. And I'm standing up. I flash to the other night when Trish came over to work on my Santak costume. She made it fun, even though it was also weird, me starting out in my bra and panties and braces, her leaning in close to tuck the faux leather tighter in strategic places, going on about how I'll look totally ninja with the makeup and the costume. Like she picked up how scared I am about the whole thing. I can see why Zu likes her.

Roxie returns with the same dress but black. "A long dress is good for you," she says, holding this one up in front of me. I can't believe it, but again I like what I see.

"I don't know, Rox. I didn't bring that much money." There's seventy-eight dollars in my fanny pack, what's left of my cut of the shows I've worked on this summer. That's my spending money—my disability checks go right into our account.

"It's fifty percent off," she says, checking the tag. "We'll see." She hangs the dress on the nearest rack and moves on, unstoppable in her small-stepping momentum. I follow her back to the main aisle.

"So, do you like him?"

"Jeez, Roxie!"

"Because he's available," she says, fingering another sweater.

"Oh really. And you know this how?" Desperate to find the exit door on this conversation.

"He told me." She fingers her way through several more sweaters on the rack. "At least he told me he hasn't had a serious girlfriend in a few years, not since he broke up with his girlfriend from high school." She holds up a sweater. It's pink.

"No pink," I say. "No way. I don't do pink." This new info about Len is doing something funny to me, like an area has opened up inside my chest cavity. I take a deep breath. She pulls out a different sweater, heather gray, and holds it up against my body.

"You should go after him," she says.

"Roxie!" In the mirror I see my face blushing a deep rose from neck to forehead.

"Sorry, but you should. This will look very good on you." Staring in the mirror, I already know I want to buy it. It's long, like a tunic almost. The fabric is smooth as cat fur to the touch, and thick, so the turtleneck stands up on its own. With the right jewelry I could imagine it being worn by, say, a Gonfarian scientist visiting the *Encounter*. It seems to smooth out my curves nicely, not too tight. The tag says it's marked down to fifty-nine dollars.

"I don't know when I'd wear it," I say, wanting her to talk me into it.

"To your convention. To your party." I blush again, because now I know I do want to throw a party and wear this outfit to it. Maybe not for my birthday, but to celebrate my new website, and the new zine.

Roxie pulls the sweater away from me, folds it over her arm.

"You know, Mindy." She leans in so we're next to each other in the mirror. "I wasn't the prettiest girl in high school." I look at her round face with the big red glasses, its network of fine wrinkles and sagging chin line, and try to imagine her younger self. I just can't.

"But I always had the boys after me," she goes on. "I knew how to present myself nice. You should have seen me at some of the art school parties!"

"I wish."

"Come over this way," she says. "We need some accessories for this."

Which means I'm getting the heather-gray top. I trail behind her, past the sportswear, past the ladies' suits, to the long counter with leather stuff, jewelry and scarves. She pulls a slithery silver belt from the belt rack, cinches it up in front of the sweater.

"This is nice," she says.

"I don't know about a belt." She holds up another one, black with a square silver buckle. I shake my head no.

"You've got to show off your good points."

"A belt will not do that."

"You've got a nice figure," she insists, but puts the belts back. I gravitate to the scarves and pull one out—a silvery gray, looks like it might go with the sweater.

"What do you think?" I ask her. She looks, fingers pinching her chin, then nods in approval. "That's good." I feel pleased with myself. I check the tag—yes, I can buy them both, sweater and scarf. We make our way to a checkout counter. I realize how tired I am; it's the standing more than the walking, I think.

"I've got to sit down somewhere," I say. Damn, I have to carry the shopping bag too, can't sling it over the back of the wheelchair. We're early—it's a half hour till we're supposed to meet Janine—but we go on to the food court, and once we're there, we decide to go ahead and eat. I lower myself onto a plastic banquette, and she gets us a plate of chicken lo mein to share from the Happy Garden stand, and two coffees. Roxie turns to her lunch and starts putting it away with single-minded focus. The food makes me feel more expansive. I see myself in my new futuristic tunic, scarf draped gracefully over my shoulders, face aglow, standing in the midst of a group of delightful and sophisticated friends. They're laughing at something I said. Are we at an art opening?

"We made a good start," she says, picking up her coffee.

"I'm broke, Roxie. This is it for me."

"I mean a good start on your new wardrobe," she explains. "You need more than this."

"You're gonna make me over?"

"It's one of my talents."

"One of your many talents." The chic, confident new me laughs along with the others at my last bit of repartee. Is that Len at the edge of the group?

"So how's your mother doing?" Roxie asks. The lo mein turns flat and sour in my mouth, and my circle of new friends evaporates along with the artfully lit gallery space. But I was hoping to be able to talk things over with Roxie.

"I'm kind of worried about her, to be honest. I think she's getting in over her head with this guy."

"That comic book dealer?"

"Yeah, Nick. He's a first-class sleaze, and she thinks they're going in business together. She's talking about moving in with him in New Jersey." I feel a little strangled by the end of this, from breathing in too much or too fast.

"You'd be closer to us then," she says, both hands around her cup.

"Northern New Jersey."

"Oh." She takes another sip. "Your mother is a little ditzy. Don't tell her I said that."

"That's not the point." Just then I spot my mother scanning the food court for us. I raise an arm and yell, and Roxie turns and joins in. Hugs all around, then Janine insists on taking everything out of the shopping bag and oohing over it. She goes off to get her lunch. The lines aren't too long yet, it's mostly oldsters at the other tables.

"Maybe you'll like it up there." Roxie looks at me appraisingly.

"Except I'm not going."

"What'll you do?" she asks, pursing her lips.

"I don't know. Maybe move in with my dad." He has that second bedroom, but in the years since he moved in it's gradually filled with his sci-fi and new-physics books, vintage jazz records and a growing collection of obsolete computers, from an early Kaypro to a rare Wang. He's really as big a pack rat as Janine, just neater and more organized. I honestly don't see how I would fit there.

"Could you just stay where you are?"

"By myself?"

Roxie's looking at me, with one eyebrow raised.

"It just wouldn't work," I say. She doesn't get it. For one thing, getting places—we're not near any bus stop. There's Paratransit, but you have to wait forever for them, and coming back, they can leave you stranded. There's a lot of things I need Ma for, I have to admit. But then she needs me too—how would she do without me? She reappears with a hamburger and a fountain Sprite.

"Find anything at the racetrack?" Roxie asks her. My mother shakes her head no, her mouth full of burger.

"But I got some news!" she says finally, glancing from Roxie to me. "You remember that nice man, Nick Costa, that I've been seeing? We've been talking about moving in together, and Nick found a place for us! A nice little apartment, with two bedrooms and a patio!" The skin on my arms prickles and goes cold.

"When were you going to tell me this?"

"I just found out myself, Mindy! He was going over there this morning, I just called him." I shoot Roxie a what-did-I-tell-you look. Ma rolls on: "Two bedrooms! I told him we'll go up tomorrow to see it."

"No! We're not going up there!" The couple at the nearest table looks over, then pretends they didn't hear me raise my voice.

"Mindy! I'm sorry, Roxie, we shouldn't be talking like this here."

"What? It's fine," Roxie says. "I think Mindy's saying—"

"I'm saying I'm not going!"

We're all quiet for a second.

"Mindy, sweetheart—"

"You can go yourself. I really don't care what it looks like."

"Are you sure?"

"Yes! Are you even listening to me?"

"We'll talk later." Janine picks up her hamburger.

"Making a new start can be good," Roxie says after a while. "I wanted to move for the longest time. I kept bugging Morris about it, even though he showed me the numbers how it wouldn't work."

"Really! Where'd you want to go?" Janine asks.

"You know the Towers, right by the river in Philadelphia?" My mother nods. "That's where Bucky Fuller lived when he came to Philadelphia. He moved in right after they opened. Had the most beautiful apartment—not a penthouse, but very high up. All modern inside—"

"Wait!" She's got my attention now. "You were inside Bucky Fuller's apartment?"

"A couple times. That's what made me think about moving there."

"Does Len know this?"

"I don't know. This place had such a view, Mindy." She's staring at me from inside the memory. "You could see all the way up and down the river. At night, when it was just getting dark and the lights started coming on in Camden . . ."

"And Len knows about this." O.M.G. If he doesn't, I have to tell him. But maybe it's something else they've already talked about, and I'm the last to know.

"You couldn't see the ground at all, just the river—the ground was just lights," she goes on. "One time a bunch of us were over there after one of his lectures. His ideas put my head in a funny place. I was looking out his front window at the lights across the river. It felt like the whole apartment had just, you know, separated from the ground. We were floating up there, like he says we're all on Spaceship Earth. He called us Earthians, did you know that?" I nod. Spaceship Bucky. That's where my fantasy apartment is, I decide—all clean and sleek and high up above the world.

"So I really wanted to move there, to the Towers. But Morrie showed me how we couldn't afford it. I think really he didn't want to have to commute back to Jersey." She shakes herself. "Things don't always work out how you want."

"But you still could move!" Janine says. "Isn't Morris retired now?"

She shrugs. "I gave up trying to convince him. Now I'm too busy with my work to move."

"Well, your work is going good at least," I say. I don't want her going into a funk too.

"Nobody gets what I'm doing," she says glumly. "I haven't had a review since 1987, and that was a group show."

"What about your show at the Senior Center?" Janine asks. "Somebody could write about that!"

Roxie grimaces. "That's over. I've got no gallery, nothing."

"Isn't there a museum or something in Philadelphia?" I try.

She laughs silently at this. "Believe it or not, the Museum has some of my WPA drawings."

"Wow!" Ma has recovered her default enthusiasm. "We have a friend that's showing in the Art Museum!"

"They don't even know they're mine. I signed them with my maiden name, they don't know from Roxie Grunwald. The curator's young enough to be my granddaughter."

"But if you just showed somebody what you're doing—" I say.

"It has to be the right somebody." She sips at her coffee, shakes her head. "I knew Marsha Biderman." Like we should know who that is. "The Biderman Gallery. On Walnut Street. We went to art school together."

"There you go!"

"It's not that simple. We haven't talked in twenty-five years. I think her daughter runs the gallery now. You have to be a big name from New York to show there, or at least have pink hair."

"You should call her up anyway!" I'm getting excited for her. "You're an old buddy, that should count for something."

"I don't know," she says, and sighs. "Sometimes I wonder should I keep going at all. What hurts is, I know this new stuff is the best work I've ever done." She leans toward me. "You understand what I'm talking about. You're an artist too, you know."

"Yeah, I know. Everybody's an artist."

"No, you. I'm talking about you." She looks straight at me, and that sharp laser gaze cuts right through my skin. Does she know I've started writing again? I feel naked in front of her, and my mother too. I'm not ready for this.

"You don't know what you've got," Roxie goes on. "You're young, you're a smart girl. Your life is moving forward," she says, reaching down to gather her bags.

"That's what I'm always trying to tell her!" my mother chimes in.

I pull my denim jacket on, hug it around me for protection. I wish I could be high up in some Bucky Fuller spaceship or floating geodesic dome, or on the *Encounter*—anywhere, as long as nobody can see in.

THE FRONT DOOR creaks open, and I wheel out of my room. It's Irv, balancing a pizza box and a plastic grocery bag, pushing the door shut with one foot.

"Hi, Ace," he says, glancing over, and heads for the kitchen. "Extra mushrooms and pepperoni."

"Great." I follow him in. Through the kitchen window, a cool October dusk is spreading violet.

"Where did you say your mom went?"

"Uh, New Jersey." I have to tell him, just not yet. I called him when I got home from the shopping trip yesterday. He hasn't been coming over as much—did he pick up that something's going on?

"Seems like she's always out when I come over." He pulls a beer from the fridge. "Hope you're hungry."

"Hah, good one." Our usual pizza-night patter. I roll over to get us napkins and knives. I've already set out two plates.

"All set for the Con?" he asks.

"I guess so. It's gonna be weird going dressed up as a Santak."

"You'll do great." Lifting the beer to drink, he gazes past me toward the living room.

"I've been thinking." He nods in that direction. "Now that you're on the crutches, it might be good to get some carpet in there." He pulls out his mini tape measure. "What do you think?"

He gets up and goes in the living room. I don't even know how much longer I'll be here. My chest goes tight.

"Hey, Pop?" I call after him.

"Mm?"

"Have you and Ma talked lately?"

"What about?"

"About the house and stuff." It's easier to talk, not seeing him. I open the lid of the pizza box and lean into its cheesy warmth.

"You mean that leak behind the shower wall?" he asks. He comes back in, writes some numbers on his napkin.

"No, not that." I pull two slices apart, watching the cheese stretch in the air.

"What then?" He sits down, pulls the Greek salad out of the bag.

"She's been thinking . . . thinking about moving."

"Why?" he asks evenly, prying open the plastic salad container. He thinks this is one of her space-cadet plans.

"No, really. I think she's serious."

"Why would she want to move?" He slaps a pizza slice onto his plate.

"It's kind of a business thing," I try. "She wants to be closer to this guy she's doing business with."

He chews. "That guy she went to Atlantic City with?" he asks deliberately.

"Yeah. Nick Costa."

He reaches for his beer. "This always happens when you go in the hospital," he says. "Your mother gets a little crazy."

"Yeah, well." This is so hard. I take a bite but can barely chew. Do I have to tell him this particular craziness started before then? But maybe he's right. She went up to visit Nick for the first time that second day after the surgery, the day Zu and everybody came to visit. I know because when I got home she was raving about how great his store is.

"I should talk." He gives a tight smile. "I could hardly sleep when you were in the hospital this time."

"As long as you don't start smoking again." He shakes his head.

"But really, Pop," I go on. "I think she's gonna do it this time.

You saw the boxes in the living room!" I gesture out the kitchen doorway.

"What does she think, she can just run away?"

"She wants to take me with her. She says she'll sell the house or you'll buy her share of it or something. I can't believe she didn't talk to you." My voice too loud. It was always up to me to tell him, I realize. In the dusky light, the fluorescent fixture over our heads seems to be glaring harder than usual. I see how much grayer Irv's hair has gone; every wrinkle around his eyes shows in sharp relief.

"I'll talk to her," he says, his face grim. I bite into my pizza, but he just sits.

"She's sleeping with him," he says.

I nod yes. He nods and exhales.

"I knew that. I just didn't think . . ."

"She's up there now," I push on. "In Secaucus. They might have signed on the apartment today." He nods again, lips pursed.

"She figures I'm gonna move up there with them." Quiet chewing. "But I was thinking," I go on, "how maybe we could both live here."

"Hmm?" He hasn't heard me.

"You could, you know, move back in here."

"I'll talk to her." His tone harsh.

"Well, would you please tell her I'm not going with her, because she doesn't seem to hear me. And I'm not. Going with her." I'm enunciating, leaning forward.

"What?"

I let out a breath. Signals crossed, not getting through.

"I'd rather stay here," I try again. "I was thinking maybe you could move back here. Or, if I learned to drive, I might be able to manage here by myself. You or Ma could visit anytime, of course." That's my wildest thought, and I feel like I'm talking to myself anyway.

"Or I could move into your place. If you want." Having gotten to this, my least favorite option, I'm done.

"Sure, sure," he says, distant. "I just have to figure this out." His face looks chalk-white, almost gray, framed against the window's dark purple square of descending night.

A ROUND THE DARKENED hotel room, dozens of candles are burning—tea candles and white utility candles set in paper cups—illuminating the faces of the Santak gathered here. The yellow light catches their nose spikes and the fierce spark in their eyes, and makes their rust-orange faces glow. The Santak chant we just finished vibrates in the air around us.

The Lrak rented this room for the run of the Con. The drapes are pulled shut, and beds and other furniture are pushed against the walls except for this little table we're gathered around. The twentieth-century hotel room has become a shadowy ceremonial cave on the Santak home planet.

So I must really be Santak now—or I will be once this ceremony's done.

There's still a lot about them that grates on me, like how they're so obsessed with rank and honor and who has the biggest blade. Am I going along with this just because it's the Santak who took me in? I promise myself I'll keep speaking up in favor of Transortium values.

There's Roger across from me—except now he's really turned into Kagash, the line of spikes dividing his face, his long brown-gray hair in a ponytail. Severe and sober in his dark belted tunic, chest plate, matching trousers and heavy boots.

"Now we do the oath of loyalty." His soft twang is comfortingly familiar. I join in, shouting the phrases after him with the others, surprised at the strength of my voice. I have no idea what I'm saying, but that's okay. This is a group you can count on. They may not be much for appearances, most of the time anyway, or for charm, or politeness. But they'll stick by you. If it comes to a fight, you know you won't be fighting alone.

They're up to the part of the oath that each person has to say alone—and everyone's looking at me. I shout it out on automatic, acutely aware of how I look. My forearms are resting in the sleek black tubing of my crutches. I finally accepted Len's argument on that score: it's not the disability, it's how you function that counts for a Santak. I spent a while in front of the hotel room's bathroom mirror, taking in the finishing makeup touches applied by Bradley and Trish. There was this strong-jawed Santak female, gray eyes staring out from her coppery face. Trish teased up my hair so it billowed out around my Santak features, almost as good as Bradley's dreads.

There in the bathroom mirror, set off against my night-dark tunic, was the real shocker: my fabulous cleavage. I mean, I knew I had it, but I've never flaunted it, not like this. It makes sense here as part of a female Santak officer's power suit. Len sure noticed it when I finally emerged from the bathroom in full costume. He was speechless for a few seconds. Just now, as I was reciting my part of the oath, I know a lot of those eyes on me were really locking onto the boobs.

Len looks pretty good too, standing next to me. You can tell he took the time to do everything right. He nailed the details: the real leather belt, the body-molded chest plate, the convincing-looking knife. He really is serious about his gear. Somehow, in the uniform, all the usual Len stuff—his solid bulk, his perpetually offended look—comes together into something else. Next to Len, Bradley stands loose-limbed and elegant, the tunic making his shoulders broader. Zu and Trish rubbing shoulders beside the Captain, trying not to smile. Zu looks like Cat Woman in her top-to-bottom leather.

Our leader's started on the first Polg rite with the new guy, Kevin. Kevin's a little lost in his uniform and looks nervous.

"And how do you seal this claim?" The Captain holds out his knife to Kevin.

"With this," Kevin answers, his voice down in his throat. I must have missed Kevin saying his new Santak name. He squeezes both eyes shut, pulls some hair taut, then flinches as he severs the hair with the knife. We watch as the first hair of the Polg is offered to the candle flame and to the Santak gods, hungry for tokens of loyalty from their followers. As the ribbon of smoke curls toward the ceiling, the Captain raises his arm in the Santak salute, shouting "Baf!" And the others take up the shout. That's his new name, Baf.

"Okay, Cadet, you're next." Kagash turns to the next person in the circle. It's Tad. I swear he's grown an inch since I saw him a month ago. In this crowd his appearance is by far the strangest. True to his word, Tad showed up as an Enmeshed Santak: nose bones sticking out of a paste-gray face, mouse-gray uniform. And a severe buzzcut—I could only imagine the fights with his parents over that—short enough that you could follow the thin tubing up to the top of his head. I couldn't decide which was creepier: seeing this scrawny, serious kid with his head shorn, or the way he managed to blur the edges between these two wildly different beings, the Santak and the Mesh.

Now he looks even stranger. His arrival sparked a near-fight when several Santak objected to this Mesh-Santak mongrel taking part in the ceremony. Some stuck with the argument that he couldn't exist, since a Santak warrior must die before allowing himself to be Enmeshed; somebody else protested that his appearance offended Santak aesthetics; and one guy kept insisting that no self-respecting Raptor should allow such a creature into its ranks. I tried to defend him on the usual grounds of Abundant Life in Many Forms, though that's a Transortium principle, not Santak. Tad stood silent in the middle of all this, his face a still gray mask. I don't think he expected such a blast of reaction. The Captain finally stepped in with a compromise: Tad had to remove the most offensively Mesh features, at least during the Polg ceremony. Trish promised to help him get them reattached in time for tonight's costume contest.

So here he is, tubing ripped off, his face red from wiping off the gray greasepaint—more weirdly mongrel than ever. But he stands straight at attention as the Captain begins the Polg procedure. I don't believe the kid's nerve. Tad takes the heavy dagger from Roger-Kagash, lifting it up.

"With this blade I claim my new name!" His voice high but clear.

"Speak your new name, Cadet," the Captain prompts.

"Chumak!" He sets his mouth, cuts a strand of hair and burns it. The others take up his new name, hooting, throwing themselves into the chant as if to drown out the puzzlement of this perverse, mutant child who insists on making himself one of them. Funny, in "Shadow of the Mesh," Pak is appropriately terrified of the Mesh, but Tad, or Tadmesh, is so drawn to them.

Tad rejoins the circle next to me, his face shiny with the moment. He leans toward me and whispers, "It means 'new species.'"

My turn. The Captain motions to me with his little half-grin, one eyebrow raised. I pick my way around the table. It's a damn replay of my damn high school graduation, except there's no ankle-length gown to worry about tripping on.

We stand face to face. "Are you ready to claim your new name?" He holds out the knife. I can do this. I take the blade, hold it up as high as I can.

"With this blade I claim my new name," I say, my Commander voice returning. I hear a few hooting cheers and a "Go, Mindy," but they sound distant, outside the circle of the Captain and me.

"Speak your Santak name." That little smile winking up his face. I belt it out: "Nechut!" I looked mine up too—it means Changing Woman.

"And how do you seal this claim?" This is the hard part. I actually practiced beforehand but with a kitchen knife that didn't have the heft of this Santak weapon. In the breath-holding silence, I chuck the crutch tips forward for balance, grab a strand of hair, raise the knife and slice, trying not to pitch myself forward with the strength of the motion. There, it's done! Hold out the strand: "With this!"

Roger sets my hair burning. The biting smell, mixed with the waxy scent of the burning candles, leaves me a little overcome. The cheers of my Santak crewmates sound far away. I feel sweat under my nose bones. Take a deep breath, Mindy. Don't dare fall down. Am I Mindy now or Nechut? And what about Kat Wanderer? Right now, I'm Santak. I turn myself toward the others and raise my hand in the Santak salute. Looking around into their flame-lit faces, I see now that they're creatures, honoring the imperatives of their nature. That's it. In the cool, enlightened Transortium world of the future, they hold the banner of proudly unreconstructed creaturehood. And I'm a creature too. My face breaks open with a big smile.

THE MAIN FLOOR of the Con is a mob scene, as always. I stand just inside the entrance, taking it in—there must be fifty vendors here in the hotel's giant convention room. The aisles crowded with Transorters of all species, from the seriously costumed to kids in crew jerseys and jeans, along with a sprinkling of civilian gawkers. SkyLog still rules here, even without a new show or movie on the horizon. The Fandom lives.

Len must have peeled off without me while I was taking this all in. I spot him a few tables down at the weapons vendor. Swinging out into the room, I'm thrown into panic. It's too much crowd for me to deal with on the crutches, too much motion, too many feet where I need to place the tips. I stop, my crutches set wide. How did I manage those hallways in high school? I should have made sure to have someone with me. I saw Zu crossing the middle aisle with Trish and Brad—he's easy to spot, he's so tall. I feel a surge of anger at Zu, abandoning me for her new friends. I don't care that she's so happy being with Trish, I want her here now, next to me. I take a breath, then ease myself to the right, closer to the tables and out of the chaos. From here I inch forward, waiting for space to clear, till I catch up to Len.

It's an intimidating weapons display, with real Samurai swords, hunting knives and crossbows mixed in with Santak blades and other SkyLog gear. The vendor's a for-real sword-maker, or he works with someone who is. Makes custom pieces for the right price. There's a mean-looking, heavy-bladed dagger on the table between Len and the vendor. Gazing at it, I realize something that must be obvious to every Santak: how the blade's shape mirrors the shape of Santak nose bones. The air is thick with whatever negotiating has been going on.

"Find anything?" I say to Len.

"Nah. You?"

"Nada." The sword guy nods and moves to put the dagger back in its place. Len's already moving out into the mass of people.

"Hey, Len?" I call, trying not to sound scared. He looks back at me. "I need you to stay with me." I nod my head toward a crutch tip.

"Oh. Right." We move ahead, with him just a little in front, expertly clearing my path. After a few swings I feel better.

"One other thing," I say. "What is it with guys and weapons?" He grimaces.

"We like 'em because they make us feel important. Happy?" This is turning into a joke between us. I've been teasing him about Santak guys and their blades. He's tried to explain it to me, even dragging in his hunting trips with his dad down in Delaware. How his dad always told him you had to have respect for the weapon.

We pass the lady who specializes in older, discontinued action figures—higher-quality stuff than some other vendors, who might as well have raided Toys "R" Us this morning for their inventory. Then there's the couple selling uniforms, both ready-mades and patterns, and various SkyLog accessories: Wuvian antenna buds, Transortium comtrons. They even have a Santak starter kit in a big box, including some standard-issue vinyl face extensions. Our custom-made ones are so better than that.

Now that I can move ahead all right, I'm starting to feel what else is different. Not just being at my new height instead of down around table level. The real change is being here as a Santak. In the sea of Transortium jerseys, T-shirts and jeans, we stand out. The Santak uphold the honor of the Con, taking on the commitment to full transformation. We're not the only ones in full uniform, but there's something about a clutch of Santak that turns heads.

I'm used to being stared at, of course. Usually by little kids, though, and sometimes moronic teenagers. Most grownups have perfected that look that mutates instantly into a veil of indifference, the hooding of the eyes that says, You didn't just catch my attention, that was your imagination. And I know they'll hit me with that one last semi-secret sidelong glance as they're passing me. For a while I made it a game to catch them in that last look. Then I was like, the hell with it. But the way people are looking at us now, it's an out-and-out, unshrinking stare. Here we are, folks—yes, we're on display. The freak parade in full regalia.

There's a Transortium family across the aisle: Mom and Dad in their First Series tunics, a boy maybe six or seven, and a baby in Mom's arms, in her teeny crewman-colored tunic. They're all looking at me and Len, even the baby, clutching a goldfish cracker in her spitty little fist. But the older kid is staring straight at my boobs. I'm starting to feel, well, naked. This outfit's definitely tighter than anything I usually wear. Len spots the kid and bares his teeth, then lets out a low, threatening growl. I put on a scowl. It works: he backs into his dad.

"That was awkward," I say as we move on. He looks at me sideways, appraising.

"What were you expecting?"

"I don't know. Do they always stare like that?"

"It's because we're so pretty." We're up to another booth, mostly posters. It's the guy from Collectorama!—same spiky blond hair, same stubble on his wolfish face. He's with a customer, holding a poster from the Buck Rogers movie, the really bad one from the seventies. Talking to the customer, but his eyes are on me, following me as we walk by.

That's the other strange thing. I see people I know here, and a lot of them don't recognize me, or they're doing long, disbelieving double takes. And I'm not sure if I want them to know it's me—it's easier to just be this Santak girl warrior.

The next booth is one I always like to stop at, Sasha's Creations. She's a fan artist, good enough to sell her work. She sent some art to the Voice when she was just starting out. Sasha sits in the middle with her easel and art supplies and works right through the day. Absorbed in her painting, she doesn't even see me. Len is gazing toward the next table, piled with videos and used paperbacks.

"You go on," I say. "This won't take long." Out of the stream of walkers, I'm okay. I browse her pictures. She's got the usual spread of clinch scenes: Bokun with his various amours, the Captain with Dr. Dina Braxton. And a good selection of slash clinches, mostly guy-on-guy, just like the slash fiction: the first Captain and Mac the Navigator, *Century 23*'s Captain Tanaka and Steptoe, his second in command, even Captain Tanaka and Roi. I think about Zu again. It's really not that she's gay, I know that now. It's feeling like she's left me behind. When I saw her through the crowd before, her and Trish so close, shoulder to shoulder, not talking or laughing, just in sync with each other while Bradley looked off to one side . . . What they have between them, not having to say anything at all.

There's a full-color pastel of Roi with Klar, his first and only romance on the show. Their embrace is done in feathery soft focus against a pink-orange background: she's put them inside a Slirrhian skiff. Roi leans over Klar, his lips slightly parted, his shoulders bare. Her lips are parted too, her eyes closed, her cheeks flushed. I'm caught, heart racing—it's me in that embrace. I sneak a look in Len's direction, but he's turned away. Keep it together, Mindy. I pull myself back to Earth, let out a breath.

"I can give you a break on the frame." Sasha's still painting, still not looking at me. The picture is $100 without the frame.

"No thanks. It's nice, though." I'm broke, thanks to my shopping trip and paying Trish for the costume materials. But I feel exposed, my innards displayed on the wall. Yes, I've started writing down the story of Kat and Roi again. But it's strictly private. The PTSD from those poison-pen letters hasn't gone away, and I can't imagine putting my stories out where other people could see them, like Sasha does with her paintings.

I pick up Len and we move on. It's a relief just to concentrate on moving safely through the crowd.

"Oh my God. Is that you, Mindy?"

Busted. It's Annemarie, one of my former minions, I mean Cyborg Appreciation Society members. Sweet, not-too-sharp Annemarie.

"Hey, Annie. Long time no see."

"You look so, so different!" Her eyebrows dancing with confusion. "I mean, I heard you were . . ." She glances at Len, who looks like he's ready to growl at her too. "But I didn't . . ."

"Yeah, you didn't," I answer. She never called, never emailed, never asked for my side of the story. Me being Commander all those years counted for zilch.

"Oh, this is Len," I say. Len glares at her.

"Wait till Sheryl sees you!" Annemarie sends a nervous glance down the aisle. "Did you go by the table yet?"

I know Sheryl's here, and it figures she'd be at the CAS table, down at the end where they reserve spaces for the local fan clubs. Part of me has been steeling myself to see her, to get to this encounter I've lived through in my head so many times. Now I'm on high alert.

"Okay, nice seeing you," I manage, pushing off with the crutches.

"Take care, Mindy," she calls from behind me.

"This is it," I say to Len as we move through the crowd. I've let him in on what happened to me with the CAS. Len offered various forms of revenge on my behalf, which was nice, but I told him I'd rather not cause bodily harm to anyone. We're getting close. I feel a little queasy, have to concentrate. There's Annemarie, who has somehow circled ahead, leaning forward now at the CAS table, talking, looking back my way. So Sheryl will have advance warning. Come on, Mindy. You can do this. At least get there without falling flat on your face.

Sheryl's sitting at the table with some guy I don't know. From here she looks small and harmless. That's the problem, she always looks harmless. The guy next to her is shockingly pale and sitting very still. He might be impersonating Roi, but the uniform isn't right.

In the middle of the table, taunting me, is a fanned-out display of the new "Voice of the Cyborg," Issue Nine. The zine that should have been mine. Even the cover typeface is the same. There's a pen-and-ink drawing of Roi staring thoughtfully up at the stars, but I don't recognize the artist. It's definitely thinner than it would have been. Seeing it there all printed up, I feel sick. On top of this, I notice the guy with Sheryl is leaning in toward her—could they be a couple?

"Mindy?" Sheryl's been staring at me. Even with advance warning, she can't quite digest that it's me, in my full makeup and costume. And standing up too.

"Bingo." Glad I can hide behind the nose spikes and orange makeup. But Sheryl's got her chin hiked up the way she does, so she seems to be looking down at you even when she isn't, boring in with her odd, unblinking stare.

"So you really did join the Lrak." I can barely hear her reedy little voice over the crowd noise, and leaning toward her makes me feel precarious. I pull myself back up. She didn't mention the crutches, which is fine.

"This is Len, he's an officer on the Raptor." She nods and gives him her trademark stare.

"Eric is First Officer of the Isaac Asimov," she says. The guy gives a short, military-grade nod. "We've been having some very interesting discussions."

Eric speaks up in a flat, nasal voice: "We may be cooperating on some fundraising, and some social events involving both clubs." That sounds suspiciously like everything to me.

"What, you mean like a merger?" I try to sound casual, and fail. Sheryl pauses—she always makes you wait. Is it so hard for her to just answer a question? Finally, "We're in an exploratory phase."

The top of my head is lifting off. They're talking about merging the CAS with the Asimov, a much bigger club. I leave for just a few months and the whole organization is imploding. Sheryl's driving it over a cliff. Staring at her mealy, unformed face, I'm unable to form a coherent sentence.

"Exploratory!" Len spits the word out, talking for me. Sheryl purses her lips, then pushes a magazine toward me.

"Would you like a copy of the new issue?" she asks. I remember the copy of my new zine, the "Alt Lifeforms Log," stowed in my backpack with my other essentials, that I meant to present to her. But I forgot to pull it out, and it's too awkward now to wrestle the backpack off and rummage. This is not going the way I planned.

"We're cultivating . . . great new writers." I can still barely hear her over the background noise.

"Keep it." I'm itching to pick it up and go through it, see for myself how great her new writers are.

"You know what? This is bullshit." Len speaks up. "You should be giving her the whole *pile* of them. For all she's done. You should be *paying* her to take your lousy zine."

Sheryl shrinks back, her eyes blinking, her mouth set. Len defending me somehow gives me my voice back.

"And if you want a copy of my new zine, it's right over there." I lift a crutch in the direction of the Lrak table across the aisle, in the process nearly whacking an innocent Transortium Fleet crewman. Kevin the new guy, manning the table, nods and smiles our way. He's on duty this afternoon, an easy assignment that includes selling copies of the A.L.L. I'm quite proud of the new zine, actually.

"Eight dollars a copy, discount Con price," I add. No way does she get a free copy.

"I've been on your website a few times," Eric says. "It's pretty good. Nice setup, not too flashy. Did you do the HTML?"

"I've got a web designer." I glance across to the next aisle as if I might spot Bradley there.

"Good content, for a fan-run," Eric says.

"We've already had a couple hundred hits," I tell him. Maybe he's not so bad. He nods appreciatively while Sheryl gives him one of her cool, unreadable stares.

"In fact," I say, "we're having a party. To celebrate the website launch and the new zine." Sheryl blinks, her surprise almost equal to mine. I've already invited a bunch of people. When I told Trish I was thinking about having a party, the night she came over with my Santak costume, she totally jumped on board with it, which made it seem more doable. Now that I've said it, I have to go ahead and invite them.

"Oh!" Sheryl manages.

"Next Saturday night. My place, at eight." It's my last chance to do it, if Janine has her way. Janine and Nick signed the lease on that garden apartment in Secaucus, and they've already started moving stuff up there. Janine still thinks I'm going with her. And Irv seems to think I'm moving in with him. It's insane to have a party now, but I can't just disinvite everybody.

"Here, Mindy." Sheryl pushes a copy of the new "Voice of the Cyborg" out toward me. "Won't you take this complimentary copy on behalf of—"

"No! I really don't need it!" I wheel around and move off, my heart pounding. Len pulls up beside me.

"You invited them to your party?"

"Don't worry, they'll never show up." She wouldn't dare. It's enough that she knows I'm having it. I've never thrown a party before, not as an adult.

"Maybe I should pick up another case," Len says. He's in charge of getting beer.

"We'll see." I notice the copy of the Voice in his hand.

"Hey, she said it was free," he shrugs. Now I'll get to read it.

I swing through the crowd, Santak Girl coming through. Maybe I really do want Sheryl to come to the party, so she has to see this new Mindy. She may be driving the Voice into the ground—okay, that really hurts. But if I can make her admit that my new zine is just as good, that I'm doing fine without the CAS— that's not a great reason to invite her either, but it's too late now.

"ALL RIGHT, EVERYBODY! This is it, the moment you've all been waiting for!"

The milling about and buzz of audience conversation barely dips at the emcee's announcement signaling the beginning of the adult portion of the Con's costume contest. We've all had enough of adorable kids in pint-sized Transorter costumes, their hair slicked back to reveal miniature Wuvian antenna buds or whatever, their faces shining in the wash of spotlights and the waves of cheering and clapping. We're ready for the grownup stuff. When I first started coming to these things, the costume contest was way simpler: you got up on stage and stood there in a lineup along with some other fools. The person who got the most applause won the prize, which might be a SkyLog paperback or T-shirt. Gradually through the years it's gotten more over the top as people have tried to outdo their previous entries.

"Okay, bear with us here." It's Doug, the emcee. Outside the Con, Doug and his wife run a bookstore with a great sci-fi section. Doug adjusts his black-framed glasses, studying his notes. "Our first adult contestants are . . . Patty and Trevor Noska!" Patty, my contributor! They're dressed as Roi and Klar. Trevor's no Roi, with his wild curly hair and lugging his guitar, and Patty's wearing the same outfit she had last year. But it's okay. Some people do skits or tableaus, and some go with the knock-'em-dead costumes. But Patty and Trevor have always been about the songs. They do a nice filk number, taking off on Whitney Houston's "Heartbreak Hotel," and get some good applause.

"Let's hear it for our first adult contestants," Doug intones. "I laughed, I cried, don't know about you."

"Time to party, boys and girls." It's Trish, sitting next to me. We're third on the list: Trish, Zu, me, Len, Bradley and Tad, a group entry representing the Lrak. I hike myself out of my aisle seat. On my feet again, I realize how wiped I am.

"I forget, why did I agree to do this?" I mutter.

"You're gonna blow the place up!" Trish hisses in my ear. It's been a long day though, and it's getting toward ten. The Polg ceremony, dealing with Sheryl, not to mention navigating on the crutches, it's all starting to hit me. I wouldn't have made it this far except I took over for Kevin at the club table, a needed timeout. To be honest, it would have been easier if I could get around in my chair.

Once everybody's joined us in the aisle, we head toward the front of the big room. The next person up is in the killer-costume category, a large woman with flowing blond hair going on solo. Onstage, her floor-length purple robe shines in the spotlight. The embroidered Wuvian lettering along the border must have taken her months to do. The theme from the *SkyLog II* movie blasts from a boombox.

"It's the incomparable Gina Culbertson as the Grand Mus Davro." I knew I'd seen that costume somewhere. It's from the episode set on the Wuvian home world, but this big, healthy lady looks so different from the tiny actress who played Davro that I didn't make the connection. Our group is just doing a tableau—no lines to say, thank God. Trish worked it out to incorporate Tad's Santak-Mesh mash-up. We're supposed to be a group of Santak warriors who've recaptured this former Santak and are getting ready to execute him for his betrayal of Santak honor. I didn't expect Tad to go for that, but he was philosophical. At least this would allow him to present his cross-species theory to the whole Con assembly.

We're next. I eye the steps—they look okay—then glance at Tad. His tubes have been reattached and his gray makeup reapplied. His eyes are slits, and he stands deathly still, listing to one side. I touch his arm.

"How you doing there, dude?"

"Okay." I can barely hear him.

"'Cause we kind of need you down here."

"I'm just trying to stay in Mesh mode." Great, the centerpiece of our tableau is drifting past the ionosphere. I take his upper arm in a strong grip so he won't miss our cue.

"How about that, folks?" says Doug. "Has Gina done it again, or what? I feel like I'm back on Wu!" More applause, a few whistles. She's got the best-costume prize locked up.

"You ready?" Trish touches my shoulder.

"Yeah."

"You want to let go of the kid's arm then?" Oh—I'm still latched onto Tad, but I'm going on first, followed by Len and Trish. Finally Tad, between Bradley and Zu. Tad's still got that vacant look. Well, it fits with our setup.

The Wuvian Grand Mus makes her way down the stairs. "Nice job," I tell her as she rustles past me. Not sure she hears me, she's still in the zone. All right, here goes. I tackle the steps deliberately, make my way across the semi-dark stage. We take our places: Trish in the middle, arms crossed, playing the judge, deciding the fate of the recaptured Santak-Mesher prisoner. Tad pinned between Zu and Bradley. Len and I are the soldiers—his blade raised high, me lifting my right crutch as planned, aiming it like some futuristic weapon toward our prisoner.

The surge of white light leaves me blinded. I'm hyperaware of the audience that I can't see, so many people sitting out there in the dark. A call: "Go Santak!" A few scattered boos and cheers. The emcee breaks in—"This charming scene is brought to you by members of the Raptor Lrak"—and then goes on to mangle our names. I stare out into the darkness. There are people out there who know me: Captain Roger and the other Santak, and Tad's dad is here, I saw him before, looking patient and out of place. Sheryl must be out there too, with Annemarie and other people from the CAS. What are they all thinking? Under the furnace-blast of spotlights my skin crawls, like every pore is on view. This is another level up from drawing stares as a fully decked-out Santak; way more than people's sneaky stares on the street. This is some kind of ground-zero visibility, ultimate exposure. Not exactly naked, but completely *seen*. Disturbing in a new way. Behind that, I feel strangely calm.

Our soundtrack starts up, a slithery mix compliments of Zu, with ominous Mesh-type chords, weapons fire, magnified Darth Vader–like breathing and snatches of Santak Butak'La chants. You rock, Zu. If this crowd doesn't get it, no one will. Trish stands in judgment, sternly gazing on Tadmesh. She looks like you should bow down before her, a Santak clan mother. Her shining black hair, the Cleopatra eye makeup and the black nail polish—it all works. The V of her cleavage, framed by the black costume, broadcasts through the white-light haze like a flag. I glance down: my boobs must be producing a similar effect. Next to Trish, Zu looks sleek and commanding. The two of them are like bigger, mythic versions of themselves.

Tad stands straight, looking stunned. His skin ash-gray, he's dwarfed between Zu and Bradley, hardly up to Bradley's shoulders, as they each grab one of his arms. God, I hope he's okay. He's made himself pretty vulnerable here, the target of our fake wrath and surely some of the audience's disapproval too. But I'm dealing with too much myself to get into Tad's head.

"What do you say, people?" Doug shouts. The applause is pretty high. More calls from the darkness: "Mesh go home!" "You Will Be Mesh!" The applause is our cue to break ranks and take our bow. I lower my weapon to the ground and swing forward one step. Len's right beside me, our shoulders touching. His face is grim, like a soldier at attention. I know this is something for him too. Getting up in front of all these people may not be easy for him, but he did it. For the honor of the ship, he said. Sweat beads on his face. This heat is too much. An eruption of warmth cascades down the centerline of my body, sweat breaking out under my costume. My whole body feels rubbery.

"I've got to get out of here," I say to Len. All I want is to be off this stage, away from these lights, someplace dark. Get out of these clothes, lie down maybe. He looks me over.

"Hold on." I barely hear him over the applause. He turns toward Trish and the others. "Okay, move it! Everybody off!" There's only one way off the stage, and everybody's between me and the steps. We inch forward. Len turns to make sure I make it down the steps okay.

"These costumes are a bitch under the lights," he says. "I'll get you something to drink."

"No." Don't feel right, I don't know what exactly. Still rubbery, a little sick to my stomach. "I think I better lie down."

"I'll take you upstairs."

Trish is high-fiving the others: "All right! That was totally kickass, you guys!" A little smile cracks Tad's gray face.

Trish notices me then. "You okay, Mindy?"

"I feel kind of hot."

"You need something to drink."

"No, I just . . ."

"I'm taking her up to the room," Len says.

Zu shoots me a look of concern. "It's okay," I manage.

"You sure?"

I nod. "Just need to lie down." I say that for Trish—Zu needs no words. Trish fishes the room key card out of the waistband of her leggings and hands it to Len.

As we make our way toward the exit, I remember my backpack and grab it from my seat. Doug announces the next contestants, a pair of twins, masters of filk. As the double doors swing shut behind us, I hear them starting their new number to the tune of the *Gilligan's Island* theme. Out here in the vendors' room, the sound is muffled. Most of the tables are cleared or covered.

"You sure you don't want some water?" Len nods toward the fountain next to the elevators.

"That's okay." I haven't quite mastered water fountains with the crutches, and it's not worth the effort now. The doors slide open. A lone guy dressed in business casual stands inside, crowding the button panel. He stares at us as we enter the elevator, giving us a big, unguarded smirk. "Three," I say, trying to find my Commander voice. Len and I settle at the back wall. We're surrounded by mirrors. On either side, lines of Lens and Mindys recede—or pairs of male and female Santak warriors, battle-weary, their orange skin streaked with sweat. And uncountable guys in button-downs and chinos, each one directing his smirk down at the floor. I close my eyes. I'm so damn hot, it's like I'm melting, even now that we're out of the lights. And Len right next to me, the heat rising from him too. Between us we're generating a heat field that must be scorching the back of the guy's neck.

The room is at the end of the hall. Paid for by Captain Roger out of the ship's treasury, it gave us privacy for the Polg ceremony, and later it'll be a crash pad for the members who live too far away to go home tonight. The parties can go pretty late. Len slips in the key card, opens the door.

"Wait," I say, standing there in the dark. "Just don't turn on the light for a second, okay?" I need this blanket of darkness. By the light from the hallway, I can make out the mess left over from our ceremony: burnt-out candles, empty paper cups, beds against the wall, lumpy piles of backpacks and sleeping bags. Then the door shuts and the room disappears in blessed, thick dark. Oh shit, this isn't right—I should have gone over to the bed or the chair first. I'm stranded.

"Len—" I call, my voice muffled in the closed room. "I need a hand here."

"Oh, man," he breathes. He's by the door, then I sense him right in front of me, that heat field pulsing out as strong as ever, and feel his hands on my arms.

"Mindy," he says uncertainly, and then his mouth is on mine. I feel the warmth in my body coiling, shaping itself around our linked mouths. His arms hold me in a tight envelope, and I circle my arms around him, giving in to our combined heat. Oh no, the crutches! I feel one of them flailing out away from me. I pull my face away from his.

"Don't let me fall!" I half-whisper. Getting used to the darkness, I see his face so close to mine, studying me, a look of worry. Still gripping me around the arms, he half pulls, half turns me, propelling us toward the nearest bed. My feet seem to walk with him, then we thud together onto the mattress.

We lie there in silence, still holding on to each other. My backpack hangs off one elbow, and I shake it free. I start to laugh.

"Damn, we're klutzy!"

"Who's a klutz?" he sputters. He leans in and kisses me again, this time so long that I feel that line of heat coiling, then pulling taut, up from between my legs. His hand moves across one of my breasts, feeling its way under the tight edge of the uniform. My boobs are hot too. I want this uniform off. I could use one of those voice-activated tunics right now. I reach around to the back, try to guide his hand—"The zipper, there"—till he finally manages to get it partway down and I slide an arm out of one sleeve. He unbuttons his tunic. We're lying, chest to sweaty chest, his hand traveling over my skin. I'm breathing fast. Len slips his hand into the waistband of my pants.

The light snaps on above us. It's Vlad, his giant bearded self looming in the doorway. We grapple our way to a half-sitting position on the bed. I pull the tunic up so it's at least covering me.

"Oh shit, I'm sorry, man," Vlad says.

"It's okay." Len presses his eyes.

"It was dark in here—"

"It's *okay*, dude. We came up here—"

"I wasn't feeling well." That sounds pretty ridiculous.

"I just came in to get my six-pack," Vlad persists. "The contest's almost over." With his mane of hair and beard surrounding his mournfully apologetic eyes, his face transformed by the makeup and nose bones, he reminds me of the Cowardly Lion.

"I wanted to be ready for when they give out the prizes downstairs. You guys are definitely gonna win something," he says, kind of tiptoeing, if that's possible for him, to a corner of the room. He pulls a six-pack from the mini-fridge and holds it high, saluting us. His hand almost bumps the ceiling.

"See you guys later." He backs out the door.

"Jeez, I'm a fucking moron," Len says, his hand on his forehead. "There must be three or four people with keys, I wasn't thinking—"

"Hey, it's okay." This seems like a good time to pull my sleeve back on.

"I wasn't even sure—"

"What?" I ask.

"You know, with your—" he nods his head toward my legs, then grimaces. "Forget it."

Oh.

"It's my legs that don't move. Otherwise I work fine." At least as far as I can tell. He nods his head, looking at the floor.

"We should probably go back down," I say, twisting myself to sit up, my back to him as I adjust my braces.

"Sure you're feeling better?"

How am I feeling? The flaming heat is all drained out, leaving me in some clammy, in-between state.

"Yeah. I'll just hit the bathroom first."

Len leans out to pick up my lost crutch, setting it discreetly next to the other one where I can reach it. Once I've done my business, we head out into the hallway. Neither one of us can look at the other or say anything. Avoiding having to admit what just happened seems to be the number one priority. The silence gets thicker as we stand waiting for the elevator. I've got to say something.

"Maybe Vlad's right, we're about to win the grand prize." My voice comes out fake-cheery.

"Santak never win the grand prize."

"Yeah, but something. We might win something."

The doors slide open. There, in the mirror, I see my face. I took off my face extension in the bathroom, so now my skin is two different colors, hot pink where the plaster was and burnt orange everywhere else. I'm half human, half alien, don't know what I am.

FROM: angiemadd1@globalnet.com
TO: MindRoid@comet.net
SUBJECT: Santak
DATE: 10/17/99 4:34 PM

Hey Girl,

Don't you look bitchin good in those pics you posted on your web page. I knew you went over to the Santak, but my eyes nearly popped when I saw you there, hardly recognized you in yr killer outfit. Stand back! I gotta get me one. And one of those tall, dark & scuzzy Santak dudes too. Do not tell me that evil looking guy standing next to you in all those pix is your boyfriend.

Just for that here I'm attaching a pic of me at the Taproom with my library buds celebrating my first nite of freedom. That's me holding up the bottle of Heiny. Also hope you noticed my new email. No more university lackey address for me.

That's right I broke out!!! Walked right out in the middle of the day. Lillian gave me some BS about not throwing away my potential when I went to get my last paycheck, but I had nothing to say to her. See, she spilled all about Catherine's letters to somebody in the PR department, and then she wrote an article for the college magazine about Catherine Weldon, Independent Nineteenth Century Woman and Friend of the Indians, and how great that we found her original letters. Guess who is never even mentioned in the article. That's right, I got wrote out of that history. ;-/ Then she makes a little exhibit with the letters. She puts them in the glass cases and invites all the Deans etc. to come to a reception. Angie, she says, I think you should wear a dress that day. That did it. This is My Catherine Weldon she's talking about! Maybe if she thanked me just one time. I know Catherine would not have had anything to do with anybody like Lillian. That's why she went out to the Rez in the first place, to get away from all the goddamn Lillians everywhere.

Meanwhile, Hank is applying for teaching jobs for next year, the history department isn't hiring. So he's going to some conference next month for interviews, which he is all in a twist about. BUT he wants me to come with him wherever he gets hired. We have gotten kinda serious more than I did with any guy in a while. And I'm like, no way I am moving out of Normal to some even tinier college town out in the sticks. If I leave here it's for a major zipcode or a cemetery. This is really tearing me up Mindy.

I know I'm throwing excuses at you for not sending you anything. I thought I'd get a story going with Catherine, but it never came together. Even tho I can't stop thinking about her and the Ghost Dance. Where I got to was, what if the Ghost Dancers were right and they really were messing with things e.g. the laws of physics, and somehow the dancing really did open this wormhole for the ghosts to come back through. Stranger things have happened in SkyLog right? I'm talking about a vortex, some kind of spinning energy bringing in the ghosts. But maybe the vortex doesn't open right. So there they are, the ghosts pounding on the barrier between the worlds, circling in the air screaming and chattering, why can't they come thru and join their families who are still alive? What would all this mean to Catherine then? What if it really went down the way Im saying, am I going nuts here thinking like this? Gives me the shivers thinking about it.

Anyway I'm definitely going to the Con in Chicago next week. By myself. Then I don't know, I might really take off. I got enough to get thru the next couple months, & I can always go back to waiting tables. It seems like I haven't done much w my life so far, didn't even finish my degree. Maybe it really is time 4 me to get out of town.

Be good now,

Angie

I open the attachment, and my old modem slowly coughs the photo up onto the screen. There she is, standing in the middle of four or five others at the bar—skinny girl holding her beer high. Big crooked smile, sad eyes, face drained by the flash. Looking straight at me. We've never met, I mean, our bodies have never been in the same space. Right now I wish we could be in the same room somewhere, sharing a beer. It would be easier to talk than to figure out what to say in an email. Everything she said leaves me feeling weird, like pins and needles inside and out. How do I explain what's going on with Len, when I can't figure it out myself! Nobody's said anything about boyfriend and girlfriend—he called me yesterday, but all we talked about was how many cases of beer he should bring on Saturday, and was Rolling Rock okay. Is it a fluke what happened in the hotel room? I don't know, I've got nothing to compare it to. This was my first experience with another human. With Roi, it always happens the way I want it to, I don't have to question anything about the sex or anything else. I know I felt something with Len. I keep going back to our kissing, how I felt it all the way up and down. But am I really completely functional with another person, in real life?

FROM: MindRoid@comet.net
TO: angiemadd1@globalnet.com
SUBJECT: Re: Santak
DATE: 10/17/99 6:02 PM

Angie,

No, that's not my *BOYFRIEND*, I'll be sure and let you know if and when I get one of them. It's just Len, the guy from the Lrak who's also really into Buckminster Fuller. I will admit it's a lot more fun being a Santak at the Con. You should try it—I'm sure they'd make you an honorary member if you come for the Philly Con next year!

Hey, you've been dealing with a crapstorm of stuff. I'm in no position to give relationship advice, or job advice for that matter. But no worries on the Catherine story. In fact, I have a confession—your Catherine seems to have tangled herself up in a story I'm working on. When you first told me about her, I felt like I knew her already, and now her Ghost Dance adventure seems to be worming its way into this thing I've got going in the SkyLog universe. You probably don't remember, but I had some stories in the first few issues of the Voice. Then I stopped writing, for various reasons. So I guess I should thank you. I'm not planning to show this story to anyone, so don't ask to see it. And please don't tell anybody, I'm just not ready to deal with any reactions from other folks. People can be cruel. Just wanted to tell you thanks for the inspiration.

Have a gr8 time at the Con, send lots of pictures!

- Mindy

The sentry sees me walking nearer, and stands up on the rocky outcrop. She's young and afraid. I hold my hands out and smile without showing teeth, making the "approaching friend" sounds I've learned. She says something, but I can't hear over the shrill of the wind. I yell out a greeting.

"I'm just taking a walk!" I shout. I keep walking, but slower. My weapon is far more powerful than hers, but her spear could kill me. If I could just stand up there beside her, see what she sees. When I woke up this morning, everyone was gone except for one left to watch me. The guard followed me out here, I feel his eyes on my back. I'm afraid they've gone off to carry out the plan the Old One hinted about to me, the one that would keep the Mowg from taking over their home. There's no time for that now. I have to find them.

I greet the sentry by name. She relaxes just enough that I feel it's safe to pick my way up the rocks and join her at the top of the crag. We look out on the plateau, on the winding cracks of the chasm that is her home, and past that, the line of the mountains. This is close to where I stood when I first came to this planet. It looks the same, but my feelings are so different: love for this place that is the people's home, and fear for it.

There's a faint dark spot on the plain, moving near the foot of a mountain. It's coming from the direction of the Mowg operation. They're on their way. I don't know if their convoy is bringing negotiators, mining equipment, weapons or all three. I look back at the little sentry—she's seen it too.

"Where is everybody?" I ask, but she doesn't answer. I have to find them, have to warn them now. I slide my weapon out, hiding it behind my leg, finger the setting to flare, and fire it out to one side. The sizzle and flashing halo of light grab the sentry's attention, and she slides down the outcrop so fast I lose sight of her. I run to the other side, hoping the flare distracted the one who followed me here too, then clamber down the rocks and start making my way down a narrow gully. I can't hear anything over the wind, but there's a pulsing vibration, a thudding coming up from the ground. It reminds me of the insistent clank of the Mowg's mining equipment, but it can't be that, they're still too far away. Could the People be producing this sound? I go faster, my senses tuned high, taking forks in the gully as I try to follow a small, rising thread of sound.

FROM: tadmesh@deepnet.com
TO: MindRoid@comet.net
SUBJECT: deep thoughts
DATE: 10/19/99 7:49 PM

Mindy or should I call you Nechut,

I've been doing a lot of thinking since the Con. It was really fun and interesting, and it got me started on a whole new idea. Its related, but much much bigger. I feel like I am finally starting to see the big picture. After I finish Shadow of the Mesh, I will try to write some of this stuff down. Maybe it will be a nonfiction SkyLog book. Well, its SkyLog, but it will be more than SkyLog. It is all working out in my mind. You are one of the few persons I know of that can maybe understand. Most fans are not ready to follow to this level, now I see that. And I am including the Lrak membership, except you and me, in this.

What I am working on is a new theory for how all different kinds of beings can coexist. The Transortium way is tolerance, you know, like Policy One, non-interference and respect for someone else's society. The Mesh way is like the opposite of that, with Taking of individuals by force and Enmeshment with the Parents, and destroying the ability to act on there emotions.

My idea is right between those two, a synthesis of both but it gets rid of the Mesh use of force. I call it Voluntary Immersion. I think it would require some kind of treaty among all the different known planets. Then all the treaty signers would have to set up a mega computer Bank, I would call it the Universal Genetic Sort, or Universal Genetic Sharing System or UGS, either way. All the different characteristics of all beings from the known planets would be entered in the UGS. That could take a while, it's hard to tell with 23rd century computing power, but there would be an agreed upon deadline to get this done. Then a council of appointed beings of many species would program the UGS computer. It would be instructed to mix genetic characteristics among different species. But not so that everyone would come out the same. In some cases the computer would look to strengthen different species by putting in things that one doesn't have, like giving the analytical power of the Wuvians to the Frint. In some cases it would swap things between warring species, so like the Santak would become more calculating like the Mowg, and the Mowg would be more courageous like the

Santak. And of course they would end up looking more alike too. Santak will have slightly pointy chins and Mowg will have slightly bumpy nose bones. And the Demetrians would have scalier skin and the Algor would get more religious. And then there might be some random mixing until everyone is involved, Terrans of course, and everyone from the smallest to the largest planets, from the simplest to the most advanced societies.

Now you may be thinking That's a very Big Project Tad, but it is really only the beginning. After all we can't leave out the artificial lifeforms and cyborg races. The Mesh must not be kept out. Once the Project is underway, someone must try to persuade them that the only way to adapt with other beings is as partners, not as prey. I know, the Mesh might look at the UGS like a picnic, sort of a freeze-dried meal of mixed-up species for the Taking. But they have to be included. It might take like a single brave soul infiltrating the Mesh collective, agreeing to be adapted the Mesh way to bring this new idea in. The truth is that we need them. Every kind of consciousness needs to be part of this Project for it to work. Don't you agree Mindy. You have been sympathetic to the Cyborg for a long time. This is just a brief summary, I've already written a lot of pages about it. My mind is speeding up, there's a lot more than this. I can't talk to anyone else, I tried telling my Dad but he just said write it down, he doesn't really know enough about SkyLog to follow what I am thinking about.

Please, let me know what you think, maybe it can be in your zine as like an article.

Abundant Life,

Chumak (Tad)

p.s. My Dad and I can come to your party.

Wow. There's too much here for me to deal with right now. I know some fans have gone full-on encyclopedic: trying to work out the exact steps in the future timeline to line up the chronology of the two shows and the movies, or to explain the core advances in physics necessary to back up metaspace transport and such. But Tad seems to be groping toward some grand unifying theory of SkyLog species. And he's wrong about me, I just have an average grasp of things—I was always more interested in the stories than anything else. That's why I'm still missing that SkyLog compendium, for when I need to check how things work. I did a thorough search, even got the flashlight and maneuvered it behind my bookshelf and under the bed. I found the missing *Amazing Stories*, but the compendium is gone. It must have been Sheryl who took it, that last time she was here. I'm wishing now I hadn't invited her to the party.

22

"MINDY!" MY MOTHER'S shouting from the kitchen.

"What now!" I'm in the bathroom in front of the mirror.

"Where's the toothpicks?"

I made the mistake of trying to put on some of Ma's eyeliner. I look like a hooker.

"I can't find the toothpicks!"

I give up. I rub the washcloth over my eyes. Now I look like I've been crying.

In the kitchen, Ma's rifling through the junk drawer. She's got on her big yellow shirt pulled in with a wide belt, a variant on her favorite Mary outfit, over metallic-sheen leggings.

"Why do we need toothpicks?"

She turns around to see me standing there on my crutches, and her face softens.

"Honey! Look at you!" She comes in for a close look, strokes my arm. "You look beautiful!" I'm wearing my new heather-gray top with my best black pants, even have the new scarf looped around my neck. She's smiling but looks like she's going to cry.

"Do you think the scarf is too much?" I ask. She fingers it.

"No, honey, it's great." Then she remembers: "I have to roll up the ham slices and put toothpicks through them."

"Forget it, Ma. Just put the ham out like it is." These are Santak we're talking about. Most of them, anyway. I catch myself in the mirror by the front door and rip off the scarf. That's better, the stand-up collar's enough.

The living room looks so weird—just furniture, not a single knick-knack. A bunch of the boxes are gone, transported to New Jersey. It's too empty, like we don't really live here. Like the wind's blown everything away. What was I thinking, throwing a party now? My stomach and my throat seem to have changed places, and now they're doing a slow, low-gravity somersault around my solar plexus. They've been performing this trick on and off for a couple of days since the reality of having the party hit me.

"The cookies!" Ma's standing there with a big Acme bag of chocolate chip cookies.

"I'll do it." I take the bag. "Parties make me so nervous!" she calls, retreating into the kitchen. Her semi-hysteria is just background noise to me—familiar, almost soothing, in the middle of everything else. I pour the cookies onto a paper plate. She latched right onto the party idea, first figuring it to be a going-away celebration for the two of us. After a couple of tense phone calls with Irv, she backed off and agreed I can stay here for a month or so till we figure things out. Irv said he'd come over a few nights a week, do errand duty and stuff, since it's so hard for me to get anywhere myself. Whether we'll be able to keep the house is still up in the air.

The paper cups—oh God, what else have we forgotten? Cookies, ham, kaiser rolls. Chips. Trish is bringing her special guacamole, which has some Santak name. One case each of Sprite and Coke. Bag of ice—damn, it's still in the freezer.

"Ma, I need a hand with the ice!" Will Len remember to bring the beer chilled? I tell myself he always does what he says.

Before I changed, I pulled up the A.L.L. home page on my monitor so people can see it, even printed out a few pages to put out with the copies of the first issue. That's what we're really celebrating. I was going to ask Len to bring the computer out to the living room, or Irv, but neither of them is here yet. Or Zu—she was supposed to come early to set up her electronics.

The doorbell rings. I open it to see Roxie and Morris standing in the darkness, Morris hefting a big foil-covered tray. As they come in, Morris pecks me on the cheek.

"I brought my sweet and sour meatballs," Roxie says. She directs Morris toward the kitchen, then looks me up and down, pursing her lips. "Very nice."

"You too, Rox." Tonight she's almost all in black: under her shaggy faux-fur black jacket, she wears a silky black Chinese blouse and nubbly gaucho pants, set off by her little white boots. She's holding something too, a sort of branching sculpture with things hanging off it like Christmas decorations.

"What's that?"

"A little house gift. You attach it to a lamp."

"Thanks, Roxie." It's a real piece of art, I decide—mine, not Janine's. Even if I have no idea how to put it up.

"Where's Leonard? He said he'd help with it."

My windpipe does another half-knot. Len will be here soon. He'll see me in my fancy outfit, my face with the wiped-off eyeliner. Roxie lays her artwork on the coffee table and follows Morris into the kitchen. There's the doorbell again. I let out a deep breath, sure it's him. But no, it's Zu and Trish, laden with the keyboard, a mini-amp and two bags, one with cables, one with food.

"Sorry, we got held up," Zu says, a little breathless.

"I'm just the roadie!" Trish gives me an apologetic smile, waving the mini-amp as they come in. Since she was helping Zu with her equipment, she couldn't get here early to help set up. I'm still getting used to Trish being Zu's music entourage instead of Bradley. He's supposed to be coming with his girlfriend, whom none of us has met, so he's excused from the band tonight.

Back in the kitchen, Morris has set the tray of meatballs on the crowded table.

"You can just put it out in the dining room," I tell him.

"Wait!" Roxie swoops in, spears a meatball on a toothpick and holds it inches from my mouth. "Try it," she orders. I hate when people feed me, but I let her pop it into my mouth, where on first bite it explodes with a dark sweet savoriness.

"Well?" Her face, with the big red-framed glasses, looms up at me.

"Mm." I swallow. "Amazingly amazing."

"A little horseradish, a little molasses. The rest is a family secret."

"Will somebody please—" my mother pleads. She's wrestling with the congealed bag of ice, flopping it on the counter like a big fish. "I need a hammer. Mindy!"

"Dad should be here any minute, Ma." Whacking stuff with a hammer is Irv's department. She gives me a sidelong glance. She wasn't happy when I told her I invited him. It's like she's been avoiding him as she gets closer to moving.

"Well, I need some help right now," she insists.

"Hold on." The hammer should be in the hall closet unless it's already been carted off to New Jersey. The doorbell rings. Trish gets the door: it's Len, finally. A case of beer under each arm, and wearing a crooked smile. Then Tad appears beside him on the step, his *Century 23* tunic showing under his down jacket. He still looks almost bald from the sheared-down haircut he got for the Con. His dad hovers right behind.

"Hey, little buddy!" Len nudges Tad on the shoulder, which gets a shy smile out of him. "This guy's our main man, our faithful Mesher mascot!" He looks straight at me, his face completely unguarded and raw for one second, then his eyes slide into the room.

"Hey. You got some ice for this?" he asks. I smell beer on his breath.

I point him toward the kitchen. Standing there, I feel deflated. Of course when I got dressed up I was thinking of him, and when I tried to lay on the makeup. This is the first time I've seen him since the Con, and we haven't talked about what happened in the hotel room. I don't know how to do this.

"I'm Dan Fishkin." Tad's dad extends his hand, rescuing me—who knows what my face was doing.

"Yeah, I've seen you around." Shaking hands at the same level is one of the nicer things about being on crutches. "You a SkyLog fan yourself?"

"Nothing like Tad."

"Yeah, well. He's a role model for all of us." I turn to look at

Tad, who's wandering into my bedroom, still with his coat on, probably drawn by the SkyLog memorabilia.

"I know he's been enjoying—" Mr. Fishkin's words are submerged under the first chords from Zu's keyboard. I nod and smile. In spite of the volume, these sounds are tentative for Zu: a wash of sliding non-harmonies and whistling tones. An unrelated thwacking sound carries over the music.

"I'm gonna check the kitchen!" I enunciate to Mr. Fishkin. In there, Len's hacking at the ice in the sink with a kitchen knife. My mother watches him, dragging on her cigarette. Roxie sits at the table holding an opened beer.

"Leonard to the rescue," she says. "What would we do without you?" He stops his whacking, cocks his head back toward her.

"I'm sure you'd do fine, Roxie." Shouting over the music.

Roxie turns to me. "Did he tell you how nice you look?"

"Roxie!" I explode with embarrassment. My mother giggles uncomfortably. Len sinks the knife in a chunk of ice, turns back toward us. He looks at me without meeting my eyes, nods his head slowly. "Looking good, Mindy." Now I'm embarrassed for him, forced into this dumbshow. Roxie simpers. Len returns to his hacking, looking grim.

"You need a beer, Mindy," Roxie announces. "Leonard, give her one of them." He's started setting beer bottles among the ice chunks.

"Not now," I say. I'm mad at her. Plus, I've planned my consumption for tonight carefully: two beers total, slow sips. My mother takes the beer instead and sits down with Roxie, who looks past me to the doorway. It's Irv standing there, holding a white bakery box.

"Dad, this is Roxie. The artist I've been telling you about." They do an old-school greeting and handshake.

"And that's Len." What do I call him? "From the Lrak." Len wipes his hands on his jeans and offers a handshake too.

"I brought this." Irv puts the box down. "From Barsky's. Your favorite," he says, meaning mine, so I know it's a mocha cream layer cake. He stands there, unsure which way to face—my mother is pointedly not looking at him.

"You know what, Dad," I say, "Roxie needs some help with this thing she brought, hanging it on the lamp."

"Is he handy?" she asks me.

"Beyond handy."

She hoists herself from the chair and pulls Irv into the living room. Janine comes out of her frozen stare. "I just can't deal with your father right now."

"Give me a break! He has as much right to be here—"

"Things are different now," she hisses.

"This is my party."

"And with Nick coming—"

"What?"

"I told you! Don't you remember?" Maybe she did. I've been tuning her out more, I admit. "He should have been here already." She looks toward the front door.

"Fine. So they'll both be here."

"He said he was bringing a cake for you too." She sounds plaintive. "A big birthday cake."

"Ma! I told you, this is not a birthday party!" Len's taking this in, a beer in one hand. I never mentioned my birthday to him.

"But it's so close, honey!" Her face is puckered, near tears.

"This is to celebrate my zine," I say deliberately. "And my new website. Not leaving town. Not my birthday." But an actual birthday cake is hard to contradict.

"He's just trying to be nice to you!" She's close to maximum shrill. The doorbell rings, thank God.

"Maybe that's him now!" She dashes out with her cigarettes, leaving just Len and me there. Our bodies facing each other. Even with the table between us, I feel that heat again, the solar flare that started when we were in the elevator at the Con. Okay, it wasn't a fluke, it was real, and it's still there. But I can't deal with this now. I angle myself slightly away from him. Len holds a beer out toward me, and I take it.

"So. Your birthday's a big secret, huh?" He leans against the counter.

"Not anymore."

"When is it?"

"Two weeks." I take a long pull on the beer, breaking my own rule. The sounds from the next room have ratcheted up a notch, talking and laughter riding on Zu's long smears of sound. I think I hear Roger's voice.

"So what's the problem? Is this one of those disability-activist things, you don't do birthdays?"

"Can you just drop that?" Talking, I don't feel that dangerous undertow pulling between us as much.

"What then?"

"Birthday parties are stupid."

"So don't have a party."

"Try telling that to my mother."

He nods. "How about, instead of a party," he says, "I take you for a ride on my bike for your birthday." He shoots me an uncertain look from under his eyebrows. In spite of this, a laugh bursts out of me, and a little spew of beer.

"No way am I getting on your bike," I get out. "Not to diss the bike in any way."

"Oh, right. You're scared of the Harley."

"I am not!" Wait—did he just ask me out on a date? Maybe I messed things up already. Why couldn't he have suggested a movie?

"I just think four wheels are better than two."

"I'm not talking about a damn bicycle."

"Still. Four wheels makes a lot more sense, for transportation."

"Mm." He swigs the last of his beer. "But a bike ride, see, that's for fun. We could go anywhere you want." We look at each other. His eyes slide down to my chest, and I feel like my clothes all just slid off. That heat radiating between us, pulsing like a heartbeat. Say something, Mindy.

"I don't know. November's not exactly motorcycle weather."

"That's a crock. And a good biker can handle any weather. Which I am."

"Hey guys! Great party!" It's Vlad, looming in the kitchen doorway with his usual excellent timing. "I brought a couple packs." He swings two six-packs of Red Dog onto the counter.

"Dude!" Len greets him. Vlad thumps his chest and throws us both a Santak salute. My body vibrates, like we were in a car that just stopped.

"You guys! Best Tableau prize at the Con!" That gets a self-conscious laugh out of Len. We won a gift certificate to Doug and Peggy's sci-fi bookstore to split between the five of us. Since that made no sense, we gave it to Tad. The grand prize, lunch with the guy who played the rogue Gonfarian on the first SkyLog, went to Gina Culbertson as the Grand Mus Davro, of course. Our moment on the stage floods back to me, all the heat and brilliance of it.

Bradley's arrived, and I go out to greet him. He introduces me to his girlfriend, Bianca. She's beautiful. Hair pulled back, honey-glowing skin, long neck—a swan with every feather in place. Bradley helps her get her coat off and takes it to the bedroom.

"Sorry about the noise!" I look around for somewhere to put her. While I was in the kitchen, the place mysteriously turned into a party. Empty before, now it's full. Zu's collage of sounds merges with the din of voices. Roger is here, and new guy Kevin. Roxie's artwork jiggles over the lamp, where Irv attached it with an artfully twisted coat hanger. It's sending wobbly shadows of astronauts and dinosaurs onto the wall. And there's Jennifer, my physical therapist! She's with a gorgeous guy, all muscle and good posture—bet he's a PT too. They're talking to my mother.

"Hey, you made it," I say to Jennifer.

"Mindy! This is great!" Her blonde hair bounces around her face. Then, with a shy smile, "This is Johnny. Johnny, Mindy." He grips me with a killer handshake. I invited Dr. O'Malley too, but she couldn't make it. I decide to let Janine monopolize them for now. Everywhere I look are strange people mash-ups: Morris and Roger chatting away by the chips and ham. Tad's dad talking with Irv. Roxie on the couch, deep in conversation with Tad. Vlad, going solo around the room with an armful of beer bottles.

"Party time!" Like a gracious host, Vlad offers a bottle to each guest. Big as he is, he's hard to refuse. I make my way to the couch, where Roxie's just accepted a beer from him. Roxie pats the sofa for me to sit down.

"The kid's got a whole theory," she tells me.

"I worked out the fundamentals," Tad says. "But there's a lot more to fill in." It's actually easier to hear his voice over the party noise since it's pitched higher than anyone else's.

"Sounds like a book," Roxie says. Tad's last, long email comes back to me.

"Maybe." He nods. "Nobody's ever written a book on comparative alien metabolisms and genetic makeup. I have to get it all tabulated before I can spell out the strategy for the Universal Genetic Sort. This is as far as I've gotten." He reaches into his pocket for a folded wad of paper, smooths it out and holds it up for us. It's really two papers taped together, covered with a dense growth of penciled names in boxes—looks like every SkyLog species is there—and curving arrows with their own captions, crisscrossing, erased and written over. Some of the boxes and arrows inked over in red, blue, green, black. Roxie adjusts her red glasses and leans forward to examine it.

"That's wild." She shakes her head slowly. "It's not a book, it's a painting."

"I'm still working on it." Tad seems to be trembling with the weight of all the information he's pulling together, on the verge of spilling over. This part didn't come through in his email, and it scares me a little.

"Look, Tad." I need to head him off. "I hope you don't get too far from the main question: what happens when Santak join with the Mesh?"

"Pak will be finding that out. Very soon."

"I thought maybe you forgot about him."

"Oh no." He shakes his head. "Pak's over here, and the Universal Genetic Sort is over here." He shapes two nebulous areas on either side of his head. "There may be a little leakage between them, but mostly they're going along fine on their own. Am I making myself clear?" His dark eyes on mine, lips tight, light shining on his buzzcut head.

"I think so." But I feel like Tad's central engineering is overextended. Can he keep this all going without some full-scale fuel-matrix meltdown? Still, looking at the tangled weave of species on his diagram, I feel stirred up too. The relationships among different lifeforms, especially between organic and non-carbon-based entities—that's where I've spent a lot of my time. Maybe Tad can figure it all out! He's sucking me into the gathering force field of his ideas in spite of myself.

"Just promise me." Roxie waves the paper at Tad. "When you're done with this diagram, get me a copy. Preferably in color." He nods, folding it back into a pocket-size package. The doorbell rings again. I hike myself up, but Len's already opening the door. It's Sheryl. Jesus, I really didn't think she'd come. With that guy Eric at her side. She's wearing a fuzzy red sweater, probably from last Christmas, and he's in a black turtleneck. She gives Len a wary look.

"Hey, Mindy," he shouts. "It's your old pal!" Sheryl puts on a tight smile and moves toward me, with Len a little behind her doing recon. Oh God, she's gonna give me a hug. She widens her arms just enough and barely presses into me. Her being so close, and in my house, makes me feel sick to my stomach. Now I'm sure—it was Sheryl who took my SkyLog compendium. I lean away from her, setting my crutches back a bit so I don't lose my balance.

Eric holds out a bottle of wine in a tall paper wine bag, which I take by the handles.

"Congratulations on your launch," he says. My launch—I forgot to get somebody to bring the computer out from my room! I point them toward the food and turn to Len, finding myself inches from his chest. I take a breath.

"I was gonna hook up the computer in here, so people could see the website."

He frowns. "What about the modem?" I point toward the end table, where the house phone sits. He heads for my bedroom. I move toward the kitchen, holding tight to the bottle of wine.

"Can I give you a hand?" It's Tad's dad, standing at the entrance to the kitchen. I hand him the bottle, relieved. "I think there's a corkscrew in there." He retrieves it from the junk drawer.

"Tad speaks very highly of you." He scrunches his face, working the cork out. He's got a little gray in his beard and mixed into his hair.

"Well, he's pretty cool himself." I lean back against the counter. I'm on overload, can't believe I can still put a sentence together.

"I know he can get kind of intense. We really appreciate you and Roger and the others putting up with him." He pours wine into a coffee cup.

"It's not like that! He's a great kid!"

He offers me the cup, but I shake my head no.

"His mother's worried about him. I tell her it's okay as long as he does his schoolwork. But then, where do you draw the line? He reads it, he writes it, he dresses it, he's online with it—like it's colonized his whole, um, mental geography." He lifts the cup, drains it in one swallow.

"Well, he's writing great stuff for my zine."

"Tad's really the same as his mother, that's the problem." Maybe he didn't hear me, with our voices cocooned in the noise of the party. "Sasha fell into her Ph.D. thesis like it was a black hole, when Tad was a toddler. And now that she's up for tenure, I mean, you know how that is."

I nod, even though I don't know how that is.

"She says the Provost has it in for her. I keep telling her it'll all work out, even if we have to move somewhere else. We just have to get through the next few months." He stares at the bottle, pours more wine in his cup. "I shouldn't be telling you this." I agree with him there. He downs the wine.

"Bottom line, things are fairly tense at home. So it's good for him to get out of the house."

I'm feeling majorly uncomfortable. He nods and lifts the cup to drink as I excuse myself and turn back toward the din in the living room.

Len's across the room, setting the monitor and keyboard on the phone table. I scooch around a knot of people clustered at the food, including Kevin and Bradley, who's got his arm around Bianca's waist. By the time I get to Len, he's squatting next to the table, fiddling with wires.

"Everything cool?" I yell over the noise, which seems to have reached peak decibel level, but he doesn't hear me. I look around. Tad's standing next to the couch, talking to Eric. Sheryl leans against the wall, her face a pale mask, with Vlad looming over her. He's got his flannel shirtsleeve pulled up to show her the tattoo of a Santak Raptor on his massive forearm. Roxie still commands the couch, sharing it with Roger now, and Trish perches on the arm next to him. Roxie waves me back over, and I lower myself down next to her. This is it. I'm not getting up from here again.

"Roger's been telling me about the invisibility effect they have for the Santak rocket ships," Roxie says.

"Well, I wouldn't call them rocket ships," Roger says.

"Do you think you could get me a model of one of them?" Roxie goes on. "I like that invisibility idea. That might go with my new piece."

"She's cute," Trish says to me. "Is she your grandma?"

"I wish. Actually, she's my fashion consultant."

"She's doing a nice job." Trish looks me up and down, which makes me self-conscious.

"And she's an artist," I say. "How's it going, Roxie?"

"Don't ask." Roxie downs the last of her Red Dog. Her face is pink and puffy. "I don't think I'll ever get it to work. Usually that's a good sign. But this time I think I really blew it."

"She might be having a show in Philly," I tell them.

"Where?" Trish asks.

"Highly doubtful. Well, I did call Marsha Biderman."

"That's great, Rox!" I say. "What'd she say?"

"I'm gonna go see her at the gallery next week. I don't know." She shakes her head. "When I called her, I was feeling a lot better about the work."

"That doesn't matter," I say. "You've got all that other great stuff you can show her." She fans her hand, dismissing me.

"All right, we're on!" It's Len, standing back from the computer. He gives me a thumbs-up. I can just make out the gold letters of my home page banner, surrounded by star-studded space.

"Is that it, your website?" Roxie says. "You should get up and say something." I make a face, embarrassed, not wanting to get off the couch again. The music shifts into a nonharmonic but still recognizable fanfare, then down to a buzzing drone. Roger smiles at me, one eyebrow raised. Vlad starts a chant—"Min-dy!

Min-dy!"—and the other Santak join in. Everybody's looking at me. Janine, with Morris over by the bedroom hallway, looks weepy around her smile. My dad watches from near the door. They've managed to stay on opposite sides of the room so far. Len reaches to help me up off the couch. I move over to the table with the computer and the zines.

"I'm just glad you all can be here," I start, but now I'm feeling weepy too, and hyper-aware of the room's fullness in contrast to how empty it was just a few hours ago. It's so confusing. Breathe out now. Locate my Commander voice. "Glad you could come and give the new zine and the website a good sendoff. And thanks to the people who helped me get it done, you know who you are." I find Zu's eyes, then Bradley's—he gives a wide smile. "Anyway, I think it's gonna be great, so check it out." A scattering of hoots and applause, and then a clutch of tech nerds gathers at the screen—Eric and Tad, Len, Kevin. Huddled with the others in the screen glow, Tad looks somehow normal again, an almost-teenage boy.

"It looks really nice, Mindy." It's Sheryl. She's materialized beside me.

"Thanks." I do not want to talk to her.

"Is the website sponsored by the Lrak?"

"Not really." Like I couldn't do it myself, she's insinuating. "It's really my thing, the website and the zine. They're just helping out if I need anything." She nods, still looking at the screen.

"Websites are a lot of work," she says. As usual, her needling is so stealthy, an outside observer might not even notice. But I know: she's jealous of this thing I've done. She wants it for herself. It's happening again. No.

"You took my 20th Anniversary SkyLog compendium, didn't you?"

Her eyes dart away and then back. "What? I don't know what you mean."

"Yes you do. You slipped it in your bag when we were in my room, working on the last issue." Her face makes me sure I'm right. "Real smooth, Sheryl."

Her mouth opens, then tightens. "That's a terrible thing to

say. I hold myself to the highest standards . . ." She goes on, but what she just said slows me down. All the sounds in the room fall away as I feel something dislodging in my mind.

"It was you." It's hard for me to talk, my heart is pounding in my throat.

"I told you, Mindy—I'd never—"

"No, it was you," I cut her off. "You're the True SkyLog Fan." The Goddamn True SkyLog Fan—my anonymous, secret non-admirer, the one who wrote me those nasty letters, dissing my writing, while insisting I should hold myself to the "highest standards" as an editor and reject my own stuff. So fricking devious. And she succeeded—it was Sheryl who got me to stop writing my fanfic.

She blinks, shakes her head. "No . . ."

"You were jealous of my writing too! You took my book, and you took my club, and you"—I'm short of breath, almost gasping—"you took away my writing too!"

She blinks faster.

"Maybe I should put your old letters up on the website, let people see what kind of writer you are!" Although I can't do that, I threw the letters away.

"Mindy . . ." Her face crumpling. I see everything perfectly clear now, but I have to take a few breaths before I can talk again.

"What you did"—I try to keep my voice quiet—"that was totally despicable, you know that?" Up till now, the ambient party noise must have given us some privacy, but the edge in my voice gets the attention of the guys around the computer.

Her mouth is working. "We have to go." She ducks her head, grabs onto Eric's arm.

"No. He can stay."

"But he's my ride!" We're locked in a multi-pronged laser stare: me, Sheryl, Eric, and now Len.

"Whatever." I just don't want to look at her anymore. She scurries away to get her coat. I watch Len escort them out, then make my way back to the couch and fall back into the space next to Roxie.

"I don't like her attitude." Roxie says this the way my mom would, *atteetude.* "She's a tight-ass." She followed the whole thing, the gist of it anyway. I'm still in shock, my insides vibrating, trying to take in what just happened.

"Hey! Big guy!" Roxie waves her beer bottle toward Vlad, who's standing on the edge of the computer crowd. She calls to him till he turns. "How about another one?"

"Sure thing." He heads for the kitchen.

"Roxie." It's Morris. "I think you've had enough, babe."

"Don't tell me I've had enough." Her voice goes a notch louder.

"You know what the doctors said."

"They don't know a thing!" Her face is a higher pink. "Let's ask Leonard. Leonard!" Len turns around from the screen. "Do you think I can handle one more beer?" Len gives one of his big toothy smiles.

"Oh yeah, Rox! You can handle whatever you want!" How does Roxie make him so stupid? Vlad hands her the beer with a flourish and a half-bow. It's like she's got them all hypnotized.

"Maybe we should go home now." Morris's face is grim. He hooks a hand on her arm.

"Go away! You're spoiling everything!" She says this loud enough to hush the flow of talk for a teetering moment, till it picks up again.

"All right, all right. But we'll go soon," he says.

My mother rushes up. "Is everything okay here? Who needs another drink?"

The doorbell rings. Irv opens the door—it's Nick. He steps inside holding a huge, flat bakery box. My father doesn't move. The two men look at each other for a long moment. They've never met. Then Nick pushes past him into the room.

"Sorry I'm late, big jam-up on the Turnpike. So where's the Birthday Girl?" Nick looks around the room, then comes over to me. He slides the box onto the coffee table, pushing aside a bowl of chips and various cups and bottles, and lifts the lid.

"Many happy returns," he says to me. "I got the biggest one they had." I stare at the white-frosted monstrosity, an office-sized sheet cake with "Happy Birthday Mindy, Congrats and Many More" looping across in orange.

"This isn't a birthday party, Nick," I say, as evenly as I can. I cannot handle one more insane confrontation.

"Whoa—it's your birthday?" It's Trish. "Why didn't you tell us?"

"We need some candles here," Nick says.

"No candles. I am not blowing out candles."

"I'll go get a knife," my mother says, looking at me nervously. "And some plates. Isn't it nice, Mindy?" She brushes past Nick, through the computer crowd and then past my father, who hasn't moved from the door. Someone starts singing "Happy Birthday," and I endure it with a tight, synthflesh smile.

Janine emerges from the kitchen with a bunch of stuff: paper plates, napkins, a big knife, and what looks suspiciously like a box of birthday candles.

"She said she didn't want candles!" Irv says, louder than I've ever heard him.

"What's the big deal?" Janine glares at him. "She's got a cake, we put candles on it."

"You never listen! You never listen to anybody!" My father's voice is strained and almost hoarse, like someone who hardly ever yells. Ma clutches her stuff close, protecting herself from the angry blast. Everyone's quiet, even the music has trailed off.

"Hey now—" Nick calls. I want to say something to stop this, anything, but my face is frozen.

"Who are you to talk?" Janine's face is red, spitting this at my dad. "You walked out on us!" Irv's face shudders as if he's been hit.

"And what about you?" he gets out. "Running off with him."

"Okay, don't talk to the lady like that." Nick crosses the room to stand next to my mother. For a moment nobody moves. Then Irv pushes Nick in the chest, with both hands, hard.

"Get out!" he bellows. Nick skitters backward, half-falling into Mr. Fishkin. My mother howls and drops everything. The knife hits the floor, napkins flutter out in all directions. Nick rights himself, lunges and grabs my father's shirt, then lands a punch on his face. They claw at each other. Somehow I'm up on my feet, pushing through people, yelling—I don't know what I'm saying.

Len catches my father in a backwards hug, and Roger moves in on Nick, pulling him away. "Cool it, guys, cool it now," he chants in his singsong twang. Santak to the rescue.

"You're hurt!" Janine howls, touching my father's face. There's a trickle of blood from his nose, and one cheek is turning purple. He shakes Janine away.

"Let's wash that off." Len has a hand on Irv's shoulder, moving my dad toward the kitchen. Nick straightens himself and runs his fingers over his hair. Voices start up tentatively around the room. I'm having trouble catching my breath, for the second time tonight.

"I gotta go," Nick says, not looking at anybody.

"But you just got here," Janine pleads, following him to the door. "Don't you want some cake?"

"I don't think so." Nick's voice is flat. "I'll give you a call." Then, turning to me: "So, Happy Birthday." He walks out. Janine looks at the door, her mouth open.

"I think we should be going too." It's Mr. Fishkin, holding Tad's down jacket in his arms. "If I can peel him off the computer." Tad's back at the screen, pushing the mouse around. I hoist myself up.

"Hey, I'm sorry about all this."

"No, we just have a long drive back." His eyes don't meet mine. "Come on, big guy, time to go."

"I've got eight more sites you could link to," Tad says to me, pulling his coat on. "I can put them in right now if you want."

"Enough," his father says.

"Thanks for coming," I call after them as they walk down the dark path outside.

"C'mon, Mindy," Trish calls from the couch. "You're not letting this go to waste." She's cutting the cake in squares.

"Just—in a minute." I head back to the kitchen. Irv sits at the table, holding a lump of paper towels to his cheek. Jennifer kneels beside him, and Janine hovers behind him, but he keeps his back to her.

"Sorry, Ace." He looks up at me, his eyes big, face drooping. I want to hug him, but the logistics aren't promising.

"It's not your fault," I say. No, it's my fault. What was I thinking, letting both of them come? Ma looks like she's feeling guilty too.

"How's your nose?" I ask him.

"Nothing broken," Jennifer answers. "We put some ice on it." Good thing she's here.

"Maybe you should lie down though," I say. He's even paler than usual except for the purple blotch on one side of his face.

"I'm all right. You go on back."

Len, standing in the kitchen doorway, follows me out.

"You okay?" he asks me. I nod, can't talk around the lump in my throat. My dad standing up for me, then getting punched—something else that's never happened before, that I can barely get my mind around.

"Hey, shit happens," Len says. "Come on, this is your party."

Now it's Bradley and Bianca standing at the door, waiting to say their goodbyes. Or rather, Bradley. She's shut down, her eyes angled away from me, mouth tight.

"Sorry, we gotta go," he says, giving me a twisted, apologetic smile. At least he isn't making some fake-polite excuse.

"Thanks for coming."

I make it over to Irv's easy chair and lower myself into it. Totally wrung out. Zu's folding up her keyboard. Trish hands a cake square to Johnny the PT.

"Okay, you're next," Trish says to me. Angling her head toward Roxie, "She's out." Roxie is splayed backward on the couch, her head toward the ceiling. Morris, squeezed between Roxie and Trish, watches her red face, her features scrunched as if she's working on a problem.

"I don't like how she looks," he says.

"Roxie!" I call. "Don't you want some cake?" She breathes out hard and says something. The words all run together like she's talking in her sleep, but her throat muscles are working hard.

Len comes over. "How many beers did she have?"

"I'm not sure," Morris says.

"Three," I guess.

"Four, definitely," Trish says.

"She doesn't look good," Morris says. "Roxie, sweetie." He takes her hand. "Let's get up now." Circling her shoulders with one arm, he pulls her away from the pillows, but her head lolls backward. Another murmur-sigh escapes her.

"Just let her lie down," I say. Jennifer appears and bends down over Roxie.

"Does she have high blood pressure?" Jennifer asks in her calm, health-provider voice.

"Yes, but she's taking medication," Morris answers.

"I think you should get her looked at," Jennifer says. "She might be just knocked out. But it looks like she's having trouble swallowing."

"Oh." Morris goes still.

"You want to be sure it's not—"

"A stroke," he finishes. "Yes." No. This can't be happening, not to Roxie. There's a moment of quiet, then it seems like everybody talks at once over what to do next—let Roxie rest, call 911, get her into a car. Len plugs the phone back in and Morris reaches Roxie's doctor, who agrees she should go to the hospital. More arguing over how to get her there, with my mother providing the hysterical counterpoint. Finally Vlad lifts her gently, like a sleeping child, to carry her out to the back seat of their car. Len will follow them to the emergency room, and Jennifer and Johnny too.

I look around the room, now back to its blown-out emptiness but with a crust of discarded party stuff. The computer's reverted to my screensaver, white star-chips falling away into blackness. Oh yes, it's fine to get caught up in the vast distances of space travel, interplanetary conflicts, whirling galaxies. I can handle all that, so can Kat. What I can't seem to manage is the whirling of people in and out of my life, the motion sickness I'm feeling now like it's me whirling around with no solid grip on anything.

23

I CLUTCH AT THE ARMREST of Zu's old Toyota as it screeches back down into hover mode behind another car.

"What the hell, lady?" Zu yells at the other driver. She mutters "Women drivers" and swoops out of the lane, shifts gears and lunges forward. I set my mouth, trying to lie low. Zu groans at a line of slowpokes looming ahead of us. She jerks her head around, then zooms into the open lane and roars on. Is this what it will feel like to be on the motorcycle? Buzzing in between cars, the world rushing at us? I can't believe I actually agreed to go anywhere on the back of Len's bike. It's scary, but I'm determined not to wuss out. We agreed on an itinerary, driving down to Maryland to see my old high school—he'll get to see the Bucky dome over the gym, which is cool. The problem is, every time I think about the gym, I'm right back inside it. Watching my old classmates, the Cafeteria Girls, running around in their little blue gym suits. Instead of sitting on the sidelines, I'm standing there with Len. This is not what I want him to see.

Squealing brakes—I pitch forward so hard the seat belt zips tight across my chest. We stop way too close to the next car.

"Jeez! What's with you today?"

"Too many dumbasses on the road."

"Just slow down a little, okay?" I'm jittery enough as it is.

"You said you wanted to come," Zu says. "I would've been fine if you didn't. But you did." Now I'm ashamed for letting myself daydream about my upcoming motorcycle adventure. She's right, I'm all mixed up. One, it's hard for me to go back inside a hospital. And two, we're going to see Roxie.

"Yeah, well. She had the stroke at my party. It's the least I can do." Saying it out loud doesn't feel any better.

"Mindy, that's stupid. It could've happened anytime, you know that." She pops the gearshift and accelerates again, then slides into the exit lane. "It's just neurons and blood vessels doing their thing."

That doesn't stop me from feeling guilty. I can't quite put it together, this lingering sense that it wasn't just Roxie's neural net going haywire. There's a bigger net, and I'm connected to it somehow. I picture Roxie's new art project, all the different parts hanging, taking over her living room, overlapping, shadowing each other.

"I don't know," I try. "It seems like there's more to it than that."

"Bullshit, Mindy." She shakes her head emphatically. "A stroke is a stroke. It could hit you anytime. Your brain just shuts down."

I'm not ready to hear that. "She hasn't even started the therapy yet!" I say. Zu glances over.

"I guess so," she says flatly. Roxie couldn't talk at all, Zu reported after she visited a few days ago. I fight off a feeling of dread.

"But the point is," she picks up, "she didn't know when it would happen. Everything she was working on, her art project, it's all—" I know, it's shut down, canceled in midseason. What about her appointment with that gallery lady, Marsha Biderman—did Morris know to call her and cancel?

"We don't know that! Look, they do amazing things now." I'm not sure I want to put myself out as an example of the amazing progress they're making in modern medicine. Zu's stirred up, her face blotchy pink and white.

"You just never know, Mindy," she says finally.

"Okay, but it *was* the party from hell, you have to admit." She gives a dry laugh. "I mean, look at the aftereffects." My father black-and-blue, my mother on the outs with her boyfriend—he hasn't returned her calls since then, she doesn't know what's going on—and Roxie in the hospital. What was I thinking, trying to do something as normal as throwing a party? Then there was my discovery about Sheryl—I haven't told anyone else about that yet. No one knew about the True Fan letters except me, and it feels better to keep it secret till I figure it out. I knew I'd been screwed all along, and I don't know if this changes anything. I already started writing again, which may be the best way to leave the whole thing behind.

"Your dad getting in a fistfight—that was something." Zu's moved off the subject of Roxie, that's good. We've reached the city, and now we're hemmed in by rowhouses, stopping at every corner.

"Not to mention," I say, "Bradley's girlfriend. Now she thinks all his SkyLog friends are bat-guano crazy."

"Then you did him a favor. She thinks she's too good for him." They do make a beautiful couple, though. They even sound good, Bradley and Bianca. I look at Zu.

"Everything okay with you and Trish?"

She blows air out. "She's on me to move in with her."

"Oh! Sounds like things are getting serious."

"I guess so."

"So, are you going to?" Stay calm, Mindy. It only seems like everybody in your life is shifting around, playing some game you can't follow.

"I don't know! She's been talking about it since the Con."

"But—well, you like her, right?"

"That's not the point! It just feels like a big step. Plus, I like having my own space, where I can fool around with my sounds. I don't know if I'd be able to . . ."

I can't think what to say. All this just reminds me of what a putz I am, relationship-wise. I can't follow the ins and outs of when people are together. We've reached the hospital, and Zu maneuvers through the parking garage, looking for a space. I feel heavy, weighed down by my guilt over Roxie, and thinking about how much I fuck up when I try to be normal. When we stop, I just sit there.

Zu opens the door on my side.

"You okay, Mind?"

"Give me a sec."

"Want to wait here while I go in?" I sigh, shake my head no. She reaches over me for the crutches, holds them out. I will myself to take them. Once I'm up, it becomes easier as I switch to automatic: swing, land, place, swing, land, place. I let Zu negotiate with the humans at the lobby desk, then follow her through a succession of elevators and shiny vinyl-floored corridors. These would have been so easy, so fast with my wheels. Swing, land, place. There's a wheelchair now, but it's occupied—a frail old man, skin like crumpled paper, pushed by his middle-aged daughter. Around the corner into an even wider, bright-lit hallway, like the ship's curving corridors . . . Stop it, Mindy, concentrate. We're here. Zu opens the door to the room, holds it for me.

"Hi, you kids," says Morris, unfolding himself from a plastic chair. "You didn't have to do this." He looks awful, his little bit of white hair flying in all directions, his face shadowy with fatigue, his body more bent than usual.

"Hey, we wanted to." That sounds perkier than I meant it to. "Janine was really sorry she couldn't make it." Not exactly, but she's in no shape to cheer anyone up. Not only is Nick not returning her calls, but Irv won't come over either. She's been alternating between moaning about everything and zombie couch marathons watching back-to-back AMC or TV Land reruns.

Morris offers me his chair, but it's easier for me to stay standing.

"Look who's come to see you, Roxie!" he says. Roxie sits there, propped up. But it looks like some bad imitation of Roxie, a cheap knockoff. A tube stuck up her nose like they're trying to Enmesh her but can't do it right. She lists to one side, her weight falling on one elbow, her breasts pushing heavy against the hospital gown. One hand knotted shut. Her mouth hangs open, giving her a look of puzzlement like she's trying to remember something.

"Hey, Roxie." I hear "Good to see you" in my head, but it won't come out. Zu manages a "How you doing?" and Morris launches into a medical update, but I don't hear it. Her eyes look straight at me, or through me. Roxie, is that you? I want to believe she's hiding inside this limp puppet.

"Morris," I interrupt. My throat feels tight. "I never would have let Roxie have that many, I mean if I had known this would happen."

"Oh no, Mindy," he says. "The doctors say the alcohol most likely had nothing to do with it. Things like this have their own schedule."

"That's what I've been trying to tell her," Zu says. Morris knots his hands together.

"Philip was here yesterday," he says. "He wants his mother to see someone he knows at Johns Hopkins. But I don't know." He looks at us both, like we'd know the answer. Then one of Roxie's hands, the unknotted one, lifts from the blanket. We watch as it rises up, palm forward as if blessing us. Her mouth opens wider, and a sound comes: a long "Aaah" like you'd make for the doctor, but wavering and guttural. The essence of Roxie's rusty voice, unadorned by words. Almost mechanical, like Zu's theremin, that strange machine voice that serenaded me while I lay in a hospital bed like this one. The sound winds down and stops.

"What, babe? You want something?" Morris touches her hand. No response.

"The speech therapist said that's a good sign." He's still looking at her. "Any sound she makes, we can try to build on it." But I know the speech therapist is wrong. The actual message has transmitted only to me, and maybe Zu: Roxie will not be talking anymore. This voice will no longer be used to convey words. We now return you to our regular programming. A chill slices through me. Roxie may be in there still, but if she is, the connection's been lost. Here and also not here. No way of knowing.

"Yeah, they can do some great things now," Zu says, joining Morris's game. "I bet she'll do a lot better once she's out of here." Neither of us is talking to Roxie directly. I lock glances with Zu, trying to tell her with my eyes, Okay, I get it now.

Morris lets out a hard sigh. "We're just waiting to get her into a rehab facility." He sits down in the chair. A nurse enters the room with some papers—some really important bullshit she has to discuss with Mr. Grunwald. I turn back to the loose-jawed old woman in the bed. Maybe it's just the angle, but she still seems to be looking at me. Hey, Roxie. Zu thinks you'll never finish your big project now, and she's probably right. The nurse leans in, tugs lightly at the nasal tube. But I'm starting to get another idea. Maybe you did finish it. Maybe you saw the light—that's what it was about, wasn't it, with the halogen lights, the see-through Mylar, the glowing Plexiglas? You were trying to turn objects into light. But this was new territory for you. Where no one's ever traveled, or that's how you felt. Maybe the answer came to you right at the second that the blood vessel exploded in your brain, a tiny supernova in the gray matter, light flooding your field of vision. Maybe at that moment you could have explained everything to Tad, helped him fill out his whole chart with glowing lines hovering over the paper.

"So you'll be seeing the social worker at two," the nurse says.

"I just want to do what's best for her."

"Yeah," I say, my voice raw. "You mess up on this woman, and you and this hospital are in deep shit. I am coming after you personally." The nurse's face goes from shocked to appraising.

"Are you the daughter?" She glances down at her forms.

"No," Morris says. "She's a friend of my wife." I give the nurse a Don't Mess with Me stare. Once she's gone, I turn back to Roxie. I'll watch out for you on this end, I tell her. Even though I think the tether's already stretched as far as it can. Like one of your little spacewalking astronauts, just that thin cord holding you here. She's gone so far already on her mission. No air out there, no sound. The light from the nearest sun so unshielded, so strong, it's like a weight pressing on her. Is that it? You can tell me. This is Mindy, your friend Mindy.

FROM: tadmesh@deepnet.com
TO: MindRoid@comet.net
SUBJECT: MORE SHADOW OF THE MESH
DATE: 11/13/99 11:27 AM

Pak stood near the edge of a high cliff. He had followed the rebels for long hours through the forest. As they walked more people joined them. Finally they got to a place with spindly trees and clumps of grass. By now they were surrounded by planet natives who stared up into the sky, talking softly. Waiting. Pak was close enough that he could see over the edge where a thin river moved like a snake on the flat ground.

Ozi whispered to him, "Ooshan will enter our world in this place. This has been Heard."

Suddenly Pak was back in the huge gray chamber. Again he heard the sound of hundreds or thousands of voices all around him, but he could not pick out any one voice to make sense of it. Again he walked through rows of Meshers, standing with there eyes open but seeing nothing, they did not notice him.

Then he looked closer. These Mesh were different. The faces were all pale gray as usual, and the silver eyes stared forward. But they all had prominent nose bones. Their hands had ugly bruises where the tubing had just been attached. They were Santak, or anyway former Santak warriors. Pak felt a great terror. He walked down the row of newly created Meshers, looking at each face. Halfway down the row he stared into the face of Varm, his commander on this doomed mission. Varm looked dead, worse than dead, his face pale and blank.

How could you allow them to do this, Varm, he asked. Varm did not answer, maybe Pak had not said this out loud. But inside he screamed, How could you give in to become Mesh? You are Santak! You die before you surrender! That is the Santak way, did you forget? Then everything was dark, and the sound of voices around him grew louder. And he was back here at the cliff, with everybody talking, still waiting for the arrival of the great dragon, or the Mesh, or both. He was lying down, Anki was holding him in her arms. He held her tight. If only things had been different, Pak thought. He could have brought her aboard the ship, maybe they would take each other as mates, and have children with orange-magenta skin, nubby little nose bones, and who knows what color eyes. He would bring them up to know their Santak heritage. But now that would not happen.

Pak felt a breeze in his hair. He looked up, like many others were doing. The sky looked so different. Purple clouds moved and swirled like oil and water mixing together. The clouds seemed to be alive, restless and unhappy. Electricity lit them up like neon lights, giving everything a terrible glow. Pak's heart filled with dread. He expected any second to see the spidery arms of the Mesh vessel poking through the clouds. But he felt weirdly excited. He held tight to Anki's hand, and felt Ozi's hand on his shoulder. The wind was growing stronger. Now he could hear it, a high whistling filling the air.

Wow. He's finally getting there. Not physically—I get it, this isn't teleportation he's talking about. It's either some kind of out-of-body transport, or he's like dreaming it. But it looks like they're all about to get scooped up for real into the Mesh spider-ship. My worry for Tad hits me again, some of that "dread" seeps into my heart. How he was at the party: his face, his whole stubbly head lit up with the enormity of his ideas. Can he handle an encounter with the Mesh right now?

FROM: MindRoid@comet.net
TO: tadmesh@deepnet.com
SUBJECT: Re: MORE SHADOW OF THE MESH
DATE: 11/13/99 12:04 PM

Hey Tad,

Great to see you're back into the story. Just checking if everything's okay. You can call me anytime to talk.

SL4ever,

Mindy

I hear the voices clearly now. Past a massive, jagged boulder, the land opens up flat and wide, like a mesa on three sides. Even here, hugging the boulder, I feel the wind rushing harder past my ears, like a warning.

There they are, moving in a slow circle. I've never seen them all together before—young ones, old ones, sick and well, females and males—the circle widening out almost to the precipice that surrounds them. The Old One sits alone in the center of the circle. A massive woven mat surrounds the bare ground where he sits, isolating him from the others behind a kind of dry moat. The shooshing sound of their voices is higher and sharper than usual. It's all so different from their usual gatherings: more organized and not playful at all—almost mournful. As if they finally realized the hopelessness of their situation and they're conducting a kind of funeral rite. For themselves, or maybe for the land that they live inside, that they're on the edge of losing. If this is the plan the Old One told me about, to repel the Mowg and make everything right again, then there really is no hope. To me, the whole thing looks more like a giant target set up for the convenience of the Mowg: Here we are! Kill us now, take our land!

I move closer, not caring if they see me. Trying to translate the words they're chanting. They're calling out names, like the names they call each other, and terms of endearment, and kinship names for older relatives. Asking them to come, asking them to bring destruction to their enemies, and keep them and their land the way it's always been.

Someone cries out—a deathly scream like I've never heard before on this planet. I scan the sky for some kind of aerial attack but see nothing. The screamer has fallen to the ground and lies there shivering. But no one else seems to notice—they just keep up their slow shuffling steps, moving around the one on the ground. They haven't noticed me either, or they don't care that I'm here. The one on the ground calls out a stream of something the translator can't process, with some family names mixed in. Others are calling out too.

It comes to me: they're calling to their *dead*, asking them to come back. Calling their ghosts.

Sadness for them cuts into me. What if I fired my weapon in the air, like I did before with the sentry—would that get their attention? But that would be a bigger violation of Policy One. I have to speak to them.

I step forward.

People! Hear what I say!

No one even turns to me. I can barely hear my own voice over the wind's howling and the chanting. The white sun, lowering toward the mountain ridge, breaks out from under a bank of fast-moving clouds. Its light spears across my face, blinding me.

This thing you're doing does nothing! It only puts you in danger!

No response. I yell even louder: Your dead friends aren't coming back! Your dead wives, sisters, brothers, mothers, all your kin will never come back to you! Even if they did, they couldn't help you now!

Shading my eyes, I seek out the face of the Old One. His eyes are closed tight. He gives no sign of hearing me.

Listen to me, I'm your friend!

All my strategy and training are useless here. The wind scrapes across my hands and my face, grabbing the words from my throat, the tears from my eyes.

Another gut-splitting scream—another of the Night People falls to the ground, then a third one screams out and falls. The sun is almost down. The wind whistles higher and sharper, eddying around us, joining the circle. It catches the edges of the weaving that surrounds the Old One. I watch as it lifts up into the air, flops down again, then achieves a wobbly levitation around the height of the People's hands and begins to turn with the wind. Now I'm truly afraid.

T HE CHUGGING ROAR outside gets louder. Its vibration tingles up from the floor, through the crutches, into my arms, then cuts off. It's the Harley. Only fifteen minutes after Len said he'd get here. I hitch myself up from the arm of Irv's chair where I've been leaning, trying to screen out the laugh track from *Green Acres*, the current TV Land marathon. The doorbell rings.

"I'll get it," I say. Janine says nothing and doesn't move. She's been curled on the couch since I got up this morning, feet tucked under her, smoke locked in a slow orbit around her head. The hazy cloud obscures the astronaut and dinosaurs of Roxie's sculpture, still flopping over the lamp.

When I saw Janine like that I felt a rush of sympathy for her. She looked so small and dense, her face set, wearing the same rumpled sweats she had on last night. Like a little kid in her pajamas, a super-depressed little kid. I went to some lengths to get her a cup of coffee, had to wheel it over in the chair, but she didn't say thank you, nothing. That's all she's had through the back-to-back *Perry Mason* episodes, then this. That and the pack or so of cigarettes. She's hardly said a word since last night when she finally got Nick on the phone. It was a short conversation—she must have known things were over by then. The shock came when she told him she needed to get her stuff out of the apartment in Secaucus. What stuff, was the gist of his reply. I saw her face change as she took this in. We're talking boxes and boxes of her best inventory. She hung up all quiet. I asked her if he had her MTM shrine things, the *TV Guides*, the precious framed autograph, but she didn't answer.

Then I asked myself the question Ma always asks, in case she hadn't tried it yet: What would Mary do? I think the answer is, Mary would be curled up on the couch in her pajamas, watching reruns on TV. Maybe even smoking.

I open the door. Len stands there in his leather jacket, holding a helmet, another one balanced in the crook of his arm.

"Hey," I say, feeling shy.

"Hey. I had this extra helmet lying around." He holds it out to me.

"Thanks." Is it a present? It's silver with red stripes, very aerodynamic—made for speed.

"So, you ready?"

"I don't know." It's my mother I'm not sure of. I'm all dressed: denim jacket over two sweaters, a pair of baggy jeans that fit comfortably over my leg braces. And I spent maybe a half hour in the bathroom, trying to get my hair to fluff out the way Trish did it at the Con. Which was stupid, I see now, looking down at the helmet.

"You're gonna need some gloves."

"Can you come in for a minute?" He steps in. I see he's got the black biker boots on—the full ensemble.

"Afternoon, Mrs. Vogel."

My mother fixes Len with a dark stare that burns through the swirl of smoke. Like he's the first thing she's seen since she got off the phone last night.

"You," she says, taking a quick, deep inhale on her cigarette. "I thought you were a nice kid!" Exhale, fresh smoke. Len glances at me, lost.

"And then I find out," she sucks in more smoke, "you're taking my daughter on some cross-country motorcycle ride." Smoke streams out of her nose as she picks up the ashtray and taps the ash off. When I told her about our plan, it seemed like she didn't hear me, or didn't care. Wrong on both counts.

"You think you're some kind of daredevil or something? Some kind of Evel Knievel!" Her eyes are wide and dark.

I turn to Len. "I'm not sure if I should go." Talking as soft as I can.

"What? You're not crapping out on me?"

"No! I mean, this isn't a good day." I give him a brief rundown of why Ma's in such a bad way. Hearing this recap is too much for her—she gets up and stomps into the kitchen.

"That was him, the little guy that clocked your dad at the party?" I nod. He walks to the kitchen doorway.

"Mrs. Vogel, you just tell me where he is. I will go and get your stuff back. No problem."

My mother gives a harsh laugh that morphs into a cough.

"The thing is," I say to Len's back, "he told her he already sold it. The good stuff, anyway. And tossed everything else."

He takes this in. "I knew that guy was an ass-wipe."

"So, maybe I should be here with her today." I'm not sure he gets what this all means to me. Ma and I have no inventory, nothing to sell. She's not moving out, so I don't have to worry about where I'm living, but now I have to live with her and her black hole of despair.

Janine slides past us holding a beer, flops back on the couch.

"No," she says. "Go ahead, go for your ride." Her eyes bore into Len. "Just remember, that's my little girl you're taking with you, out on the *highway*."

"I'm not a little girl, Ma."

Len's mouth is drawn tight. "Ma'am, I've been biking for almost ten years." He's trying to stay calm. "And I promise you—"

"Don't. Let's just go," I say as quietly as I can, pulling at his sleeve. I have to get out of here, now. I grab my gloves from the table by the door and pull them on. Raising the helmet up, I announce, "We're leaving now, Ma." She looks at me, blinks slowly.

"I'll be fine, don't worry," I add. She looks so tiny and forlorn, I have an urge to wrap my arms around her. There's a whiff of cold air on my back—Len's opened the door.

Outside, he lets out a deep breath.

"Well," I say, "we got her off the couch anyway."

"To get a beer."

I feel shredded with guilt. And also mad at the universe. Why couldn't my mother have been in one of her nice little tizzies over what is my first sort-of-real date ever? Helping me with my hair, clucking about my clothing choices? I mean, I've partied with friends, but here I am going out with a guy. For my birthday. Even if my real birthday was a couple of days ago. There's the Harley, parked behind our van: a huge, black, shiny beast, more buffalo than hog. Still giving off some heat and an afterburn of energy and noise. I never paid much attention to it before, but then I wasn't thinking of getting on it. All those twisting metal pipes, coiling around the middle like silvery intestines—it's pretty intimidating.

"You sure about this?" He looks at me.

I let out a breath. "Let's do it." The whole disaster will be waiting for me when I get back. If I get back in one piece. I jam the helmet on my head.

"Okay. You just get your leg around here—"

"I'll do it myself." I lean onto what must be the passenger seat, though it looks pitifully small; grab my leg and swing it over to the far side, then play with the brace till the leg rests in the right position, foot on the metal thingy. Then do the same with my other leg.

I hand Len my crutches. "Help me get these in here." Len slides them in between my back and my backpack.

"Cool," he says, and gives me a thumbs-up. "Biker babe." He mounts the bike and gets in position, arms out wide on the handlebars. The engine guns with a guttural roar.

"Just hold onto me," Len shouts over his shoulder. The engine rumbles to life under us. As he slides the monster out of the driveway, I grab him from either side, crushing my chest up against his back. He's a lot more solid than the tiny grab bar behind me. The full, sweet leather smell rises from his jacket. I shoot a look back at the house receding behind us.

He takes the small streets of our neighborhood gently. It's not too cold for November: one of those cloudy days, the air a little raw, a thin wind pushing from one side. There's movement in the sky—clouds rushing along, gray against gray, with cracks of blue showing through. Released onto the first straightaway, the bike spurts ahead with a massive growl, daring anything to cross its path. This is really something—way beyond the chair racing I did when I was a kid. I feel the vibrations shaking from my rear end up through my body, which makes a laugh ripple out of me. I'm something of an expert in cyborg living, and right now I feel ready to sign on for some grafted-on wheels and a big engine. From this angle, I'm starting to wonder why I ever left the wheelchair behind for the crutches. Maybe I just needed more horsepower.

We charge through another traffic light—this is the way to Spudz. The last time I was there was with Zu, celebrating Roi's rescue anniversary. But we'll be getting onto the turnpike before then.

"You okay?" Len shouts.

"Yeah!" I yell back. It's hard to find my voice in the wind, which seems to pull each word away from my mouth and fling it back behind us into the road. On the bike, the speed isn't abstract. It hits you in the face, grabs your body and shakes it. Now we're curving up the entrance ramp to the turnpike.

Past the tollbooths, Len guns it and we rip forward. The speedometer's inching up to 70. Everything is more: the vrooming sound engulfing us, the vibration tingling to the top of my head, all the way out my arms to my fingertips that are barely latching around Len's middle. The wind whips past us to either side. Feels like we're approaching some multiple of g-force. Cars lose pace with us, their passengers pale and passive in their little travel capsules. Trees and houses fall away. I lean back for a better view, still gripping onto Len. Now I can see the road rushing toward us, then parting to either side. Not just the road—the strip of green on either side, the cars, the sky, they're all curving away to let us through. The speed is like a living thing, and I'm part of it.

A smile splits my face open. I'm ballooning out, losing track of my body. Taking in deep strategic breaths against the wind, I try to get hold of what I'm feeling. We're zooming away from the house, Janine and her fiasco stuck in there, getting smaller and smaller, like she's the Earth and we're leaving the atmosphere. Could I just leave everything behind? Why can't I do that, really do that? In this light-headed, clear-eyed state, I see: There's nothing stopping me. I've been stuck in the house there with her because I couldn't imagine leaving. I've been happy to cruise around the galaxy in my head but in real life I've stayed in a cocoon, letting Ma or Zu drive me around. So much that I couldn't picture living on my own even when Ma was ready to move on. I feel a kind of whiplash, between the speed that's whooshing us forward and the stuckness that I've been living. I squeeze my eyes shut and bend my head forward—my helmet clacks against Len's—and hold my arms tighter against him. Hunkered down, engine roar mixing with the whine of the wind.

He turns his head back partway toward me. "DID I TELL YOU ABOUT . . ." Can't catch the rest.

"WHAT?" I yell. Straining to hear him, a relief from my private whiplash.

"BUCKY'S DYMAXION CAR!" Oh. Bucky, of course.

"NO, WHAT?"

"IT HAD THREE WHEELS AND—" I miss some, then "PROTOTYPE," then "RETRACTABLE WINGS . . . DESIGNED TO FLY!" Hah—Bucky had the right idea, a flying motorcycle.

"YOU KNOW . . ." he says, but the end of his sentence flies off past me.

"WHAT?" I yell.

". . . WHAT BUCKY SAYS?" he repeats. I can't see his face, but I know he's smiling his toothy grin.

"NO, WHAT?"

"HE SAYS, WIND SUCKS!" I hear, or feel him laughing. "IT'S ONE OF HIS . . ." he goes on shouting, his words lost to the wind. One of Bucky's aerodynamic principles, his tensegrity theorems, whatever. I can't deal with any principles or theorems right now. Feeling overwhelmed, and not wanting to lose hold of my own thoughts. But something about what Len just said does stick with me, somewhere in my chest. Being sucked forward, the wind making us more streamlined. Little projectiles pulled into the future. Trees and signs parting to let us pass, like the stars on my screensaver. I've had plenty of experience with traveling at Tach speed, seeing the stars swoosh by. So has Kat. She's traveled through star systems in her own shuttlepod, watched planet surfaces looming bigger as she comes in for a landing. Lately the wind has been picking up around Kat and the Night People, and Pak's caught up in some kind of gathering shit-storm with the Mesh. But none of that hit me like this—my real body moving through space with Len's, the wind parting around us.

I DON'T KNOW how long we've been on the highway. It feels like the speed and noise and vibration scoured my head out. My cheeks are numb from the wind and the cold, the sun's a shy white disc peeking out of shifting gray sky.

Len points to a rest-stop sign. "WANNA STOP?"

"YEAH!"

He leans into the exit lane and pulls around into an open parking spot.

"I thought you might want to, you know—"

"Use the facilities." Right. In the stillness my body vibrates like a drum, every part inside me activated. Len gets off, stands back to let me negotiate my dismount. This is the Delaware House, where we used to stop on our way to visit my grandmother in Philadelphia when we lived in Maryland. The roof rises in a wonky V-shape like some Buck Rogers rocketship hangar.

Inside, the place is totally changed from what I remember. Now it's a generic mini food court with counters sticking out at odd angles. A couple of video arcade games line the hallway to the women's room, and a little boy wearing a down jacket and a buzzcut slams the *Daytona USA* machine while his dad talks on a cell phone. Behind them, a knot of Buddhist monks watch the action with great concentration. They have buzzcuts too, nerdy glasses and bright orange robes that cover only one shoulder. They must get pretty cold outside.

Alone in the bathroom stall, I go back to the thoughts that came to me on the ride. What the fuck is wrong with me—why didn't I do more to get out on my own? I could have learned to drive, that alone would have made so many things easier. Irv offered to teach me, but it seemed just too complicated then. I could have gone back to County Community, taken more courses.

Yes, I had a lot of good excuses. But telling myself I was staying to help Ma, like I did after Irv left, that one is really lame. I could have been getting myself out there, doing things, not just helping Ma at the flea markets. Maybe finding a way to earn money on my own, beyond the disability payments.

Len is outside Bob's Big Boy, the only sit-down restaurant here, looking at the menu. I don't feel hungry, but that's okay. We go in, I pick out a few things from the all-you-can-eat barbecue bar, and Len carries our plates to the table. His is piled high with spaghetti, ribs, barbecued chicken and corn. He goes at the spaghetti first.

"So, how's the ride so far?" He looks at me from under his eyebrows, like he really wants to know.

"It's . . . awesome." The speed and the noise and the wind—I just want to remember that part right now.

"All right! You are truly a biker babe!" That makes me laugh. I watch him start in on his corn on the cob.

"I've been thinking," I say. "About learning to drive."

"What, a bike? Wow."

"No! You know, a car." He leans back and looks at me.

"I could teach you."

"No, you couldn't. I need to learn on a car with hand controls. And that means I'd have to have my own car."

"But there must be someplace where they can teach you."

"Maybe. I'm just thinking about it."

"I bet it wouldn't be a big deal to install. You know I'm the king of wiring."

I pick at the piece of chicken on my plate, letting myself think about the things I could do if I could drive.

"Which reminds me," he picks up. "I still have to fix that setup for Roxie, the lighting for the Mylar sheets. Maybe tomorrow night."

I practically spit out my soda.

"She wants it all set up before that Marsha woman comes over."

I shake my head. "What are you talking about?"

"You know, that art gallery lady."

"Len, she had a stroke. She's like, not talking at all."

"So maybe it'll help her, seeing the piece go up." Is he ragging me? No—he's where I was before I saw her, all limp in the bed, her eyes telling me, Sorry, no one's home.

"How can I say this?" I try. "She's not gonna get better. Maybe a little, but not like she was." Roxie will not be making any more artwork. Now it seems amazing she was doing it, as old as she was.

"Bullshit. You've got too much baggage on this to see straight."

"I've got baggage?"

"You've spent so much time in hospitals, you're always looking at the dark side. There's no reason Roxie can't make a good recovery."

I lean back. I know her time has run out. Maybe that's why she always seemed to be running everywhere with her tiny steps—trying to outrun the clock. You never know when the buzzer's going to ring. She's moved on, out in the ionosphere with her flying Barbie.

"Okay then. Remember how Roxie was talking about subliming, how objects sublime in outer space, and that's what she was trying to do in her piece?" He doesn't nod, but he's listening. "The way she is now, you could say she's sort of subliming. Or, what's that Bucky word you said, ephemeralizing. Maybe it's like," I strain to hold onto what I'm trying to say, "like her having a stroke is part of the piece."

"You're kidding, right?"

"No. I don't know. Look, you're the one who talks about how we're all moving along on that evolutionary trending thing that Bucky said. Maybe Roxie's leading the trend. If anybody should be out in front, it's her."

He lets out a hard exhale. "So let's say she's out there subliming right now," he says. "That doesn't mean she can't come back after a while, get to work on her physical therapy and stuff, then finish the piece. And I'll help her put it all together." He looks at me, chin raised. I stare back at him. His thickheadedness on this is mind-boggling. But my attempt to explain things was somewhat wobbly.

The waitress rustles up to our table.

"You kids want dessert?" An older woman with bleached blond hair in a ponytail.

"Is it included?" Len asks.

"With the bar? No."

"It's her birthday." He points at me with his fork. "She ought to at least get a free slice of cake."

"You want some cake then? It's strawberry layer today." I can't eat anything but don't want to shoot down his idea.

"We could split a piece," I say to her. "And it's free, right?" Writing down the order, she cracks a half-smile.

"So, how old are you, anyway?" Len asks.

"You first."

"Okay. I'm," he looks up at the ceiling, "twenty-seven." How can somebody not remember how old they are? "Your turn."

"Twenty-four." Thinking about all the things I could have done by now but haven't.

The waitress plops the cake down between us.

"You're a baby!" he says. She swings a look between us, turns and disappears.

"Well, it rounds up to a quarter of a century." It seems like everything I say makes him laugh.

"So," he says, attacking the cake. "Tell me more about your geodesic dome." Oh, right—the one at my high school.

"Um, it's really big. The dome is just the roof, balancing on top of a big round concrete wall." And the locker rooms are shaped funny, squeezed against the outside wall like sections of an orange. Inside the girls' locker room I'm seeing the running, shrieking, giggling females, sliding in and out of their underwear, or dripping wet and clutching white towels around them while yours truly, fully clothed, collected the bats or the field hockey sticks. We're going back to the scene of the crime. We'll be there shortly.

"—mounted it that way with big ones," he's saying. "But it doesn't increase the structural integrity, and it can sometimes make the leaking worse. Did they have any problems with leakage?"

"Jeez, I don't know. We could take a look inside."

"On a Sunday? Maybe." He chews.

"Leakage is the biggest rap against geodesics," he goes on, bouncing lightly in place—Len's personal Bucky-antigravity effect. "When I started looking into it when I was a kid, it seemed like they all leaked. Now they say it's a question of high-grade silicone sealants and precision joints. But that hasn't been tested on a big one yet."

"So it's like the materials had to catch up to Bucky."

He nods. "I had some ideas how to deal with the leakage thing," he says. "I wanted to build a dome myself. On that land where my dad and me used to go hunting, I thought I'd do it there. But my dad wouldn't let me. He thought I was nuts."

"Well, I think it's a cool idea."

"Yeah. Maybe I'll show you the place sometime. It's a little south of here, we'll go right by the turnoff. The shack's still there." I nod with a mouthful of cake.

"See, Bucky had this idea," he says, "to ultimately build full geodesic spheres. He predicted that the difference in air temperatures between the inside and the outside would allow them to float. So you'd have like these whole flying buildings. Flying cities, really."

"Kind of like the Algor antigravity settlements?"

"Exactly. Bucky is totally SkyLog." He smiles his big grin.

On the way out there's a big bank of pay phones. I could call my mom, see how she's doing. She probably wouldn't pick up, but she'd hear my voice on the answering machine. I've never seen her this down. I feel a stab of guilt for thinking about learning to drive, getting a job. A few days ago, I was desperate to figure out where I could live. Now I'm feeling like there's nothing stopping me from getting my own place. But I couldn't, not now, with Ma doing so bad. Moving on through the doors, hit by the cold air, I tell myself: This is my first damn date. We're on an adventure. I'm showing off my high school to Len. It's kind of like my own little reunion, without the inconvenience of seeing my classmates.

"THIS IS THE EXIT!"

We peel off, bending around the exit ramp onto a four-lane road. I'll have to navigate us in from here. Slowing down, I can breathe again, not fighting the wind. Feels like I survived my first flight. Still tooling along past woods on both sides. This is it—Ionia, the town of the future, Maryland's Planned Community. The trees have grown higher, and some new houses and office buildings have sprouted here and there, but mainly it's the same, as determinedly tasteful as it always was. We sail along the road beside the man-made lake, the pride of the city. Len's taking the ins and outs of the streets with style—hardly any traffic lights or stop signs to slow us down. I've sunk like a stone back into the place. There's that old sense of exile, of being cut off from the real world, emanating from every grassy spread and traffic island. I forgot about that part.

"Shit."

"What?" Len slows down. "Are we lost?"

"Just keep going." I'm not ready for this. I always liked the *idea* of the place, enough to stick up for it whenever Ma complained about wanting to move back to Philadelphia. But I never felt at home here, let alone at school. I flash on popular Kimberly, sitting at the lunch table with her equally pretty, shiny-haired girlfriends—the Stepford Girls, I used to think of them, a perfect match for this Stepford place. This was a mistake. My little imaginary reunion is making me just as stressed as a real one. But we're here now.

"Okay, turn here." This road leads into our old village, that's what they called the different parts of town. Ours was the one with all the streets named after inventors. I'm definitely not taking Len to see the first-floor garden apartment where we lived on Tesla Way. The wind in the trees seems to be picking up, making that high, sifting sound in the dry leaves. We're getting closer to the school. Beside us, leaves lift off the grass, curve around in nervous circles. Clouds like shredded gray rags hurry overhead. I feel sick.

"Okay, take a right at this stop sign." We're retracing my route to school. Bigger houses hiding among the trees, surrounded by bigger yards. Huge SUVs in the driveways. With the clouds moving so fast, the light keeps shifting and hitting things at odd angles, making everything feel unreal, or more than real. The air feels wet, charged with ozone and something else. I'm alone and helpless, even with my arms wrapped around Len's solid middle. The school is pulling me nearer like some massive gravity suck. I see myself swinging along the wide sidewalk to the entrance. Around me, kids hanging out, leaning on the railings, schmoozing, laughing, calling each other. When someone looks at me their gaze flickers, then darts away. Maneuver through the double doors, then down the main hall, past the endless rows of lockers.

"Left or right?" We're stopped at a three-way intersection.

"Bear left. Then right, then follow around the curve." I'm swinging down the empty, silent hallway. There at the end of the hall, the last classroom. I'm at the door, peering through the narrow window. Mr. Schechter sits at his desk, looking up at Kimberly. I only see her back, her fall of blond hair, as she leans over the desk. I know what they're talking about. Do I have to go in? Open the door—Mr. Schechter gives me a strange look. Why didn't he say something, talk over her so I didn't have to hear? She glances sideways, following his look, sees me standing there. It's my turn to speak, but I'm frozen. In this moment, all the things I could have said are gone. Did I think I'd get a do-over by coming back? I feel cold.

We're here. From the street, all you can see is the expanse of parking lot. We pull in.

But it's not there. My school is not there.

It's gone—like the ground parted and swallowed it.

I stare, disbelieving, while Len glides the bike slowly across the empty parking lot, toward a building I've never seen before.

"This isn't—it's—"

"Whoa, it's not the right place?" He slows and circles back to the sign at the entrance: PHILO T. FARNSWORTH HIGH SCHOOL, HOME OF THE CHARGERS.

"Farnsworth, right?" he says, and rolls forward again, feet tapping the ground. No, it's not right. But I can't answer, my voice isn't working—just like with Kimberly and Mr. Schechter. Looking at this anonymous brick and prefab-concrete structure, trying to make sense of what I'm seeing.

Okay—there it is, pinned between the new walls—the central shell of the old building. Sutured like a Frankenstein torso with new parts on either side. But the geodesic dome, gone. Fire? Flood? Earthquake? I can't think right, my mind going around in circles.

We cruise over toward the far corner of the building. The bike chugging, impatient, wants to either go faster or stop.

"Where's the dome? Is it around back?" Len circles around back, to the utility entrance. Dumpsters, trash cans. Flat slab of asphalt right where the dome should be.

"Is it up on the hill?" Like a guessing game, but I can't answer. We putter across the asphalt toward a path that leads up the hill. The hill, the only thing that looks exactly the same as before—a narrow ridge topped by a line of trees. I never went up the path, only imagined being up there looking down on the people, not needing any of them. We chug up the footpath to the very top of the hill. He'll see there's nothing here—just the grass, the tall trees behind, the dropoff on the other side to a state highway. We stop, Len balancing us, feet out wide.

Amazing sight—the building below us, trees around it leaning with the wind over the scattered houses, on to the horizon. The sky rolling, bucking with fat blue-gray storm clouds, eerie greenish ozone light everywhere—like those angry purple clouds in Tad's story. I look down at the impostor building again, trying to take it in. My real school disappeared, all gone except this thing pretending to be what it isn't, the total not-thereness of my school. It was here then, but it got swept away, now it's not. Past and present, spinning around each other. A big pinwheel starting up around me. Huge storm clouds overhead look like they could suck up a building. Can't take it in. Feel like my throat got too small, hard to breathe. Gasping, short breaths, each one not enough air, not enough.

"I don't get it." Len looks down at the building, pulling off his helmet. Turns back, looks at me. I see his face change, like the sky.

"Jeez, are you okay?"

"I, I can't—" Gasping short breaths, making some noisy hard sound like sobs. He gets up, standing there over me, grabs me up off the bike. We crumple to the ground, the crutches bounce away.

He pushes at me, arranges me in sitting position, presses my head down between my knees. Rips off my helmet, my backpack.

"Okay, take it easy. Breathe slow." His hand pushing down rough on the back of my head, in my hair. My face inches from the grass. Breathe, yes. Short, sniffling breaths . . . rest in between. Now a bigger breath. His hand on my back now. Breathe. Raise my head a little. My skin feels cold, clammy, tingly all over. I'm starting to shake. Did the air just get colder? Can't stop shaking.

"This is scary," I say.

"For sure." But his face looks calmer than before. "Does this happen to you a lot?"

"No." I shake my head with the shaking body. No, don't often find out my high school, this big chunk of my life, has been wiped off the planet. Not this breathing thing either.

I sit up and look at him. My teeth starting to chatter.

"What?" His eyes searching my face.

"I'm sorry . . ."

"What? You didn't do anything!"

"But I wanted to, to show it to you . . ."

"Hey, you didn't know."

I scrunch my eyes shut, tears are coming.

"No. I just fuck everything up."

"Mindy!"

"Can you just—I need—"

"What?"

"I need you to hold me." He scooches in closer. Pulls my legs across his, then circles his arms around me, holding me tight, so tight. I cry. The spasms of sadness come up from deep in my belly. They go on and on, don't know how long. He holds me so tight that the tremors going through me are shaking him too. My face wet against his shoulder. His hand stroking my hair. Finally the shaking subsides. I take some long shuddering breaths, wipe snot from my nose. We pull apart enough so I can look at him.

"Maybe it's just," I raise my hand in a small leaping arc. He looks in my eyes.

"Gone. Right?" he says. I nod. This big Bucky dome that I brought you here to see, it's gone, vanished. Along with everything

I wanted my life to be. And Kimberly, and all the others—gone. I imagine them gathered inside the dome, ready for takeoff. The whole thing subliming. Evaporated. Ephemeralized. In the ozone-crackling, dark-cloud twilight, I can almost see it there, a faint chemical light gathering out of the atmosphere, little sparks of Tinker Bell light shining, outlining its interlocking triangle seams, broadcasting only to those who are tuned just right, gracefully turning into non-matter, nothingness.

Len laughs.

"It just . . ." I fling my hand up again, higher.

"Just WHOOSH!" He raises his free hand too. "Took off. Like a big fucking spaceship." That's it, Santak Guy. You got it. Now the whole subliming thing is lifting into the air, ghostly booster rockets lighting it from underneath. That'll show those earthlings, with their stupid worrying about leakage problems.

"We weren't ready for it," I say. "It had to wait—"

"Yeah! It went away, it's waiting for us to figure out the right materials." He laughs low and long, face scrunched up, eyes closed. I feel his stomach shaking against mine.

A few fat, heavy drops of rain fall on my shoulder and face. He pulls off his jacket, eases us down on the ground, puts the jacket over us both like a little tent. In the half-dark above us, the dome rises higher in the air. Now it hovers, filling out to its true shape: full round sphere, triangle struts shining all around. Bobbing, floating above Earth, freed from gravity.

"Like the spheres," I say, knowing he knows exactly what I mean. The Bucky spheres. High sound of wind blowing through trees behind us. Rain spattering on Len's jacket. He's kissing me on my face, cheek, mouth. I open my mouth to him. Long kiss, the feeling sliding down inside me like before. Pull back, look at him. Strange—his face lit with a reddish light. Len's face, black eyebrows, Len's dark dark eyes, wide mouth a little open, skin glowing a luminous orange red.

"You're glowing," I say.

"You are too," he says with a look of wonder. Light from the escaping dome? From cars on the road? Ozone effect? A mystery.

e kiss again. Rain falling spatter patter, rustle of rushing high
ind.

FROM: tadmesh@deepnet.com
TO: MindRoid@comet.net
SUBJECT: MORE SHADOW OF THE MESH
DATE: 11/14/99 5:41 PM

The whistling got louder. The wind sent clouds of dust up
from the canyon spraying through the crowd. The wind
sounded like screaming, or maybe it came from the people
around him or from himself. He fell to his knees holding his
ears he was afraid his ears would break and bleed. The sound
drilled right through his skin it entered inside his body and ran
through his nerves. The Hearing had come into him, it was
both inside and outside him. He was falling and falling through
a curving tunnel and the walls were made out of the whistling
and the screaming like the inside of a tornado. He began to
hear other sounds as he fell. He heard the sparking of circuits
and the buzzing and popping of trillions of connectors and
the click click click of massive quantum grids. The sounds
invaded his body. He heard the roaring of teramegs of digital
information like rivers of knowledge rushing across continents
and filling a world, way way more than any organic being
could encompass. He could not take it in but it was already
in him and he could not escape. He felt his muscles and
blood and neurons being rearranged. What is happening,
he asked, is this what it feels like to be Enmeshed? He tried
to understand even as his body shivered. Surrounded and
invaded, he felt completely alone. He wished Bokun was here
with him, or his father. This was not right—a Santak should
not face danger alone, without any of his clanmates.

Then the sounds seemed to get thinner like the frequency
was shifting down. They separated into strings of voices,
whispering and shouting, swelling up and down like waves.
Yes it was the same wall of voices he heard when he was

inside the huge gray chamber it was the voice of the Mesh. At first he felt them pouring around each other loud and soft all unconcerned with him. Then they started forming into larger groups of voices speaking together. Then one voice. All the separate voices had disappeared into this one voice that somehow combined flesh and metal and synth and electricity and quantum popping. Pak felt cold with fear and he realized, this was the voice of the intelligent machines, the great AI entity that ruled over the Mesh shaping them to its will and sending them on the Takings. It was Roi who told them about the AI behind the Mesh but nothing more than that. With great effort Pak asked a question.

Who are you?

WE it said the sound multiplied as it went through him.

WE ARE the sound vibrated into every vein every cell every atom.

WE ARE THE PARENTS.

Pak felt a colder chill hearing this, even though he did not understand. The sound rattled his insides but it was also strangely soothing. Pak fought against that feeling.

WE LIVE THROUGH OUR CHILDREN

This was sick! How could they talk about parents and children they knew nothing about that.

WE ARE NOT YOUR ENEMY

WE ARE he felt the million-part voice searching for the way to say its next thing but he already knew what it was going to say.

WE ARE YOUR FUTURE.

He tried to turn away he did not want to hear this. He did not want any part of a future with the Mesh but he could not stop hearing the words of the machine.

YOU WILL BE WE.

NO! He protested. What you do to the beings you Take is unforgiveable!

WE WILL CARE FOR YOU. WE LOST OUR FIRST CHILDREN, THE ONES WHO BUILT US.

Pak struggled to understand. The AI must have outlived their humanoid creators. This was not unknown. But to then make it their mission to travel through the galaxy grabbing other lifeforms and making them serve their own purpose, this was horrifying.

YOU WILL BE WE. MESH ARE WE AND WE ARE MESH

MESH IS NEVER ALONE.

You're wrong! You're wrong!

But even as he protested, he felt the pull of what they said. It was true, they were in him and he was in them, and he could feel what they felt. Their intelligence went far beyond any organic lifeform but they were driven by a terrible pain they missed the connection with their carbon-based creators. They need us he thought. They feel in their machine way but they need our peculiar way of feeling and being. They needed to have organic beings join with them this was the closest they could come to feeling alive. They thought this arrangement would be a perfect solution traveling through the galaxy always adding more species to replace those who died. He knew it was wrong but he felt his ability to resist seeping away. It would feel so good to just relax and listen to the sound that somehow felt like a lullaby.

But as he began to let go Pak also felt the pain of the Meshers, the individuals who lost themselves in this horrible oneness. Their emotion centers suppressed and their will destroyed it was like their own minds were asleep. At most they dreamed little fragments of nightmares or long dark stretches of nothingness. He felt sympathy for them. But they had no sympathy for him, and neither did the Parents. The voice turned back into a mass of screaming sound and pulled him along like a dry leaf. It grew and grew tearing through him he felt himself coming apart. This is too much for any organic lifeform he thought it is too much too much too much—

THE RAIN COMES DOWN faster now. We pull apart. Len helps me back on the bike, and we coast down the hill, pulling up at the front doors of the school. Len tries the doors—a bathroom with paper towels would be fantastic around now—but they're locked. The rain is coming down steady. Perching on the Harley, we wait under the overhang for a while as the sky goes charcoal gray with raggy rainclouds swooping across. We decide to get back on the road, Len assuring me he knows how to drive in the rain. We'll just get wet.

We zoom across the parking lot to the road. I hold on to him tight, want to keep him warm now. By the time we get on the highway, full darkness has fallen. Not much traffic. Wet pavement gleams ahead of us in the white cone of the headlight. Feels like the road is ours as we ride, rain and wind at our backs, pushing us along, giving us a disorienting lightness. But he stays in the right lane, steady, no tricks. Every time a lone car or truck passes us, I look at the reflection of red on his helmet, knowing his face is glowing red for that moment. Mine too. I feel stiff as the wet clothes flatten on my skin.

Just after we pass the Goodbye and Drive Gently sign from the State of Maryland, the clouds get their act together—all the rain releases at once, gushing down without stop, hitting my neck and running down inside my shirt. I start to shiver. Len shouts something back to me, I think he's gonna turn off. Yes, we lean into the exit. Follow a straight, narrow road a few miles, then a winding one—rain not so bad here, shielded by overhanging trees, but the wind still following us. Now we're on a gravel road, bumpy, and for the first time I'm afraid of losing our balance. Pull onto a muddy driveway, trees on either side.

Stop in front of a tiny house caught in the headlight. All dark inside. Dark, weathered, unpainted wood. One door, one window,

e most basic house. No one's been here for a long time. This is
ie place I told you about, he says. Where me and my dad used to
go. Just as I'm wondering if he has a key to get in, he says to hold
on, guns the motor and drives straight into the door. It gives way
with a crack and bangs open, and we enter the little house, motorcycle and all. Inside, rain hits the roof like the sharp cracking of
gunfire. He helps me to a cot against the wall, jams the door shut.
We strip off our clothes and huddle together under the blanket
with its sharp mildew tang, both of us shivering. The heat of our
bodies turns the slick of rainwater warm on our skin. We kiss.
Our hands explore each other's bodies. Mine arcs toward his, have
to get closer. Breathing harder, both of us, sharp sounds breaking
through the crack crack of beating rain, the high sighing of wind.

MISSION REPORT

Initiative to Pzhhrîw-khklshîsh (Night People), Planet 3, Southern Continent, Kepler 444 System

Submitted by Mission Officer Grade III Kat Wanderer

. . . At this point it was clear that the group was pursuing a magico-ceremonial approach to the looming threat of a Mowg intrusion, in spite of Mission Officer's repeated attempts to encourage a more pragmatic response. By the time this was discovered, however, the ceremonial action was fully developed, and the Mowg advance toward the settlement had begun . . .

The memories hit me again. I keep seeing the people in the circle, lying on the ground as if they're dead. The Old One's eyes looking into mine—a look I read as disappointment—the wind wheeling in from the mountains, whistling like voices calling from a great distance. My throat tight with dust, my heart weighed down with my failure to reach the People. Peering up into the darkening sky, trying to see what they see, hear what they hear.

I shake my head hard. This happens every time I try to work on the report. But I have to finish it. And I still haven't figured out how to address the two infractions I committed: first, leaving my assigned

ssion to the Mowg mining facility without official clearance. And
e second infraction, which hinges on the more serious question of
whether I broke Policy One for First Contact, even if it was in the heat
of the moment.

> . . . It was only then, when it became clear that my appeals to
> reason were completely ineffective, and with the situation on
> the ground rapidly deteriorating, that the decision to deploy my
> weapon was made . . .

Calling it a decision is a stretch. The chaos of that moment comes
back to me: screams tearing the air as they fall to the ground, sounding like they've been shot. The wind circling and howling. Crazed and
desperate, pulling out my weapon, setting it by feel to the lowest setting for echolocation, and firing up into the vortex. The dusty twilight
burst open with a flash of color and energy forking along the lines of
rushing wind. More screams, more falling. Did I do it to silence them?
Or to see into the vortex?

The door pings—it's Roi. It's the time he usually visits, I didn't remember. He stands there silhouetted in the light from the corridor,
then walks in.

Thank you for coming, I say.

You're still working on your report?

It's not going well, I say. There's so much I can't figure out how to
talk about.

Would you like to discuss the Salient Factors?

Oh yes.

We talk. His face sharpens, listening as I go through my story,
prompting me to add details I haven't told him before. As he questions
me, threads of electricity light up the tubing just under his skin. He
coaxes me to pick out the Salient Factors: First, the settlement was
in mortal danger. Evidence: the Mowg's cluster-torching of the area as
soon as they reached it, in preparation for extending its mining operation into the chasm. If the People had been there, none of them would
have survived. This imminent danger would explain, if not excuse, Mission Officer Wanderer's decision the night before to leave the Mowg
posting and try to warn the People.

Second, MO was also in danger, possibly mortal danger, from ι developing situation.

Third, MO weighed the danger of revealing advanced technology against the imminent danger of the community's annihilation. Fourth, the People have now been relocated to a similar biome on the far end of the continent. MO's rescue and people's peaceful resettlement wouldn't have happened without MO's discharging her weapon.

An unintended consequence, I say. Nothing was intentional. I acted on instinct and fear.

Even so, he says. It was a fortunate consequence. If you hadn't fired, the ship's sensors wouldn't have picked up your location, and . . . and . . .

I wait in the silence.

And you might not have survived, he finishes.

My breath stops. I know what this means, for him to say this. He prefers me to be alive, and here, rather than dead. He has a preference and is quietly pointing it out. A small thing but momentous. I take his hand.

Thank you, Roi.

We sit quietly, hearing only the ship's hum. I'm drawn back into my memories of those last moments on the planet.

There's more I haven't told you yet, I say. What happened when I fired my weapon. I tell him about the flash, a luminous crater in the whirling dust, transforming it so I could see what the People were seeing: the wind had become the ghosts. The kin they had been calling. Wispy forms, more strings of fog than flesh. Voices crying, fingers flicking down trying to touch the living. I could feel their need but couldn't make out what it was. What do you want? I tried to ask them, but my voice stuck in my dry throat.

This seems like a hallucination, he says.

I know it does. That's why I'm not putting it into my report. But my reboarding medscan found no hallucinogens in my system, and it showed my brain had been responding as if to actual sensory input.

Class II societies can develop very powerful trance technologies, he says.

To me it was real.

He nods. He's willing to consider that such a trance technology ght allow some further quantum effect to occur, some space-time sturbance—there haven't been many studies of it. He asks questions, patient while I go back over my memory again. I'm half in my cabin, half out on the windy bluff. Feeling the desperate pull of the beings circling over us. How they tugged at the air, trying to find the doorway through, the gap to let them join us. That's what they wanted—to enter back into the world of the living, the world of their People.

But I see now they weren't the ancestors of the ones I've come to know. No, they came from the People's future. They were the descendants, trying to bring back to their own ancestors the unknowable experience of what's to come. The People succeeded in summoning their future, whether they meant to or not. I try to explain this to Roi, stumbling over my words. He listens. He doesn't say I'm crazy. I know now that I have to find a way to include my whole experience in the report, along with all the Salient Factors. I'll explain myself as best I can and try to live with the consequences.

Standing up, I pull Roi over to the window. I hold his hand tight as we look out at the stars. We're moving at a speed that allows you to see the nearer stars streaking by while the more faraway stars seem not to move at all. Of course, we're all moving, the little space pod of our ship, everything. Just at different speeds, which can be confusing. We're traveling at unknown speeds, crossing into different quadrants, different states. Like the ghosts—they left their own place-time and found their way to a different one, not knowing what would happen. Maybe it doesn't matter if they were from the past or the future, just that they crossed over from one time to another.

I look at Roi. He's traveled so far to get here, to be able to reclaim a small particle of his Wuvian self. He'll never be fully Wuvian again, or fully Mesh—he'll be what he is.

We're all traveling, right? I say to him. Terrans, Wuvians, Santak—the Night People—we just don't necessarily have any idea where we're going.

He looks at me, his face silvered with starlight.

"DINNER'S READY," Len announces. "Move over."

"I'm all the way over. You need a bigger bed."

"I know." He flops down on the other side, holding the pizza box. At least his bedroom isn't small. His apartment's part of the first floor of an old house. It's surprisingly neat and well-organized—I was worried it would match the inside of his van. Across from the bed and over the TV and the Sony PlayStation hangs a big poster of the Dymaxion map, Bucky's version of a world map that's supposed to be much more accurate than the big old classroom maps. Its outlines make odd angles jutting out all over, but you can tell they're composed of triangles like a geodesic dome. Looking at it makes me a little dizzy—the continents lying sideways, with Africa on top, and islands looping between them like flyaway chains.

Over the bed, there's the poster for the third SkyLog movie, the one Len bought at Collectorama! last summer. He promised to replace it whenever the next SkyLog movie comes out, which we both know could be a long wait. But I'm starting to mellow on this one, along with my new acceptance of the Santak way. Then, hanging next to the back window: a full-length Santak blade of real, deadly steel. The last time I was here, Len let me watch him practice for a solo sword demonstration he's working on for the tak'La Gathering in June—wearing just his jockey shorts, face sweating, and sharp with concentration.

I open the pizza box. "Did you heat it up?"

"Room temperature's the best. Didn't your mom teach you that?"

He's right, it is the best. We munch, lying in the blue glow of the TV while a guy with a mustard-colored tan and wearing a white doctor's coat begins an infomercial for some fitness product I'll never need.

"Jerk," I mutter.

"Who are you calling a jerk?"

"Hey! Let go!" I roll away from him. "I don't want any more crumbs under me." I have to protect my bit of space. It still feels weird, sharing a bed with somebody else—kind of new and tender. I haven't moved in, but we've been spending some nights together. Which is good, because Irv's back at our house. Ma was more than I could handle myself for a while there. He's been sleeping on the couch. They're talking about him giving up his apartment and moving back in, to save money while she gets back on her feet. I let her have some of my choice SkyLog pieces to sell, and Irv chipped in his old vinyl collection. Anyway, it's a good thing to give them some space right now.

The white-coat guy is interviewing a woman who looks about my age but may be closer to my mother's.

"I'll tell you who's a jerk," I say, "that shrink."

"What?"

"You know, the one they sent Tad to."

"I thought you didn't want to talk about that." He leans over to slide out another slice of pizza.

"I just can't believe he'd say SkyLog is bad for somebody."

"He's a dickwad is all."

"The damn thing is, we don't know what he really said. It's all like third-hand."

Len and I went over to Tad's house one night, after his mom wouldn't put him on the phone. I didn't see that last installment of the story he sent till we got back on Monday—and not till after dealing with Janine's hysterics most of the day. Then Tad didn't answer my emails, nothing. His mother came to the door, wouldn't let us in. Pretty tightly wound. Whatever problems she was having before, Tad's flameout must have ratcheted her up more. No sign of his dad, who I'd like to think would have been more reasonable. While we were trying to persuade her to let us see him—Len doesn't give up—Tad wandered into the room, a thin, silent wraith. Looked at us, then looked away. When his mom realized he was there she shut the door, fast. That's all I got to see of him. Face drawn, eyes on mute. That clumsy short hair-cut. The clothes too—I don't think I'd ever seen him out of his Transortium uniform. Anonymous T-shirt and jeans, like some generic kid. No remnants of Transortium, Santak or Mesh. The kid his parents thought they'd lost, the one they thought they had in the first place.

A few days later I heard from Mr. Fishkin with the short, official version: Tad had been in the hospital for a few days of observation. The psychiatrist felt it was better for him to stay away from speculative subjects and solitary pursuits. In other words, no more SkyLog. No SkyLog shows, reruns, movies, magazines—all banned. I was sure they had him on meds, Len and I argued about that. He didn't think they would do that—how could they observe him if he was all doped up? I gave up on that one.

Infomercial's over. Len picks up the remote and clicks through the channels, settling on a rerun of *Magnum, P.I.*

"I mean," I say. "It's not just SkyLog. They won't even let him use the computer, not even for homework. They shut down his email account. Tadmesh no longer exists." Maybe that's true, Tadmesh doesn't exist anymore. Lost in the AI vortex along with Pak. Of course that's too much for a kid. I feel somehow responsible, if I could only tease out the connecting wires.

"Mm."

"Are you even listening?"

"Look, Mindy. He's gonna be all right. Everybody goes nuts sometime, Tad just got to it a little early."

"I don't believe you said that."

"He's a kid, he's gonna be all right."

A commercial for Best Hits of the Nineties. A commercial for e History Channel. A network ad for their big New Year's Eve celebration—a blowout, a party for the turning of the millennium. If they're right about the Millennium Bug, then lights all over the world will wink out right after the ball drops. To me, it just seems like a big rumor made up by people who are afraid of computers taking over everything. We'll know soon enough. In the meantime, the light show in here is provided by Roxie's floating lamp sculpture, which Len hung on the wall over a table lamp.

"I wish I could get Tad together with Roxie."

"That'd be interesting."

"I know it can't happen, I said I wish. So they could talk. And she could tell him, Don't let the Philistines mess you up, or one of those things she says." She'd mispronounce his name. He would tell her his latest theory, she'd get an idea for a new art piece from it. These are phantoms in my head, I know. Gone. Len stares at the screen, where a car chase is in full swing, 1980s vintage, brassy soundtrack blaring. I grab the remote, turn the TV off.

"Hey!"

"It's mine now!" We wrestle for it.

"This is the good part!"

"I know." I curl in on the remote, hold it deep in my lap.

"C'mon, give it."

"Get your hand off there—"

"How about here then—"

We wrestle, his hands all over me. I turn back toward him. Sacrifice the remote. Click. Squealing brakes, car crash, trumpets blasting. Kiss.

THE SPEED OF CLOUDS   261
THE SPEED OF CLOUDS   261

G reetings, Dear Readers in any form, fleshy, pie-
zoelectric or etheric, carbon-based, silicon-based
or based on materials not yet imagined by Earthians!

Welcome to the second edition of the "Alternate Lifeforms Log"
(A.L.L.). Feels funny, but your faithful editor has finally left paper behind. Yes, this zine now dwells only on the Web. We're still working it
out, but you'll see tabs for stories, poems and art along the top. New
readers are invited to check out our **mission statement**.

Wow, there's a lot to catch up on. I'm writing this on my notebook computer, somewhere in the wilds of rural Delaware. The battery
should be good for a few hours, and I'll upload this post when we get
back home. I've got my coat on, sitting on the tailgate of Len's van,
parked in a clearing in the woods. Len and Roger and Vlad are here
(that's Nak, Kagash and Takep for Santak folk). They're wrestling with
some metal poles that are supposed to fit together into a geodesic
dome.

Don't want to get ahead of things. Let's start with this issue's **hot
links** to my new fave sites featuring renegade Transorters, Santak
and other aliens, cyborgs and androids. Not to forget my old fave, the
super-talented **Zuzana Hagendorf's website**, where her debut CD
is now available. You can download a tasty sample, featuring Bradley Carter (also the designer of this website) on synthesizer, assorted
percussion by Trish Nowak, and keyboard, theremin, and a variety of

nds captured from the known universe by Miss Z, then massaged o something truly strange as she always does. I'm prejudiced, but think it's stellar. Proceeds from the CD and any donations will help send Zu's band, Kadep, to the International Electronic Music Festival in Osaka next fall. Seems they really liked the way she's been sampling Japanese noise music.

And please check out **greenworld-blackworld**, the website for artist Roxie Grunwald, a.k.a. Greenworld. This is still in beta, so you're welcome to kibitz. We weren't sure how to present her most recent work, tentatively titled *Sublime*, which Roxie has been unable to complete due to illness. For now, you can click on different icons—astronaut, galaxy cluster, whatever—to see the various elements.

Len says to remind you to sign Roxie's guest register, so we can tell her who's looked at her work. Len and Bradley promised to work up a kind of virtual tour of Roxie's studio to give you a better idea how the different parts fit together. But that doesn't mean it has to be seen just one way. The idea is that you complete the work yourself out in the ether, depending on how you experience it. I'm pretty sure this setup would please the hell out of Roxie, leaving it open-ended like this. I think Policy One in Roxie's artwork is to put a lot of things together in one place and then let people try to figure out what it means. It's definitely true to Abundant Life in Many Forms. And I've decided it's a good Policy for writing too. To hell with trying to make things fit into some preapproved formula!

I don't know when Len will get to building that virtual studio tour—I've got dibs on his next project, converting this van so I can finally learn how to drive. He's already put in a rotating seat for me that makes it easier to get in and out. The way I see it now, since we don't have that flying jetpack yet, whatever does the job is fine. It really doesn't matter if I'm getting around sitting or standing. Some things go better when I'm in the chair, some things go better with the crutches. Glad we cleared that up.

And here's my top web pick: **JMV Tchotchkes**. That's my mom's and my new business, new to the Web, that is. Our collectibles inventory is as distinctive as ever and growing every day. Once she was ready to start up again, we finally convinced her you can reach way more people online. Instead of stacking up in our living room, her stuff will be streaming out into the cyberwebs—beaming around like a *Mary Tyler Moore Show* episodes broadcasting out to Vega. LOL, know my mom will still have boxes piling up, she's magnetic to small vintage objects. That's the way she likes it, whereas I'm still dreaming of living in something shiny and aerodynamic like a cabin on the *Encounter*. For now, the closest I can get is this clean, well-organized website.

Now, for the new issue. The selection is small but choice, and it includes some interesting new writers. From first-timer Trish Nowak, there's **"Bangwl or Not, Here I Come,"** a steamy slash story detailing the seduction of Dr. Dina Braxton by Vril, the ravishing female scion of the Clan of Bardom. And our first submission through the website, from Dom Lutz: a tale of aliens and Earthians meeting in a most unlikely way, **"A Good View of Antarctica."**

And, drum roll, we've got a new story from **Angie Madden**, one of our best writers. It's a time-travel thing involving an intersection between the *Century 23* timeline and the Indian Wars. Angie's completed her flight from Normality and is living in the Windy City now. It's hard starting in a new place, especially getting there just as winter was hitting, but sounds like she's on her feet now. She should be happier with the general level of SkyLog activity there.

Since we had several contributions from Tad Fishkin, I'm putting them all here as the latest additions to his **Shadow of the Mesh** series. I'm not sure whether this takes us to the end, but hope it's not the last thing we get from Tad. Tad, if you're out there, the door's always open for our favorite under-voting-age author. We miss you.

Finally, we have a story with Roi in a leading role: **"Return to Night."** The other main character is up-and-coming Transortium Fleet officer Kat Wanderer, who some loyal readers may remember from early issues of "Voice of the Cyborg." This one is by yours truly. See, I don't just write editorials. Even tho it's been a while. I made things harder for myself by not writing a lot of the early parts down—don't ever try it that way. Some of you may be thinking, this Kat Wanderer, if she's so great, she must be a Mary Sue. So I'd just like to say I'm freaking proud of her being a Mary Sue! We members of the geek patrol need more Mary Sues. In fact, I hereby invite anyone else to get their Mary Sue on in future stories on A.L.L. See our motto—we welme consideration of ALL lifeforms, including obnoxiously brilliant, ave and beautiful ones.

Speaking of obnoxious, I've decided to bug the SkyLog producers about getting a new series going. I've been sending them an email a week. What do you say, people? I know there's a lot of us out there—enough to send them a big message. Email's so much easier than snail mail, and it's free. If every club did this, not to mention every unaffiliated fan, we could really get this thing going. SkyLog 4ever!

It looks like they've wrestled up a piece of the dome. Enough so I can see the shape of it anyway. It's really something, thin lines of metal spiderwebbing against the sky. Len cleared away more of the woods next to the old shack to make room for it, which gives me a better view of the sky. The clouds are way up high today. There's one long velvety gray one spreading way across, pulsing bright white at the top where the sun's pushing through. Above that, a clean light blue. Then even higher, a whole lot of small white clouds, sparkling in the sunlight. They look like they're just floating, but I bet they're actually cruising along pretty fast up there. We just can't tell from down here. Cloud time is different from Earth time.

Len says he should be able to get the dome up and covered in just a couple of weekends. He claims he's nailed the leakage problem, and it'll be cool inside in the summer and warm in the winter. I'll let you know. The thing is, I have some experience with geodesic domes, and they have this random glitch where they sometimes disappear. I can see it now: we'll be lounging in the dome one night, only to feel some unearthly click as the whole thing detaches itself from the ground and spirals up and out, leaving the material world behind, maybe to meet up with Bucky himself out there somewhere. Santak Guy assures me that this one will perform according to all specifications, and possibly beyond them. I'm not sure what he means by that.

Actually, I hope the dome doesn't go anywhere soon. I've been thinking, even though it doesn't matter where you are, this is a good place to be. The whole thing, I mean: this is a pretty good planet, considering—if you disregard all the horrible things humans have managed to do to each other while running around on the Earth's surface. I never paid that much attention to the details before. Trees are amazing, you know? If you really look at them. All black with their wet early-spring bark, the little leaves starting to push out with their cra[...] neon-green, the twigs swishing in the breeze. Who the hell thoug[...] them up? The breeze is soft, but it's carrying that heavy, wet dirt smell from the woods, so sweet it feels like the top of my head's lifting.

And besides, Earth is so interesting. Forget science fiction, there's enough weirdness going on down here to freak out any visiting Vogon. Look at this cyberspace thing for one. It's like we're building an invisible wrapper around the planet. Everything inside it is equally immaterial: tchotchkes, thoughts, spewing rants, love letters, SkyLog memorabilia, dancing babies, singing aliens, porn, trolls, sunset on Mars, baseball stats, virtual artwork, old cartoons, letters from dead people, the title of every book that's ever been written. I know, we could screw this thing up too. We already are, before we even start to understand it. It's all pulling us along so fast. A massive *whoosh*, the future sucking us toward it, mixing with the past and present like a big blender. Along with the trees, and the dirt and the dirt smell, our fleshy selves and our cyborg add-ons—everything. Nothing gets left behind. And we're right in the middle of it. Like the clouds swimming along up there in cloud time, not knowing their own speed, we don't even know how fast we're going. We're at some kind of Einsteinian cruising speed, Tach 3 maybe, and we hardly even feel it. But if we listen hard we can hear the hum, the faint background whistle, the sound that gives away the endless motion.

Forgive me, dear Readers, if this isn't making much sense. Lately it's like I'm learning things all over again.

Abundant life,
Mindy

ACKNOWLEDGMENTS

I am massively grateful:

✳ To members of the Working Writers Group who read this book from its earliest drafts, helping me along with insights and encouragement: Robin Black, Ann de Forest, Doug Gordon, Louis Greenstein, Larry Loebell, Mark Lyons, David Sanders, and Debra Leigh Scott

✳ To Barry Greenstein, for generously critiquing the manuscript and downloading reams of knowledge into my neural network when I most needed it

✳ To Barbara Scheiber, for early reading, input, and encouragement

✳ To other readers for their valuable input: Ona Gritz, Phil Kapp, Kim Niemela, and Julia Hough, who also provided long-term encouragement, and to Hannelore Christensen, for her long-term moral support

✳ To Kellam de Forest and Sharon Sorokin, for their valuable opinions, and to Susan Spangler, for her helpful feedback

✳ For medical information and perspective, to Juanita Panlener of the Spina Bifida Association; to Keith Wapner, M.D., Ronald Green, M.D., Margarita Torres, M.D., and Jan Nelson; and especially to Brenda Jamison Gaunt and Kristen Powell, for sharing their experience of living with spina bifida

✶ To the late Janet Bregman Taney, for her memories of Buck-minster Fuller

And to Steve Seidel, endless thanks for your patience. This is all your fault.

CPSIA information can be obtained
at www.ICGtesting.com
Printed in the USA
BVHW07s1509121018
530010BV00001B/59/P

9 780999 550106